Co

## RULES OF ENGAGEMENT

"The author of *DEFCON One* flies again."
—*Kirkus Reviews*

"Weber is a master of cockpit chatter and ready-room cross talk." —*Publishers Weekly*

## TARGETS OF OPPORTUNITY

"Weber continues to write great flight scenes."
—*Kirkus Reviews*

"Suspenseful and crisply written." —*Booklist*

"Highly recommended." —*Library Journal*

## HONORABLE ENEMIES

"Takes Michael Crichton's *Rising Sun* a step further . . . brisk and exciting." —*Publishers Weekly*

"Weber obviously knows his stuff."
—*Lincoln Star-Journal*

# PRIMARY TARGET

## JOE WEBER

BERKLEY BOOKS, NEW YORK

PRIMARY TARGET

A Berkley Book / published by arrangement with
the author

PRINTING HISTORY
Berkley edition / December 1999

ISBN: 0-425-17255-4

BERKLEY®
Berkley Books are published
by The Berkley Publishing Group,
a division of Penguin Putnam Inc.,
375 Hudson Street, New York, New York 10014.
BERKLEY and the "B" logo are trademarks
belonging to Penguin Putnam Inc.

PRINTED IN THE UNITED STATES OF AMERICA

10  9  8  7  6  5  4  3  2  1

# Acknowledgments

As always, I wish to thank those who provided assistance and wise counsel during the creation of this book. To Jeannie for her encouragement and steady input; Natalee Rosenstein for her kind support and professional guidance; Adele Horwitz for her keen eye and endless patience; Joyce and John Flaherty for their friendship and help.

Other friends and contributors to the book include Colonel Bill Lehman, USAF (Ret.); Mike Hodgden; Nicole Gislason; Christopher P. Baclayon; Timothy K. Kyomya; Larry and Vivi Hodgden; and Captain Terry Chafee.

The novel is the product of my imagination and should not be interpreted as expressing the views of anyone listed above.

Treason doth never prosper: what's the reason?
For if it prosper, none dare call it Treason.

—Sir John Harrington, English courtier

# Prologue

## Russia

With communism a distant memory and oligarchs corruptly seizing hundreds of billions of dollars, political leaders in Moscow faced difficult decisions. The motherland, suffering from an industrial collapse and economic meltdown, was on the brink of social explosion. Would the government be able to overcome the robber barons and their massive security forces before the military took control of the country?

If the tycoons and Mafia were thwarted, would the politicians embrace a Western-style democracy with a market economy, or would they accept a quasidemocratic style of capitalism? Many of the deputies in the Communist party, as well as a large segment of the Russian people, were nostalgic for the cradle-to-grave days of communism. A few of the stouthearted politicians and military leaders openly called for a return to authoritarian rule, whether Communist or fascist, blended with nationalism and militarism.

Thus far, attempts at economic and political reform had been distorted and sabotaged by oligarchs and politicians still faithful to the old Soviet system. Corruption plagued Russia's fragile economy, from rising crime rates to Mafia ties in the Kremlin. A vast majority of Russians believed that old-line Communists and the KGB secretly transferred billions of dollars out of the country when the reforms were implemented.

The Russian Federation, widely known for questionable election practices, was still considered a menacing and de-stabilizing force in the world. A force with a powerful military showcased by nuclear-tipped ICBMs and an impressive strategic nuclear submarine fleet. Although the Russian armed forces appeared to be in a state of chaos, the admirals and generals were still actively engaged in preparing for nuclear war with the United States. Unfortunately, the NATO bombing campaign in the Balkan states had exacerbated the situation and soured U.S. relations with Moscow.

# 1

## Moscow

On the birthday of Soviet founder Vladimir Lenin, blowing snow and bone-chilling temperatures paralyzed Moscow. Thousands of the poor and homeless were standing in government-organized soup lines, shivering as they inched their way toward steaming kettles full of thin, near tasteless broth. They were literally a stone's throw from where President Nikolai Shumenko would be paying his respects to their deceased founder.

A sense of foreboding, some would call it despair, permeated the frosty air during this miserable day in April. Chaotic political upheavals, combined with a hair-trigger military desperate to compensate for the erosion in the Russian command and control system, were pressuring "hard-liners" like Shumenko to make fateful decisions.

The homeless and oppressed Muscovites watched as Shumenko and his entourage arrived at Red Square in their shiny black limousines. After the officials stepped out of their cars, Shumenko momentarily made eye contact with one of the dispirited men. The stooped man had hollow eyes and a twisted, angry look. The thickset president nodded respectfully, then looked away and walked in silence. Unable to stifle his bitterness, he turned to his friend Yegor Pavlinsky, a former first deputy prime minister.

"Look at these wretched people," Shumenko grumbled. "I will *not* allow the Americans to continue to wipe their feet on us," he said venomously as they approached Lenin's granite tomb. "Their State Department has slashed funding for another twenty-two agencies in Moscow, and President Macklin has publicly humiliated me about our ties to Iran and Iraq."

Shumenko gestured toward the soup line. "All this while the economic reforms the technocrats insisted on have impoverished millions of our people."

*"Da,"* Pavlinsky said angrily. "The Mafia and the corrupt elite also share the blame for this disaster." A fervent hardliner and consummate political dealmaker, Pavlinsky cleared his throat. "My friend," he said morosely, "our crisis, Russia's crisis, has reached the breaking point. The Americans are catnapping while our economic and political instability represents the greatest threat to global security today."

Pavlinsky took a quick breath. "If we are to survive, we must infuse more money into our economy, and we must do it quickly."

Pavlinsky's impassioned words prompted Shumenko to speak bluntly. "More money," he growled in protest, "for the mobsters to take to their offshore banks. More money for the corrupt bankers and businessmen to steal and send to Zurich."

Shumenko's eyes narrowed and his jaw tightened. "They have systematically looted the Central Bank and sent the money to a variety of phony asset-management companies. We might as well pour the money into the sea."

"We have no other choice," Pavlinsky shot back. "The economy is free falling. We're bankrupt! We must stand together and do what's best for our motherland," he exclaimed.

"Lower your voice," Shumenko said firmly. "We're riding a hungry lion. Speak quietly and calmly."

"If we don't do something drastic to improve our economy," Pavlinsky said through clenched teeth, "we will lose political control and the country will collapse in anarchy."

"Nineteen seventeen," Shumenko said angrily.

"What?"

"We have all the ingredients for another revolution."

Pavlinsky paused, then lowered his voice. "We can avoid

an overthrow and return our country to a position of global prominence," he said with deep emotion. "We can provide Russia with great wealth and strategic leverage, if you'll listen to me."

"I'm listening," Shumenko said mechanically.

A virulent anti-American, Pavlinsky's angry voice suggested ominous intentions. "The millions of dollars Washington sprinkles on us, and the billions of dollars we make from Iraq, Iran, and other countries is nothing compared to the four-trillion oil-and-gas bonanza in the Caspian Sea."

Shumenko's eyes hardened, challenging his friend. "Keep your voice down," he insisted in a coarse whisper.

"Working with Iran and Iraq," Pavlinsky said in a low, raspy tone, "we can provide a nuclear umbrella for a pipeline through Iran to the Persian Gulf. Russia, not the U.S. or the West, will control a key point of distribution and we can drive prices much higher."

"We're running out of time." Shumenko sighed in frustration. "As long as the Americans are entrenched in the Gulf region, your idea will only be a wistful dream."

"We can force the Americans out of the region," Pavlinsky said with a distinct harshness in his voice.

Shumenko's eyes grimly reflected his impatience. "I suppose you have a foolproof plan?"

"*Da,*" Pavlinsky said stiffly. "The Persian Gulf will be our salvation." He paused, then turned to face Shumenko. "If we fill the void when the Americans withdraw."

"Yegor Ryzkovich," Shumenko said with passion, "think about how many people have underestimated the Americans in the past two hundred years. Do you *really* believe the U.S. will pull out of the Gulf region?"

"*Da,*" Pavlinsky declared, seeing the surprised look on Shumenko's face. "Allow me to explain how we can contribute to—"

"Wait, wait a second," the president interrupted as he stole a glance at members of his security detail. "Not here," he said under his breath. "We'll have dinner at my dacha."

"As you wish."

Shumenko's wife, Anna, along with their three grandchildren, had been shepherded through the snowdrifts to the guest quarters to allow privacy in the massive dining room of the dacha. A bodyguard added logs to the crackling fire, then quietly left the room when Shumenko and Pavlinsky seated themselves at the dining table. They made small talk and ate a few bites of the array of caviar, smoked trout, sliced beef, and stuffed cabbage. When the maid and the chef retreated to the kitchen, the men shoved their plates aside and Shumenko poured generous amounts of Stolichnaya vodka into their glasses.

"We have to be very cautious with the Americans," the president began in a tight voice. "We've already irritated Washington with our campaign to end sanctions on our trading partners. Now the State Department is forcing more sanctions on us for helping Iran with their missile technology —technology which is transforming the balance of power in the Gulf region."

"Advanced missile technology," Pavlinsky said dryly, "which is our sovereign right to provide to any nation. The United States has no right to tell us what to do with our technology."

Shumenko slowly shook his head. "I understand, but look at the condition of our country and our people. We can't afford to poke the tiger too many times."

Grim and exasperated, Pavlinsky took a sip of vodka and looked his friend straight in the eye. "Nikolai Kopanevich, how long have we known each other?"

"Since we were in the Komsomol Youth League."

"Have I ever betrayed you?"

"Not that I'm aware of."

Pavlinsky raised a bushy eyebrow and spoke in a clear, firm voice. "The American military forces have diminished while the demand on their services is continuing to increase. Look at the Gulf region, the Balkans, the Western Pacific, South Korea, and other commitments."

"They're still in much better shape than our decaying military," Shumenko said glumly. "While the Americans continue to launch improved satellites to monitor our military forces, we don't have the money to replenish the early-warning satellites we need to monitor their missile fields and the world's oceans."

Shumenko's voice turned flatter. "Our decision makers are

blind, which greatly increases the risk of a major miscalculation."

Pavlinsky ignored his friend. "In the foreseeable future, as Admiral Loshkarpov and I view it, the demand on the U. S. military will exceed the Americans' force structure."

Dubious, Shumenko blandly nodded. "Yes, their plate is full, but their cupboard is well stocked."

"My friend," Pavlinsky went on with raw emotion in his voice, "their pilots, Navy and Air Force, are leaving the military in droves."

Impatience flashed in Pavlinsky's eyes. "Major aircraft programs have been realigned or canceled, they're running out of high-tech missiles and bombs, and budget squeezes are having an adverse effect on recruiting, personnel retention, and morale. They're trying to maintain a superpower spread from one end of the globe to the other and it isn't working."

Pavlinsky squeezed his fist into a knot. "Their aircraft carriers are going to sea without a full complement of sailors. When the 6th Fleet battle group deploys to the Persian Gulf, U.S. forces in the Mediterranean will have to make do with one submarine and four surface vessels. That's absolutely insane," Pavlinsky declared loudly. "It's an open invitation for disaster."

Shumenko paused a moment, a faint glimmer of hope in his eyes. "At a time when the U.S. is enjoying a reasonable amount of economic stability. How stupid of them."

"That's my point." Pavlinsky tossed back the rest of his vodka. "In addition, we know the U.S. is having a problem with forward basing in the Gulf region. Host nations like Saudi Arabia, Oman, Turkey, and even Kuwait are becoming more reluctant to permit key U.S. air operations to originate from their sovereign territory."

"Undermanned or not," the president interrupted, "you're forgetting about the Americans' aircraft carriers. They have their own *floating* sovereign territories—100,000 tons of diplomatic persuasion."

"Ah, yes." Pavlinsky smiled thinly, the look in his eyes full of malice. "But they don't have enough carriers to handle *all* the potential problem areas. If one or two carriers were damaged or destroyed, and say a crisis developed between

North and South Korea, or India and Pakistan, or China and Taiwan, or another crisis erupts in the Balkans, someone would have to fill the void in the Persian Gulf."

Shumenko reached for more vodka. "Someone who is welcomed in the Middle East—say a benefactor who isn't despised by Iran or Iraq?"

Pavlinsky nodded in agreement. "A benefactor who can offer stability to the region." He paused to allow his message to register. "Admiral Loshkarpov suggested that we send the cruisers *Pyotr Veliky* and *Peter the Great*, along with our Navy's flagship, *Admiral Kuznetsov*, to the Persian Gulf for an extended goodwill cruise."

"Have you discussed this with anyone else, other than Loshkarpov?" the president anxiously questioned.

"No, of course not."

"Let's keep it that way," Shumenko said bluntly. "So, my friend, what is your plan?"

Pavlinsky answered with an air of enthusiasm. "I've scheduled a meeting in the near future with Bassam Shakhar. I'm proposing to you that we supply the kindling in the Middle East and let someone else light the fire."

A sudden frown crossed Shumenko's face. "I'm not so sure that's a good idea—too much instability and too many variables."

"Trust me," Pavlinsky said with a gleam in his eye. "Others—factions that hate the U.S. presence in the Gulf region—will confront the Americans. All we need to do is provide the critical mass."

"Critical mass," Shumenko quietly mused, then caught his friend's eye. "A self-sustaining fission chain reaction?"

*"Da,"* Pavlinsky said firmly. "Our hands will be clean, I promise you."

Shumenko remained quiet while he contemplated the pros and cons of the ambitious and risky undertaking. Finally, he looked at Pavlinsky for a long moment, then spoke forcefully. "Officially, I'm not going to endorse what you have suggested—and I don't want to be involved."

Pavlinsky quietly nodded. "As it should be."

"We never had this conversation," Shumenko insisted.

"You can count on me," Pavlinsky said with a sly smile.

An awkward silence filled the room.

"I know I can," Shumenko finally said, despite the anxiety he felt in his chest. "I'll recommend sending our ships to the Gulf for a goodwill cruise, show the flag and all."

Pavlinsky's puffy eyes expressed his great satisfaction. "Leave everything to me."

# 2

## Tehran

Dressed in a long dark cloak and white turban, Bassam Shakhar entered the austere chambers of his closely guarded office complex in the heart of the city. The thickly bearded multimillionaire, his lips barely covering his protruding teeth, was a fierce defender of the hard-line clergy. When the power struggle between Iran's moderate president and the conservatives turned ugly, Shakhar had prodded agents from the Intelligence Ministry to assassinate over a dozen dissident writers and politicians.

Without looking directly at the Russian politician, Shakhar raised his arm and motioned for Yegor Pavlinsky to take a seat on the opposite side of the conference table. Pavlinsky quietly sat down and folded his hands on the table.

Shakhar, an intractable and humorless man with a permanently furrowed brow, stiffened ever so slightly before he sat. His pinched eyes were deep brown, and when he became irritated or excited, the right one tended to turn inward. A dangerous and unpredictable man, Shakhar's complex character reflected generous portions of aggression, grandiosity, paranoia, and narcissism. The combination of traits was accentuated by a total lack of conscience.

Muffled sounds of jeers and shouts from Shakhar's growing league of followers permeated the building. "Death to the

Americans!" the crowd of Islamic militants chanted while they burned a dozen U.S. flags. "Death to the enemies of Islam!" Acting on the orders of Shakhar, the fanatical throngs of anti-American militants were creating factional violence not seen since the revolution in 1979.

Additional devoted followers, estimated at 17,000 and rapidly growing, were venomously protesting against America in various countries, including Saudi Arabia, Somalia, Kenya, Afghanistan, Pakistan, Kosovo, Montenegro, Macedonia, Sudan, Libya, Bosnia, Yemen, Egypt, the Philippines, Chechnya, and Malaysia.

Bassam Shakhar, one of the masterminds behind a series of terrorist bombings and hero to legions of Islamic fundamentalists, was a strong advocate of using terrorism to drive the United States military out of Saudi Arabia and the entire Persian Gulf region. To expedite his ambitious plans, the murderous psychopath had developed a growing infrastructure to train and indoctrinate hard-core terrorists, including a sizable cadre of "throwaway agents" known as suicide bombers.

A powerful figure in Iran, Shakhar had openly and loudly declared that the United States was "the enemy of the Islamic Republic" and called for the Iranian leadership to reject any dialogue with Washington. He had gone on to explain that "talks or relations with the United States would have no benefit for the Iranian people." He had concluded his bitter remarks by reminding his vast audience about the 1988 shoot-down of an Iranian jetliner by a U.S. Navy cruiser, then blamed Washington for another incident in which fifty-two Americans were held hostage for 444 days.

Determined to bring America to its knees, Shakhar later used state-run radio and television, along with major newspapers, to declare a personal *jihad* against U.S. military personnel in the Gulf region. Three weeks after his announcement, he and members of the Iranian secret police planned and supervised a car bombing in Riyadh, Saudi Arabia, that killed six American advisers to the Saudi National Guard.

Emboldened by the results of the Riyadh attack, Shakhar provided financial backing to the terrorists who bombed the barracks building in Dhahran, Saudi Arabia, that killed nineteen members of the U.S. Air Force and wounded 386 servicemen.

While the Pentagon was shifting U.S. air operations from Dhahran to other bases with better security, Shakhar continued to use the conservative newspaper *Islamic Republic* (*Jomhuri Islami*) to threaten U.S. military forces and their commander in chief. Using Islamic newspapers based in London and newspapers in Egypt, Libya, the Philippines, Italy, and Jordan, Shakhar urged Arab leaders to unite in a *jihad* against the "master of the world."

Undeterred by the "Great Satan's" power projection in the Gulf, Bassam Shakhar was eager to take his personal war to the shores of the United States. In an interview broadcast live by CNN, the international financier boldly promised to use his vast resources to terrorize the heartland of America if all U.S. military forces were not withdrawn from the Arabian peninsula. Shakhar ended the interview by calling the American president a coward and a bully. His vituperative rhetoric panicked conservative emirs, crown princes, kings, and sheiks in the Middle East.

With the CIA-based Counter Terrorism Center tracking a number of his terrorist cells, Shakhar became enraged when one of his deputies suggested that Shakhar's satellite telephone calls were being monitored by U.S. reconnaissance spacecraft.

Five weeks later, with the approval of his consultative council (*majlis al shura*) Shakhar supported another major terrorist organization in their bombings of U.S. embassies in Nairobi, Kenya, and Dar es Salaam, Tanzania, that killed more than 250 people. On the heels of the bombing, Saddam Hussein sent word that he would back Shakhar with money and weapons to terrorize the U.S. military.

Less than two weeks after the tragic bombings, the United States Navy launched a barrage of cruise missiles on suspected terrorist infrastructure and related facilities in Sudan and Afghanistan.

As tensions mounted in the Gulf region, the American president reinforced his commitment to "dual containment" of the "pariah" states, Iraq and Iran. He delivered a stern warning to both countries; U.S. forces were going to keep them in check, *and* the U.S. military was going to maintain a long-term presence in the Arabian deserts and Persian Gulf waters.

Saddam Hussein, enraged by the dressing-down from his nemesis, and determined to avenge his humiliation in the Persian Gulf War, decided to test the resolve of the United Nations and the United States. He expelled the UN arms inspectors who were attempting to investigate his biological and chemical weapons capability and threatened to shoot down U-2 reconnaissance planes.

Saddam, convinced that U.S. military forces were shallow in depth, overextended, and demoralized, had laid the groundwork for a new kind of terrorist game: the cat-and-mouse search for secret weapons of mass destruction.

After a whirlwind of diplomatic endeavors, overt threats, and, finally, an agreement to end the standoff brokered by the United Nations secretary-general, Saddam decided to put the diabolical genie back into the bottle for the moment. However, Hussein had never conceded defeat in the Gulf War and he fully intended to continue causing headaches for the White House and the Pentagon.

As usual, Saddam proved to be a predictably unpredictable foe. He strongly condemned UN sanctions and the United States government, then invited the UN arms inspectors to leave. The dustup culminated in U.S.–British airstrikes on Iraq.

Shortly after the operation was canceled, Saddam demanded that the United States and Britain end their "illegal" patrols over the "no-fly" zones in northern Iraq and south of Baghdad. When the demand was ignored, Iraqi surface-to-air missile systems began "illuminating" coalition aircraft patrolling the northern zone. Saddam's game of constant torment was clearly designed to erode the will of the UN and the U.S. to continue sanctions against Iraq and to maintain a military presence in the region.

Listening to the muffled chants from the militants in the street, Yegor Pavlinsky kept his gaze level and his expression pleasantly gentle. *Get straight to the point.* "Our countries could greatly benefit if we could collectively take advantage of the opportunities in the Gulf region."

Motionless and frowning, Bassam Shakhar quietly stared at the center of Pavlinsky's forehead.

"Unfortunately," Pavlinsky went on, "the presence of the U.S. military is having an adverse effect on the economy of both our countries. From our previous conversations, it is my understanding that you have been working on a plan to drive the Americans out of the region."

"Is your country," Shakhar began slowly, "prepared to assist me with my assault on America?"

Pavlinsky quietly nodded, then looked straight into the dark, sunken eyes of the terrorist leader. "Yes, in any way we can—covertly, of course," he quickly added. *This is the opportunity we've been waiting for.*

"At the request of your government," Pavlinsky went on, "we are sending fighter tactics instructor pilots to enhance the skills of your pilots. Additional scientists and engineers will be arriving soon to help with the missile development program, and we've had a number of experts helping to train your submarine crews. If there is anything we can do to help facilitate the removal of U.S. forces from the region, we stand ready to provide assistance."

"What about the nuclear warheads?" Shakhar abruptly asked. "Without the warheads, everything else is useless."

In silence, the two men stared at each other.

"I have made arrangements for the nuclear warheads to be delivered to you," Pavlinsky answered, suppressing an uneasy feeling in the pit of his stomach. "Working together, we can drive the Americans from the region."

Shakhar's jaw clenched and the pupil of his right eye began to drift toward his nose. "It is my destiny," he said boldly as he shifted his bovine gaze to the crowds in the street, then back to Pavlinsky. "To be subservient to the infidels is to be not a man."

Shakhar remained impassive. "It is time to give President Macklin an ultimatum—a deadline for removing his military forces from the Islamic world. I will issue the deadline soon. If the president refuses to cooperate," Shakhar said in a scratchy voice, "he will become my *primary target.* I will have him assassinated."

Amazed at the visceral hatred in Shakhar's voice, Yegor Pavlinsky remained expressionless.

# 3

## Over the Gulf of Oman

After extending the Tomcat's refueling probe, Commander Garner Stockwell inched the throttles forward as he carefully maneuvered the sinister-looking F-14 closer to the KC-10 tanker. With his eyes riveted on the refueling hose and drogue, Stockwell concentrated on flying while his radar intercept officer, Lieutenant Alan "Skeeter" Jeffcoat, scanned the skies for other traffic.

After stabilizing the airplane behind the drogue, Stockwell eased the sleek fighter toward the basket. Adding a touch of power, the commanding officer of the VF-32 "Swordsmen" gently guided the airplane forward until the probe smoothly plugged into the refueling receptacle. Once the nozzle was mated with the drogue, Stockwell carefully maintained his position directly behind the tanker.

"You're takin' gas," the sergeant in the boom operator's station radioed in his deep whiskey voice.

"That's what we like to hear," Stockwell drawled.

"Commander," an urgent voice interrupted, "this is Major Labrowski."

Instinctively, Stockwell and Jeffcoat tensed. Labrowski was the aircraft commander of the KC-10 Extender.

"What's up, Ski?"

"Sir, the AWACS that was scheduled to rendezvous with

you just had an engine problem," Labrowski said, then paused to listen to an air traffic controller who was communicating with the Boeing E-3 AWACS crew. "They're headed back to base, and the spare bird won't be up for another thirty to forty-five minutes."

*Shit!* Stockwell swore to himself. *This mission is a White House priority—a request directly from the president. I sure as hell don't want to be the one who scrubs it.* "Stand by."

"Roger."

With the SR-71 Blackbird downed by a line-item veto, and the venerable U-2 "Dragon Ladies" temporarily grounded after a mysterious crash, the carrier-based F-14 Tomcat had been called on to provide war-ready strategic reconnaissance for the White House and the Pentagon.

Countering the effects of the turbulent air, Stockwell deftly worked the control stick while he quickly analyzed the situation. Although an Airborne Warning and Control aircraft wouldn't be available to provide advance notice of hostile aircraft or missiles, Stockwell remained confident about flying over the *denied area.*

The sleek Tomcat carried the latest technology in Electronic Counter Measures equipment. Recently released from the secretive "black world," the highly sophisticated defensive system could electronically jam enemy early-warning radars and missile sites, making it almost impossible to obtain a firing solution on the TARPS-equipped fighter.

The Tactical Airborne Reconnaissance Pod System with a digital imagery (DI) camera would image the targets and transmit the information to the Joint Task Force–Southwest Asia headquarters in Saudi Arabia for positive identification and analysis. Forty minutes later, the president of the United States and his secretary of defense would have the recce photographs in their hands.

The near-real-time imagery of the TARPS-equipped Tomcats expanded the reconnaissance role of the F-14 during crisis situations. The aircraft delivered aerial photos so incredibly clear you could read street signs and license plates. Although "national systems"—Pentagonese for spy satellites and intelligence-gathering aircraft such as the U-2 and Rivet Joint—were excellent platforms for gathering vital information, they occasionally malfunctioned or were not in a proper position to spy.

When time is critical, a call to an aircraft carrier in the vicinity of a potential target allows the president the luxury of assessing the threat in a matter of minutes or hours. In addition, with aerial refueling, the manned Tomcat could provide increased flexibility for the commander in chief and his military advisers.

"I appreciate the heads-up," Stockwell said flatly. "We're going to press on with the mission."

"Understand you're going to continue?"

"That's affirm."

A short pause followed.

"Ah . . . Roger."

Skeeter Jeffcoat keyed the intercom. "Skipper, the place is crawling with missiles and fighters. Are you sure you don't want to abort?"

Stockwell hesitated a few seconds. *I don't want to screw this up with the whole air wing watching.* "Normally, I'd go home, but this mission is a White House priority. I'm goin' for it, unless you're uncomfortable."

The seasoned naval flight officer faltered a few moments before he answered. "I'd be lying if I said I don't have some reservations, but if you want to march on, I'm game."

"Then let's do it."

"Yessir."

*Piece of cake,* Stockwell told himself as he played the controls and watched the hose and basket. The delicate ballet continued while Jeffcoat monitored the sky. Approaching a full load of fuel, Stockwell's throttles began creeping forward.

"Time for an adjustment," he said to himself.

Flying as smoothly as possible, Stockwell added power to maintain the proper refueling position. He counted the seconds until the F-14 was full, then keyed his radio. "Thanks for the drink."

"Anytime, sir."

Darting a final look at the boom operator's station, Stockwell disconnected the probe and eased the Tomcat aft and down from the KC-10. Clear of the tanker, he retracted the probe and pushed the throttles into minimum afterburner.

Long, white-hot flames belched from the turbofans as the multirole fighter raced away from the tanker and rapidly climbed toward the bright midday sun.

The previous day, Stockwell and Jeffcoat had flown the same route to capture their primary targets in the long shadows of early morning. Now, after another request from the president, they would be photographing the sites with the hot midday sun directly overhead.

Passing 36,000 feet, Stockwell advanced the throttles to maximum afterburner to rapidly build airspeed for the final climb.

Ascending through 43,000 feet, Jeffcoat prepared to engage the Defensive system. "Ready for the DEF gear?"

"Shoot her the juice."

"You got it."

Jeffcoat energized the state-of-the-art system and the Tomcat immediately experienced a power surge that momentarily caused the enunciator panel in the cockpit to light up like a Christmas tree.

"Ho-leeee *shit*," Stockwell exclaimed as he fought to calm his nerves. "What the hell is going on back there?"

"Sorry, boss." Jeffcoat quickly turned off the faulty system. "The DEF gear went haywire."

"Jesus," Stockwell muttered as he sucked in a breath of oxygen. "My heart won't take another shot like that."

"I've got it secured."

"Yeah, forget it." Stockwell sighed, feeling the effects of the adrenaline rush. "The damn thing only works on training flights."

The demon named *Fear* had slipped out of Stockwell's subconscious, taunting him, coiling around him like a boa constrictor, squeezing tighter and tighter until it was so palpable that he had trouble swallowing. The snarling, hissing distraction possessed the power to erase a pilot's judgment and skill. During his long career, Stockwell had successfully conquered the demon many times.

"What d'ya think, skipper?" Jeffcoat asked with a trace of anxiety in his voice. "Press on, or get out of town?"

Stockwell stared at the horizon while he fought the impulse to cancel the mission and return to the carrier. *Maybe we should abort, or wait for another AWACS.* He considered the knowns and unknowns. *If we loiter and wait for an AWACS, we'll have to refuel again. The timing will be off because the sun won't be directly overhead.*

"Why me?" he quietly asked himself, then allowed a thin smile to crease his face. "Skeeter, the president is waiting. I'm committed, unless you're dead set against it."

Jeffcoat took a deep breath and slowly let it out. "We can hack it, sir." *Just concentrate on the mission.*

With their pulse rates winding down, the two men remained quiet while the F-14 climbed through 54,400 feet, then accelerated to the "speed of heat" and leveled off at 54,000 feet. High above most of the other air traffic traversing the busy Gulf of Oman, the Mach 2.34 Tomcat was back in its environment. In less than fifteen minutes, they would be photographing the first of two recently constructed missile sites along the coast of Iran.

Spacecraft imagery and electronic data indicated the new launch pads were being equipped with Shahab-3 and Shahab-4 missiles. According to dissidents in Tehran, the Shahab-3 could deliver 1,650 pounds of explosives over 860 miles, allowing Iran to inflict severe damage to Jerusalem and to U.S. forces at bases in Turkey, Kuwait, Bahrain, and Saudi Arabia. A few Shahab-3s carrying anthrax could easily kill the majority of American troops in the Gulf region. More powerful, the Shahab-4 had the range to hit cities in Egypt.

With the assistance of Russian, North Korean, and Chinese engineers and technicians, a third generation of Iranian ballistic missiles was being manufactured at Hemat Missile Industries, which contained a production facility thirty feet underground.

The news had caused a mad scramble at the Pentagon, and frayed nerves at the White House and the State Department. Capable of reaching Paris or London, the state-of-the-art missiles were equipped with thermonuclear warheads.

Other Chinese and Russian advisers headquartered at the Shahid Bagheri Industrial Group in Tehran were in the final stages of developing a 6,300 mile missile that could strike Washington, D.C., and New York City. The Iranian weapons of choice for the U.S. were terrorists to disperse anthrax, followed days later by missiles with thermonuclear warheads.

Jeffcoat punched the play button on the small portable CD

player he had modified to plug into his helmet. A few seconds later the greatest hits of Hank Williams filtered through his earpads. Jeffcoat adjusted the volume while he listened to "Hey, Good-Lookin'," then glanced at the horizon and tilted his head back.

The bluish dome of sky turned dark blue as his gaze traveled higher. Far below the spy plane, the sky was powder blue and filled with fluffy white clouds that resembled puffs of cotton randomly scattered about.

After studying the curvature of the earth for a few moments, Jeffcoat turned his attention to his instruments in an attempt to ease his growing uneasiness. The increased pressure to accomplish this particular mission was subtle, but it was there. Jeffcoat closed his eyes and sighed. *First the AWACS—now the DEF gear. What next?* He unconsciously tapped his foot to the beat of the music. *We're hangin' it out on this pass.*

Mulling over the possibility of being attacked by the Iranians, Jeffcoat finally shrugged off his concern. He keyed his intercom. "What d'ya think, skipper—is the commander in chief about ready to teach the big shots in Tehran a lesson?"

"I wouldn't bet against it." Stockwell quietly chuckled. "Giving us a deadline to have our troops out of Sandland *wasn't* a stroke of diplomatic genius."

"Yeah," Jeffcoat said, "and now they're threatening to close the Strait of Hormuz if we don't get out by the deadline."

"It may come down to a shoot-out." Stockwell paused while he glanced at the Persian Gulf and the coast of Iran. "They're sure as hell flaunting their muscle—trying to intimidate us."

"Not a smart idea," Jeffcoat declared.

"True, but you have to remember who you're dealing with." Stockwell made a slight heading adjustment. "After watching Bassam Shakhar threaten us on CNN, the president may want to give him and Tehran a demonstration of who *really* runs the show in the Gulf region."

Skeeter nodded in agreement. "Yeah, it might get noisy down there before too long."

"*Real* noisy," Stockwell said with conviction. "And then *real* quiet."

"Like Stone Age quiet," Jeffcoat suggested.

"Yeah, something like that."

Skeeter closed his eyes and sighed while the lyrics of "Your Cheatin' Heart" floated lightly and smoothly through his headphones. "Wake me up if you get lost."

"You'll be the first to know."

Stockwell pointed the Tomcat toward the initial point of the photo run, then made a sweeping left turn to align the aircraft with the desired track to be photographed. Traveling at twenty-six miles a minute, there was no room for miscalculation or pilot error.

Feeling a sudden chill race down his spine, Stockwell scanned the curvature of the horizon and thought briefly about Francis Gary Powers and the U-2 Affair. *I wonder what he was thinking when the missile hit him, must'uv been a major* "OH, SHIT!" *for sure.*

Checking his instruments, Stockwell tried to quell his uneasiness. *I hope we slide through this without becoming the center of an international incident.*

During the previous two days, Tehran had repeatedly threatened to shoot down the reconnaissance planes if the "provocative acts" continued. To bolster their declaration, Iranian fighter planes equipped with the latest generation of Russian-made air-to-air missiles were patrolling the skies. The heated threats from members of the Supreme Council for National Defense were being shown on MSNBC and CNN against a backdrop of Iranian fighter pilots manning their planes and preparing for takeoff.

Stockwell breathed deeply, enjoying the cool oxygen. *Well, God never loved a coward.* "Are you ready, Skeeter?"

Jeffcoat hit the pause button on the CD. "Skipper, I was born ready."

"We're goin' for it," Stockwell said with a tinge of apprehension in his voice. "Keep me honest."

"I won't even blink."

Twenty seconds later, they blasted over the southern coast of Iran. Flying at a speed of 1,560 mph, they were thundering over hostile territory at an altitude in excess of ten miles. Time seemed to expand as the minutes slowly passed. With their survival instincts keyed to a high degree of intensity,

Stockwell and Jeffcoat concentrated on flying a flawless pass over the missile sites.

"That's one down and one to go," Stockwell declared as they flew over Bandar-e Abbas.

"I feel like we're swimming in molasses," Jeffcoat commented in a hollow voice.

"I've got the throttles two-blocked." Stockwell's voice reflected a display of false bravado.

"It still isn't fast enough for me," Jeffcoat said, then counted the time until the TARPS recon pod began documenting the missile site at Bushehr.

"Uh-oh," Jeffcoat said as the radar warning receiver began to bleep. "Someone's painting us, no shit."

"We're about through," Stockwell observed in a soothing voice. "Another thirty seconds and it's Miller time."

Jeffcoat's heart stuck in his throat as the time slowly passed. *This ain't good.*

"That's it," Stockwell said boldly.

Twenty-three minutes after the fuel-thirsty F-14 started the recce sweep over Bandar-e Abbas and Bushehr, Stockwell began a shallow left turn to coast out over the Persian Gulf.

"They're still on us," Jeffcoat said in a tense voice. "Now, ah, it's intermittent, but someone's tracking us."

"Okay, Skeeter," Stockwell said as he forced himself to relax, "you can start breathing again."

"Yeah, that's a wrap." Jeffcoat punched the play button on his CD player an instant before the Tomcat exploded in a horrendous yellow-orange fireball. Rendered semiconscious by the violent blast, Stockwell and Jeffcoat sagged in their ejection seats while the F-14 shed the right wing and right engine, then broke in half and exploded a second time. The twisted and scorched remains of the fighter tumbled out of the sky, trailing flames and blazing jet fuel.

## High Above the Persian Gulf

Easing the throttles out of afterburner, Iranian Air Force Major Ali Akbar Muhammud gently banked his Soviet-built MiG-29 Fulcrum as he and his wingman rapidly descended from 52,000 feet. Muhammud's first missile had malfunctioned and gone ballistic, but his second missile had destroyed one of the Great Satan's reconnaissance planes.

Smiling with unbridled satisfaction, he glanced at his wingman. Although the Iranian Air Force had greatly increased the number of aircraft patrolling their borders, Muhammud's flight was the first to make contact with the "hostile" recce planes. A few primary radar returns on an air traffic controller's screen had made the difference. It had given the MiG pilots a basic heading to intercept the intruders.

After descending to 2,300 feet, Muhammud leveled off and watched the fuselage of the Tomcat plunge into the Persian Gulf. Scanning the hazy sky for parachutes, the MiGs flew a sweeping circle around the impact area as more debris splashed into the water. Unable to spot any sign of the downed crew, Muhammud and his wingman added power and banked toward their base at Shiraz.

En route to the airfield, Muhammud recalled the emotional pep talk their squadron commander had given the pilots. *The infidels are going to have to face reality; the Islamic Republic of Iran will no longer tolerate the intrusive acts fomented by the president of the "capital of global arrogance." Today marks the emergence of a different, more powerful, more determined Iran.*

Muhammud swelled with pride, knowing that he was the first of Iran's elite fighter pilots to strike a deadly blow to the Americans.

# 4

## Alaska

Scott Dalton stumbled sideways in the Kenai River when a king salmon snagged his line. Thrashing wildly, the powerful fish almost jerked the rod out of Scott's hands. He quickly found his footing and regained his balance while line screeched off the reel. This was Dalton's third attempt at landing a king salmon and he was determined not to let this one get away, especially not in front of his longtime friend and fishing buddy, Greg O'Donnell.

The former Marine Corps Harrier pilots had a standing wager. When they rendezvoused in Alaska for one of their fishing trips, whoever caught the first fish of the day enjoyed dinner at the expense of the loser, and the winner of the biggest fish of the day received free drinks for the evening. The traditional rivalry had been pretty much a wash thus far, with Dalton buying most of the drinks and O'Donnell paying for the majority of their dinners.

Enjoying the cool of early morning, Dalton fought the fish and stole a glance at O'Donnell's king salmon lying on the edge of the riverbank. The gleaming trophy was a rare beauty that Scott figured would tip the scales at 40 to 45 pounds. He looked at the sun rising over the picturesque river, then cast a look at a moose and her calf. He decided that life couldn't get any better. The day was in glorious bloom, the birds were trilling, and the salmon fishing promised to live up to the reputation of the Kenai River.

The descendant of a disciplined Confederate general, and the son of a hard-charging Vietnam-era Marine Corps brigadier general, Scott Johnston Dalton was a strapping native of Nashville, Tennessee. Broad-shouldered and strong-willed, Dalton was an intelligent, intense man who had learned to take time out for a few of life's pleasures. He enjoyed flying aerobatics in his Great Lakes biplane and sailing his immaculate Morgan 33 around Chesapeake Bay. At six feet even, with dark hair, he was ruggedly handsome and had startling blue eyes that exuded charm and wit.

A three-year varsity quarterback for the "Commodores" of Vanderbilt University, Scott had been Greg O'Donnell's flight leader during a number of combat missions in support of Operations Desert Shield and Desert Storm. When Captain Dalton's Harrier was shot down over southern Iraq, O'Donnell flew cover for him until an Army rescue helicopter could reach the injured pilot. Shortly after he returned to flying status, Scott made the difficult decision to leave the Marine Corps and pursue a different career.

Less than six months later he reported for initial training at the Central Intelligence Agency. During his first years at the Agency, he established a solid reputation for successfully completing the most complex and hazardous assignments. After he qualified as a counterterrorism-strike-force team leader, many of Scott's daring and courageous feats made him an instant legend in the CIA. As his reputation grew, the White House began calling on him to conduct special covert operations in various corners of the world.

Following several years of political infighting within the Agency, Scott elected to resign and start his own security consulting firm in the Crystal City complex near Ronald Reagan Washington National Airport. Specializing in corporate security measures, which many of his former associates knew was a sophisticated front, Dalton also accepted "sensitive" assignments for the Terrorism Warning Group within the Counterterrorist Center.

Reporting to the CIA director, the CTC was designed to bring all elements of the intelligence community together to collect and analyze information about terrorist groups from all over the world.

In his role as a private citizen and consultant to international entrepreneurs, Scott could circumvent certain obstacles that might prove embarrassing to the White House or the Pentagon if one of his covert operations went awry. In addition, Scott's activities were not subject to the cumbersome congressional reporting requirements that accompany CIA-directed covert operations. Scott's assignments centered around one basic element of covert operations, no fingerprints and no headlines.

To that end, Greg O'Donnell often provided pilot services for Dalton's far-flung expeditions. The off-the-record excursions, sometimes as a jet captain and sometimes as a jump pilot, provided a sound financial base for Greg's Learjet charter service.

"Grab the net," Scott yelled as he waded farther into the rushing current. "This one weighs at least fifty pounds."

"In your dreams." The stocky redhead laughed as he snatched the net and splashed into the swirling river. O'Donnell lost his balance and plunged forward into the frigid water. "Holy mother!" he said in a high-pitched voice. "I'm awake now."

"That's good, 'cause I need some help," Scott declared as he continually hefted the rod, then reeled down. "This guy is strong."

"Hang on." Greg laughed as he regained his footing.

The battle continued while Scott desperately tried to maneuver the thrashing fish closer to shore. Finally, he waded toward the salmon until ice-cold water poured into his hip boots.

"Net him!" Scott gasped.

"I'm trying."

O'Donnell made two attempts at snaring the hefty fish before he stepped in a hole and had to swim back toward the muddy bank.

"Anytime you're ready!" Scott laughed while he struggled with his catch. "I hope there aren't any *serious* fishermen watching this."

O'Donnell lunged again and scooped the thrashing salmon into the net. With his thinning red hair plastered to his head and water gushing over the tops of his waders, the freckle-faced aviator proudly displayed the big fish. "Are you implying that I don't look like a professional outdoorsman?"

"You look like Howdy Doody coming out of the rinse cycle."

Scott's comment was interrupted by the familiar *whop-whop-whop-whop* of a Sikorsky helicopter. Less than fifty seconds later an Air Force H-60 swooped low over them, then pulled up in a sweeping turn as the pilot circled to land near the riverbank.

O'Donnell studied the helo, then turned to his friend. "You're not in some kind of trouble, are you?"

Scott flashed his mischievous grin. "I'm always in trouble."

Carrying the salmon toward the riverbank, O'Donnell shielded the bright sun from his eyes while he watched the helicopter descend. "Maybe they think we're lost."

"With a bright red Explorer parked on the road?" Scott asked with a chuckle. "Somehow, I don't think that's it."

They watched as the Night Hawk slowed to a hover and settled into a small clearing by the edge of the river. A moment later Dalton saw two figures exit from the side door as the main rotor began winding down. He immediately recognized Hartwell Prost, his former boss at the Directorate of Operations. *What the hell is he doing here, and who's the woman?*

"Greg," Scott said in a barely audible voice, "I believe my vacation is about to come to an end."

Shifting his gaze to the strangers, O'Donnell's aqua-blue eyes widened. "Is that Hartwell Prost?"

"None other."

Greg raked an unruly cowlick from his forehead. "What's your guess?"

"I don't know, but it isn't good news," Dalton quietly replied. "My secretary wouldn't have told anyone where to locate me unless there was a major problem."

Prost and the young woman stopped on a rise, her arms on her hips while he waved to the two fishermen.

Returning the friendly gesture, Scott and Greg sloshed out of the river and met the couple on a gravelbar below the vegetation line.

The president's national security adviser had fatigue-induced bags under his olive-gray eyes and a firm set to his angular jaw. Medium in stature, Prost had wiry salt-and-pepper hair and a warm, fatherly demeanor that made him look very professorial.

Born to a life of wealth and privilege, Hartwell Huntington Prost IV had eschewed a secure career in his family-owned investment empire. Instead, much to the dismay of his father, Hartwell joined the CIA after graduating with honors from Harvard Law.

Now a retired chief of the elite Directorate of Operations—known to insiders as "the DO"—Prost was still regarded as one of the most ingenious spymasters in the history of the Agency.

The attractive, darkly tanned woman was wearing a khaki jumpsuit that complemented her athletic figure. Allowing a hint of a smile, she made brief eye contact with Scott.

*Interesting,* Dalton thought as he gave her a friendly smile and casually checked her military-style name tag. In bold letters under a set of embossed Air Force wings was the name JACKIE SULLIVAN. The name and face seemed vaguely familiar, but he couldn't remember from where or when.

Although O'Donnell had met Prost on two previous occasions, introductions were quickly exchanged. Since Greg was not "officially" in the loop, Jackie glanced at Dalton to see how he was going to handle the situation.

Diplomatically, Scott smiled at his friend. "Greg, why don't you take the Explorer back to the cabin. I'll catch a ride in the helo."

"Sure," the friendly man replied with disguised relief, then turned to the visitors. "If you have time, stop by for some fresh salmon."

After Prost and Sullivan thanked him for the invitation, O'Donnell lugged the two large fish away while the trio walked to a log at the edge of the gravel bar. A tense, restless energy filled the air, the strain showing on Prost's face.

"Your secretary"—Prost quietly chuckled—"is a very cautious woman."

Scott struggled to wipe the grin off his face. "She's, ah . . . what I would describe as mission-oriented."

"A former Marine, huh?"

"Through and through."

"That's what I thought."

Once they were seated, Prost cast a glance down the serpentine river, then turned to Dalton and apologized. "Well," he began, and raised his voice a little, "I sure know how to ruin a perfect day for fishing."

Displaying an understanding smile, Scott overcame the awkward moment. "Don't worry about it. What's up?"

"Iran," Prost said contemptuously. "It looks like they may have shot down a Tomcat—a TARPS bird."

Scott's smooth face, chiseled in strong, clean lines, was devoid of expression. "What about the crew?"

"We don't know anything yet. They just disappeared into thin air, no Mayday or anything that—" Prost paused in midsentence. "At any rate, that's not what I came here to see you about."

Prost turned sideways and threw a leg over the log. "Before we discuss why I'm here, maybe I should bring you up to date on the Iranian situation. We—actually the Agency and the State Department—have irrefutable evidence that Tehran has a stockpile of nuclear-tipped missiles, *and* Russia's fingerprints are all over the warheads."

Casting a quick look at Sullivan, Scott paused a moment. *Where have I seen her?* "How'd they confirm it?"

Prost allowed a slight smile of satisfaction to spread across his face. "One of Sandia's remote monitoring systems detected a breach in security at a nuclear weapons storage vault near Moscow. When our people arrived, they found fourteen nuclear warheads missing. They also discovered that the arsenal was being guarded by a group of homeless, desperate soldiers.

"The soldiers, including the officer in charge, were moonlighting at menial jobs and foraging for their basic necessities. They hadn't been paid for three months, so they turned their heads and pocketed enough money to keep them going for a while."

Prost gazed at the river. "To no one's surprise, the senior officers and bureaucrats who were behind the theft had taken their payoff and were long gone. Our friends at Sandia said it had to have been an inside job."

"That seems to be happening on a regular basis," Scott said lightly. "We're going to see a number of 'rogue' countries with nuclear weapons in the near future."

"I'm afraid you're right," Prost admitted. "Less than four days later the Agency traced the weapons to Taganrog."

"On the coast of the Sea of Azov?" Scott asked.

"That's right," Jackie interjected with an air of confidence. "The place has become a magnet for weapons exporters, and a clearinghouse for Russian scientists and engineers who have the ability to construct nuclear weapons."

Dalton's quick glance studied the sparkle in her eyes, quietly sizing her up while he focused his attention on Prost.

"At any rate," Prost continued. "One of our informants spotted the truck carrying the warheads when it entered the ship repair yards. A few hours later we had an unmanned aerial vehicle monitoring the stolen weapons. Shortly after midnight, the warheads were loaded on a small cargo ship which sailed with the tide."

"Russian?" Scott asked.

"You guessed it," Prost confirmed with a frown. "The Agency stayed on top of the situation until the *Vasily Proshkinov* left the Black Sea and entered the Bosporus Strait. Between the flotilla of fishing boats, oil tankers, cargo vessels, and the fog, the ship simply vanished, or so it seemed to the Agency."

Prost shook his head in mild disbelief. "Three weeks later one of the NRO's advanced KH-11s spotted the *Vasily Proshkinov* as it lay at anchor in the Strait of Hormuz near Bandar-e Abbas. The 5th Fleet dispatched a destroyer and a frigate that were conducting interdiction ops near the Shatt al-Arab waterway. By the time the ships arrived on the scene, the nukes were gone."

"Do you have any idea where they are?"

"Oh, yes." He chuckled very weakly. "They're sitting atop missiles on the launchpads at Bandar-e Abbas and Bushehr."

"Out in the open—not even camouflaged?"

"That's right. Our spacecraft data, and the photos from the recon flights show most of the details. The Tomcat that went down was photographing the launch pads with the sun directly overhead."

Tilting his head down, Prost seemed to search for the words he wanted to say. "Their nukes can easily reach all of their regional enemies, including our military units in Tur-

key, Bahrain, Qatar, Kuwait, and Saudi Arabia." Prost caught
Scott's eye. "And, they're daring us to do something about
it."

"Well, I'm not surprised," Scott said as he struggled to
contain the remark he really wanted to make. "When we
didn't take a tougher stance against Iran for helping Saddam
circumnavigate the oil embargo, what did we expect? Same
with Saddam's cheat-and-retreat strategy."

"I agree." Prost nodded. "It made us look like fools."

"And," Scott added, "our lack of determination encouraged the boys in Baghdad and Tehran to be more aggressive
toward us. Hell, Saddam is still playing rope-a-dope with us
while he continues to strengthen his nuclear capability."

"I'm with you," Prost said hastily. "While everyone was
focused on Saddam, Iran has been busy stockpiling advanced
weapons, including nukes. Look, we all know that the Arab
leaders never wanted Iraq too weak because their real nightmare is Iran, not Baghdad."

Scott paused a moment. "We can be sure of one thing,"
Dalton said as he glanced at Jackie. "Our nuclear deterrence
isn't going to stop a bunch of fanatics set on martyrdom."

"No question about that," Prost said in a low voice. "We
can't prevent people from committing suicide."

Scott's glance locked with Prost. "If the Iranians launch
their nukes at our forces, the entire Gulf region would be
uninhabitable for hundreds of years. If they lob a few nukes
on Tel Aviv at the same time, the Israelis will turn downtown
Tehran into one gigantic smoking hole."

"Gigantic *radioactive* hole," Prost added. Tilting his head
back, he studied the blue Alaskan skies and turned to Scott.
"That's the dilemma the president is struggling with. This is
very different from the Cold War era. The Soviet premiers
and their military leaders had wicked intentions, but they
were at least rational, and somewhat predictable. They didn't
really want to have a nuclear exchange with us and risk losing the fragile control they had over their people."

Prost continued with a sense of dread. "Iran is an entirely
different anomaly. It is, without a doubt, the greatest non-
deterrable threat we face, and Tehran now has the capability
to deliver chemical, biological, *and* nuclear weapons. One
miscalculation and the Middle East could erupt into a war

that might set off North Korea—and other rogue nations—and force us to use our nukes."

"Take away their options," Scott suggested.

"That's what the president is considering," Prost said emphatically. "Have you heard the latest threats from Bassam Shakhar?"

"I haven't heard a thing for the past three days."

Before leaving on his fishing vacation, Scott had seen extensive news coverage of the wealthy militant shouting threats at the United States, desecrating the American flag, and burning the U.S. president in effigy.

"The last I knew, Shakhar was threatening to assassinate the president if we didn't pack our trash and get out of the Middle East."

Prost slowly exhaled. "That hasn't changed," he said with a grimace, "but Shakhar added a new twist yesterday morning—a globally televised reminder of our deadline."

Scott let it run through his mind, then shook his head. "Shakhar is backing himself into a corner."

"He doesn't think so." Prost raised his arm and studied his wristwatch. "According to Shakhar, we now have less than four hours to begin removing our military forces from the Arabian peninsula, or his *premier* terrorists cells will assassinate the president of the United States and begin downing U.S. airliners. In fact, Shakhar brazenly stated that his *primary target* is President Macklin."

"He actually said that?" Scott asked with an anxious expression of disbelief.

"*Live* on CNN and MSNBC," Prost groused. "If the U.S. attempts to retaliate in any way, Shakhar said the Iranian Navy will close the Strait of Hormuz and starve the West of oil. He also said Iran has prepositioned a wide variety of biological and chemical agents in all major U.S. cities."

The first warning light flashed in Scott's mind. "The guy is crazy—he's a madman who needs to be institutionalized."

"Crazy or not, he *is* a major player in this whole scenario, *and* he has a sizable fortune at his disposal."

"Is the president going to back down?"

"No way." Prost's voice was quieter, flatter. "He thinks they're bluffing, and he intends to call their bluff."

"What do you think?" Scott asked.

"Bassam Shakhar is not a man who makes idle threats." Prost tossed a pebble in the river. "If they've prepositioned nerve agents, botulism, or anthrax in our largest cities, it would be easy to pollute our air and municipal water supplies. However, we don't have any evidence to substantiate his claim—at least not yet."

Prost picked up another pebble. "On the other hand, Shakhar knows our commercial aviation security system—for the most part—is inadequate and disorganized. It's nearly impossible to develop and maintain security areas around congested urban airports. He also knows airports and airliners are vulnerable to sabotage, and shoulder-fired antiaircraft weapons."

"And," Jackie said with feigned nonchalance, "the terrorists understand the primal fear that airline crashes strike in the hearts of millions of people who—by necessity—have to fly commercially."

"Absolute fear is their primary goal," Prost agreed in a sad voice. "If Shakhar can drop a dozen U.S. airliners, *and* orchestrate the assassination of the president, the members of the Supreme Council believe Americans will fall to their knees in fear and confusion."

Jackie looked straight into Scott's eyes. "We may think it sounds wacky, but they truly believe it."

"I have no doubt. An assassination, combined with the airlines going bankrupt, would certainly put us in a bind."

"If Shakhar isn't bluffing," Prost went on, "we're a little late on the draw. We're going to have to take some major risks, and we're going to have to do it quickly." He glanced at a moose ambling toward the river. "That's why I'm here."

As he saw the deep concern written on Prost's face, Scott's entire body suddenly tensed. His glance sliced to Jackie, then back to Prost. "Okay. What's the plan?"

"We've penetrated a few of the terrorist groups," Prost confided triumphantly. "During the past sixteen months, our undercover agents—including a number of Islamic recruits—have infiltrated the Hezbollah of Hejaz, al-Gamaat, al-Islamiyah, Hamas, and the Organization of Islamic Revolution at the Imam Ali Camp in east Tehran. It's like playing the lottery: you have to dump a lot of money in, but every now and then someone hits the big prize."

"And we hit the jackpot," Jackie announced with pride in her voice. "One of my colleagues—also a *civilian* agent—successfully infiltrated one of the main training camps for the central faction of Islamic Jihad."

Scott merely nodded.

"About eight months ago," Jackie continued, her voice filled with exuberance, "Bassam Shakhar began spending three to four hours a week at the training camp. He's surrounded by heavy security and comes and goes at random times, but he *is* the kingpin behind the anti-U.S. military operation."

Scott felt a tingle of excitement. "The agent—is he still there?"

"*She,*" Jackie informed him in a pleasant voice. "Her name is Maritza Gunzelman. She's still at the camp, but she recently came under suspicion, and they're closely watching every move she makes."

"Why do you think they're suspicious of her?" Scott asked.

"I really don't know for certain." Jackie paused, eyeing Scott briefly. "She sent us a short message about three weeks ago. She's gleaned a lot of important information about Shakhar, his plans, and his team leaders. Unfortunately, since they've become suspicious of her, we aren't able to communicate with Maritza like we did before. She's trapped there and we're going to have to mount a covert operation to rescue her."

Although he was intrigued by what she had divulged, Scott's curiosity about Sullivan's role was quickly getting the best of him. There was a bold and adventurous spirit about her—an air of courage that was both sensuous and reckless. About five and a half feet in height, she had dark brown hair swept back in a wedge, and seductive gray-green eyes that didn't miss anything.

"No offense," Scott said, aware that Prost had a tendency to be absentminded around attractive women, "but I'm a little confused about Ms. Sullivan's role."

"I apologize," Prost hurriedly replied. "It's been a long night for us. We left straight from the White House and went to Andrews to catch a flight to Elmendorf. Jackie and Maritza are former clandestine intelligence officers with the Defense

Humint Service, and, like you, she and Maritza have become *civilian* consultants."

Suddenly the synapse hit Scott like a two-by-four. *I invited her to go sailing with me.* His face flushed as it all came rushing back from the previous year. Her hair had been longer and she had been wearing a stunning black cocktail dress, but it was definitely the same woman he had met at an elegant restaurant in Georgetown.

Jackie and three of her girlfriends had been enjoying a lively birthday bash at 1789. Scott and another former Marine pilot had introduced themselves to the quartet, then hosted after-dinner cordials for the group. Later, when Scott managed to get Jackie alone, he'd invited her to go sailing. She accepted the invitation, but Scott left the following day for Buenos Aires, and during his quest to capture an international terrorist, he misplaced Jackie's name and phone number.

Scott tilted his head down. *I hope she doesn't remember who I am.*

"Besides speaking six languages," Prost continued, "and being an excellent markswoman, Jackie's an expert in counterterrorism and international weapons proliferation."

Scott cast a quick look at her and noticed the guarded, aloof poise she maintained. He assumed a guise of nonchalance while she eyed him with close curiosity. *If she remembers, she's hiding it well.*

"She's a former Air Force F-16 pilot who also flies helicopters, and she teaches a course in high-speed evasive driving."

Scott gave her a casual glance, then cleared his throat. "Okay"—he paused—"where do I fit in?"

Prost's eyes hardened and a forced smile highlighted his cheeks. "President Macklin and I would like you—working in conjunction with Jackie—to extract Maritza Gunzelman from the terrorist compound." The words came out as a challenge. "We have to know what Shakhar is *really* up to, find out if he's bluffing."

Scott's response was stony silence for a few seconds, followed by a slow grin. "That's a mighty tall order."

"That's why the president sent me to talk to you in person," Prost confided. "This is *extremely* important. Our intel—CIA, the Brits, and Mossad—indicates a flurry of activity in the Shakhar camps, but Maritza is the only operative who has firsthand knowledge of his intentions."

"It's critical," Jackie asserted. "We have to find out what Maritza has learned about Shakhar's specific plans."

Scott arched an eyebrow, but remained silent while he contemplated the scope of the operation.

"President Macklin," Prost went on, "asked me to tell you that you have carte blanche to carry out the mission."

Prost placed his hands on his knees. "Scott, we have every reason to believe that Ms. Gunzelman has critical information that is vital to our national interest. We have to know what their plans are."

Scott's eyes shifted from Prost to Sullivan.

Jackie's expression was intense. "Maritza had originally planned to disappear from the Bekaa Valley during one of her weekly trips to the marketplace. Now she isn't allowed to leave the compound."

Scott slowly shook his head. "I can't perform miracles."

"She's in real jeopardy." Jackie's voice took on a sense of urgency. "We can't storm the place, and there are too many obstacles in and around the camp to risk a simple helicopter extraction."

"It sounds like a suicide mission," Scott said. "The terrorists are well armed and ruthless, but that's only part of the problem. That entire valley is a center of international drug production. The druggies and their security teams are also well armed, and they shoot at anything—and I mean *anything*—that threatens their billion-dollar business."

Scott paused, then smiled ruefully. "Another *minor* problem is the thousands of Syrian troops in the valley. Target practice is their favorite pastime, night or day."

"I'm fully aware of everything you've just mentioned," Jackie retorted with a flash of anger. "I don't know what else to say, except that I'm going after her—with or without you."

Scott experienced a faint twinge of guilt.

"We *really* need your special skills and experience," she implored.

Scott gave her a brief nod, then turned his attention to the man responsible for coordinating the activities of the National Security Council. "I'll give it a try—on one condition."

"It's your show," Prost said, knowing how Scott operated. "You call the shots, no questions asked. Whatever you need—just extract Ms. Gunzelman from the terrorist camp."

Scott and Jackie exchanged glances.

"Is that acceptable to you?" Scott asked. "I make the final decisions?"

"Fair enough," she said with a sly smile. "Unless, of course, you make *faulty* decisions."

Scott saw the self-satisfied gleam in her eyes. He sensed that she was going to be a formidable challenge.

Prost broke the undercurrent of tension. "Scott, do you want to use O'Donnell as your drop pilot?"

"Absolutely," Scott replied as he shifted his gaze to Prost.

"Ah, yes, the brotherhood," Jackie deadpanned.

With his eyes reflecting a devilish trace of humor, Scott turned to her. "Now that's what I like—a woman who is direct and honest."

Refusing to take the bait, she smiled serenely and changed the topic. "Are you acquainted with Ed Hockaday?"

"I know of him," Scott admitted with apparent indifference. "But I've never met him."

Edward "Eddy" Hockaday was an eccentric and savvy English-born journalist who covered the Arab world. In addition, he pocketed a second income as a freelance spy for the Agency.

"I have arranged a meeting with him in Dallas late this afternoon." Her eyes never wavered from his. "He's been in the compound and has interviewed Shakhar for CNN, and he spoke at length with Maritza. He'll be able to give us a detailed description of the training facility and the surrounding area."

"Is he in Dallas for the seminar on terrorism?" Scott asked.

"Yes, he's one of the guest speakers."

"I'm looking forward to meeting him."

"Then let's get moving." She reached down and retrieved two American Airlines from a pocket on the leg of her flight suit, then handed one to Scott. "The Air Force has a plane standing by to fly us to DFW as soon as you've packed your gear and briefed O'Donnell. He can fly back to Washington with Hartwell."

"Whoa—wait a second," Scott said, smiling faintly. "That assumes Greg will join the show."

"You're former Marine jet jocks, aren't you?" she taunted.

"That's right."

"He'll go," she said with undisguised cockiness. "We'll meet Eddy at DFW and fly back to Washington with him. If everything goes as planned, we'll leave the following day for Athens—our staging area."

She tilted her head to meet his gaze. "Any questions?"

"Not at the moment," Scott said lightly.

Prost signaled the helicopter crew and started walking toward the helo.

"Well," Scott said as he glanced at her, "we better not keep Mr. Hockaday waiting."

"You're the boss," Jackie demurred with practiced ease.

# 5

## Khaliq Farkas

Monitoring the A-4 Skyhawk's Global Positioning System, Khaliq Farkas noted his progress and the course to his final destination near Huntington, West Virginia. This was real flying; exactly how he remembered the sensation during his jet transition training at Tampa International Airport. In a matter of seven weeks, he had mastered both the Cessna Citation II and a civilian-owned former Navy TA-4J Skyhawk.

To Farkas, this was the ultimate experience in the world of aviation. He was captivated by the exhilaration of flying high-performance military aircraft to the edge of the envelope—and sometimes beyond.

Considered one of the world's most dangerous and cunning terrorists, Khaliq Farkas had successfully eluded an international manhunt for over sixteen years. During that period, in addition to learning how to fly jets at the expense of Bassam Shakhar, Farkas had mastered the art of building remotely triggered bombs while he and his devout followers watched the bounty on his head steadily increase to $4.35 million.

Operating with various special action cells of Islamic Jihad, he had been the mastermind behind numerous ambushes and bombings, including the suicide truck bombing on the U.S. Marine barracks in Beirut in 1983.

More recently, Farkas had assisted Shakhar in planning and executing the bombing of the Khobar Towers military housing complex in Dhahran, Saudi Arabia.

Farkas was also directly responsible for the bombings of two U.S. embassies and the kidnapping and assassinations of a number of political and religious leaders. Along with his record of murder, torture, and bombings, he proudly took credit for downing two U.S. airliners and a French corporate jet. Now, with the strong encouragement and considerable financial backing from Bassam Shakhar, Farkas was stalking new prey in the heart of America.

Known as a merciless chameleon by his pursuers, Farkas lived for the banishment of American and French influence from the Middle East. An explosively bitter little man, his hatred of "Western imperialism" was a crippling emotion that sometimes blinded him from reality. His campaign of zeal and fury would not end until the Americans and their cultural "pollution" disappeared from the Persian Gulf.

A thin, energetic man with dark, deeply set eyes, Farkas was a cruel, cold-blooded sociopath who could kill without compunction. At times he frowned and his eyes glazed over before he would suddenly smile so horribly that people would step back from him. The father of the "human bombs" suicide battalions, Khaliq Farkas was the frightening product of an extremist ideological culture.

Farkas unsnapped his oxygen mask and took off his crash helmet. He rubbed his scalp to stimulate the blood flow and watched the scattered clouds rush under the compact fuselage of the single-engine, single-seat Skyhawk. Refreshed, he donned his helmet and snapped the mask in place.

A moment later he grinned while he raised the Skyhawk's nose fifteen degrees above the horizon and completed an aileron roll to the left. Stopping precisely upright with the wings level, he then executed a snappy roll to the right. In his mind, there wasn't any comparison to the thrill of flying a military jet—except perhaps the thrill of flying one loaded with live ordnance.

Farkas had flown the restored McDonnell Douglas A-4 attack jet from a short, narrow airstrip near Portland, Oregon.

Even with the two auxiliary "drop tanks" empty, the departure from the restoration complex had required every inch of available runway and full power from the moment of brake release. A cold shudder ran down his spine when he remembered the charred wreckage of another jet that hadn't cleared the tops of the trees at the end of the less-than-adequate airstrip. The inexperienced pilot had overestimated the power of the jet fighter, and his own flying ability. He died a fiery death in the blazing cockpit of his F9F-2 Panther.

Due to his light load of fuel on departure, Farkas had been forced to make an en route refueling stop at Casper, Wyoming. The gray and blue Skyhawk, complete with two operational Mk-12 cannons and wing stations for two heat-seeking Sidewinder missiles, had attracted unwanted attention at the airport.

Outfitted in a dark gray flight suit, Farkas had made every attempt to be friendly to the curious onlookers at Casper Air Service. He tried to keep his distance whenever he could, but the immaculate warbird had piqued the curiosity of the local hangar fliers.

Now, in less than a half hour, the airplane would be in the barnlike hangar at its new home. Checking his high-altitude navigation chart and the GPS, Farkas decided to wait a couple of minutes before he began his descent.

His base of operations had been selected by drawing a boundary line from Washington, D.C., to Seattle, then a line connecting the nation's capital and Mobile, Alabama. Approximately 300 miles west of Washington, D.C., and close to equal distance from the parameters of the boundary lines, was the ideal place to set up a staging area to shoot down *Air Force One*. Although the president's 747 was equipped with electronics that could create false echoes to divert radar guided missiles, *Air Force One* remained vulnerable to heat-seeking missiles and twenty-millimeter cannon fire.

The location of the airstrip was predicated on the range of the Skyhawk, and the necessity for the airplane to disappear as quickly as possible after the attack. Normally, if the president traveled west or southwest from the capital, *Air Force One* would be in range of the airstrip. Situated in the far western corner of West Virginia, the landing field was a sim-

ple grass strip a short distance from the confluence of the
Ohio and Guyandotte rivers.

Slowly and methodically, trees and bushes had been
planted thirty to forty feet from the sides of the runway.
Other varieties of camouflage had been carefully planted to
deceive curious observers. Viewed from the air, or from the
ground, the landing site blended in with the rest of the Mountain State countryside.

Although the Internet provided flight-tracking services for
aircraft operating on instrument flight plans within the contiguous U.S., Farkas and his team would have to rely on two
operatives for flight information about *Air Force One*. Real-
time flight data on military flights, Drug Enforcement
Agency aircraft, civilian operators who request anonymity,
and *Air Force One* is filtered from the Internet.

Farkas relaxed and let his mind drift, then stretched his
legs and prepared to begin his descent profile. He didn't want
to draw any unnecessary attention to the airplane or to himself. As far as the Air Route Traffic Control Centers were
concerned, the attack airplane was a Sabreliner corporate jet.
He had taken off VFR from Casper, then filed an instrument
flight plan en route. The air traffic controllers wouldn't know
the difference, unless another aircraft flying near the A-4
pointed out that it was, in fact, a military jet. From experience, Farkas was confident that no one would finger him.

He waited patiently for a radio frequency change for the
upcoming sector, then switched to the next controller.

"Indianapolis Center, Sabre Sixty-Seven Alpha Kilo with
you at three-seven-oh with a request."

"Six-Seven Alpha Kilo, Indianapolis. Say your request."

"Alpha Kilo would like to start down."

"Roger, Sabre Six-Seven Alpha Kilo. Descend and maintain three-three-zero, and I'll have lower for you shortly."

"Down to three-three-oh, Alpha Kilo."

Keeping the power where it was, he lowered the nose and
began a series of rolls while he descended to 33,000 feet. A
minute later, the controller cleared him to begin a descent
toward his destination. Out of 12,000 feet, Farkas began
slowing to 250 knots and canceled his instrument flight plan
out of 10,000 feet. He squawked 1200 on his transponder—
the standard code for visual flight rules—and blended in with

the other VFR traffic on the controller's radar scope. Less than thirty seconds later Farkas turned his transponder off and became a semistealthy radar image. No one would be the wiser that a corporate Sabreliner had suddenly metamorphosed into a lethal military attack jet.

Ten minutes later the A-4 arrived at the secluded private airstrip. Farkas made a firm landing, brought the airplane to a halt at the end of the grass strip, then raised the flaps and retracted the speed brakes. He quickly taxied the Şkyhawk directly to the hangar and stopped next to a freshly painted corporate jet.

After Farkas climbed down from the A-4, two members of his special action cell used a John Deere utility tractor to park the airplane in the hangar. In the back of the hangar sat three containers of Sidewinder air-to-air missiles and fourteen cases of shells for the Mk-12 cannons. Eight Iranian-supplied Swedish Bofors RBS-70 portable antiaircraft missiles completed the arsenal. Before the day was over, the Skyhawk would be loaded with cannon shells and two heat-seeking missiles.

Farkas noticed a new container sitting next to the cannon shells. He opened the box and smiled with great pleasure. *These should be considered weapons of mass destruction.* The nine Russian-built GPS jammers could immobilize military and civilian signals, including Russia's own *Glonass* Global Orbiting Navigation Satellite. When winter storms engulfed the major airports along the East Coast of the United States, Farkas and his group of terrorists planned to create nightmares for pilots, passengers, and air traffic controllers.

After a quick snack and a change of clothes, Farkas threw his canvas bags into the gleaming white and blue Cessna Citation I/SP and headed for his next destination. If the White House ignored the deadline for the U.S. military to begin leaving the Gulf region, Shakhar had ordered Farkas to deliver an immediate and resounding response.

# 6

## En Route to Dallas–Fort Worth International

The C-37A Air Force Special Air Missions VIP transport, a modified military version of the long-range Gulfstream V corporate jet, cruised quietly at 41,000 feet as it neared the southeastern corner of Colorado. Relaxing in the spacious cabin, Scott and Jackie were the only passengers on the specially configured plane.

An hour and a half ahead of them in another Air Force VIP jet, Hartwell Prost and Greg O'Donnell were going over the details of the rescue mission. They would be back in Washington, D.C., before Scott and Jackie arrived at Dallas–Fort Worth International.

Scott was finishing the report Jackie had written about Maritza Gunzelman's surveillance activities. Setting the confidential report aside, he reached for Maritza's dossier. From the variety of photographs of Gunzelman wearing different disguises in different settings, it was easy to see how she could blend into almost any environment.

Maritza could pass for Spanish, Mexican, Portuguese, Egyptian, Indian, Italian, or a native of the Gulf region. Dressed in a solid black *chador* with her arms and legs hidden, hair and forehead concealed by scarves, she looked amazingly like the archetypal Islamic woman.

She was well versed in the Muslim religion and spoke

several Persian dialects, including Farsi. Covered in traditional Islamic garb and espousing fierce opposition to the Israeli occupation of southern Lebanon, Maritza had methodically worked her way close to the senior Hezbollah activists operating in the Bekaa Valley.

Scott read a little further, then paused and leaned closer to Jackie. "How did she manage to break through—to actually become a member of the Islamic Jihad?"

"It wasn't easy," Jackie answered with considerable satisfaction. "She gained the attention of the militants by preaching day and night about exterminating the infidels and making Islam the sole religion on earth. She even spent entire days chanting outside the compound about the fury and breadth of Islam's revenge."

Scott shook his head. "Incredible."

Jackie smiled to herself. "Slowly they began to trust her, including Bassam Shakhar. After she was invited to join the terrorist group, Shakhar personally challenged Maritza to prove her loyalty by murdering a man charged with being a heretic."

"That sounds like Shakhar," Dalton quietly commented, his expression unchanged. "Welcome to the psycho ward."

Jackie paused and made eye contact with Scott. "She carried out the execution flawlessly."

Scott avoided stating an opinion.

"That solidified her acceptance by the group, and Shakhar invited her to move into the compound."

Scott was about to reply when the aircraft commander stepped out of the cockpit to give them an update on the weather situation in the Dallas–Fort Worth area. The present conditions were reasonable, but the weather was expected to deteriorate as a powerful line of thunderstorms neared the metroplex. The pilot explained that they would be descending soon, then excused himself and turned to speak with the pilots who had flown the leg from Andrews Air Force Base to Elmendorf AFB.

"Interesting," Scott said as he handed the report and dossier back to Jackie. "She's a gutsy woman."

"She's one of the best," Sullivan said as the command pilot returned to the cockpit. "Like any good actress, she thoroughly prepares for the part she's going to play."

"Tell me again," Scott inquired with idle curiosity, "what caused them to become suspicious of her?"

"It's only a guess, but I think someone may have heard Maritza speaking English when she was ostensibly being interviewed by Ed Hockaday. That's the only logical thing I can think of."

"They probably bugged the room."

"Well, that may be the case, but it's academic now. The day after Eddy visited with Maritza, Shakhar told her that she wouldn't be allowed to leave the compound until certain issues were resolved. He said it was for her own safety and protection."

"What issues?"

"He didn't say—still hasn't, as far as we've heard."

Scott searched Jackie's face. "What about Hockaday?"

"What about him?"

"He could be a double agent."

Surprised by the blunt statement, she gave him a look of skepticism. "If he is—which I don't believe is the case—he has more guts than brains." She gave Scott a hard look. "Before you start tossing out insinuations or accusations, you should do your homework."

"That's good advice," Scott said evenly, and changed the subject. "How do you communicate with Maritza?"

"Satellite-phone."

"You're kidding," he protested in mild disbelief. "She just whips out her sat-phone and calls you from a Hezbollah stronghold."

"Not exactly. Maritza has a matchbook-size experimental phone. It slips into a recess in her clothes and rests on her right shoulder. If she's outside, or near a window, she can push a small button, then turn her head and speak softly into the microphone."

"Can you contact her?"

"Yes, but obviously the phone doesn't ring." Jackie smiled.

"Yeah, that could cause some problems."

"It vibrates."

"How often does she contact you?"

"Before they became suspicious of her, she would send us very short messages once or twice a week. She called at random times and left brief messages on a designated line in our office. We have some basic info about Shakhar's plans, but the details of his assault on us were just beginning to gel a few days before Eddy's interview with Shakhar."

Scott's uneasiness grew as he considered Maritza's predicament. "If they catch her or even suspect . . ."

"I know," she said with a dismissive shrug. "Since Shakhar and his followers have become suspicious, she's only been able to contact us twice in the past three weeks. The last message—less than seven seconds long—was a clear plea for help. She has a lot of crucial information and wants out of there as quickly as possible."

Scott didn't underestimate the odds of rescuing Maritza. "Will you risk contacting her by voice to let her know when we're coming to get her?"

"You bet," she said firmly. "Once we commit ourselves, all of us have to know exactly what's happening. We'll make contact with Maritza twenty-four hours before we go in to get her. I'll brief her on exactly what we're going to be doing."

Scott fell silent for a moment, then spoke quietly. "You realize this extraction is going to be next to impossible."

"Well," she said under her breath, "that depends on how you define impossible. I wouldn't be here, and you wouldn't either, if you didn't think it was possible."

Scott nodded, then changed course. "What do you know about the compound? How well is it guarded?"

"Ed Hockaday can give you more detail than I can, but the place is surrounded by a high steel fence, and it's heavily guarded on all sides. The buildings are constructed of low-grade concrete blocks, and very crude by our standards. There isn't any way to gain access to the compound, except from the air."

Jackie hesitated as her mouth curved in a warm smile. "That's—of course—why I asked for your help."

Scott gazed at the clouds, then turned to Jackie. "I suppose Hartwell gave you my bio?"

"Yes." She smiled. "And I'm *not* into parachuting into confined areas in the middle of the night."

He studied her expression, sensing a bond of trust developing between them. "That's good, because I'm not into flying helicopters."

"That's probably a wise decision," Jackie said matter-of-factly, and raised an eyebrow. "How did you manage to get permission to go through the Army's HALO School?"

The High Altitude, Low Opening School is designed to train Special Operations forces to infiltrate enemy lines by air without being detected.

"The Agency arranged it." Scott chuckled. "You know, one of those 'career enhancement' opportunities."

"Does O'Donnell fly all your drops?"

"Every one," Scott declared with obvious pride in his voice. "When I was shot down during Desert Storm, Greg kept the Iraqis off me until a rescue helo arrived."

"Yes, I've read about your exploits together."

The look in his eyes was both serious and sincere. "He's one of the best pilots—maybe *the* best—I've ever seen."

"Second to you, of course," Jackie suggested in a faint taunt.

Scott managed to keep his ego just below the surface. "Actually, you're right." He smiled broadly.

"I thought so," she said, then turned toward the window to keep the smirk from showing.

With a slight reduction of power from the twin Rolls-Royce fanjets, the C-37A began a shallow descent toward DFW.

Turning back, she leaned close to Scott's ear and spoke in a low, cultured voice. "Have you done much sailing lately?"

For a stunned second Scott was speechless while he tried in vain to hide his embarrassment. "I was hoping you'd forgotten about that," he said with a sheepish grin.

"No," she replied, smiling sweetly. "In fact, I remember every detail about the evening, *and* the invitation."

Scott took in a slow breath. "Look, Jackie, I apologize for not calling you, but I was in the mid—"

"Let me guess," she interrupted with a cool smile. "You lost my name and phone number, right?"

"It's the truth," Scott said with a straight face that involuntarily turned into a smile. "How can I convince you it's true?"

"You can't, so don't even try," she said with conviction,

then abruptly changed the subject. "Do you think you can pull this off?"

"I thought this was a dual effort," Scott challenged.

"It is," she murmured with strained politeness. "But *you're* the mission commander."

In mock seriousness, Scott turned to Jackie. "Are you one of those 'I have to be equal to men' types?"

"Not even close," Jackie said evenly. "It's been my observation that women who aspire to be *equal* to men," she said with a touch of sarcasm, "lack ambition."

"Touché."

# 7

## Coral Gables, Florida

Massoud Ramazani finished his short conversation with Khaliq Farkas and placed the portable phone on his kitchen table. The reception from the Cessna Citation's newly installed Flitefone had been exceptionally clear. Farkas was ahead of schedule and the next step in their ambitious plan to assassinate the president and bring down U.S. airliners was unfolding nicely.

The deadline for the Americans to start their military withdrawal had just expired without any movement on behalf of the United States. Now the foolish president and his naive countrymen were about to receive a message they weren't likely to forget. The stage was set for Shakhar's rebellion against the *tahajom-e farangi*, America's cultural aggression.

Outwardly a mild-mannered college professor with no strong views on the trouble spot known as the Middle East, Massoud Ramazani was leading a double life. In his heart, he lived for the day when the complete destruction of the state of Israel, the "Little Satan" as he referred to the close ally of the Americans, would be complete.

When not on campus, Ramazani spent most of his spare time educating himself on the weaknesses in the capability of the U.S. to deal with international terrorism. In addition to his surveillance activities, he and Farkas had established several terrorist footholds within ethnic communities in Atlanta, Dallas, Kansas City, Houston, Los Angeles, New York City, San Diego, Seattle, and Chicago.

After organizing the new "religious charity" arms of Islamic Jihad, Ramazani and Farkas had used a war chest of over $24 million to establish a base of operations to support terrorist attacks throughout America, including Alaska and the Hawaiian Islands. Bassam Shakhar had spared no expense in his efforts to build the foundation for an all-out assault on the "capital of global arrogance," and the arrogant U.S. president. Ramazani and Farkas would play key roles in the attacks. The first step in the aggressive scheme would be to change America's course from the new world order to complete disorder.

After five years of teaching economics at the University of Miami, the undeclared war between the U.S. and Iran had spelled the end of Ramazani's facade. At the behest of Bassam Shakhar, the soft-spoken, thirty-four-year-old, Oxford- and Yale-trained Ph.D. would be resigning from his teaching post to devote his full efforts to the goals of Islamic Jihad. The time had arrived for Ramazani to exploit the weaknesses he had so carefully and patiently studied.

Well traveled and sophisticated in the ways of the Western world, Ramazani would assume his new duties as the number-two man in the expanding terrorist organization. Working in conjunction with Khaliq Farkas, Ramazani would concentrate on wreaking havoc on American citizens and assassinating their president.

In addition to his primary objectives, Ramazani would be in charge of sixty-three special action cells that had been filtering into the U.S. during the previous five months. The nearly bald economist would be trading his conservative coat and tie for the expensive business suits favored by the sheikhs from Saudi Arabia. Ramazani's new persona would be that of a wealthy prince who enjoyed socializing with his American friends.

He would be relocating to his new base of operations in the Florida Keys. Complete with a helicopter and a refurbished 126-foot motoryacht, the luxurious estate on a private island reflected the type of accommodations a young sheikh would expect. If he handled his role carefully, no one would suspect that the friendly man from the oil sheikhdom of Saudi Arabia was in fact a highly educated Iranian terrorist—a terrorist with a deep feeling of resentment toward the United States. Ramazani's father had been a passenger on Iranian Air Flight 655 when the U.S. Navy mistakenly shot down the airliner.

Ramazani leaned back and smiled in his cynical way. *The feckless infidels are about to have their "civilized" lifestyles explode in their faces.*

### Fort Worth

After landing at Meacham International, Khaliq Farkas had the gleaming Citation filled with jet fuel, then borrowed a courtesy car from the fixed-base operator. On the way to the Dallas–Fort Worth International Airport, he checked into the Holiday Inn on Meacham Boulevard, then called American Airlines to find out the departure gate for his flight.

Pleased with himself, he shaved and changed into an airline pilot's uniform. Complete with an ID badge and a chart case, Farkas was now American Airlines Captain Manuel Gervasio.

A half hour later Farkas was parked near a security entrance to DFW. When a catering truck appeared in his rearview mirror, he stepped out of the car and flagged down the driver.

"Son, my car quit, and I'm running late for my flight," Farkas said without a trace of an accent. "Would you mind dropping me off at my gate?"

The pimply-faced young man hesitated. "Captain, we're not supposed to allow anyone in the trucks when we're making—"

"I understand," Farkas interrupted with a radiant smile as he handed the driver a folded $100 bill. "I won't say anything, but I have to make my flight. Let's get going."

"Uh, okay," the wide-eyed youngster uttered as Farkas grabbed his chart case and climbed into the passenger seat.

"You saved the day." Farkas beamed.

# 8

## The White House

The mood was somber when President Macklin walked into the basement Situation Room to join Pete Adair, his secretary of defense. Neither man smiled as they exchanged perfunctory greetings.

The chief executive was tall and thin, with a prominent nose, perfectly coiffed gray hair, and deeply set blue eyes. Impeccably attired in a dark gray suit, custom-tailored white shirt, maroon tie, and highly polished black leather shoes, Cord Macklin looked the part of the consummate politician. Like many ambitious men before him, he had coveted the highest political office in the land.

Boisterous and stubborn-natured, the former F-105 Thunderchief pilot was one tough customer. He was also a highly decorated survivor of the Vietnam War. While flying a Route Pack Six mission to Downtown Hanoi, First Lieutenant Macklin had been forced to eject from his "Thud" when it was destroyed by a surface-to-air missile. After a splash landing in a rice paddy near a small village, he evaded his angry pursuers for three days before a gutsy Jolly Green helicopter pilot saved him from an extended stay in the Hanoi Hilton.

Behind his tortoiseshell spectacles, Macklin's eyes were red and irritated. He politely dismissed two Secret Service agents and sat down at the head of the wide conference table.

The president motioned for Adair to have a seat near him. "What's the latest on the Tomcat—any sign of the crew?"

"Yessir." There was a telling hesitation. "Their bodies were recovered about two hours ago."

Saddened by the mysterious accident, Macklin said quietly. "Have the families been notified?"

"Yes, sir. About half an hour ago."

The president nodded as he went through the ritual of lighting a maduro cigar. "I want to call them later this evening."

"I'll make the arrangements."

"Do you have a salvage team out there?" Macklin took a deep drag from his prized Onyx.

"They're en route, and we've dispatched two ships to secure the area around the crash site. They're the ones who recovered the bodies, and they've also recovered quite a bit of floating debris."

"I want you to stay on top of this, Pete," the president insisted. "If it was hit by a missile, it's an act of war."

"I understand, sir."

Born on a small farm in the Oklahoma Panhandle, Peter McEntire Adair was an island of integrity and honesty in a sea of lickspittles. An ex-Green Beret captain and former bull rider, Adair enjoyed high-stakes poker and skeet shooting. Stocky and in excellent physical shape for his fifty-five years, Adair's friendly personality and boundless enthusiasm crackled like a lightning storm.

Adair glanced at the detailed map displays of Iran and the other Persian Gulf states. Numerous intelligence sources in the region were convinced that Israel had become so vulnerable that the Muslim world was planning its destruction. The only thing standing in the way was the 5th Fleet and other U.S. military forces in the Gulf region.

SecDef checked his wristwatch and frowned. "Well, the deadline is past and we haven't heard anything from Shakhar or his cronies."

"Let's pray that cooler heads prevailed."

Adair was nervous and it showed in his eyes. "Prost and Chalmers should be here anytime." He glanced at the empty chair normally occupied by Fraiser Wyman, Macklin's chief of staff. "Where's Fraiser?"

"Recuperating from oral surgery."

Clasping his fingers together, Adair stared at his briefing folder. For the first time since he'd accepted his position as secretary of defense, he was facing an imminent threat from the premier state sponsor of international terrorism—a sponsor who now had Russian-made supersonic antiship missiles and nuclear-tipped missiles to augment its biological and chemical weapons.

In answer to the continued U.S. military buildup in the Gulf, the Iranian Supreme Council for National Defense had quadrupled Iran's long-range surface-to-air rocket sites and surface-to-surface missile pads. Provided by a leading Swiss armament company, Oerlikon-Contraves AG, the top-line weapons posed serious threats to shipping and air traffic in the Gulf region.

Many scholars and analysts were convinced that Iran planned to take control of the Persian Gulf, now referred to as the Arabian Gulf, so it could blackmail the West. At the U.S. Naval War College, the annual war games featured Iran—not Baghdad—as the number one menace among potential adversaries.

Arriving by helicopter from Andrews Air Force Base, Hartwell Prost walked into the Situation Room and gave the president a thumbs-up. No handshakes were proffered while the president and Pete Adair exchanged pleasantries with the national security adviser.

"Dalton is onboard," Prost announced triumphantly. "But we have to be conservative about our expectations. They're taking a hell of a risk."

"I understand," Macklin declared, experiencing a moment of concern. "Just make sure they have all the support we can give them."

"I've got it covered."

"Good," Macklin said as Prost sat down.

Following on the heels of Prost, the chairman of the joint chiefs of staff, Air Force General Lester Chalmers, entered the quiet room. During his first tour at the Pentagon, Chalmers had developed the ability to absorb a series of questions and extemporize rational answers that addressed each subject.

"Good afternoon, Mr. President."

"Have a seat, Les."

"Yes, sir."

The tanned, athletic-looking general had twinkling hazel eyes that squinted through narrow slits. His cheekbones were pronounced and wide, with thin lines etched down his cheeks. A full head of close-cropped gray hair and a slow smile added to his handsome features. An even-tempered man who seldom made a political blunder, General "Lucky" Les Chalmers was the embodiment of a senior military leader. He was also a former classmate of cadet "Cordy" Macklin. They had attended the Air Force Academy together.

The president studied the men's faces before he spoke. "The first item of business is the ultimatum from Shakhar."

Macklin switched his focus to Pete Adair. "From the day he issued his threat, I've made it clear that we have no intention of removing our military presence in the Gulf. With that in mind, I don't think we should underestimate him. Even though his first deadline has passed, we may get another one—we need to be extremely cautious, and we need to be prepared for any contingency."

When he faced the president, Adair was dead serious. "I have every confidence in our military leadership."

Macklin glanced at Chalmers, then turned to Prost. "Hartwell, what are we doing about overall security?"

Prost glanced at his notes. "All government agencies— plus our foreign embassies in the Middle East and Indian subcontinent—have been ordered to take increased security measures. The FBI is sending additional undercover agents to every major airport in the United States, including Alaska and Hawaii."

Tired from his trip, Prost spoke in hushed words. "Every airline that flies to U.S. locations has been informed of the terrorist threat, and the FAA is on notice. Our airports are at Level Three now, so unattended vehicles are being towed to inspection points, unattended bags are being confiscated, and passengers must show proper IDs and answer questions about their luggage. As you know, all baggage is being matched to the boarded passengers."

"What about more police patrols?" Macklin asked.

"They're working on it as of this morning," Prost said, then added, "The FBI is coordinating their efforts with local law enforcement agencies to patrol airports and to search warehouses—anything suspicious—for biological and chemical agents. We're taking every step that we feel is necessary to preserve the safety of our citizens, both domestically and abroad. And, the FBI is working with the Immigration and Naturalization Service to investigate Iranian students who are attending school here. They plan to expel any suspicious diplomats or students."

Prost paused, then turned to face Chalmers. "Do you have anything to add, General?"

"No, sir," he replied. "Our forces are still being mobilized."

Although Cord Macklin appeared to be calm and unconcerned, inside he was nervous. Possessing the ego of a fighter pilot who now presided over the lone superpower, he didn't want to discuss the threat of assassination. It simply wasn't good form. Satisfied for the moment, he took a long drag on his cigar and slowly exhaled.

"Gentlemen," Macklin began slowly, "the next item on the agenda has to do with the question of Iran's recent emergence as a nuclear player. Moscow's fingerprints are all over this development, including the Russian Space Agency and the Central Aerohydrodynamic Institute. I want your input, and don't pull any punches."

Silence filled the room.

Pete Adair was the first to breach the void. "We all know the Russian foreign minister is openly anti-American. He has demonstrated that he will do anything to elevate Russia on the world stage. I think Moscow and Tehran are betting we won't cross the 'Mogadishu Line.'"

Prost removed his glasses and quietly nodded in agreement. "They're taunting us," he said in his clipped eastern accent. "After watching third-rate powers stand up to us, they're convinced we don't have the stomach for boots-in-the-mud warfare."

The chief executive narrowly eyed Prost, then spoke slowly. "They—the powers in Moscow and Tehran—figure we're too squeamish to do anything unilaterally, especially if it means taking casualties and getting bad press?"

"That's a reasonable inference," Prost said, with the confidence of a man who was accustomed to being the most intelligent person in a room. "They've closely watched us since Desert Fox and the Kosovo crisis. They honestly don't believe we would undertake a military action that risks more than a few lives, or a few thousand cruise missiles and bombs."

Pete Adair felt a sudden tenseness. "They know our military is half the strength it was during the Gulf War, and, they know we're stretched mighty thin. They figure there's no way we'll go it alone."

"What's your inclination?" the president turned and asked Adair. "Do we rely on ourselves to destroy their nukes, or do we try to build an alliance to work with us?"

SecDef paused a moment, combing his fingers through his rumpled hair. "In my judgment," Adair said reluctantly, "*we* have to deal with the problem. Our NATO allies and Arab friends have gone soft on us, and we don't have time to play games with the UN or NATO."

The president eyed Prost. "What do you think?"

"I agree," Hartwell declared. "Because of their business ties to Iran, some of our allies want to offer *more* incentives to the Iranians. They simply don't want to face the fact that Tehran has no moral compunction against using any type of weapon, including nukes."

Macklin quietly nodded.

"Hell," Prost went on, "we've tried to work with the Security Council. We've encouraged other countries to increase diplomatic and economic pressure on Iran, and we all know it's been a pitiful failure. All it's done is cause a tremendous backlash. The Arab nations believe that we use the 'dual containment' of Iraq-Iran as a way to reinforce our position as a superpower."

Hartwell paused for his message to have an impact. "Sanctions aren't going to solve *this* problem. They just provoke the power structure in Tehran and make them more intransigent. *We're* going to have to stand up to Iran, like we did to Iraq in Desert Storm."

There was a moment of hesitation while all eyes were on Prost.

"I may be wrong," Hartwell's voice resonated, "but I don't think anyone else is going to dive into this snake pit with us. We're going to have to be sensitive to our allies and our

Arab friends, but in the end, we're going to have to swim up this river alone."

The president still hoped to come up with a less forceful way to deal with the crisis. "Before we start lobbing ordnance at the Iranians, we have to establish some form of meaningful dialogue with Tehran."

Prost sighed heavily, betraying a dry patience. "Sir, as of two hours ago, we don't have diplomatic representation with Iran. We can't even muster a contact at the level of chargé d'affaires, let alone pursue critical dialogue with the foreign minister."

"That's ridiculous," Macklin said with open irritation. "Brett and Dave are on their way to the Gulf, and you're telling me that we can't communicate with anyone in Tehran?"

"Not at the moment, sir."

Vice-President Dave Timkey and Secretary of State Brett Shannon were en route to the Gulf to meet with members of the Gulf Cooperation Council and the assistant secretary of state for Middle East affairs. In addition, Timkey and Shannon hoped to persuade the Saudi Arabian leaders to allow U.S. Air Force aircraft stationed there to fly cover for the naval vessels in the Gulf.

"Mr. President," Hartwell said firmly, "we've tried everything. We even appealed to the Russian and the French ambassadors to intervene on our behalf. They both refused, citing their strong financial ties to Iran. Israel isn't going to get onboard either. They're afraid of getting nuked if things go south."

With a look of disgust on his face, Macklin stared at Prost. "Tell Tehran that the president of the United States is calling."

Hartwell hesitated for a few seconds. "We, ah . . . already tried that, sir."

"And?" Macklin prompted, his eyes narrowing.

The muscles along Hartwell's jaw stood out in ridges. "The message was quite clear; they despise us for attempting to turn their oil industry into their Achilles' heel. After the harangue, they pulled the plug."

Macklin bristled, then spoke in a tight voice. "What an absolutely insane region—beyond comprehension."

"Mr. President," Pete Adair said hastily, "we're clearly on a collision course with Tehran. The powers that be would like nothing better than to see you get on CNN or MSNBC and beg them to negotiate with us, especially after you've formally declared Iran a slum of global society."

Macklin's neck and face reddened, a clear signal to back off.

Adair paused to measure his words carefully. "Sir, we *have* to eliminate their nukes before some zealot in Tehran decides to rearrange the topography of Israel, or some other place in the neighborhood.

"And," Adair went on, "one of those neighbors is sitting on the world's richest oil field. Alarm bells have been ringing all over Saudi Arabia, especially after the terrorist bombings there."

"Pete's right," Prost quickly added. "We all know that tensions in the region have been growing since the Gulf War, primarily because of the increased presence of our military forces, and the westernization of the region."

"It's an assault on traditional Arab culture," Adair asserted. "We're viewed as the bad guys, no question about it."

Prost nodded in agreement. "Another factor we have to consider is the national instability facing Saudi Arabia, and the possibility of a political shake-up within the House of Saud. Between the royals' succession issues, the disaffection in the middle class, and the passions of the Islamic puritans, the monarchy could literally collapse overnight."

Pausing to gaze at each man, Prost continued. "Then, gentlemen, we'd have a bunch of squabbling ministates ripe for Iran and Iraq to fight over. Of course, if Iran uses their nukes, the entire Gulf region could become a huge ghost town."

"And," Adair quietly added, "we'll be out one fifth of our oil imports."

The president suddenly looked tired. "If we launch a unilateral, preemptive strike on Iran's nuclear stockpile, they'll unleash the terrorist factions on us—we know that. They could use crop dusters to spray chemicals all over this country and remotely activated atomizers to disperse biological agents almost anywhere."

With a look of confidence, Pete Adair countered. "They've already threatened to terrorize us if we don't pull our troops out of the Gulf. I'm convinced we have the capability to deal with their thugs, and we have the military muscle to keep the Strait of Hormuz open."

"Their *thugs* may not respond to your deterrence calculus," Macklin retorted, and shifted his gaze to the Air Force general. "Les, what do you think about this? I want to hear your thoughts."

Chalmers answered without hesitation. "I agree with Secretary Adair and Mr. Prost. There'll never be any insurance against human folly. We're dealing with people who don't behave rationally, at least not according to our accepted principles of logic. They've been accustomed to arbitrary rule for nearly 3,000 years, so I seriously doubt that Tehran—at our request—is going to peacefully destroy their nukes and become model citizens."

Macklin glanced at Prost and Adair, then fixed the JCS chairman in his gaze. "What do you recommend?"

Chalmers spoke in a confident, clear voice. "Sir, Tehran is the real threat in the region, not Baghdad. Iran has already demonstrated their ability to launch cruise missiles from the air, sea, or land. I recommend we take away their nuclear capability, before our conventional power becomes checkmated."

Chalmers poured himself a glass of water. "With the aid of certain Islamic fundamentalist groups, Tehran may feel that the time has come to purge the United States from the Holy Land, then destroy Israel."

"He's right," Prost declared. "The Israelis have been passing out gas masks and updating their emergency kits."

"Nuclear missiles," Chalmers continued, "or even conventional cruise missiles, are a surefire way to take advantage of the situation and destabilize the whole peninsula. If we, or one of our allies, take a major hit, then cut and run, the fanatics in Iran will be doin' the boogie-woogie right down Main Street, Tehran."

The president eyed him skeptically.

"We have to consider every possibility," Chalmers stubbornly persisted. "If Saudi Arabia is ruled by Islamic extremists, we're going to see an oil shock that'll dwarf the one of the seventies. But that'll pale in comparison to the tremendous oil wealth the Islamic extremists will devote to anti-American terrorism worldwide."

Chalmers leveled his gaze at the president. "When you consider the proliferation of weapons of mass destruction to Islamic extremists, transnational terrorism quickly emerges as our primary national security threat. It isn't *if* they'll use the weapons, it's a question of *when* they'll use them . . . and where."

A hint of worry crossed the president's face as he rested his cigar in an oversized crystal ashtray.

"We can't deny the obvious," Chalmers persisted. "Terrorism is rapidly engulfing our world, and that includes the heartland of America. There are millions of zealots—Islamic or otherwise—who believe they're the agents of Allahu, or some other God. These kooks see terrorism as a way to punish their enemies in God's name."

Macklin slumped in his chair and quietly tapped his fingers on the table.

Chalmers spoke slowly and clearly. "We have to take away Iran's nuclear capability, and we have to do it now . . . before we're caught in a crossfire in the Gulf."

The president leaned forward and folded his hands on the table, then caught Chalmer's eye. "They aren't going to take this lying down. We're a major target for states or terrorist groups whose ambitions are frustrated by our superpower status."

"Sir," Chalmers said as his mouth tightened, "we have the biggest and heaviest hammer on the block. I'm not overly concerned about Iranian reprisals once we destroy their nukes, *and* I'm damn sure not worried about keeping oil flowing through the strait."

"Les," the president said impatiently, "this situation is ripe for miscalculation. I don't mean to sound like the harbinger of doom, but those people *are* going to strike back—and strike back with a vengeance. There's no doubt about it. They're absolutely convinced it's their moral responsibility to attack their tormentors. If we're not careful, we could find ourselves backed into a very uncomfortable corner."

Macklin gritted his teeth. "If we get drawn into a major regional conflict—like the Gulf War—we could be vulnerable to aggression by a host of potential enemies." The president narrowly eyed his former wingman. "Enemies who might be convinced that we lack the military capability to oppose them."

Prost quickly intervened. "Sir, if we become paralyzed with fear, then the terrorists have already won the war."

"Dammit," Macklin exclaimed in frustration. "We have to consider the consequences of our actions. We're dealing with a primary supporter of terrorism here. Forget about their submarines, antishipping mines, cruise missiles, *and* nukes. No other *thug* regime on the planet employs terrorism more effectively as an instrument of national policy."

Prost became rigid with indignation.

"Terrorism," the president went on contentiously, "that reaches every corner of the globe. There was a time when the World Trade Center bombing would have seemed unthinkable. Now, the friggin' terrorists are crawling in our back doors, *and* they have chemical, biological, and nuclear weapons. Think about it. One nuke concealed in a truck or car could take out Los Angeles or New York."

When no one said a word, the president realized his voice had trembled in frustration. He quickly gathered himself together. "Gentlemen," he said with a wide smile, "enough of this discussion."

With a trace of embarrassment, Macklin took a slow, deep breath. "We'll discuss our options after dinner."

Pete Adair and Les Chalmers exchanged a brief glance. They had known the president for many years and he wasn't his usual self.

Seconds later Attorney General Sandra Hatcher and Jim Ebersole, the director of the FBI, were quickly ushered into the Situation Room. Sensing trouble, Macklin braced himself against the tension in the air.

"Mr. President," Sandy Hatcher said without hesitation, "we have a serious problem."

# 9

## Dallas–Fort Worth International Airport

The dark cumulus clouds were turning an angry greenish black when Scott and Jackie finally arrived at the airport. Running late, they had been delayed by a mix-up in arrangements for their ground transportation.

"You go ahead," Scott said as they neared a set of rest rooms. "I'll catch up with you at the gate."

"We don't have much time."

"I'll be right behind you."

Suppressing a growing concern about the weather, Jackie quickly made her way to their gate. With the exception of a few stragglers, including Ed Hockaday, most of the passengers had boarded American Airlines Flight 1684 to Washington, D.C. Jackie and Ed saw each other at the same moment.

"Jac*kay*," exclaimed the robust, jolly giant.

"Hi, Eddy," she exclaimed, hurrying to greet him.

Sporting a green-and-white polka-dot bow tie and a thatch of hair best described as fire-engine red, Hockaday's bulldog features invited a cheery smile. "I daresay you've given me a bit of a fright." He beamed as he opened his arms to hug her. "I just *knew* I was going to miss the pleasure of your company."

"Well, we made it—barely." Jackie laughed as she

squeezed the friendly bear of a man. "It's so good to see you."

"Likewise, my dear."

Scott walked up as she and Hockaday were reminiscing and Jackie introduced the two men.

Turning to Scott, she smoothly slid an arm under and around Hockaday's forearm. " 'E's honest, 'e's loyal, but 'e can be bought for a pint or two."

Hockaday belly-laughed and hugged her around the shoulder. "For a Beefeater martini, I'd even do your windows."

Scott smiled and started to speak when he was interrupted by the ring of Jackie's cell phone. She plucked it out of a pocket on the leg of her jumpsuit and snapped it open. "Sullivan," she answered tersely, then gave Scott a concerned look.

"We're about to board our flight," she challenged the caller, then changed the tone of her voice. "I understand," she said in a mild state of surprise as she absently closed the phone.

"Scott," she said with a sudden intensity. "Hartwell has an urgent message for us, but he won't discuss it over a cell phone. We have to find a pay phone, call him at the White House, then wait for a return call in about ten minutes."

"The White House?"

"Yes."

Dalton nodded, but remained quiet. *I wonder if we've squared off against the Iranians?*

A gate agent with a flattop haircut lifted a microphone. "All passengers holding confirmed seats on American Airlines Flight 1684 nonstop service to Ronald Reagan Washington National should now be onboard."

Jackie gave Hockaday a sad look. "Eddy, we're going to have to take a later flight. I'll give you a call when we get to D.C."

Hockaday glanced at the airline agent who was about to close the door to the jetway passenger boarding bridge. "Sounds good," he said cheerfully as he started toward the door. "Give me a ring when you get settled in."

"I'll do it," she said, and waved good-bye, then turned to locate a phone.

"What's going on?" Scott asked as he fell in step.

"You know as much as I do," she answered as she spied an empty stall. "If it's any consolation"—she shrugged indifferently—"they tried your phone first."

"I never take it on vacation," Scott said, then quietly waited while Jackie picked up the receiver. When she was sure she would not be overheard by passersby, she called and left their number.

Less than two minutes later Jackie flinched when the phone rang. "It's for you," she said without rancor.

Scott reached for the phone and surveyed everyone around him as he quietly spoke to Prost. The conversation was short and tense. When he hung up the receiver, Scott stared at the phone for a moment, then closed his eyes. *Farkas is just the opening act.*

"Bad news?" Jackie asked, knowing the answer.

"Well . . ." He hesitated and shook his head. "Are you familiar with a terrorist named Khaliq Farkas?"

For a split second she froze as the line of her mouth became grimly straight. "I sure am," she said in disgust. "I'd like to get my hands on that—"

Scott's eyes grew large.

"SOB." She softened. "What's he done now?"

"Nothing yet." Scott's nerves were suddenly on edge. "He was spotted in Wyoming this morning, but that isn't the bad news," Dalton said as his gaze wandered around the immediate area.

"I'm waiting."

"He was seen flying an A-4 Skyhawk complete with missile racks."

Jackie drew back. "Missile racks?" she asked, trying to make sense of the fragments of information. "Wyoming?"

"That's right," he quietly said. "Hartwell said the attorney general just briefed the president and he wanted us to be on guard."

"Wait a second," Jackie queried with a suspicious look. "I think I missed something. Maybe you better start from the beginning."

With the hair standing up on the back of his neck, Scott glanced around the area. "Some local pilots at the Casper airport took pictures—Prost said videotape—of the plane and pilot when he stopped for fuel early this morning. The people at the airport became suspicious of Farkas and contacted their local FBI office. The agents viewed the tape, and after picking themselves up from the floor, they called Washington."

"Are they positive it was Farkas?"

"No question about it. He's clean shaven now, but Hartwell said that they don't have any doubt. And, surprise surprise, the Skyhawk didn't have any registration numbers on it. That's probably what made the people at the airport suspicious."

"No markings of any kind?"

"Not a thing, except for a blue-and-gray camouflage paint scheme."

"Fearless Farkas has surfaced again," Jackie said with cold frustration, then glanced around the concourse. "This is absolutely crazy. There's a multimillion-dollar bounty on him, and he's blissfully flying around *our* skies in a military jet. Go figure."

"Yeah," Scott said as he studied the other travelers, "he's definitely a gutsy little bastard, but he won't be able to elude us forever."

A brilliant flash of lightning caught her eye. "Do they have any idea where he's headed?"

"All the witnesses at Casper agreed that he initially headed southeast, then turned due east about three miles from the airport."

The sound of rolling thunder suddenly drifted through the terminal.

Stiff and tense, Jackie stared at Scott. "He'll do anything, and I mean *anything*, to complete his mission—whatever it is."

"Or to escape being captured," Scott said, pointing to a small reddish scar on his neck under his right ear. "A little souvenir from a recent encounter with Farkas."

Her eyes opened wide in disbelief. "You're kidding," Jackie said as she examined the scar.

"No."

"I didn't see anything in your records."

"That's because I didn't say anything about the wound."

"What happened?"

Scott allowed a lazy smile to touch the corners of his mouth. "I was in Tel Aviv on a tip that Farkas had been spotted in the area. I was checking security systems when we literally bumped into each other at the entrance to a hotel. He fired three or four shots at me, one of which grazed my neck."

"Were you armed?"

"Yes, but I couldn't return fire. There were too many people in the way. He grabbed a pedestrian and used her as a shield until his driver pulled up beside them. Farkas shoved her away, then jumped in the car and disappeared in the traffic."

"I'm amazed that no one recognized him?"

"He was masquerading as an Israeli general."

"That's what I mean," Jackie declared with a shake of her head. "He isn't afraid of anything, and he gets away with murder—literally."

"His day is coming," Scott said mechanically. "He knows I've been dogging him ever since our unexpected meeting."

"Well, he's here now," Jackie said, restless with energy. "You may get a chance for a second meeting."

"I would like nothing better."

She picked up the solemnity in his expression. "Let's change our reservations," she said on a high note. "Then how about a drink?"

"You've got a deal." A thunderbolt of lightning prompted Scott to study the dark clouds. "I hope this weather clears before we take off."

"That makes two of us."

# 10

## American Flight 1684

Relaxing in the first-class section, Ed Hockaday flinched when a loud clap of thunder boomed across the airport. A nervous flier in the best of conditions, he glanced at the dark storm clouds, then tilted his glass to finish the last of his double martini. He loosened his seat belt and relaxed slightly as the effects of the alcohol took hold.

By the time the terrorist conference was over, Hockaday and the other experts had made one point abundantly clear to their audience; in the past, when terrorists wanted to attack U.S. forces or American citizens, they did it overseas. Now, with the growing animosity between the West and the Iranian leadership, the rules had changed. More and more attacks would likely be taking place on American soil.

Citing the Defense Department study *Terror 2000: The Future Face of Terrorism*, a specialist in the Office of the Assistant Secretary of Defense for Special Operations and Low Intensity Conflict predicted that Iran's network of state-sponsored terrorism would rapidly progress to larger-scale operations in the United States.

The experts also believed that incidents that caused few fatalities would no longer have the shock value the terrorists desired. They would concentrate their efforts on inflicting mass casualties, the kind likely to capture U.S. media coverage for extended periods of time. Expressing their mounting fears, Ed Hockaday and most of the conferees agreed that open warfare would have to be waged against terrorists and their supporters.

Across the aisle from Hockaday, Senator Travis Morgan signed an autograph for an exuberant flight attendant assigned to the coach section. After the vivacious young woman thanked Morgan and returned to her duties, the chairman of the vice-president's task force on terrorism took a sip of his bourbon and resumed his conversation with his wife. The smiling couple held hands as they quietly discussed their new grandson.

Morgan had delivered the keynote address in Dallas, noting the serious problems stemming from the spread of terrorism. When he called for open discussions, a lively exchange erupted between law enforcement officials and antiterrorist experts.

When Senator Morgan felt the jet being pushed back from the gate, he asked for another bourbon on the rocks, then opened his *Wall Street Journal* to skim the political news and the op-eds.

A spattering of warm rain was pelting the terminal building at DFW when Captain Chuck Harrison taxied the twin-engine jetliner away from the passenger boarding bridge. Harrison was in command of Flight 1684, a McDonnell Douglas MD-80-series aircraft. Scheduled to depart Dallas–Fort Worth at 4:50 P.M., the nonstop flight was running a few minutes late as a result of weather-related traffic slowdowns.

The former B-52 aircraft commander and his copilot, First Officer Pamela Gibbs, surveyed the ominous rotor clouds as a massive storm began to engulf the northern perimeter of the sprawling airport. Placing her personal handheld GPS in the side pocket of her flight bag, Gibbs watched the advancing greenish-black squall line, then glanced at Harrison. "I'm just waiting for a funnel cloud to drop out of this mess."

"I wouldn't be surprised," he said with a concerned look at the swirling rotor clouds. "Definitely not an ideal day for aviating."

"Ditto," she said with a hint of reservation in her voice. "This looks like a good day to go Amtrak."

Even though this time of year was considered to be the height of thunderstorm season in northern Texas, both pilots were surprised to see such a powerful weather system develop so quickly. Brilliant, searing flashes of cloud-to-cloud lightning flickered back and forth as the towering storm blocked the light of the sun and turned day into night. The air was thick and heavy with moisture, promising to spawn even more savage storms before the evening was over.

Carefully merging the heavily loaded plane with a half-dozen other jetliners, Harrison felt the gnawing pressure to get airborne as soon as possible. If they could get off the ground before the intense storm rolled over them, Harrison felt confident he could give his passengers a comfortable ride to their cruising altitude.

In an attempt to suppress her concern about the mounting intensity of the storm, Pam Gibbs turned to Harrison and smiled. "Did you have a chance to meet the senator?"

"Yeah," he answered as he released the brakes and moved forward in concert with the other pilots. "We chatted for a minute. He seems like a pretty decent guy . . . for a career politician."

Pam chuckled to herself and looked at Harrison. "What," she said with mock surprise, "no tirade today?"

"I had to stop watching C-SPAN." Harrison smiled as he gently applied the brakes. "It was causing a blood pressure problem."

Reading a report from the House Task Force on Terrorism and Unconventional Warfare, FBI terrorist expert Marsha Phillips glanced at two other special agents seated in the back of the coach section. Chatting quietly with the director of the Department of State's Antiterrorism Training Program, the agents appeared to be totally at ease.

Marsha was anything but at ease. She'd spent countless hours mentally preparing herself for the flight back to Washington. A recent experience had reinforced her gripping fear of flying, and had cost her more than a few sleepless nights. The turbulent flight had left her physically ill and terrified of being confined in a fragile metal tube blasting through the sky at over 500 miles an hour.

Marsha looked up from her report long enough to see the threatening clouds and lightning outside her window, then she folded the papers and closed her eyes. She couldn't wait to get home, curl up on her couch, and watch the adventure movies she had taped before leaving for Dallas.

Approaching the southern end of Runway 35 Left, the pilots completed the remaining items on their takeoff checklist before Pam switched the radio from ground control to the control tower frequency for the parallel runways on the east side of the airport.

The ex-Navy P-3C Orion pilot again observed the black clouds and the flickering veins of lightning. She noticed that her hands were cold and damp. Pam wondered how much of her anxiety stemmed from her concern about the weather— and how much stemmed from being in the cockpit with Chuck. He was an easygoing, okay guy who happened to be divorced and available, and she was attracted to him.

She glanced at Harrison. *What the hell—I might as well be straightforward and take the initiative.* With a certain amount of trepidation, Pam steeled herself and turned to Harrison.

"Chuck"—she tried to sound nonchalant—"I was wondering if you might be interested in coming over for dinner tomorrow evening? I have a great recipe for lobster with coral sauce . . . if you haven't made other plans."

He gave her a slow, quizzical look. "No, I don't have anything planned. Dinner sounds great," he said, letting his special smile show through his surprise.

"Good."

"Want me to bring the wine?"

"Sounds good." She smiled in return. *Yes!*

"Regional Tower," Gibbs radioed as she mentally planned the evening with Harrison. "American 1684 is ready to go."

"Ah, roger American 1684," came the crisp reply from the female controller. "Delta 728, fly heading three-five-zero, cleared for takeoff."

"Three-fifty on the heading, cleared to go, Delta 728."

Two superheated streams of powerful jet exhaust belched dense black smoke from the huge engines as Harrison and Gibbs watched the heavily laden jet begin to accelerate down the long stretch of semiwet runway.

"If the weather keeps building at this rate, we could be in for some real excitement," Pam said dryly.

"Yeah, it's gonna be a challenge."

"All aircraft be advised," the tower operator said as a bright bolt of lightning flashed overhead. "We have, ah, low-level wind shear alerts from all quadrants. Repeat—we have—we're recording low-level wind shear from all quadrants."

The tower personnel, concerned about the intensity of the approaching storm, closely monitored the terminal Doppler weather radar. The short-range, high-frequency C-band radar is specially designed to detect dangerous microbursts that cause strong downdrafts capable of forcing airliners to the ground.

Harrison and Gibbs exchanged concerned looks while streaks of blue-white lightning crackled and thunder rumbled in the distance. The weather picture was rapidly deteriorating and Harrison knew that the airport was going to have to cease flight operations at any moment. *We've gotta play, or fold our cards. Let's go, tower . . .*

"American 1684," the tower operator said after a long delay, "taxi into position and hold."

"Position and hold, American 1684," Gibbs read back, then again keyed her mike. "Say winds."

"Winds are now zero-four-zero at twenty-three"—the controller paused—"with peak gusts to forty-five. Low-level wind-shear alert in northeast quadrant, three-two-zero degrees at nine, northwest quadrant one-four-zero degrees at five."

"Copy, American 1684," Gibbs replied as the former Air Force bomber pilot swung the nose of the jetliner around to align it with the centerline of the runway. She studied the thin, swirling vortices slinking from the bottom of the foreboding clouds and cast another dubious look at the captain. "Chuck, this weather really looks questionable."

A short pause followed while he thought about the situation. Hell, he'd flown through lots of tough weather, including a full-blown hurricane. Dealing with inclement weather was just another facet of being a professional aviator.

"Yeah, it's a little messy," Harrison replied in a voice he hoped sounded more confident than he felt. "Once we get airborne and out of the area, we'll be okay—just gotta get on top."

Pam started to respond, then stopped herself before she said something she might regret.

Avoiding her questioning eyes, Chuck Harrison watched Delta 728 slowly lift off the runway and disappear into a solid black mass of clouds. Feeling a sudden surge of adrenaline, the pilot forced himself to be calm as he keyed the PA system.

"Ah . . . ladies and gentlemen, this is Captain Harrison." He paused while his concern about the weather conditions weighed on his conscience. "We're presently number one for takeoff. It looks as if we're going to have to work our way around a few thundershowers this afternoon, so please keep your seat belts securely fastened. I'll turn off the seat-belt sign when it's safe for you to move about the cabin; however, I ask that you please keep your seat belts fastened when you're occupying your seat."

He tossed a quick look at the dark, churning clouds. "And, on behalf of the crew, we thank you for choosing American."

Harrison focused on the spot where the runway disappeared in the torrential downpour. *I hate to put these people through this, but we have a schedule to keep.*

A few feet behind the cockpit door, Travis and Julie Morgan frowned at each other and leaned over to look out the cabin window. They were seasoned fliers who weren't usually concerned about weather conditions, but this particular storm looked extremely severe. The darkened sky had taken on an eerie, greenish cast and the intensity of the rain was increasing.

Senator Morgan knew from past experience that a storm of this magnitude could easily contain severe turbulence, heavy rain, strong updrafts and downdrafts, intense lightning, severe icing conditions, and heavy hail.

During his illustrious political career, he had flown through every imaginable type of miserable weather. After a number of hair-raising flights over the years, Travis Morgan had drawn a clear conclusion; thunderstorms were the worst kind of torture. They concerned him more than any other hazardous weather condition.

The senator had read a variety of National Transportation Safety Board accident reports about aircraft that had flown into thunderstorms and encountered catastrophic turbulence.

He knew the resulting high G-loads on the airframes had led to loss of control, causing structural failure and an inevitable crash. Without a parachute, the chances of surviving an in-flight breakup were nil-to-nonexistent.

Senator Morgan folded his paper in half and gently patted his wife's arm. "I don't think I'd describe those clouds as thundershowers, but what's the poor guy going to say?"

"Well," she replied in her usual confident tone, "they're trained to do this, and I'm sure they know what they're doing."

Her hushed comment didn't convince either of them.

"Let's hope they do," Morgan said as he opened his paper and tried to concentrate on the political comments in the editorial section. A few seconds later he turned toward the window to study the approaching mass of black clouds.

Ed Hockaday also felt a sense of apprehension, but he kept his eyes closed and mentally reassured himself that everything would be fine.

# 11

Chuck Harrison attempted to appear confident when he glanced at his normally relaxed, effervescent copilot. He'd flown with her enough times to know when she was uncomfortable, and she was definitely tense. It showed in her eyes and in her mannerisms. Small, subtle things.

*If she's this nervous, maybe I should taxi back to the gate.* He started to suggest a prudent retreat, then immediately talked himself out of it. *This'll be a rough ride, but I can handle it.*

"Pam, I think it's a good idea if we climb at Vee Two plus twenty to give us a slight cush on speed."

"Good idea," she said with more than a trace of anxiety in her voice. "You might want to consider adding a little more speed—in case we go through some shear or a downburst."

"I think we'll be okay." His attempt to reassure her seemed to have no effect. "It'll be a bit bumpy, but we'll be out of it fairly quickly."

Pam nodded valiantly and cinched her seat and shoulder restraints tighter. "We're going to have *lots* of white knuckles in the back." *Chuck, you might want to reconsider this and taxi back to the gate while we still have an option.*

"American 1684," the pleasant voice said, "wind is zero-two-zero at twenty-seven with gusts to forty-seven, runway three-five left, cleared for takeoff."

With her mouth as dry as sawdust, Pam took a deep breath and held it momentarily in an effort to loosen the knot that had formed in her stomach. She was an extremely confident pilot, but loud warning bells about wind shear and microbursts were going off in her mind. Wind shear and thunderstorms are unforgiving killers and she rated them at the top of her "fear factor" list.

"American 1684, cleared for takeoff three-five left," Pam repeated while she fought the paralysis that gripped her throat. The bright warning lights continued to flash in her mind and her senses were crying out for rational intervention, but no action was being taken. *I'll be glad when this day is over.*

"Let's go for it," Harrison said boldly as he released the brakes and gripped the twin throttles. "Lights on."

Pam studied a whirling mass of debris crossing the edge of the runway. *Yeah, let's go for it.* The feeling of helplessness was almost overpowering. *Jesus, what are we doing?*

Harrison slowly walked the throttles forward while Gibbs closely monitored the engine gauges and the airspeed indicator. The two jet engines smoothly spooled up to the predicated power setting on the takeoff data card. With 11,388 feet of runway available, there wasn't any reason to rush the normal sequence of events.

Marsha Phillips closed her eyes and silently prayed as the thrust from the powerful engines pressed her against the seatback. This was the moment she'd been dreading since the breakfast meeting. Every terrifying second was suddenly compressed into one stomach-wrenching desire to scream out in protest, to yell, Stop the plane! Let me off!

Facing the stark reality that she didn't have any control over the situation at this point, Marsha thought about her fiancé. Forced to accept the fact that her fate was in the hands of someone else, she stole a quick peek at her engagement ring. Her husband-to-be had surprised her with the ring the night before she left for Dallas. Two rows in front of her, a baby cried out as Marsha prayed. *Dear God, give me the courage I need to get through this flight.*

"Set takeoff power," Harrison ordered while Pam worked to fine-tune the engine power settings.

"Power is set," came the terse response from a highly experienced pilot under tremendous pressure.

"Thanks."

Pam studied the engine instruments. "Power looks good."

"Okay."

Gibbs inched the right throttle forward to make a small correction. "Just a tad low on number two."

"Whatever it takes."

The clouds abruptly spilled their contents and a gigantic waterfall collided with the windshields.

Harrison unconsciously gripped the control yoke tighter. "I'll take the wipers when you get a chance."

"Wipers coming on," she replied behind a superficial barrier of calm professionalism. "Everything's lookin' good."

"Okay."

The runway markers were flashing past the wingtips when the Super-80 reached takeoff decision speed.

"Vee One," Gibbs reported in a strained voice as the intensity of the rain suddenly increased. The loud noise was similar to the pounding sound of light hail on a tin roof.

Harrison shot a quick glance at the engine instruments. All indicators were within normal parameters.

Shortly thereafter, the long, sleek jet accelerated to the speed at which the pilot would rotate the aircraft to the initial climb attitude.

"Vee R," the first officer sang out an octave higher than usual. The butterflies in the pit of her stomach were beginning to take flight as she watched Harrison ease back on the control column. *We're committed, no turning back now.*

At the same moment the deck angle increased to the takeoff attitude, Gibbs felt an unexpected decrease in velocity. Her eyes flashed to the airspeed indicator, which confirmed a fifteen knot deceleration in airspeed.

*Oh, shit!*

"You're losing speed," Pam shouted. "The airspeed is dropping! We're going through a microburst!"

"I know!"

"Hang on to it!" Pam urged.

"I've got it!"

Harrison felt the airplane buffet and instinctively pushed

the throttles forward to maximum power. *No sense sparing the engines if it looks like we might crash.*

"Call my speed!"

"It's coming up," Gibbs yelled as they rocketed through the downburst created by the massive thunderstorm. Four seconds ticked by in slow motion. "Vee R plus five!"

"We're almost there," Harrison exclaimed through clenched teeth. "Just gotta nurse it nice and easy."

Aborting landing approaches or takeoffs is among the toughest decisions captains have to make. They are instinctive decisions in most cases. Things happen so quickly that there isn't time to consult and exchange ideas when a split-second decision has to be made.

Pam felt a pang of real doubt begin to creep into her mind. *We need to abort—even if we go off the end of the damn runway.*

"We're running out of runway," she blurted.

"—gonna make it."

"I don't know . . ."

The 3,000-foot "runway remaining" marker flashed past as Harrison gingerly worked the control yoke and shoved on the throttles. "Come on, baby . . . climb. Don't give up on me now."

Pam gripped the glare shield and held her breath while she fixated on the airspeed indicator. *This isn't good.*

Concerned about the unusually long takeoff roll, Senator Morgan squeezed his wife's hand and darted a quick look out the window, then attempted a reassuring smile.

She remained quiet and looked down at her lap.

"We're going to be in Lewisville," he scoffed under his breath, "if they don't get this thing off the ground."

Julie squeezed his hand so hard her wedding ring dug deep into her finger. "Something's wrong—I just feel it."

Morgan clasped his wife's tightly balled hand. "Just relax," he reassured her. "Everything is going to be fine."

"I don't think so."

"It'll be okay," he insisted.

"We're out of runway!"

"Relax."

On the other side of the aisle, Ed Hockaday's hands were glued to the armrests. He opened his eyes and slowly turned his head to look out the window. *We're at the end of the airport!* The pounding in his chest was excruciating and unrelenting. Taking deep breaths in an effort to calm himself, Hockaday closed his eyes and tightly gripped the armrests. *Gents, it's time to get the kite in the air.*

The right main landing gear of the MD-82 skipped twice before the struggling airliner staggered into the disturbed air mass. The wings rocked back and forth as the long fuselage yawed left, then right. The hapless travelers were being slung from side to side as a number of overhead bins popped open and spilled a few items on top of them. A murmur of frightened voices could be heard throughout the cabin. The passengers, even the uninitiated ones, knew that this takeoff wasn't normal.

"Positive rate," Gibbs breathlessly announced as the aircraft approached takeoff safety speed.

"Gear up," Harrison ordered, and winced at a bright flash of lightning.

"Gear coming up—Vee Two."

The pilots could see that they were only seconds away from another wall of water that appeared to be more intense than the last one.

After Pam raised the landing gear, she watched in horror as the altimeter suddenly stopped climbing and slowly reversed its direction. "We've got a sink rate going! We're going down!"

"Son of a bitch!" Harrison said as he pulled on the control column. He could feel the severe sink rate and his heart raced like a trip-hammer. *Don't give up, stay with it!*

Pam's face turned pasty white.

A microsecond later the ground-proximity warning device sounded. "*Whoop, whoop, pull up!*"

Waiting for the expected impact with the ground, Harrison maintained the proper deck angle to fly out of a wind shear condition and continued to push on the throttles. He had practiced the same procedure many times in the flight simulator.

"*Whoop, whoop, pull up!*"

Pam braced for the impact.

"Don't let this happen to me," Marsha Phillips moaned aloud, and tightly gripped the armrests. She glanced up the aisle and saw some of the other passengers doing the same thing. Listening to the baby cry more loudly, Marsha allowed her gaze to drift to the window, then recoiled in sheer terror. The runway was no longer under them and the shuddering airplane was only a few feet above the ground. Unable to contain her fear any longer, Marsha began praying out loud. "Dear God, please give me strength . . . please don't let anything happen."

"Brace yourself!" a flight attendant ordered over the PA system. "Get your heads down! Assume the crash position *now!*"

Marsha winced when someone screamed. Her worst fears had suddenly materialized and she couldn't wake herself from this horribly frightening dream. She was about to die. *No, no, no not me, please, God.*

Both pilots slowly let their breath out when the airplane began accelerating and the shaking finally ceased. They could feel the stimulating effect of the adrenaline coursing through their veins. It would take a few minutes for their vascular systems to recover from the sudden shock.

The ride through the heavy downpour was extremely rough, but it couldn't have been sweeter to them. Little did they know that the red-hot exhaust gases from the two Pratt & Whitney engines had literally scorched the ground at the end of the runway.

The pilots busied themselves with the after-takeoff checklist while their heart rates slowly began to return to normal. Neither wanted to say anything to the other. The decision to take off into the teeth of a raging thunderstorm had been ill-advised and they both knew it.

"Just another fun day at the office," Harrison finally muttered.

"Yeah." Pam sighed and glanced at the rain streaking off the windshield. "I wonder if I could make it as a topless dancer?"

Chagrined as well as frightened, Harrison didn't respond to her comment. "We better tell the tower what happened."

"As soon as I find my voice."

Allowing a thin smile, Harrison grudgingly turned his gaze toward her. "Don't ever let me do that again."

"Trust me," Pam said as her glance slid to Chuck. "I'm gonna carry a hammer from now on."

Julie Morgan could tell by her husband's sallow complexion that he, too, had been traumatized by the terrifying experience.

"I think we need a double bourbon and water," she commented in a weak voice as she tilted her head back against the headrest.

"I'll take mine straight," he said, letting out his breath, then slowly glanced at his wife. "I wonder what the hell was going on up there?"

"Who knows?" she answered with her own sigh of relief. "Just be thankful it's over and we're safely airborne."

He shook his head. "I'll feel a lot safer when we're on the ground in Washington," he replied with a hint of irritation in his voice.

"I'm sure the worst is over."

"Don't bet on it," he said sarcastically. "We aren't there yet."

Wide awake and on the verge of panic, Ed Hockaday felt beads of perspiration on his forehead. He placed his right hand over his heart. It was pounding so hard, he thought he was going to faint.

Looking around the cabin, Hockaday could see the raw fear in people's eyes. *Something is wrong. Get out of the storm and land this thing!*

"Regional tower," Pam said evenly, "American 1684 lost fifteen to twenty knots at rotation."

"Copy, 1684. We're shutting everything down until the storm passes. Contact departure, one three five point niner two, good day."

"Switchin' departure, American 1684."

"Flaps up," Harrison ordered.

"Flaps comin' up," Pam said, reaching for the lever.

Marsha Phillips hesitantly opened her eyes and tried to slow her rate of breathing. *Never again, . . . never, never, ever again.* Her knees were shaking uncontrollably and her neck was as rigid as a steel post. *I could drink an entire pitcher of water.*

A nervous flight attendant attempted to calm the frightened passengers. "Ladies and gentlemen," she said over the PA, "please stay seated. Captain Harrison will turn off the "fasten seat belt" sign just as soon as he feels it's safe for you to get up and move about the cabin."

Marsha tuned out the announcement when she noticed her hands. They, too, were trembling uncontrollably. With a feeling of nausea sweeping over her, she closed her eyes and began taking deep breaths and exhaling slowly. After a few seconds she gripped the armrests to keep her hands from shaking and then slowly opened her eyes.

She glanced around the cabin and noticed the same strained looks on the faces of the other passengers, including a handsome young Navy lieutenant with gold aviator wings adorning his white uniform. He shook his head in disbelief and displayed a taut smile as he flexed his fingers. Marsha returned his smile. *Even the topguns get scared.* Somehow, she found that reassuring.

With their seat belts still fastened, many passengers were collecting their personal effects from the aisle. Most were grumbling to themselves and to others while they gathered their possessions.

"Regional departure," Pam said in a calm voice, "American 1684 is with you out of twelve-hundred, goin' to one-zero-thousand."

"Roger American 1684, good afternoon, radar contact. Turn right, heading zero-seven-zero and maintain one-zero-thousand. Expect filed altitude in eight minutes."

"Ah, zero-seven-zero on the heading, and up to one-zero-thousand," Pam replied, then flinched when a blinding streak of lightning flashed in front of the windshield. "Sixteen-eighty-four can expect our filed altitude in approximately eight min—"

A deafening, blinding explosion ripped the cockpit to shreds and sent a powerful shock wave through the passenger cabin. The thunderous blast killed Harrison and mortally wounded Gibbs. The first officer remained semiconscious, but she couldn't lift her shattered arms high enough to grip the twisted control yoke.

The aircraft pitched nose up and slowly rolled to the right, rapidly bleeding off airspeed while total chaos erupted throughout the passenger cabin. Bloodcurdling screams and anguished cries of terror added to the trauma and confusion.

The intense explosion had blown the cockpit door into Julie Morgan's lap, cutting her face and arms. Her heart pounded so hard that she could barely catch her breath.

Hearing a strange ringing sound in his ears, Senator Morgan sat back in shock and stared wide-eyed at his bleeding wife. "Are you all right?" he uttered before realizing he could not hear the sound of his own voice. "Are you okay?"

Julie mouthed what passed for a yes and then stared in disbelief at the fragmented remains of the cockpit. She could see the magnitude of destruction on the pilot's side of the mangled flight deck. Julie couldn't see the copilot, but the captain was slumped in his seat with his chin resting on his chest and his right arm dangling on the crushed throttle quadrant. There was no question in her mind that the pilot was dead.

Frozen with fear and disbelief, Ed Hockaday's legs turned into rubber and his right hand shook uncontrollably. An intelligent man, he knew he was about to die, but his mind refused to accept his fate.

The senior flight attendant in first class finally found her feet and struggled to the cockpit entrance. She gasped aloud at the condition of the pilots, then stumbled back in horror. From looking at the pilots and the twisted remains of the flight controls and throttles, the dazed woman knew they were doomed.

"Travis," Julie sobbed, and wiped the blood from her mouth. "We're not going to make it."

He held her close to him and cupped her head in the crook of his neck. "We'll always be together, I promise." For the first time in his long and distinguished political career, the senior senator was powerless to correct a problem. In one horrifying second, money and power and influence had become completely useless.

A chorus of howls and screams filled the cabin while the sleek jet—at climb power—rolled steadily to the right until it was inverted, then slowly pitched nose down to a pure vertical attitude. Full of jet fuel, the airliner was now an out-of-control bomb plummeting toward the ground.

Powerless to stop the deadly plunge, Gibbs made a last survey of the shattered flight instruments. She willed her lifeless arms to grasp the bent control yoke, then felt warm tears as she slipped into unconsciousness.

Marsha Phillips screamed in desperate anguish as the airspeed rapidly increased to 330 knots.

Slumping in agony, Ed Hockaday felt like he was being suffocated. He convulsed twice, then gripped his chest and died of a massive heart attack.

Travis Morgan hugged his sobbing wife with all his strength and closed his eyes for the last time. Behind the first-class section, the piercing screech of a small child rose above the other anguished screams.

A moment later the MD-80 slammed into the ground and exploded in a mushrooming orange-and-black fireball. The kinetic energy of the impact compressed the fuselage to a length of seven feet at the bottom of a twenty-foot crater. Mercifully, no one onboard felt anything when the plane hit the ground. In less than a nanosecond everyone was gone.

# 12

"Here you go," the friendly airline agent said as she handed Jackie and Scott their revised tickets. "Your flight should be boarding in about an hour."

"Thanks," they said in unison at the same moment Jackie's sat-phone rang. She answered it while they walked to a quiet area out of the mainstream of passenger traffic.

Scott double-checked their tickets while Jackie spoke in a hushed voice, then frowned and slid the cell phone into the leg pocket of her jumpsuit.

"What now?" he asked.

"That was my office." The look on her face was dead serious. "They just received a short message from Maritza."

"Is she okay?"

"Physically, she's okay for the moment, but they intend to take her to Tehran in five or six days. That was all she said before the call was terminated."

Dalton remained quiet a few seconds while he computed how soon they could launch the rescue attempt. *It's going to be close.*

"Well," he remarked in a flatly serious voice, "we had better redouble our efforts."

"We don't have much choice," she dryly countered.

With their revised tickets in hand, Scott and Jackie were

about to walk into the concourse cocktail lounge when they heard the first muted shriek of sirens. They made their way to a viewing area, then stopped to watch the twinkling lights of a fleet of emergency vehicles as they raced across the airport. Although Jackie and Scott had a good vantage point, it was difficult to see the crash trucks and other vehicles through the torrential downpour.

"I think someone ran off the runway," declared an army sergeant to his pregnant wife. "Man, they get to slippin' and slidin' in this here stuff and they're flat gone—I mean clean off in the pasture."

A hush suddenly settled over the waiting area as people rose from their seats to find a better view. A college student wearing a T-shirt emblazoned with Embry-Riddle Aeronautical University was intently listening to his small aviation radio. His anxiety mirrored the feelings of others as he methodically scanned the radio frequencies.

Glancing at the raging storm, Scott's expression was troubled and his eyes were dark with concern. His instincts told him it was Flight 1684.

"Look," Jackie said as she pointed toward the ramp. "A few of the planes are taxiing back to the gates."

"They must have closed the airport."

Jackie studied the slowly moving jets, then noticed two American Airlines agents walking rapidly down the concourse. Their expressions were strained and one of them was nervously talking into a handheld radio.

As word of the accident swept through the crowded terminal building, the young man from Embry-Riddle finally broke his silence. "There's been a crash," he announced in a loud voice as he continued to scan various frequencies. "American . . . they're saying American sixteen-eighty-four went down—crashed just north of the airport."

"What was the flight number?" boomed another young man.

"One-six-eight-four—sixteen-eighty-four."

A murmur carried through the concourse as Jackie and Scott locked eyes. In the horror of the moment they felt stunned, saddened, and relieved to be alive. His face was close to hers, examining the deep pain in her eyes. The caring and concern she saw in his expression broke the paralysis of shock.

"Oh, God." She trembled uncontrollably. "Eddy was on that plane—we would've been there, too."

Scott's senses were on full alert and the hair on his neck stood up. "Let's go find out how bad it is," he said solemnly as he gently took her by the arm. "Come on, just start walking."

Visibly shaken by the incident, the young college student lowered his transceiver from his ear. He caught Scott's eye, then spoke in a hollow voice. "According to the reports I'm hearing, they went straight in."

"My God," Jackie said in a soft, flat voice. Her lip quivered as she remembered her friend's infectious smile and eccentric bow ties. "Eddy," she murmured with a sob. "That could have been us in . . ." She trailed off, unable to get the rest of it out. "Oh, my God . . . why?"

When Scott reached for her, she gratefully embraced him and buried her face in the hollow of his shoulder. He held her close and absorbed the shudders that shook her body. Fate had intervened. By the grace of God, they had dodged the Grim Reaper.

Horrified and shaken by their close brush with death, Scott looked around the immediate area. His instincts were screaming, Khaliq Farkas. *He's here, I can feel it in the pit of my stomach. The sick little bastard just took out a plane full of antiterrorist experts.*

Scott cupped the back of Jackie's head and held her more tightly to his shoulder. *Did Farkas know we were scheduled to be on the plane?*

"Jackie," he said in a barely audible voice. "Look at me." He paused to compose himself. "I don't think the crash was caused by the weather. I think—" He stopped when she pulled away.

Jackie stifled a sob and looked into his eyes for a long moment. The realization suddenly hit her, causing her stomach to twist into knots. "You think it was sabotage?"

"Yes," he said in a calm voice that left little doubt about his conviction. "I'm almost positive."

"Farkas?" she asked as a sense of terror gripped her.

Scott frowned. "Think about it. He was spotted in Wyoming—flying a military jet—and now a plane full of terrorist experts crashes."

"You're right," she said weakly, staring into his eyes. "Did he know we were going to be on that flight?"

"That's what we need to find out."

Dalton studied the throng of people in the concourse, then turned to Jackie. "He prefers explosives that are triggered by radio control transmitters—the type used for model planes and boats."

"I know," she said, meeting the narrowed probe of his gaze. "He would have to be fairly close to his target to detonate the charge."

"If he did it, he isn't far away." Scott's eyes traveled to a young couple who were obviously from the Middle East. "He could be watching us as we speak. Keep an eye out for anything strange."

She shivered, then cautiously looked around the immediate area. "Let's get moving—we don't have a second to lose."

He took her by the arm and headed toward the entrance to the concourse. After working their way through the crowd, they raced to the area where transportation was available for arriving passengers. Jackie cast a glance at the line of taxicabs and limousines while Scott surveyed the crowd.

"I'd like to shoot him on sight," Jackie said with a mixture of pain and bitterness. "We need to find out if there's an A-4 Skyhawk here at DFW, or at any of the other airports in the area."

"You're right," Scott agreed, then stopped dead in his tracks. He was staring at a familiar face, but something was strangely out of kilter. The man was dressed in the uniform of an American Airlines captain, complete with an ID badge and a chart case hanging from his left hand. Farkas saw Dalton at the same instant and stared in disbelief.

"Oh, shit," Scott exclaimed in shock as Jackie whirled around in total surprise. "It's him!"

Farkas drew a handgun from the chart case, then ran twenty yards to a waiting taxi and yanked the front passenger door open. Scott started toward the cab and then shoved Jackie behind a minivan when Farkas fired three shots at them. Two rounds ricocheted off the side of the van inches from Scott's face. The third bullet shattered the windshield of a Toyota, narrowly missing the startled driver.

After a moment of disbelief, the shocked bystanders began running in every direction as the taxi made a jackrabbit start, then sped off. Scott could see that Farkas had his gun shoved against the driver's head.

"He's getting away," Jackie shouted in frustration.

Without hesitating, Dalton raced toward a new Lincoln Town Car that had been temporarily deserted by its frightened owner. The engine was running and the trunk was wide open, waiting to receive a set of luggage stacked neatly on the curb.

"Notify the authorities," Scott yelled to Jackie as he slid behind the wheel and placed the car in gear.

"I'm going with you," she exclaimed as she jumped into the front seat. "We're right on top of him! *Go!*"

"Hang on!" Scott said as he floored the Lincoln. The car lurched to the left at a forty-five-degree angle and careened off the side of a shiny red Jaguar.

"We're off to a helluva start," Jackie said breathlessly as she hurriedly buckled her seat belt.

"Yeah, that's always a crowd pleaser," he deadpanned. "Next time I steal a car, remind me to point the front wheels in the direction I want to go."

"I'll work on it."

With the headlights on and the windshield wipers flailing, Scott drove with wild abandon through the maze of airport roads. After bouncing off a curb and sliding through a grassy area, they spotted the commandeered taxi in the midst of dozens of flashing lights.

Accelerating on International Parkway, Scott rapidly closed the distance between the Lincoln and the cab. Both cars were dodging law enforcement and emergency vehicles as a steady stream of flashing lights rushed toward the crash site. To Scott's amazement, the police were ignoring the speeding cars. Approaching the curve to Northwest Highway, the taxi began to swerve violently back and forth across the wet parkway.

"They're struggling," Jackie said a moment before the cabdriver's side window exploded into a million glass fragments.

"He shot him," Scott shouted above the screaming engine.

"Don't get too close!" she warned.

"I'm going to ram him!"

"No."

A few seconds later Farkas shoved the taxi driver out of his car. The mortally wounded man tumbled and flipped like a rag doll.

"Watch out!" Jackie warned.

Scott yanked the wheel to the left, barely missing the driver. The Town Car skidded sideways as Scott fought for control. Once he corrected the slide, he nailed the accelerator and started closing on Farkas.

"Fasten your seat belt," Jackie advised as she gripped the dashboard and braced her other hand against the roof.

"I'm working on it." Scott latched his seat belt, then reached between his back and belt and slid his nine-millimeter Sig Sauer to Jackie. "If we get close enough, shoot him."

As she reached for the handgun, her expression froze into a kind of stiffness. "How did you get this past security?"

Scott swerved to avoid a slower-moving car. "Thanks to Hartwell, I have credentials from both the CIA *and* the FBI."

"How convenient," she said as she checked the sidearm. "Is there anything else I should be aware of?"

"Nothing that comes to mind."

With the trunk lid bouncing up and down, Scott worked hard to stay directly behind Farkas. They were banging fenders with other vehicles as Farkas used the battered taxi to bulldoze his way through traffic. Cars and trucks were sliding off the side of the road as angry drivers mashed their horns, cursed, and shot Farkas and his pursuer the middle-finger salute.

"He thought we were dead," Jackie said through clenched teeth.

"He thought *I* was dead."

Her throat felt tight as she gripped the Sig Sauer in her right hand. "You could see it in the look on his face."

"No doubt about it." Scott slammed on the brakes, then pressed hard on the accelerator when Farkas's taillights flickered an instant before he swerved to miss an ambulance. "Take a shot when I get closer."

Jackie hit the switch that lowered her window, then grasped the weapon with both hands and leaned out of the car. Deluged by rain and spray, she waited until Scott was less than twenty feet from the cab. Barely able to see through the downpour, she aimed for the back windshield and gently squeezed the trigger.

*Boom! Boom!*

Two fist-sized holes appeared near the top of the rear windshield as it shattered in an explosion of glass particles.

Jackie wiped the water from her eyes and squeezed again.

*Boom! Boom!*

Stunned and cut by the flying fragments of glass, Farkas swerved back and forth while he pointed his weapon rearward and blindly fired every round in his clip.

Two shells went through the Town Car's radiator before three rounds shattered the windshield, blowing the rearview mirror into the backseat and spraying Scott with glass.

Jackie yanked her head inside the car. "Are you okay?"

"Couldn't be better," he exclaimed, stomping on the accelerator. "Okay, you son of a bitch, it's time to show your hand!"

Consumed by rage, Scott pulled up to the taxi and rammed the trunk on the driver's side. He kept the throttle buried, turning Farkas slightly sideways. "Come on, lose it."

"Be careful," Jackie said as she subconsciously pushed on the floorboard. "We've already cheated death once today."

Scott backed off a few feet.

Farkas steered into the slide, then jammed the brake pedal to the floor, causing the Lincoln to smash into the trunk of the taxi. Scott eased back a couple of car lengths seconds before Farkas sideswiped a new Corvette convertible, spinning the sports car completely around.

"Take another shot!"

"Next time I'll drive—you do the shooting!"

Jackie leaned out and fired three quick rounds, hitting the trunk twice and shattering the driver's-side mirror.

"Lucky shot," Scott said lightly as Farkas yanked the car to the right, then back to the left. "That got his attention."

She wiped her face and glanced at Scott. "How did Farkas know? Who gave him the information about the flight?"

He darted a look at her. "Who knows?" he answered without hesitation. "An Iranian operative—an agent who follows the Washington scen—"

"Watch it," she shouted as Farkas whipped the taxi to the left to pass a Mayflower moving van. Scott started to follow, then stood on the brakes when he saw that the road was partially blocked ahead. The right front fender of the Town Car clipped the moving van, throwing the car out of control.

"Sonuva—" Dalton gasped as they tried to brace themselves before the car flipped over and slid on its roof, popping the shattered windshield out. There was a wrenching tear of metal while the pavement ground away the roof. When the crashing, crunching noise finally stopped, it was a dazed few moments before Jackie and Scott realized they were alive and in one piece.

"Get out!" Scott said as he detected the odor of gasoline. "We're leaking fuel—get out! *Now!*"

Terror overcame her as she tugged frantically at the seat belt buckle. She saw flashing lights and heard voices coming closer as Scott released her buckle. Then she recoiled when she saw the first reddish-yellow flame dart from beneath the smashed hood. She heard a muffled sound a second before the small fire blossomed into a roaring inferno.

"Let's go!" Scott said as he kicked out a backseat window. He pulled Jackie partially through the jagged opening before she got a foothold and pushed herself clear of the burning wreckage. They scrambled away from the blazing car, then stumbled across the road before the Lincoln exploded in a massive fireball. Amid the confusion and chaos of the moment, Khaliq Farkas had disappeared in a sea of flashing lights and emergency vehicles.

Wet, muddy, and shaking, Jackie gave Scott a troubled look and shook her head. "You need some driving lessons."

He looked at her smudged face and glanced at the burning car. "Well, I just happen to know a woman who is an *expert* instructor in high-speed evasive driving."

She forced a weak smile. "I was thinking you might want to begin at a demolition derby, and work your way up."

"Hey, even Richard Petty had off days."

Jackie started to respond, then paused when she caught sight of the multitude of police officers approaching them. "I suppose you'd like to handle this situation."

"Sure," he said with a confident smile, then reached for his credentials. "This is going to cause a mountain of paperwork."

# 13

## The White House

The shocking news from the attorney general about the sighting of Khaliq Farkas in Wyoming had been the central topic of conversation during the working dinner. The decision to keep the frightening discovery as understated as possible was unanimous. No one wanted to stir the media into a feeding frenzy, causing a nationwide panic.

The military services, Coast Guard, and several government agencies, including the CIA's Counterterrorist Center, the CIA's newly opened Global Response Center, the Secret Service, and the Federal Aviation Administration had been informed about the threat posed by Farkas and his A-4 Skyhawk. While hundreds of airport managers and fixed-based operators were being alerted, scores of aircraft were already searching for the camouflaged blue-and-gray attack aircraft.

After dinner and dessert, President Macklin and his advisers returned to the White House Situation Room. When everyone was comfortably seated around the expansive table, Hartwell Prost cautiously confronted the chief executive.

"Mr. President," Prost said in his crisp Ivy League monotone. "This whole thing bothers me."

With a weary effort, Macklin leaned back in his chair.

Prost hesitated, then continued. "I consider it my duty to recommend that you move to an undisclosed location until we have a handle on things. You know as well as I do, it's next to impossible to defend the White House against an air attack. With Farkas on the loose, I think it's prudent that we take swift action to ensure the safety of you and the first lady."

For a moment Macklin appeared surprised by the suggestion. But his skepticism was obvious to everyone.

Prost stared straight at the chief executive. "In addition, Mr. President, we need to increase your Secret Service protection, and we should place additional SAMs on the roof."

"Wait—slow down a minute," Macklin said in a low-key voice as he raised a hand. "I'm not going anywhere, Hartwell. If I run for cover every time some nut threatens me, the terrorist groups would be falling over each other to get here."

The president shook his head. "No," he said emphatically, "I'm not going anywhere. Take whatever measures you feel are necessary to increase our security, but we're not going to abandon the White House."

Prost paused to steel himself. "Sir, with all due respect, one of the most feared men in the world is flying around this country in an A-4 Skyhawk. With that in mind, Bassam Shakhar has publicly declared that you're his primary target."

A long silence followed.

"Mr. President," Prost said impatiently, "I have no doubt that Farkas has orders to assassinate you."

"Goddammit, Hartwell, I'm not going into hiding." They locked eyes. "That's final—end of discussion."

"Yes, sir," he said politely, refusing to be intimidated. "New subject?"

"New subject," the president said without any visible emotion.

Prost swept Macklin with cold eyes. "Iran's nuclear weapons are a real and immediate threat. I think we need to neutralize them first, *then* deal with the terrorist issue."

Inclined to be dubious, the president stared over the top of his spectacles and spoke to his national security adviser. "Hartwell, we know Iran *has* the capability to smuggle biological, chemical, or nuclear weapons into our country. Hell, the terrorists could as easily turn Fords and Buicks into low-budget stealth bombers. If we take it on ourselves to single-handedly deal a major blow to Iran, it could create so much regional instability that *everyone* would turn against us—including our spineless allies."

"Do you think the Iranian-controlled nuclear weapons are *creating* stability in the Middle East?"

Macklin's eyes flashed with anger.

With his rebellion announced, Prost continued. "Tehran and their terrorist groups are a strategic threat to Israel, to everyone in the Arab world, and now to the West. We have to neutralize their nuclear capability, before our worst fears become a reality."

"*We* don't have to do a damn thing," the president retorted, trying to conceal his growing irritation.

"Look at Qaddafi," Prost demanded. "We know he still keeps his hand in the terrorist game, but since Reagan thumped him on the head, we haven't heard much out of him."

"Qaddafi retaliated against us," the president suddenly blurted. "Remember Pan Am 103? If we 'thump' Iran, we could trigger a whole series of Pan Am 103s, or worse. Think about TWA 800," Macklin said curtly. "Although we can't disclose the truth to the public, we know the attack was retaliation for shooting down Iran Air Flight 655. Hell, hundreds of eyewitnesses, including professional pilots, saw a missile strike TWA 800. We may not be able to cover up the next act of retribution."

Prost ignored the remarks. "Sir, the people of this country, and the free world, are looking to the United States for leadership. It's time to show our resolve—time to set a precedent. Obviously, we need to confer with our allies, but it's up to us to take swift and decisive action against Iran."

Prost waited while the president's political handicapping process computed the various odds of increasing or decreasing his popularity rating.

General Chalmers covered his mouth and quietly coughed.

"Les," the president said with open irritation, "I recognize that cough. Tell me what you think."

"Well," Chalmers began slowly, "I've been informed by luminous minds that war planning is much too serious a thing to be left to military men, especially generals. With that in mind, it's my opinion that peace is much too important to be left to diplomats."

"Excellent point," Prost declared.

Chalmers continued as if Prost had said nothing. "Together, we must solve our predicament—if we want to avoid a nuclear holocaust in the Middle East. Once someone tosses a nuke or two across the pond, we won't be able to quarantine the hysteria. There'll be a global anxiety attack that'll create political and military chaos beyond anyone's comprehension."

The air crackled with tension while the president rubbed the bridge of his nose, then made eye contact with Chalmers. "You're telling me that I don't have any other choice—is that it?"

"Sir, I wish I could provide a half-dozen options, but we're dealing with Iran." Chalmers spoke with a hint of frustration. "This is more sensitive and potentially more catastrophic than dealing with Saddam Hussein. We *have* to intervene to maintain stability in the Gulf region, and to ensure that Iran doesn't close the Strait of Hormuz."

Macklin quirked an eyebrow. "Les, we're a nation built on democracy. We can't go around inter—"

"This doesn't have anything to do with democracy," Chalmers interrupted. "It has to do with oil—with the economic well-being of the industrialized world. And," he said more softly, "it has to do with power. If we ignore this blatant threat, the credibility of the U.S. forces in the region will go straight to hell."

"And my credibility with it . . ." The president trailed off.

"That's right." Chalmers looked him straight in the eye. "You're the commander in chief, the most powerful man on this earth. You have to look at the *big* picture—what's best for the entire planet."

Macklin showed no emotion. "What about radiation contamination?"

"Negligible to nonexistent," Chalmers said firmly. "The nukes aren't armed to detonate until they're airborne."

Finally, the president swiveled to face his advisers. Their obvious unity was infectious and had the clear markings of an emerging policy change.

Macklin took a deep breath, then slowly exhaled. "I'll

stand by your recommendation," he said in a quiet voice, "but we better be prepared for the consequences."

Chalmers gave the president a forced smile. "You made the right decision, sir."

Macklin shrugged his shoulders in resignation. "Like you pointed out, I don't have a choice. Now, what's your next step?"

"I plan to reposition two more mine countermeasures ships to the Gulf, just in case the Iranians attempt to blockade the Strait of Hormuz. I'm also going to assign another five ships to Destroyer Squadron 50 and station an additional attack submarine in the Gulf and one in the Gulf of Oman."

The president nodded in silent approval.

"We'll make the operation appear to be routine, then go on alert just before our submarines initiate their attack on the missile sites. The skippers have their orders, and they're en route to the Gulf of Oman."

Macklin gave him a questioning look. "Do you think it's wise to commit to this plan with just one battle group in the Gulf?"

"Yes, sir. *Roosevelt* and her battle group are en route to the northern Arabian Sea if we need additional firepower. We'll be able to counter any retaliation from Iran—against our forces stationed in the area, or our allies."

"With just two battle groups?" the president asked with a look of skepticism in his eyes.

"We'll have more than two carrier air wings and their escorts. I intend to use F-15s and 16s from Turkey and Saudi Arabia to assist in providing air cover for the carrier groups."

The president worked hard to keep his concerns from showing. "Realistically, what kind of resistance can we expect?"

Chalmers paused when he noticed the anxiety written on Macklin's face. "They'll probably scramble fighters and their guided-missile patrol boats. Another thing that could be a problem is the threat of their cruise missiles, SAMs, and surface-to-surface missiles. It's a concern, but we expect to successfully counter any type of retaliation."

"How can you be so sure?" the president queried with undisguised apprehension. "We're already in an undeclared war with Tehran."

"Sir, they're going to be caught off guard in the early hours of the morning. We have battle groups operating in the Gulf on a regular basis, plus we have scores of other ships patrolling the Gulf, so our presence isn't going to appear to be anything other than business as usual."

"Are the other chiefs in total agreement with you?" Macklin inquired.

"To a person, and our intel people at Rand are onboard."

"Think-tankers," the president mused without any warmth. "Hartwell, what's your assessment? Will the Iranians put up any resistance?"

The line of Prost's mouth became grimly straight. "They *have* the capability to inflict a lot of damage," he answered coldly. "*Will* they? None of us can answer that question."

Chalmers smiled to himself and looked at Macklin. "As usual, Mr. Prost makes a good point. That's why we're not going to take an invasion-size force into the Gulf. We're going to make it look like a routine training exercise—business as usual."

"Okay, you're the expert," the president said in a resigned voice. "However, I want the rules of engagement to be simple," he asserted. "If the Iranians show hostile intent, our folks are free to defend themselves."

Chalmers suppressed a grin. "I'll make that *very* clear."

"One other thing, Les."

"Sir?"

"After the contrast between the Gulf War and the Balkans fiasco, the American public expect a quick, decisive operation with few civilian casualties." Cord Macklin rose from his chair. "Although we have overwhelming firepower and technical supremacy, we're not invincible. Let's keep that in mind—no mistakes."

Chalmers straightened, surprised that anyone would question his professional competence. "Sir, with all due respect, we haven't forgotten the lesson of Vietnam."

"We can't afford to," Macklin declared.

"Yes, sir," Chalmers said firmly as he rose from his chair. "If you'll excuse me, I have work to do."

"Sure."

The president waited until the general left the Situation Room. "Pete, do you think we should consult with the congressional leadership before we take any action?"

"I wouldn't advise it, sir. If this leaked to the media before the strike, it could have disastrous results."

"You're right," Macklin replied, then rubbed his chin. "You can't keep anything secret in this town."

"My recommendation," Adair continued, "would be to notify the speaker and majority leader while our weapons are en route to their targets. The same with our allies."

"Hartwell?" the president asked.

"I concur."

Macklin leaned back and studied the ceiling before closing his eyes. "Why do I have an uneasy feeling?"

The question went unanswered.

Outwardly, the president showed a steely calm, the years of military discipline and fighter-pilot bravado coming to play. Inwardly, he didn't feel comfortable with his decision. Macklin opened his eyes and stared straight ahead. "Well, if we're going to champion freedom and democracy, we sure as hell can't cower in fear."

Suddenly General Chalmers reappeared at the door. "Mr. President, my aide just informed me that there's been a major crash at DFW."

The stunning news caused a moment of hesitation among the solemn-faced men. Everyone looked to Macklin.

"Turn on the television," the president ordered as Adair reached for the remote-control unit.

"He said the plane was bound for National," Chalmers continued, "and apparently crashed shortly after takeoff."

Transfixed, the men stared at CNN's live coverage of the accident scene west of Interstate 35 East. Although it was early evening in Dallas, the sky was so dark and hazy that motorists had been forced to turn on their headlights. In spite of the rain, wind, and reduced visibility, it was obvious that no one could have survived the crash. The entire airplane had simply disappeared in a muddy, smoking hole.

Moments later the president's personal phone rang. Adair walked to the phone and answered the call, then listened in shocked disbelief while Fraiser Wyman told him the sad news about Senator Travis Morgan and the Washington contingent of terrorist experts.

As the president's chief of staff continued to explain the

tragic situation, Adair took an involuntary half step backward and went numb, thinking that Wyman must have made a mistake.

A moment later raw logic sobered Adair. He glanced at his wristwatch, then stared at it in silence; the Iranian deadline for the commencement of U.S. troop withdrawals had long passed.

With the United States on the brink of open conflict with Iran, the tragic death of Senator Morgan and the other terrorist experts wasn't a coincidence. The reprisals had begun. Adair's mind raced to make sense of the situation. *Someone—maybe Khaliq Farkas—murdered them.*

"Hold on a second," Adair said, then cupped the phone receiver in his hand and turned to face Macklin. "Mr. President, I don't think we have to be concerned about our plans triggering retaliation from the terrorists."

Macklin slowly turned and gave Adair a puzzled look. "What the *hell* are you talking about?"

"The terrorists just declared war on us," Adair said as a frown creased his forehead. "We're looking at the results of the first salvo. Travis Morgan and a group of terrorist experts were on that plane."

"Damn," Prost suddenly blurted. "Dalton and Sullivan were booked on the same flight, but canceled to wait for a call from me."

Silence suddenly filled the room as all eyes again turned to the president.

"Farkas?" Macklin asked.

"It's highly possible," Prost replied.

Overwhelmed with grief and anger, the president's eyes reflected blazing fury. "If it's true, they've made a serious mistake." Macklin's rage was reaching the boiling point when he looked at General Chalmers. "If this crash was the work of terrorists supported by Iran, I want those gutless cowards to pay a severe penalty."

Chalmers nodded his head. "They will, Mr. President. They will."

### Global Response Center, McLean, Virginia

Behind a heavy door on the nondescript sixth floor of the CIA headquarters, the stunning revelation about Khaliq Far-

kas had sent a chill through the command post for clandestine
war on terrorism. While computer screens flashed dispatches
and warnings, secure phones rang with alerts from operatives
at overseas locations. With its array of video monitors and
high-tech workstations, the antiterrorism center looked remarkably like a state-of-the-art military command center.

A small group of dedicated analysts studied dozens of up-
to-the-minute spy-satellite photographs while nineteen counterterrorism specialists monitored the continuous flow of
highly classified information about the whereabouts of Farkas
and other widely known terrorists.

In a secluded executive conference room, the director of
the CIA spoke by secure phone to a senior foreign intelligence official. The conversation was loud and strained. No
one, not even field operatives who observed Farkas on a daily
basis, could explain how he was still in Tehran at the same
time as he was seen flying an A-4 Skyhawk in Wyoming.
Embarrassed by the professional blunder, the director finally
had to admit that Farkas had deceived them once again. His
stand-in was a carbon copy.

# 14

## Athens, Greece

After spending an exhausting night in Dallas, Scott and Jackie arrived at Ronald Reagan Washington National Airport late the next morning. Pressed for time, they hurriedly packed their gear and caught a flight to Kennedy International Airport. With only minutes to spare before departure time, they boarded Olympic Airways Flight 412 bound for Athens and immediately fell into a deep sleep.

The bright sun was high overhead when their Olympic Airways 747 landed at the international airport. Using passports and credentials provided by the CIA, they quickly cleared customs and secured transportation from the airport, then checked into a luxury hotel with a spectacular view of the Acropolis.

While Jackie unpacked her luggage and indulged herself with a warm bath, Scott took the time to thoroughly inspect one of his custom-designed black parachutes. The chute's rectangular "ramair" canopy provided Dalton a high degree of control and accuracy after a precision free fall. Using night-vision goggles, and a wrist-mounted Global Positioning System satellite navigation instrument, Scott consistently landed within three feet of his target.

After a quick shave and shower, Dalton called Hartwell Prost and received a thorough brief on the status of the prepositioned equipment needed for the rescue mission. They also covered emergency contingencies and, once again, the subject of identification. Scott and his team would go in sterile. No one would carry any form of ID or wear any type of identifying jewelry or clothing.

In addition, all articles of clothing and footwear had to be free of identifiable tags or logos. As far as the White House and the Agency were concerned, Scott, Jackie, and Greg were mercenaries with no ties to the U.S. government.

The two helicopters and the single-engine airplane they had at their disposal were not insured and were not registered with any agency or government. In addition, the Bell LongRangers and the turboprop Cessna Caravan didn't have serial numbers on their airframes or engines. They had been written off as either destroyed or lost at sea.

When he was satisfied that his jump gear was in order, Scott took a leisurely nap, then went to the rooftop restaurant and requested a table with a panoramic view of the city.

After he was seated, Scott enjoyed a Chivas and soda while he waited for Jackie. When she entered the elegant dining room, her trim figure and striking good looks stopped a number of conversations. Smiling pleasantly, she caught sight of Scott and spoke quietly to the maître d' as she walked toward Dalton's corner table.

He rose from his chair and greeted her with an approving smile. *Wow.* "That's a very nice dress."

"Thank you," she said, noting the warmth of his smile.

He seated her, then gave the waiter a slight nod. "How about a drink before dinner?"

"Sure," she said with a hint of a smile. "I could use one."

"Rough day?"

"I just can't seem to get the crash off my mind. Every time I think about it, I visualize Eddy's face twisted in sheer terror." Jackie's pain was still fresh, but she maintained control of her emotions.

There was a slight pause while Scott considered Jackie's comments. "I know," he said in a comforting voice. "I can't stop thinking about Farkas, the innocent people he killed, and divine intervention—why we were spared at the last moment."

The waiter took her drink order and she turned her attention to Scott. "What's the latest from Washington?" she asked in a deliberate attempt to change the subject.

"Greg will be arriving early in the morning. After he gets here, a Navy helo will fly us out to the container ship. Two LongRangers are already onboard the ship."

"*Two?*"

"That's right. Hartwell believes in having spares whenever possible. And, like we requested, both helos and the jump plane have extended range tanks mounted inside the cabins."

"That's a relief," Jackie remarked, smiling vaguely at Scott. "What about my gear and the NVGs?"

"Hartwell assured me that everything you requested is there, including night-vision goggles, plus UHF and VHF radios."

"I'm impressed."

"Hartwell doesn't miss much," Scott declared. "After we drop you off on the ship, Greg and I will continue to Cyprus. The airplane has already been flown to Larnaca and topped off with fuel, so we're ready to launch on arrival."

Jackie smiled at Scott's contagious enthusiasm. "Any problem with getting permission to operate out of the international airport?"

"None whatsoever." The answer was simple and direct, emphasizing his expertise in covert operations. "The State Department explained that we're investigating the feasibility of starting an air-cargo service."

Jackie chuckled. "Surely they don't believe that."

"Hey, it gives everyone plausible deniability if anyone brings something up later. The airplane left the island and never returned. No one knows anything, except that it had a problem and disappeared. End of feasibility study—end of mystery."

"Let's hope it *is* that simple," Jackie coolly observed while their eyes met briefly.

"It usually is," Scott said as he arched his shoulders in a flexing shrug.

A hint of a smile touched her lips. "Usually—but not always," she challenged. "We can't know the odds."

"I guess I'd have to agree with that." Dalton's expression reflected a sudden concern. "Jackie, what do you think about changing our plans?"

"What?"

"I think we should eliminate the practice run and rendez-vous."

"Why?" she asked with a suspicious frown.

"Intuition," he said with a confident smile. "We need to be unpredictable—just in case someone *is* telegraphing our movements."

"I can't argue with that," Jackie admitted, eager to launch the rescue effort. "I just hope Maritza is still at the compound."

"So do I," he said firmly. *We may be risking our lives for nothing.*

She caught his eye. "If one of those crazies has a bad day, she could pay the ultimate penalty before we even get there."

Scott recognized the wayward direction her thoughts were taking her. "We have to keep the faith."

"I know," she murmured, understanding yet not liking the situation. "I'm just afraid she might be on her way to Teh-ran."

Dalton's thoughtful look hinted of compassion. "Unless we receive new information from Maritza, we have to assume that she's still there. I know she's a personal friend, but we can't afford to become distracted by what *could* happen."

Her eyes narrowed. "What would you do if Greg O'Donnell was in Maritza's place?"

"I'd follow my own advice," he replied easily, not rising to the obvious challenge. "I'd concentrate on doing my job right and try to increase the chances of succeeding."

They paused while Jackie's drink was delivered to the table.

"You have a point," she agreed, then looked him in the eye. "I'll be there when you need me," she said confidently. "I won't let you down."

"If I had any doubts about you, I wouldn't be here." Scott paused while another couple was seated nearby, then changed the subject. "Hartwell gave me an update on Far-kas," he said in a hushed voice. "A security camera caught him on video at DFW."

"And?"

"Apparently, he feigned car trouble on the perimeter of the

airport and hitched a ride with the driver of an airline catering truck."

"That figures," Jackie lamented.

"Since he was wearing an airline captain's uniform," Scott continued, "and had an official-looking ID badge, the driver never questioned anything. He drove the little bugger right through a service gate, then drove him to the boarding bridge leading to the cockpit of Flight 1684. According to a baggage handler who was near the jet, Farkas got out of the truck and leisurely sauntered up the stairs, then entered the jetway and boarded the plane."

"Wait a second." Her eyes studied his with a certain skepticism. "He would've needed a key, or some kind of code, to enter the jetway. You can't just walk up and open the door."

Scott eyed her and glanced around the room. "We're talking about *the* master," he reminded her with unabashed ease. "The bag smasher said the guy used a key to enter the jetway. Farkas obviously had done his homework."

"Or," Jackie asserted, "someone did his homework for him. It's amazing what money will buy these days."

"Yeah, that's true. The guy who saw Farkas went on loading bags and didn't think anything else about it. After Farkas planted the explosive—they believe it was Semtex, his favorite—he came back down the outside stairs and walked through the baggage-handling area. That's where the security camera tagged him. Once he cleared the area, he entered the concourse and probably wasn't far from us when he triggered the bomb."

"Amazing," she said with restless energy. "Absolutely amazing. How did he get out of Dallas?"

"No one knows."

"Did they find the A-4?"

"No," Scott said lamely. "They checked every airport within two hundred miles. No one saw anything that even vaguely resembled an A-4. My guess is he flew to Dallas in a run-of-the-mill plane."

"He might have arrived on a commercial flight," Jackie said as she attempted to conceal her frustration.

"I doubt it." Scott shrugged. "That would present too much

of a risk, and he wouldn't have been able to manage his time as well."

A frown crossed Jackie's face. "I can't believe he just vanished after our accident."

"Neither can I. The taxi—or what was left of it—was found about a mile from where we were, but he hasn't been seen since."

"That figures," she said, then absently stirred her drink with the straw. "Did Hartwell have anything to say about the crash?"

"Yes. They listened to a copy of the ATC tapes—from the tower and departure control. The first officer was in mid-sentence with the controller when the bomb was detonated. I have no doubt that the bomb was in or near the cockpit, because it incapacitated the pilots and instantaneously destroyed the radios. Forty-six seconds later the airplane slammed into the ground at approximately 380 miles an hour."

Scott reached for his drink. "Hartwell believes Farkas was going for a trifecta; he planned to bring down an airliner, kill a major segment of our terrorist experts, *and* take us out at the same time."

They remained silent for almost a minute, both thinking about how close they had come to dying.

Jackie finally broke the silence. "We have to stop him," she urged in mild outrage.

"I understand your feelings," Scott said patiently. "I feel the same way, but right now our job is to rescue Maritza. She may be able to give us a lot of information about Farkas, including where we might find him."

Noticing the concerned look in Jackie's eyes, Scott gave her a brief smile. "As we speak, the FAA, the FBI, the Counterterrorist Center, the Army's Delta Force, and the Navy's Dev Group—the Naval Special Warfare Development Group, formerly known as SEAL Team Six—are working round the clock to locate Farkas. We'll concentrate on finding him as soon as we get Maritza out of the camp. Like I said, she may know where we can find him."

Jackie nodded. "If she knows that, she may know how they plan to assassinate the president."

"Yeah, that's a possibility." Scott casually glanced around

the dining room before turning his attention back to Jackie. "Oh, I almost forgot. Hartwell gave me one other tidbit of information about Farkas."

"I hope it's good," she said with a lazy smile.

"Well, it gives us an idea of how he operates."

"And?"

"The FBI checked the ATC tapes from Salt Lake Center, Denver, Minneapolis, Kansas City, Chicago, and Indianapolis Center. From the time the witnesses said that Farkas took off from Casper, every jet the controllers handled for the next three hours was checked out and located, including a Sabreliner that *wasn't* flying that day. It was undergoing maintenance at its base in Houston."

"The *phantom* corporate jet," Jackie said in mild disbelief, then sent a glance heavenward.

"That's right," Scott declared. "The controllers said it sounded like the Sabre pilot was wearing an oxygen mask. Since he hadn't declared an emergency, they didn't question why he was wearing it at 37,000 feet."

Jackie shook her head in frustration. "Let me guess—no crews identified their traffic as being an A-4 Skyhawk? No one corrected the controllers?"

"Yup. From what the FAA and FBI have reconstructed, the A-4 was in and out of the clouds most of the time."

"Where did he land?"

"He was filed for Charleston, West Virginia, but he canceled IFR approximately ninety miles west of the city and disappeared. Where he went is anyone's guess, but the feds are scouring the airports in the area."

"I wish them lots of luck." She gazed into his eyes. "Regardless of how this operation turns out, I want to thank you for helping us."

"You can thank me later," he said with a radiant smile, then leaned closer to her. "We're going after Maritza *tomorrow* night, twenty-four hours early, so you better send her the signal tonight after midnight."

Jackie's eyes gleamed with excitement. "Are you going to tell Hartwell about our change in plans?"

"No," he admitted reluctantly.

Jackie gave him a curious look. "You trust him, don't you?"

"With my life," Scott said without hesitation. "But I don't know who might be pumping him for information."

"Good point," she said in a tempered voice, then raised her glass. "To Maritza Gunzelman, and a successful rescue."

Scott stared into Jackie's eyes and felt the blood surge through his veins. "To a successful mission."

# 15

## USS *Hampton*

Resting in the quiet darkness of his private cabin, Navy Commander Robert Gillmore dozed fitfully as *Hampton* silently slipped through the cold depths of the Indian Ocean northeast of Madagascar. With the exception of the slower-than-usual transit through the narrow Strait of Gibraltar, the long voyage from the Mediterranean to the Gulf of Oman was progressing smoothly.

Operating alone and undetected, the Los Angeles–class nuclear attack submarine was nearing its destination. Gillmore and his executive officer, Lieutenant Commander Todd Lassiter, were the only men aboard the "boat" who were privy to their secret orders. The rest of the crewmen were aware that the captain was deviating somewhat from standard procedures, but the officers and sailors didn't speculate on the nature of their mission, at least not openly. They knew the cerebral, tight-lipped skipper was not a man who tolerated scuttlebutt.

Bob Gillmore was a tall man who stooped to pass under normal doorways. In spite of his imposing size, he was adroit at navigating the narrow passageways in *Hampton*. His soft brown eyes peeked from under bushy eyebrows, and his thinning, sandy-colored hair was rarely out of place. Even in the confines of a cramped submarine, Gillmore seemed always to be immaculate and clean-shaven.

His quarters, no larger than steerage-class accommodations onboard a passenger ship, provided him with the only space he could call his own, his small kingdom away from home. To Gillmore, being here was like sitting in his living room in Groton, Connecticut—completely still, without even the slightest hint of motion. It was the only haven in the boat where he could relax and lose himself in the masterpieces of Count Leo Tolstoy.

Gillmore, a distinguished graduate of the U.S. Naval Academy and a third-generation submariner, was considered by his superiors to be one of the best and brightest skippers in the silent service. Unlike his colorful and gregarious father, Bob Gillmore drank sparingly, ate a healthy diet, and exercised on a regular basis. On duty, or at home with his family, he spent the majority of his time focused on the next hurdle in his highly competitive career. His primary goal in life centered on becoming the chief of naval operations.

To that end, the seasoned technocrat-manager was an excellent career planner. He carefully labored over every decision and how it might affect his future. As the admiral at La Maddalena had clearly explained, this operation would have to be flawlessly executed. The translation for Gillmore was abundantly clear; bungle the mission and your first afloat command will be your last. His future would be in the civilian world, not at the helm of an $870 million nuclear submarine.

At this stage of his delicate climb to the top, he cursed any involvement in operations that might jeopardize his plans. He desperately wanted to successfully finish his current tour of duty as skipper of *Hampton*, then get off the hot seat and report to the admiral's staff at New London—the heart and unofficial capital of the U.S. submarine force.

He rolled on his side and squinted at the eerie red multifunction display near his narrow bunk. The databank provided an instantaneous readout of *Hampton*'s depth, speed, course, position, and the current tactical situation.

All was well, prompting Gillmore to yawn and stretch his long legs, then roll on his back. He clasped his hands behind his head and stared into the inky darkness, carefully calculating the risks involved in the special mission, Operation Desert Phantom. A few minutes later, after reassuring himself that everything would work out to his satisfaction, Gillmore drifted into a restless sleep.

Sixteen hundred miles to the northeast of *Hampton*, the attack submarine *Cheyenne* glided through the depths of the Arabian Sea off the western coast of India. Her mission was the same as *Hampton*'s—destroy the two Iranian missile sites. *Cheyenne*'s Raytheon Tomahawk/BGM-109 cruise missiles would follow a different course to their targets, arriving minutes after *Hampton*'s Tomahawk land attack missiles.

### Gulf of Oman

The Liberian-registered freighter *Dauntless* barely made headway through the placid waters while the picket ship's thirty-nine-year old Iranian master trained his binoculars on a low-flying jet. The early-morning sky was hazy and visibility was limited, but he immediately recognized the stubby-looking twin-engine aircraft.

Known as "Hoovers" because the engines sound like vacuum cleaners, it was a U.S. Navy all-weather, antisubmarine and antisurface warfare plane patrolling for submarine activity near the approach to the Strait of Hormuz. The dull gray Lockheed S-3B Viking banked to the left and flew directly toward the rusty freighter, passing close to the fantail before resuming its search pattern.

A few minutes later, between bites of greasy lamb chops and sour rye bread, the captain watched as a mammoth aircraft carrier and her escort ships materialized on the opaque horizon. When the battle group drew closer, the skipper and his skeleton crew could see that the flattop's flight deck bristled with aircraft. The captain consulted his dog-eared *U.S. Ship and Aircraft Recognition Manual* and identified the carrier as the nuclear-powered USS *George Washington*, one of the newest ships in the infidel's Atlantic Fleet.

He raised his binoculars and studied the other vessels, recognizing the guided-missile cruiser USS *Normandy* and the destroyers USS *John Rodgers* and USS *O'Bannon*. Other escort ships included the guided-missile frigates USS *Boone* and USS *Underwood*, plus three support ships. The attack submarine USS *Annapolis* went undetected.

With tensions running high between the United States and Iran, Tehran claimed that the Americans were attempting to make their presence and vast influence in the region irreversible. Underscoring Tehran's worst fears, the "Arabian Gulf" had become the focal point of U.S. global strategy. Since the Gulf War, the crucial waterway off the coast of Iran had become the one place where the world's only military superpower openly and consistently showed its strength.

As the Iranian master knew, *Washington*'s powerful fighter planes would soon be screeching up and down the length of the Persian Gulf, swooping low over the waterway at speeds nipping the sound barrier. Occasionally, a young jet jock would nudge his sleek Tomcat or Hornet past Mach one, sending a sonic boom reverberating across the narrow Gulf. The intimidation factor was causing a great degree of angst to military and political leaders in Tehran.

At the captain's direction, the communications technician punched in a code at his console and sent a scrambled message to Tehran. After receiving a confirmation reply and further instructions, he sent a warning message to seven of Iran's aging regular Navy Combattante IIB guided-missile patrol craft.

When the last skipper checked in, the comm tech changed radio frequencies and sent a message to the eight Houdong-class patrol boats manned by sailors of the more politically favored fleet of the Iranian Revolutionary Guard Corps Navy. The skippers of the small Chinese-built warships raced to take up their assigned positions near the entrance to the Strait of Hormuz.

The communications tech would have to wait almost an hour to contact the first of three Iranian Project 877 Kilo-class submarines operating in the area. Venturing farther from port and remaining submerged longer than ever, the Russian-built, ultraquiet boats only poked their communications masts above the surface at preset times. After making contact with *Dauntless*, one of the submarines would be instructed to reposition in the southern waters of the Arabian

Gulf. The other two boats would remain on station in the Gulf of Oman and Arabian Sea.

Equipped with computer-driven weapons control systems and Russian Novator Alpha (NATO SS-N-27) antiship missiles, the Iranian Kilos fielded the latest generation of torpedo-tube-launched cruise missiles. The Russian equivalent to the antiship version of the Tomahawk, the Alpha ejects a supersonic submissile that can defeat almost any terminal defense system.

Minutes after Tehran had been notified of *Washington*'s current location, the supercarrier erupted with activity as one fighter plane after another blasted down the bow catapults and roared into the air. As the launches continued, the Iranians watched the blazing action while a few aircraft began landing on the carrier's angled flight deck. While the Iranian crew was absorbed with the air show, an F-14 Tomcat came in low from behind them and blasted over the freighter's bridge. The shocked crew ducked in unison and simultaneously cursed the cocky Americans.

The Iranians continued to watch air operations until the carrier disappeared in the dark haze. *Dauntless* and her crew would remain in the area and monitor events until the American armada left the region.

# 16

## The Mediterranean Sea

The pilots of the Navy SH-60 Seahawk were uncharacteristically quiet as their helicopter cruised at 1,200 feet above the tranquil blue sea. The flight crew's orders had been simple and straightforward; don't discuss anything with your passengers, unless there is an emergency, and don't discuss the mission with your shipmates when you return. The two lieutenants had been instructed to refuel the helo in Cyprus after their passengers departed, then immediately return to their ship.

In the back of the SH-60, Jackie, Scott, and Greg had gone over every detail of their mission. Afterward Jackie and Greg got acquainted exchanging basic information about their backgrounds. Later they went over the radio terminology and code names the team would be using during the operation.

When Scott jumped from the Caravan, O'Donnell would continue on course and monitor the radio calls. Once Jackie had retrieved Maritza and Scott, Greg would declare an emergency, then turn off his transponder and external lights as he dove for the deck and set a course for Athens.

If Greg experienced a *real* emergency that forced him to bail out or crash-land the rugged Cessna, Jackie would attempt to pick him up as soon as Scott and Maritza were safely aboard the helicopter. If the LongRanger developed problems that forced Jackie to land, she would try to make it to one of the suitable landing sites for the Caravan.

They all agreed it was a fairly straightforward plan, but they knew the devil was in the details. What had they overlooked? What had they not anticipated?

Their briefing gave way to silence as Scott and Jackie checked their personal equipment for the third time. Surrounded by enlarged land maps and aeronautical charts, Scott circled a point thirty nautical miles off the coast of Lebanon. "When you cross this fix, transmit 'Charlie Tango' and switch to your secondary frequency for our reply. If we're off the mark, I'll give you a plus or minus on our position from the Initial Point."

"I expect you to be on the money," came her dry response. "Don't naval aviators pride themselves on their split-second timing?"

"True," Dalton admitted with a crooked grin, "but Greg's been known to—occasionally—be off by two or three seconds."

Jackie gave him a sweeping glance, then lowered her head and studied the chart for a few seconds. The closeness between Scott and Greg made her feel more comfortable. *It's almost as if they can read each other's thoughts without speaking.*

She drew a circle around a checkpoint and looked up. "Greg will give me a call on primary when you leave the airplane?"

"That's affirm."

"I'll switch to your helmet radio"—Jackie looked up— "and wait for your call when you pop your chute."

Scott nodded as the helo began to descend. "That'll happen about fifteen to twenty seconds after I jump."

She could feel the excited tremblings of her nerves. "Once I confirm that you've jumped, I'll trigger Maritza's sat-phone to alert her."

"Yeah, we don't want to forget that," Scott said with a brief glance. "If either one of us has a radio failure, we operate on timing only."

"I'll be there," Jackie replied confidently.

Scott smiled briefly. "The weather looks good, so that shouldn't be a factor. If either ship has a problem—mechanical or otherwise—before I jump, call 'abort, abort, abort, charlie, charlie,' and we'll return to our bases. As we've discussed, if either ship goes down, the other pilot will attempt a rescue. If we abort, we'll plan on completing the mission the following night." Scott looked into Jackie's bright, gray-green eyes. "Failure is *not* an option."

"Speaking of options," she said, somewhat combatively. "I know we've been over this at least a dozen times, but I'm not going to leave you and Maritza there, even if I lose radio contact after you land."

"You have your instructions, and—"

"You mean orders," she interrupted.

"I expect to be on the end of the line—with Maritza—no later than ninety seconds after I hit the compound. If we're not there, head for the ship."

"Whatever you say."

"I mean it." Scott stared into her eyes. "If we're not there, get the hell out of town."

Jackie turned and stared at the wake of a cruise ship as the helo began to level off. Approaching the *Permak Express* from the stern, the Seahawk circled the reddish-brown container ship, then slowed as the pilot prepared to land.

Scott looked down at the slow-moving ship. Leased by the Agency, the neglected-looking *Permak Express* was crewed by agents who were licensed, professional mariners.

Dalton and his team fell silent while the Navy helicopter stabilized in a hover and gently settled on the ship's landing pad. Off to the side they spied two Bell 206 LongRangers under a bluish-gray camouflage netting. The helos were painted dark charcoal and bore no insignia. Jackie was relieved to see that both of the helicopters were equiped with wire strike kits and belly-mounted searchlights.

"After we get airborne," Scott said over the din of rotor-blade noise, "we'll get a radio check with you from both of the helos, then I'll give you a call with my helmet radio."

"I'll be standing by," Jackie said loudly, then tightly gripped Scott's arm. "Take care of yourself."

He locked her in his stare for a moment, then put his hand on her shoulder. "You, too."

She smiled and instinctively hugged him, then jumped out of the Seahawk. "Good luck!"

He gave her a quick, modified salute. "That's the only kind to have!"

As soon as Jackie was clear of the helo, the pilot increased power and lifted the SH-60 into the air. Climbing through 200 feet, the Seahawk entered a shallow bank to starboard and began circling the container ship.

While Jackie boarded one of the LongRangers, Scott fastened his helmet and quickly adjusted his twin boom microphones. The state-of-the-art communication system was voice-activated to allow him to keep his hands free. In the noisy helo, he would have to use the push-to-talk switch to manually override the sensitive automatic feature.

Dalton looked down at the helos and nodded to Greg.

O'Donnell raised his handheld transceiver to his mouth. "LongRanger, how copy Seahawk?"

"Loud and clear," she radioed. "How about me?"

"Five by five."

Scott then called on the discreet frequency that he and Jackie would be using after he jumped from the plane. The checks continued until the radios in both LongRangers passed inspection. Once the comm checks were complete, the SH-60 turned toward Cyprus and accelerated.

Jackie watched the helo until it was out of sight, then thoroughly checked both of the rescue helicopters for life rafts, life vests, and first-aid kits. Satisfied that everything was in order, she went about rigging two of the four 150-foot-long rappelling ropes to each ship. When she was finished attaching yellow snaplights above the six D rings hooked to the nylon ropes, she thoroughly preflighted both helos, then went to her stateroom to rest.

## Bekaa Valley

Maritza Gunzelman's shoulder muscles were tense and her stomach was churning. She had been relieved to actually hear Jackie's voice during the early hours of the morning. The message had taken only seconds, but it was like having a life jacket thrown to her in a storm-tossed sea.

The confirmation of the upcoming rescue effort had boosted her spirits and confidence, but her anxiety remained.

When the next call came, she would have to be ready to make a bold move.

From her prior training and from Jackie's brief but thorough instructions, Maritza knew exactly what she was expected to do during the extraction. When her rescuer parachuted into the guarded compound, Maritza would have to react swiftly and decisively.

If everything went as she desperately hoped it would, she would be liberated from the militants' compound before the next sunrise. Free from the unrelenting stress, free from the unsanitary living conditions, but most important, free from the fear of being found out, which meant certain death.

Stifling her growing angst, Maritza rose from the straight-backed wooden chair and walked across the cracked cement floor to one of two windows in her cramped room. She surveyed the familiar squalor and the bearded, unkempt men guarding the compound. It was not difficult to understand how the leaders of the front-line terrorist cells managed to recruit so many "suicide bombers" from the ranks of their illiterate, uneducated drones. Returning to her chair, Maritza attempted to channel her nervous energy into confidence.

The militants seemed to be growing more suspicious of her by the day, especially their leader, Bassam Shakhar. A shrewd man who prided himself in manipulating people, Shakhar had an uncanny ability to tell when someone was not being truthful.

Staring at a portrait of the late Iranian leader Ayatollah Ruhollah Khomeini, a mythical figure to the militants, Maritza quietly prayed that her rescue would be swift and safe.

Without warning, Shakhar opened the door and slowly walked into the small room. Maritza's heart skipped a couple of beats. During previous meetings with Shakhar, she had always been summoned to his quarters. This was a first for the wealthy supporter of Islamic Jihad, and it had a paralyzing effect on her. The slender man closed the door, then sat down under a yellowed banner marking the victory of the Islamic revolution in Iran.

Maritza willed herself to breathe slowly and be calm.

Adorned in his usual dark cloak and a rumpled turban, Bassam Shakhar did not say a word while he slowly examined Maritza from head to toe. Although no one would ever accuse Shakhar of being a charismatic person, Maritza could see that he was unusually solemn this day. He absently tugged on his salt-and-pepper beard and then stared into Maritza's piercing dark eyes, looking for a sign of fear that might give her away—a hint of worry that would tell him that she wasn't truly one of them.

After clearing his throat, Shakhar finally broke the silence. "We will go to Tehran tomorrow," he declared in his scratchy, strained voice. "My associates are looking forward to meeting you."

"I am honored," she said evenly as a tremendous sense of relief rushed through her. *Don't allow your voice to quake.*

Shakhar paused, then gave her a slow, crooked smile. "If you prefer, we can leave today."

Maritza's heart skipped another beat and lodged in her throat. *He's toying with me.* "Whatever you wish," she said with as little emotion as possible. "My loyalty is to Allahu, and to you," she said with conviction in her voice. "I live for Islam."

Without saying another word, Shakhar rose from his chair and walked out of the room.

Maritza took a deep breath and slowly exhaled. *Don't panic. Stay calm and think.*

# 17

Captain Nancy Jensen, USN, the first female skipper of a
Nimitz-class aircraft carrier, leaned back in her cushioned
chair and watched the last of the F-14 Tomcats and F/A-18
Hornets trap aboard *Washington*. Tall, blond, athletic, and
outgoing, Jensen was a distinguished graduate of the prestigious Test Pilot School at the Naval Air Test Center in Pa-
tuxent River, Maryland.

After leaving TPS, the vivacious aviator had flown Tomcats with the "World-Famous Fighting Black Lions" of VF-
213, served as executive officer of the "Jolly Rogers," and
later CO of the skull-and-crossbones squadron, commanded
*Nashville*, an Austin-class amphibious transport dock, then
served the obligatory stint at the Pentagon before advancing
to her present position.

Always the professional naval officer, Jensen took great
pride in the fact that she was in command of the enormous
nuclear-powered, self-contained floating airport. From keel
to mast top, USS *George Washington* measured twenty-four
stories high and weighed over 99,000 tons when loaded to
her maximum combat displacement. With a full complement
of more than eighty embarked warplanes and helicopters of
*Carrier Air Wing One*, the 1,094-foot-long-behemoth could
travel to the far corners of any ocean and be ready to fight

on arrival. Like the other U.S. carriers, *GW* provided the commander in chief with an air option that didn't need the permission of a host country.

Jensen raised her binoculars and studied the variety of ships operating between *Washington* and the opening to the channel linking the Persian Gulf with the Gulf of Oman and the Arabian Sea. Only twenty-nine miles wide at one point, the crowded Strait of Hormuz is of great strategic and economic importance, especially since a continuous flow of oil tankers passes through the narrow bottleneck. Jensen walked to the starboard side of the bridge and gazed at some of the other warships in the flotilla. Guiding the huge carrier through the narrow choke point would be a stressful time for her.

When Rear Admiral Ed Coleman, the task-force commander, left the bridge to return to the tactical flag command center, Jensen turned her attention to a Grumman E-2C "Miniwacs" Hawkeye on the starboard bow catapult. The airborne warning-and-control aircraft would orbit high above the carrier while the *Washington* battle group traversed the Strait of Hormuz and steamed toward their operations area.

Rotating shifts with three other VAW-123 "Screwtops" crews, the close-knit group would provide continuous surveillance while the warships were in the Persian Gulf. In order to enhance coordination, the tactical picture from the Hawkeyes was data-linked to Joint Task Force Southern Watch.

The "Hummer" pilot came up on the power and the "shooter"—the yellow-shirted catapult officer—gave a snappy hand signal to launch the twin-engine turboprop. The E-2C squatted, then charged down the deck in a vortex of steam.

Immediately after the Hawkeye cleared the bow, two VF-102 "Diamondbacks" F-14s taxied forward to the starboard catapult. The heavily armed warplanes would serve as the group's combat air patrol until they were relieved by two fresh crews. The bridge was hushed as Jensen watched the first Tomcat go into afterburner, then thunder down the deck, rotate sharply, and make an immediate clearing turn.

While the pilot of the second F-14 taxied into position, Jensen walked aft on the bridge to check the Alert Five birds parked behind the island. The pair of F/A-18 Hornets were manned and ready to launch on five minutes' notice. Hearing the Tomcat go to burner, Jensen returned to her chair in time to watch the big fighter blast down the deck and claw for altitude.

"Howszitgoin'?" a familiar voice asked.

Jensen turned to greet her executive officer when he stepped beside her elevated captain's chair.

"Well, we haven't been gassed or hit any mines yet." She smiled, absently tapping her Naval Academy ring on the side of the armrest. "What more could I ask for?"

"Yeah, life couldn't get any better." The XO chuckled as he glanced at the departing F-14. "I thought you could use a change."

"Thanks, Jim," she said, accepting a steaming mug of freshly brewed coffee. "I've had about all the tea I can stand."

"Same here." A smile twitched his mouth. "It's starting to taste like warmed-over jet fuel."

Captain Jim Lomas, a dashing Hornet pilot and fast-tracker on his way to flag rank, was a likable man who had no qualms about Nancy Jensen's history-making status. "I hope the folks in the puzzle palace know what they're doing."

"So do I," she admitted with icy calm.

Lomas studied *Washington*'s escort vessels and the two mine countermeasures ships, then turned his attention to the continuing action on the crowded 4.5-acre flight deck. "I'm sure uncomfortable about taking our boat into Sindbad's sea."

"You think *you're* uncomfortable." Jensen chuckled under her breath. "I'd like to know how many of these dilapidated tankers and tramp steamers are actually floating bombs?"

She pointed to a nearby bulk ship going the opposite direction. "If that rusting hulk came hard over to port, he'd nail us straight through the bow."

"You're right about that," Lomas declared. "But I'm more worried about our Achilles' heel."

"Getting through the choke point?"

"Right," he said, and lowered his voice. "We have a deck full of armed and fueled planes, and we're looking at dozens of new Iranian surface-to-surface missile sites along the straits."

He picked up a pair of binoculars and studied the shoreline. "They've been enlarging their underground facilities and at least nine of the caverns are equipped with Scud-C missiles. We're sitting ducks if someone gets trigger-happy."

She sipped her coffee and nodded in agreement. "I'm more worried about their new Shahab-3s. Fire enough ballistic missiles around the Middle East and all our troops are in trouble."

"Deep trouble," Lomas drawled.

Jensen glanced at the cruiser *Normandy*, their lead ship in the battle group, then scanned the array of ships funneling in and out of the Gulf. "We've been spoiled by blue-water operations."

"I like being spoiled," Lomas said as he watched the destroyer *John Rodgers*. "I'll take maneuvering room and wind over the deck anytime."

"And," she said with a smile, "plenty of warning time."

"You bet." Lomas's pleasant expression turned solemn. "With all these ships confined in an area approximately 440 by 155 nautical miles, we might as well be floating around in a farm pond."

Jensen nodded and gazed at the escort ships. "If the cannonballs start flying, it's going to be like Dollar Day at the Mustang Ranch."

"Yeah." Lomas grinned. "Everyone gets screwed."

Concerned about a supertanker that appeared to be closing on the carrier, Jensen concentrated on the advancing ship, then glanced at the officer of the deck. He ordered a slight course correction and the oil tanker also turned away from the carrier.

Jensen turned to her XO. "You look like a man with something on his mind."

"Nothing important," he said evenly, noticing the fatigue etched on her smooth face. "Any chance I can talk you into catching a few winks while I drive for a while?"

She smiled wanly. "I really appreciate the offer, but I better stay on the bridge until we get through the strait."

Lomas grinned uneasily. "Don't trust me, huh?"

"You know I trust you." She laughed quietly. "You wouldn't be able to sleep either."

"I can't deny that." Lomas chuckled and glanced at the hatch leading to the flag command center. "How often does the ol' man drop by?"

"Oh, I'd say about every thirty to forty-five minutes," she answered without any obvious emotion.

Rear Admiral Coleman, a man of prodigiously false humility, didn't leave any doubt about what he thought of women serving on ships, let alone allowing a female to *command* an aircraft carrier. The pairing of Nancy Jensen and Ed Coleman had not happened by chance.

"Well, don't let it bother you," Lomas said, somewhat self-conscious. "He's a leftover from the steam-gauge era."

Jensen simply nodded, adding to the sudden uneasiness of the moment.

"I'll keep the coffee coming," Lomas said, turning to leave the bridge.

"Jim."

He stopped and turned back. "Yeah."

She smiled warmly. "Thanks."

"You're gonna do fine," he said with a rush of enthusiasm.

### Persian Gulf

Darkness had quietly settled over the Gulf when the captain of the Iranian guided-missile patrol boat *Neyzeh* cautiously closed on the starboard side of the American aircraft carrier and her nine-ship battle group. Ordered to shadow the mighty warship and her flotilla of cruisers, destroyers, and frigates, the skipper was nervous about getting too close to *Washington*.

On a previous reconnaissance of *Enterprise*, he had ignored several warnings from an escort vessel and ventured too close to the carrier. In response, U.S. Navy warplanes put on an aerial firepower demonstration that left everyone aboard *Neyzeh* paralyzed with fear.

Other than viewing the latest in military training films, the men had never seen anything so frightening and devastating. The thunderous display of overwhelming firepower left an indelible impression on the young sailors. An hour after the patrol craft docked, every officer and sailor in the Iranian Navy knew about the incident.

Although the young captain of the *Neyzeh* didn't know it, his counterpart in *Shamsher*, the other Combattante IIB-class guided-missile patrol boat, was even more concerned. By the time he'd heard the embellished story of the awesome American firepower, F-14 Tomcats purportedly walked cannon shells along the side of the craft. Matching the speed of the formidable battle group, *Shamsher* remained over two miles away from the port side of the giant carrier.

The patrol-boat commanders were aware that the Americans were monitoring and recording all messages they sent to Tehran or received from headquarters. Likewise, Iranian intelligence specialists were receiving a steady stream of information about the movements of the American ships.

In addition to his anxiety about the U.S. warships, the captain was equally concerned about the sudden concentration of American surveillance aircraft over Iran and the Persian Gulf. According to senior Iranian military leaders, signals intercept and spoofing were being carried out by intelligence-gathering aircraft like the U.S. Navy's EP-3s and the Air Force's RC-135s. Along with the manned aircraft, the medium-altitude, long-endurance, all-weather Predator unmanned aerial vehicles were sending real-time sensor data to the Pentagon and to the carrier battle group.

Sporting forty-eight-foot wings, the 1,873-pound UAVs contained a payload sensitive enough to monitor low-power radio transmissions, including small handheld walkie-talkies, cell phones, and messages flowing between microwave towers. Equipped with real-time video, synthetic aperture radar, and infrared sensors, the Predators allowed controllers to see through clouds and operate at night. The radar could also be directed under metal buildings and be reflected with enough energy to reveal aircraft or missiles inside.

Shouting matches had broken out in the Baharstan Palace when one of the unmanned intruders repeatedly buzzed the seat of the Majles. The members of the Iranian parliament angrily ordered their military forces to destroy the American's *toy* airplanes.

High above Iran, another advanced unmanned reconnaissance aircraft was busy vacuuming electronic signals of interest. Loitering at 62,000 feet, the stealthly UAV was preparing to depart the country after being on station for twenty-eight hours. Joining the bow-tie pattern, another UAV took up station as the first aircraft rolled wings level and flew toward the Gulf. Roughly the size of a medium corporate jet, the highly classified reconnaissance planes represented the latest generation of UAVs.

The skipper of the *Neyzeh* cast a long look at his Chinese-made antiship missiles. With a range of sixty-five miles, the C-802 Silkworm was Iran's first new sea-launched missile since the United States sank an Iranian frigate armed with American Harpoon antiship missiles. The captain of the *Neyzeh* fervently hoped Tehran would not order him to fire the Chinese missiles at the American armada. He knew that attacking the U.S. forces would be tantamount to committing suicide.

# 18

## Aboard *Permak Express*

With a keen sense of both excitement and trepidation, Jackie securely fastened her twin-cell airline-style life vest. She looked up at the moonless, star-filled sky, then donned her flip-down night-vision goggles and waited for her eyes to adjust to the greenish artificial light. The night-vision aid amplified ambient light 1,200 times, allowing her to conquer the dark.

After she felt comfortable with the goggles, she carefully checked the helo's instrument panel and engine gauges one last time before she lifted the LongRanger off the container ship and flew alongside the bridge. With the transponder turned off and the exterior lights extinguished, the dark charcoal helo was almost undetectable as it flew low over the smooth Mediterranean Sea.

Satisfied that everything was functioning normally, Jackie set the radar altimeter for 100 feet, then added power and set course for her first navigational fix. She had flown the rescue mission in her mind dozens of times. She knew the circuitous route to the terrorist enclave like the main street of her hometown, and she had memorized every obstacle she expected to encounter, including three major centers of drug production and distribution. She was also acutely aware that the origins of illicit narcotics in the Bekaa Valley were fiercely protected by men armed with powerful weapons, including portable air defense missiles.

In Jackie's view, the toughest part of the flight would be her descent into the valley that separated the Lebanon Mountains and the Anti-Lebanon Mountains. No matter how she approached the terrorist training camp, she would have to fly directly over concentrations of Hezbollah militias and encampments of Syrian soldiers.

Jackie smiled to herself when she touched the Hermès scarf tucked under the neck of her flight suit. Her father, Dr. E. Raines Sullivan, always sent her a dozen assorted scarves on her birthday. As much as she loved her pipe-smoking aristocratic father, his elitist and sexist values had driven her away from the family and all the trappings of inherited wealth. When she announced she had joined the Air Force, Dr. Sullivan abruptly canceled his annual pilgrimage to the Prix de Diane, France's most exciting horse race, and vented his spleen at Jackie for two days and nights. Always an elegantly dressed and eloquently expressive man, E. Raines had had what he would later describe as an "indecorous lapse in manners."

Without warning, a bright light ahead of the helo blinked on and off twice, then disappeared. Jackie changed course a few degrees and scanned the horizon looking for a boat or ship. The more she moved her eyes, the more she felt off balance. When the insidious "leans" began inducing the first stages of vertigo, she removed the NVGs and tossed them on the life raft behind her. She flew strictly by instruments for a few moments, then began sweeping her eyes across the sea for any sign of a ship.

After two minutes of fruitless searching, she altered course again and added a touch of power to make up the few seconds she'd lost. *I must be seeing things that aren't there. Concentrate.*

Jackie's nerves settled down as she continuously checked her time and position. She was hitting her coordinates precisely on time and on course. Sixty miles from the container ship, Jackie's sense of well-being was shattered when she felt a shudder run through the LongRanger.

"What the hell was that?" she said under her breath, then quickly scanned her instruments. Everything appeared to be in order. *Okay, take a deep breath and get a grip on your nerves.*

### Larnaca, Cyprus

Wearing a parachute, Greg O'Donnell coaxed the fuel-laden Cessna Caravan into the night sky and began a very shallow climb to their assigned altitude. While Scott exchanged his cargo-pilot uniform for his black jumpsuit, body-armor vest, modified rappelling harness, and paratrooper boots, O'Donnell switched radio frequencies and pointed the big single-engine turboprop toward Damascus.

After Dalton zipped up his boots and donned his helmet, he looked at the huge ferry tank bolted to the cabin floor, then stepped forward to the dimly lighted cockpit. "How much are we over gross?"

"You don't want to know." Greg quietly chuckled. "Let's just say that I have enough fuel to fly from the valley to Athens, with plenty left over."

"Well, as the British say, you can never have too much petrol."

"Unless you prang the ship," Greg quipped.

Scott checked the time and the Caravan's GPS. "Jackie should be about twenty miles south of us."

"Let's hope so," Greg replied with a slow grin. "How's the chemistry between the two of you?"

"Chemistry?"

"Are you attracted to her?" Greg asked innocently. "Are you bonding? That kind of chemistry."

After Scott gave it a moment of thought, he proclaimed, "I'd say that we get along just fine. In fact, I wouldn't mind developing a *much* closer relationship with her."

Greg adjusted the power and gave Dalton an understanding glance. "You mean, if you live through this, right?"

"Well," Scott said as he strapped on his assault knife, "I try not to dwell on the negative aspect of things."

"Seriously, Bubba," O'Donnel said with a grim look. "This gig isn't gonna be easy."

"What could possibly go wrong?" Scott piped sarcastically.

"Well, we could start with the fact that you stood up your rescue pilot."

"What?"

"She told me about the sailing date." Greg laughed out loud. "Or should I say, the sailing date that didn't happen?"

"I'm guilty as charged," Scott admitted as he tucked his Sig Sauer into the compact nylon holster strapped to his thigh. "However, I wasn't purposely shirking my responsibility."

"You don't have to convince me," Greg said with mock innocence.

"I thought you might put in a good word for me." Scott chuckled as he donned his black, custom-made parachute. He snapped two grenades and a quick-don rappelling harness to his assault vest, then tugged at his multigrip gloves. "There's something about her, something that makes the hormones churn."

"Tell me about it," Greg declared in a suggestive voice.

Scott sat down and closed his eyes. *She is captivating, no question about it. Intelligent, attractive, articulate, and she has a good sense of humor. This definitely has long-term possibilities . . . if we live through this extraction.*

### Near the Ancient City of Sidon

Jackie closely monitored her flight instruments and the GPS until she was precisely thirty nautical miles due west of the coast of Lebanon. With an eye on the radar altimeter, she keyed the radio. "Charlie Tango," she announced, and immediately switched to the secondary frequency.

"Transco twenty-seven on the numbers," Greg O'Donnell radioed in his clipped fashion. The Caravan was on course and on time.

"Charlie Tango," she said in the same abbreviated style.

"Copy."

With her confidence growing, Jackie searched for the faint glow of lights marking Sidon, the Mediterranean terminus of the Trans-Arabian Pipeline. She would make landfall south of the piers and oil-storage tanks, then remain on course for another seventeen nautical miles. At that point she would turn left seventy degrees at the power plant south of the Qa-

raaoun Reservoir at the southwestern edge of the Bekaa
Valley. From there, it was a straight shot over the drug dealers and military troops to the terrorist camp.

After squelching her growing anxiety, Jackie finally caught
sight of Sidon, also known as Saida. Nearing the city, she
glanced at the thinly scattered lights of the boats moored in
the picturesque harbor. The small port was surrounded by
orchards of oranges, banana, and loquat trees.

She allowed a small grin to crease her face as she initiated
a climb to clear the mountain ridges leading to the Bekaa
Valley. Jackie slowly moved her head from side to side in
order to ease the tension in her neck. *Just a few more
minutes.*

### Beirut, Lebanon

Approaching the gateway to the ancient world, Scott and
Greg were treated to an unforgettable experience as the ambient glow of Beirut slowly gave way to a vista of shimmering lights. In the distance, the mountains rising behind
the legendary city were paintbrushed with softly glowing
lights that blended into a sea of twinkling stars.

At this early hour of the morning, most of Beirut's 1.5
million residents were fast asleep. The air traffic was sparse,
and, for the most part, the pilots and controllers exchanged
very little in the way of casual conversation.

Passing almost directly over Beirut International Airport,
Greg checked the Caravan's Global Positioning System
against Scott's portable unit. Both receivers were in harmony.

"Six minutes, thirty-five seconds to go," Greg announced
as he punched the timer. "Recheck your gear and fittings."

"Workin' on it," Scott said as he methodically smeared his
face, neck and ears with a camouflage stick, then went
through the familiar routine of rechecking his equipment.
While he was tightening his parachute harness, random
thoughts began to drift through his mind.

"The last time I was in Beirut," Dalton said calmly as he
inspected the two grenades attached to his assault vest, "I
spent an entire afternoon at a cliffside café. I met a girl who

was going to med school at Tulane, and we had a great day just knocking around and—"

"Hey, Bubba," Greg interrupted. "I don't mean to throw a damper on your party, but it's time to start focusing on the present."

"I'm trying to relax," Dalton said, then opened the Caravan's modified cargo door. "I'll focus on the present when I jump."

"Partner," Greg said emphatically, "this is the Super Bowl of jumping. If you screw the pooch on this deal, you only get penalized once—I'm talkin' about graveyard dead."

"I suspect you're right," Scott said while he checked the strap over his thigh holster. Despite his seemingly calm demeanor, Scott's heart was beginning to pound. "Thanks for the comforting words."

"Semper fi," O'Donnell said firmly as he donned his night-vision goggles. *We've gone too far this time. I should've talked him out of this crazy shit when we were in Alaska.*

### The Hezbollah Camp

The sounds were muffled, but Maritza recognized voices outside her spartan quarters. She quietly made her way across the darkened room and peeked through one of the small windows. What she saw frightened her. Instead of the usual two or three men standing guard at this early hour, there were at least a dozen armed militants walking around inside the perimeter of the compound.

*What's going on?* she nervously asked herself, then moved away from the window. She carefully removed a bundle of wooden sticks and paper from her makeshift closet, then opened a small tin of matches and stuffed them into the compact bundle. When she was finished, she shoved the package under the foot of her wood-framed bed. *Something is wrong with this picture.*

A moment later Maritza held her breath when she heard footsteps near her door. With her heart pounding, she slipped into bed and waited for the door to open. Ten minutes passed without another sound. She reached under the bed and gripped her Glock nine-millimeter semiautomatic, then slid the weapon inside a pocket sewn into her Islamic garb. Maritza was about to swing her legs over the side of the bed when she heard footsteps walking away from her quarters. *Be patient.*

## Approaching the Terrorist Compound

Greg O'Donnell eased the throttle back and began slowing the Caravan. "Twenty seconds," he announced, darting a glance at the GPS while he stabilized the big turboprop. "Negligible wind drift."

"I hope you're right."

"I'm always right."

Scott made a final adjustment to his night-vision goggles, patted the flap over his Sig Sauer, then gripped each side of the door frame. "I'm ready to do it—let's go."

"Ten seconds," Greg said over the wind noise whipping around the back of the cabin. "We're almost over the target."

Dalton's heart was thumping like a trip-hammer. *Concentrate . . . take it one step at a time.*

Greg continually tweaked the elevator trim as the Caravan slowed to just above stall speed. "Five seconds."

Scott took a deep breath, then—

"Four."

—sharply exhaled.

"Three."

"Two."

"One."

"Go!" Greg said as Scott flung himself out of the airplane and disappeared into the moonless night.

O'Donnell slowly added power and keyed his radio. "Ball four—he's taking a walk."

"Copy the runner going to first," Jackie said hastily.

"Roger that," O'Donnell calmly replied.

She checked to make sure that all of the helo's exterior lights were off, then quickly switched to the frequency for Scott's helmet-mounted radio. *Come on, don't keep me in suspense.*

Fumbling with her sat-phone, she punched in the code that would signal one of the Low Earth Orbit (LEO) satellites in near-polar orbit to trigger Maritza Gunzelman's miniature phone. When the connection was made, Jackie spoke slowly and clearly. "Take the midnight train."

"Copy train," Maritza replied in a tense voice. "You're flying into an ambush. There's at least a dozen armed men waiting for you."

"Say again."

"We need to abort," Maritza said as loud as she dared. "It's an ambush!"

Stunned by the unexpected revelation, Jackie finally found her voice. "What's going on? Give me a sitrep."

"I don't know what to tell you, except that the compound is alive with armed men. We need to abort."

"Negative!" Jackie's heart raced as she thought about Scott. "The jumper is on the way down. Get ready to go."

"I'm all set," Maritza whispered as she heard a faint noise near her door. "Gotta go," she said, and terminated the connection.

Jackie snapped the sat-phone shut, then concentrated on flying the helo as close to the ground as she could. While she waited for Scott's radio call, she continually scanned her instruments and the rising terrain. Something didn't feel right. She couldn't locate any of the telltale landmarks she expected to see by now. *Is the GPS giving me erroneous readings?*

Without warning, the bright stars at her twelve o'clock position vanished. Startled by the sudden change, she flicked on the 30 million candlepower searchlight and gasped as she froze on the controls. She was staring straight at an outcrop of rocks surrounded by dense vegetation. Jackie desperately pulled on the collective, then rolled the helo to the right to avoid colliding with a cemetery at the top of the ridgeline. With her hands shaking, she leveled the LongRanger and quickly turned off the powerful "Night Sun" spotlight. *You're making too many mistakes. Get it together.*

A few seconds later the stars appeared to rise above the ridge, prompting Jackie to let out a sigh of relief. She cleared the mountaintop by twenty feet, then turned to her original heading and began a rapid descent into the bowels of the Bekaa Valley. The topography of the valley provided a wide variety of landing strips for helicopters and rugged light planes.

Less than two minutes after entering the valley, Jackie was startled when a stream of tracer rounds flashed past the right side of the LongRanger. She jinked twenty degrees to the left, made an abrupt descent, jinked to the right, then climbed steeply. She continued the evasive maneuvering as more tracers slashed by the left side of the helo, then stopped as quickly as they had begun.

After tumbling head over heels a couple of times, Scott finally stabilized his body in a classic free-fall position. He looked straight down and tried to locate the terrorist camp, but the vertigo-inducing counterclockwise rotation he'd developed was causing him to lose his situational awareness. He attempted to orient himself, then gave up and pulled the rip cord.

The parachute opened with a muffled report, snapping Dalton upright. He peered at the ground through his night-vision goggles while he completed a 360-degree circle.

*Where the hell is it?* Scott asked himself as he spiraled down toward the valley. He was about to yank the NVGs from his helmet when he finally spotted the compound. Able to clearly see the camp, Scott removed the goggles and tossed them away. He gazed at the surrounding countryside and quickly oriented himself to the irregular clusters of lights.

"Charlie Tango, bull's-eye," he radioed to Jackie.

"I'm over the hump," Sullivan replied as she chewed uncertainly at her lower lip. "Three miles and . . . ah, rapidly closing."

"I'll be on the ground in about a minute," Scott replied.

"We have approximately a dozen armed guards waiting for us," Jackie said as she squinted to locate the compound.

"Shit!" A long pause followed. "Maritza confirmed that?"

"Yes. She's standing by."

Disturbed by Jackie's tone, Scott looked down at the dark compound. *She doesn't sound very confident.* "Are you okay?"

"I'm not sure about the GPS. It seems like—"

"Give me a quick flash on the searchlight!" Scott said firmly. A second later he saw the powerful spotlight flick on, then off. "Come left about ten to fifteen degrees, and hustle the descent."

"I'm on my way," Jackie said as she increased her rate of descent, then flexed the yellow snaplights attached to the two nylon rappelling ropes. She shook the colored lights and quickly released the 150-foot ropes. "I have the camp in sight, and the lines are out!"

"Good work," Scott radioed in a hushed voice. "Better hustle."

"If I go any faster," she said with a great deal of tolerance in her voice, "I might run over you before you're on the ground."

"I'm almost on the ground," he said as he approached the compound. "I should've popped the top a little earlier."

"I'm comin' down like a brick!" Jackie had to force the words out, knowing that Lady Luck held their lives in her hands. "I'll be there!"

# 19

## The Camp

Maritza Gunzelman's throat was tight as she covered her nine-millimeter Glock with a thick pillow, then walked across the darkened room and cautiously opened her door. What she encountered did not surprise her. She silently maligned the lineage of the armed terrorist standing guard four feet away. The lanky, bearded militant was carrying an Intratec semiautomatic pistol with a thirty-six-round detachable magazine. An assault weapon, the TEC-9 was popular with gangs, drug dealers, and terrorist groups.

With her mouth as dry as sawdust, Maritza stepped outside and approached the young Shiite. Bred by a culture of violence and inhumanity, the man was a typical example of the crass and servile followers found in the terrorist camps.

She spoke in a Persian dialect. "Come quickly. I must show you something," she said urgently as she motioned for him to follow her. "It is very important. Come quickly."

The man hesitated, unsure about her earnest plea. He started toward the open door and looked back over his shoulder. No one was paying any attention to him.

"Hurry," she coaxed with a no-nonsense edge to her voice. She preceded him into the room, then closed the door. "Look out the other window," she whispered with determined urgency.

While he cautiously approached the window, Maritza reached under her pillow and quietly retrieved the Glock. Gripping it tightly, she raised the semiautomatic high above her head and slammed the butt of the weapon against his temple. He dropped to his knees and fell forward, smashing his face into the cement wall. Maritza quickly grabbed the TEC-9 and tossed it on the wooden table.

Stepping out of her cumbersome Islamic-style clothes, she slipped the Glock into a baggy hip pocket of her fatigues. She struck a match and set fire to the large bundle of dry sticks and paper stuffed under her bed, then scooped up the assault weapon and hurried to the door.

Squaring her shoulders, she stepped outside and immediately heard the reverberating sound of helicopter rotor blades. Holding the TEC-9 at the ready, she listened for a moment as the sound grew louder. Moving slowly and silently along the perimeter wall, Maritza was startled when a diaphanous ghost suddenly appeared out of the inky darkness. She felt a sudden chill as Dalton flared his parachute for a flawless landing in the middle of the courtyard.

Simultaneously, a trio of militants caught sight of Scott as he quickly released his canopy risers from his harness. The silence was shattered when the three men opened fire at the same instant Dalton spotted Maritza.

Running toward Scott, she sprayed a steady stream of rounds at the startled Shiites. Two of the shadowy figures crumpled to the ground while Dalton drew his weapon and dropped the third man in his tracks.

"Get down," Scott shouted to Maritza.

She sprawled in the dirt and kept firing.

Indoor and outdoor lights flicked on as the beat of the helicopter's mainrotor blades grew louder and louder. Scott dropped to a prone position and fired at two men who were scrambling for cover behind an empty flatbed truck. Dalton scrambled toward a stack of wooden boxes as he fired at three other men.

Ignoring the blinding hurricane of dirt and debris being sucked up by the LongRanger's powerful downwash, Scott pumped three rounds into a side-mounted fuel tank on the flatbed. Without warning, Dalton's discarded parachute canopy swirled overhead as Maritza low-crawled the final few yards to join him.

"We don't have time to get you into a harness," he shouted as rounds kicked up dirt and ricocheted around the compound. He shoved his Sig Sauer into his nylon holster, then yanked the pin from a grenade and lobbed it close to the truck. The vehicle exploded in a huge fireball.

"Cover me till I get a ring hooked," Scott yelled above the swirling dust storm. "When I've got it latched, throw your arms around my neck and your legs around my waist and hang on!"

"Got it," Maritza shouted as she fired the last rounds from the TEC-9. She reached for her Glock at the same time Scott lobbed his last grenade at two men who were charging them from behind the main barracks. The terrorists were cut down by the violent blast.

Muzzle flashes began to twinkle as Jackie slowed the helo to a crawl while she trolled for Scott and Maritza. With the element of surprise gone, she listened to Dalton as he instructed Maritza and fired at the militants. While Jackie attempted to maintain the proper altitude to allow Scott to see the glow of the snaplights, an AK-47 round pierced the helo's chin bubble and grazed her ankle. The sensation was akin to having a branding iron sear her bare flesh.

"Hold it," Scott yelled over the radio as he crawled toward the rappelling ropes. "Hold it! Hold it! *Stop!*"

Jackie grimaced in pain and concentrated on the blazing truck as she slowed to a motionless hover.

"Stay down!" Scott said to Maritza as he struggled to latch his parachute harness to one of the D rings. He lurched toward the nearest snaplight and felt the exhilarating tug of success.

"Maritza," he bellowed as he drew his weapon and fired twice at an unarmed terrorist who was running straight at them. One of the rounds knocked the man to his knees as Maritza holstered her weapon and lunged toward Scott. She leaped on him and held his neck in a death grip while she locked her legs around his waist.

*"Go,"* Dalton shouted to Jackie as the back of his body armor stopped a round, partially knocking the breath out of

him. "We're aboard!" he blurted in a hoarse croak. "*Go, Go!*"

Staggering to his feet, the bleeding terrorist charged Scott and Maritza as the rope became taut.

"I'm slipping," Maritza exclaimed as they left the ground.

Before Scott could answer, the militant slammed into him. Screaming at the top of his lungs, the powerful man wrapped his arms around Dalton's lower legs.

Scott struggled to get a leg free, but the crazed man held him in a viselike grip. Seconds later a round caught the terrorist in the head and he plummeted into the side of the burning truck.

Applying full power and a prodigious amount of collective, Jackie tripped the "Night Sun" searchlight. Petrified by cold fear, she hoped it would blind the militants long enough for her to escape being shot down. As the helo struggled to climb, she heard several rounds rip through the Long-Ranger's thin aluminum-and-magnesium fuselage. Time seemed to stand still as another fusillade shattered the cockpit windshield and showered her with fragments of Plexiglas and aluminum.

Turning to avoid overflying the burning truck, Jackie was shocked and temporarily blinded when the truck exploded in another thunderous fireball. She blinked her eyes several times as she struggled to read her flight instruments, then realized that she had slung Scott and Maritza straight through the middle of the blazing inferno.

"Scott," she frantically radioed, "do you read me?"

The radio remained silent.

Jackie killed the searchlight. "Scott, do you copy?"

The silence was deafening in the windy cockpit.

"Hang in there!"

Angered by knowing that someone had set them up to be ambushed, Jackie stared at the shattered instrument panel as she climbed away from the terrorist camp. A few heartbeats later she again triggered the powerful spotlight and rotated it downward, then leaned to her right to see if Maritza and Scott were still attached to the line. Although she could barely see them, they were hanging from one of the ropes. Jackie was ecstatic. "Give me a thumbs-up if you can read me."

When the searchlight was directed downward, Dalton holstered his weapon and looked up at Jackie. His eyes conveyed a sense of urgency that bordered on desperation. Swinging in the wind, Scott repeatedly jabbed his thumb toward the ground.

*Something's wrong*, Jackie told herself as she abandoned the plan to land at the original site to take them onboard. She switched off the searchlight and looked for an alternate place to set down.

"Charlie Tango," Greg O'Donnell calmly radioed from the Caravan. "Do you read the umpire?"

"That's affirm," Jackie shot back. "They're on the hook, but I'm going to have to stop short of the dock. Stand by."

"Copy," Greg said, glancing at his GPS. "I'm going to have to make my move soon."

"Give me a couple of minutes," she said loudly. "We've taken some hits, and I don't know how much damage it's caused."

"Do you need assistance?"

"We may need some help," Jackie said as she felt the helo shudder and start to vibrate. "Stay with us."

"I'm not going anywhere."

Scott was holding Maritza with both arms, but she was beginning to slip as the wind whipped them in tight circles. During the harrowing escape, his twin boom microphones had been ripped off by the rappelling rope, making it impossible for him to communicate with anyone.

"Hang on," he said to Maritza. *Jackie, get us on the ground!* "We're going to make it," he continued in a soothing, calming voice. "Just another minute or two."

"My arms are going numb," she said, keeping her head buried against his neck. "I can't feel them."

Hanging by the upper right side of his parachute harness, Scott strained to hold Maritza next to him. If she lost her grip on him, it was going to be impossible for him to hold her very long. If they didn't land soon, Maritza would fall to her death.

As the seconds passed, Maritza struggled to keep her legs around Scott's waist. The more she strained, the more she slipped and the heavier she seemed to become.

Dalton gripped her with all his strength, but he was rapidly losing the battle. He closed his eyes and willed himself to keep her from falling, but it was useless. *Land this thing!*

Rapidly slowing and descending, Jackie triggered the bright spotlight, then adjusted the focus of the beam slightly ahead of the LongRanger. She brought the helo to a slow halt and gently settled toward a grassy knoll.

"We're almost down," she said to Dalton, hoping he could hear her over the beat of the main rotor blades.

Without warning, a shoulder-fired SAM missile flashed past the helo's shattered cockpit.

"Oh, shit!" Jackie swore as she instinctively ducked her head. *We've gotta get out of here.*

A few seconds later Maritza lost her grip around Scott's neck and her legs swung wildly downward. Another missile slashed by as Dalton caught her under the arms.

"Land this sonuva*bitch*," he shouted as Maritza slowly slipped through his hands and fell.

# 20

Enjoying his notoriety as the killer of the American's F-14 Tomcat reconnaissance plane, Major Ali Akbar Muhammud led three MiG-29 Fulcrums as they circled their airfield at Shiraz, then turned west toward the Persian Gulf. One of the pilots in the formation was Major Viktor Kasatkin, a renowned Russian fighter pilot and advanced tactics instructor. A graduate of the Kharkov Higher School of Pilots and the Gagarin Air Force Academy, Kasatkin was honing the skills of the Iranian pilots.

Muhammud, having received reliable up-to-the-minute information from the auxiliary patrol boat *Gavatar* and the Iranian corvette *Naghdi*, was prepared to confront the Americans if they attacked Iran.

Equipped with *Flash Dance* radars, air-to-air missiles, and thirty-millimeter cannons, the MiGs represented the most advanced of the flyable fighters in the Iranian Air Force. Major Muhammud adjusted his cockpit lights to enhance his night vision and darted a look at his Iranian wingman, who had been selected from the best the Iranians could muster. He was tucked in close to his leader's wingtip.

Muhammud, the politically powerful son of an Iranian Air Force general who was killed in a 1995 JetStar crash, was considered by his peers to be one of the most talented fighter pilots in the Iranian Air Force. But then again, during mock dogfights, no one was stupid enough to seriously challenge the cocky and temperamental pilot.

Not far behind, three more MiG-29s joined in trail and followed Muhammud to their patrol sector between the coastline and Khark Island. The well-educated pilots came from Iran's upper classes; however, their aviation training wasn't up to the standards of the West. The Iranians could demonstrate passable displays of air combat maneuvering, but their basic dogfighting capabilities were considered to be limited at best.

In addition, the aviators weren't as young and proficient as they once were. A lack of flying time had eroded their skills and prevented the training of new pilots. Almost to a person, the Iranian pilots dreaded the thought of pitting themselves against the highly competent, younger, and better-trained Americans. A bootlegged video of the movie *Top Gun* had added to their anxiety, especially the scenes of "fangs out" aggression that unfolded during combat training engagements.

From the first briefing after *Washington* and her battle group neared the Strait of Hormuz, there had been a strange sense of foreboding among the Iranian pilots. Something seemed different from previous alerts. Most of the younger aviators sensed that their superiors were also more tense than usual. Thanks to the Russian fighter instructor pilots, the Iranian aviators were improving. However, they knew they were up against some of the best-trained fighter pilots in the world.

With both flights in close proximity, Muhammud entered their assigned patrol area and waited for further instructions. The mission plan was highly modified from the usual sorties they flew, which heightened Muhammud's sense of anticipation. If nothing happened in the next twenty minutes, they would begin cycling planes to a coastal airstrip for refueling.

Seventy-three miles south of Muhammud's position, seven additional MiG-29s were steering a circuitous course toward Hendorabi Island. The American carrier battle group was steaming southwest of the island. Eight miles behind the MiG fighters, three cruise-missile-equipped Dassault Mirage F-1s were prepared to attack the carrier if ordered to do so. Slightly above and a mile behind the F-1s, two aging

Bushehr-based F-4 Phantom jets were positioning themselves to attack. Both fighters were equipped with Chinese-made C-801 Sardine antiship cruise missiles.

If hostilities erupted, the Iranians' strategy would be to lure the U.S. aviators close to their homeland, or over any of the seven Houdong-class guided-missile patrol craft, where surface-to-air missiles would be used to make the fight more deadly. Few of the Iranian pilots were willing to discuss the fact that Iran's SAMs couldn't identify friend from foe. A senior pilot who had questioned the tactics disappeared from the base. No one would openly speculate as to his whereabouts.

## Saudi Arabia

Four U.S. Air Force F-15 Eagles from the 33rd Fighter Wing's 58th Fighter Squadron taxied into position on the dark runway and held their brakes. Based at Eglin Air Force Base in Florida, the flight crews were completing the last two weeks of a routine rotation to Saudi Arabia.

Normally, the seasoned fighter pilots enforced Operation Southern Watch, the United Nations–mandated "no-fly" zone in southern Iraq. This early morning wasn't any different for the "Nomads," except that these four highly experienced pilots were preparing to take off on a special mission.

Their commanding officer and flight leader, a former Thunderbird demonstration pilot, was about to take the pride of the Air Combat Command's 9th Air Force to the Persian Gulf. The pilots' collateral mission was straightforward; fly cover for American warships while the U.S. Navy sent Iran a message.

A veteran of the Persian Gulf War, Lieutenant Colonel Trent McCutchin took in the panoramic view from his cockpit. Behind the tightly secured fence lines, motion sensors and surveillance cameras mounted atop a watchtower scrutinized the flat, barren desert for miles.

Turning his head toward his wingman, McCutchin glanced at Sting Two in his F-15. Bathed in the soft glow of his cockpit lights, Major Tim Cotton appeared to be an alien sitting in the clear dome of a flying saucer.

Satisfied that Sting Two was in the proper position,

McCutchin checked his warning enunciators. Loaded with AIM-120 Advanced Medium Range Air-to-Air Missiles, AIM-9 Sidewinders, and 940 rounds for the M-61 Vulcan cannon, the powerful F-15s were ready to add another page to the record book. With over 100 confirmed air-to-air kills— with no losses—the Eagle was considered by many to be the best air superiority fighter in the world.

McCutchin set the flaps and keyed his radio. "Sting One, radio check."

The other pilots replied in clipped voices.

On McCutchin's next call, he and his wingman shoved their throttles forward and released their brakes. Belching tongues of white-hot exhaust from the afterburners, the F-15s blasted down the dark runway. With the precision of a seasoned aerial-demonstration team, the two Eagles lifted off the runway in a shallow climb.

Spewing flames from their afterburners, Three and Four were rapidly accelerating to rotation speed.

Seconds later, after the four fighters were aerodynamically clean, McCutchin initiated a smooth transition to a steep climb. Behind his oxygen mask, the flight leader smiled to himself. He was surrounded by some of the best fighter pilots in the U.S. Air Force.

Back on the runway, eight F-16 Fighting Falcons taxied into position. Cleared for takeoff, Fang Flight and Rock Flight immediately thundered down the runway in sections of two.

### Incirlik Air Base, Turkey

A U.S. Air Force Fast-deploying Air Expeditionary Force, including F-15s from the 1st Fighter Wing, Langley Air Force Base, Virginia, F-16s from the 388th Fighter Wing, Hill AFB, Utah, and the 20th Fighter Wing, Shaw AFB, South Carolina, would join F-117s from the 49th Fighter Wing, Holloman AFB, New Mexico, to provide a powerful response if Iran mounted an aggressive counterattack.

Navy and Marine aviators would patrol along the southern coast of Iran. The flight crews would act as a barrier between Iran and the *Washington* battle group. Other U.S. warplanes based in Oman, Qatar, Bahrain, and Kuwait would provide additional cover for the U.S. warships. If the pilots were confronted by Iranian aircraft, or Iranian surface-to-air missile sites, the rules of engagement were clear. They were free to respond to any threats.

# 21

## Near Lake Qaraaoun

Scott flexed his knees and closed his eyes when the LongRanger's downwash began whipping the ground and slinging debris in every direction. When his feet hit the ground, he ran from under the helo and quickly detached himself from the D ring on the rappelling rope.

While Jackie maneuvered the damaged helicopter off to the side, Scott turned to search for Maritza. He shielded his eyes and ran toward the inert form lying a few yards away. When he knelt beside her, he was convinced she was dead. When the lifeless body moaned, Dalton almost shouted in relief.

"Maritza, can you hear me?"

"Yes," she gasped in excruciating pain. She was staring straight up at the stars and struggling to breathe. "I think my back is broken."

"Save your strength," Scott said as he held her hand. "I'm going to have to carry you to the helo, okay?"

She nodded weakly as Jackie rushed to Maritza's side.

"Oh, God," Sullivan uttered as she brushed grass and dirt out of Maritza's hair. "We're going to get you out of here."

"I know," Maritza said with a convulsive intake of air.

Without warning, a series of gunshots rang out and the

LongRanger's bright searchlight exploded in a puff of smoke.

"Let's go!" Scott said to Jackie as he started to lift Maritza. To his surprise and amazement, she turned over and struggled to her knees before he could help her to her feet.

"Your back isn't broken," Dalton exclaimed as Maritza took a step and almost fell against him.

"That's the good news," she said, trying to get her wind back. "But my ankle's shattered."

He scooped her into his arms and ran for the helo. Seconds later Jackie added power as Scott gently placed Maritza in the back of the cabin, then scrambled in beside her.

More shots rang out as Jackie lifted the LongRanger off the knoll, then lowered the nose to transition into high-speed forward flight. As the ship climbed away, a round went through the tail-rotor gearbox.

While Scott tended to Maritza, Jackie kept the helo's forward speed up and maintained a shallow climb.

"Uh-oh," Sullivan said to herself when the helicopter started a steady series of vibrations. Subtle at first, the vibrations grew more intense as the helicopter ascended. She gently nursed the cyclic, collective, and tail-rotor pedals. When the tail-rotor controls didn't respond normally, she knew that something was on the verge of failing. "Just stay together," she pleaded out loud as she gently reduced power.

"What's wrong?" Scott shouted from the wind-whipped cabin.

"We have a problem."

Dalton covered Maritza with a thin blanket and tucked the edges under her shoulders and legs. "How bad is it?"

"I don't think we can stay in the air much longer," she said in a resigned voice, then keyed the radio. "Umpire, Charlie Tango."

"Go," Greg O'Donnell shot back.

"I have a major problem," Jackie said tersely. "I'm going to try for the dirt strip between the power plant and the south end of Lake Qaraaoun. We need assistance ASAP."

"Site Delta?" O'Donnell asked.

"That's affirm."

"I'm on my way."

Greg adjusted the dim light above his kneeboard, then

flipped the selector switch to the number-two radio. "Transco Twenty-seven is on fire! Transco Two-Seven is on fire!" he said in a panicked voice as he pulled the power and rolled the big Cessna into a step turn, allowing the nose to drop straight toward the ground.

O'Donnell kept the transmit switch keyed. "Transco Twenty-seven is going down. Mayday! Mayday! Mayday!" he continued as he flicked the external lights off.

"Transco Twenty-seven is on fire! Going down, out of control! We're going in," he shouted, switching back to the number-one radio while he turned off the transponder.

From what the air traffic controllers saw on their scopes, Transco 27 had vanished from radar over the peaks of the Anti-Lebanon Mountains.

Pulling out of the steep dive east of Dahr al Ahmar, Greg steered a direct course for the emergency landing strip at Site Delta.

Jackie's cautious expression dissolved when the Long-Ranger suddenly started vibrating violently laterally and vertically. She was instantly afraid that the main rotor blades would disintegrate, causing a catastrophic failure that would send them plunging to their deaths.

Wide-eyed with fear, Sullivan concentrated on stabilizing the ship and turned to Scott. "I have to put it down!"

"You're the pilot."

"Umpire," Jackie said over the radio, "I have to set it down here." She looked at the GPS and gave O'Donnell the coordinates.

"I've got it firewalled," he assured her, and read back her position. "Keep me informed."

Before Jackie could reply, there was a resounding vibration and banging that shook the helo so hard that she couldn't read the instruments. Reacting to the terrifying crisis, Jackie eased off the power at the same time something snapped in the tail-rotor gearbox. The LongRanger immediately began oscillating from side to side as she desperately fought the controls.

"Tail-rotor failure!" she cried out as she frantically lowered the collective and rolled off the throttle to keep the ship from rotating out of control under the main rotors. Jackie entered an autorotation and, before she thought about it, hit the switch for the searchlight.

Nothing happened.

"Great," she said as she stared down at the black hole they were descending into. "Brace yourselves," she shouted to Maritza and Scott.

"Umpire," Jackie said urgently, "we've had a tail-rotor failure. I'm autorotating near the south end of the lake."

"Roger that," Greg advised. "I'm hurrying."

Without the powerful searchlight, Jackie was having a difficult time seeing the edge of the shoreline.

"Scott, are you and Maritza strapped in?"

"We're all set," he said as he covered Maritza's head with a pair of folded blankets. "It's too late for me to strap her into a seat."

"This is gonna be a rough landing," Jackie warned as she fought to control the plummeting helicopter.

"It couldn't be as bad as my last one," Maritza deadpanned.

Watching the radar altimeter, Jackie was about to begin a flare over the edge of the reservoir when the helo hit an unseen electric power line. A bomb burst of blue-white sparks flew in every direction as one of the wire strike cable cutters snagged the high-voltage power line.

The LongRanger entered a violently pitching, spinning, disorienting, out-of-control maneuver. The spinning created a centrifugal force that pulled Jackie forward toward the shattered windshield.

For a few seconds the helicopter hesitated precariously in midair and then crashed into the shallow lake. The megavolt power line separated and dropped into the reservoir as the LongRanger rolled over on its right side.

Dazed and gasping for a breath of air, Scott could feel electrical shocks coursing through his body. He struggled with his restraining straps while the helicopter sank below the surface of the reservoir. The cool water was pitch-black and he was feeling light-headed. Finally, after what seemed like minutes, Dalton cleared his head enough to snap the quick-release buckle open and free himself from his restraints. He tried to move, but something was holding him back.

• • •

From a distance of seven miles, Greg O'Donnell saw the pyrotechnic display from the power-line strike. He glanced at his chart. Sure enough, the high-voltage lines exiting the power plant ran along the southern edge of the lake. His heart sank to the pit of his stomach as he selected 121.5, the emergency frequency, on his number-two communications radio.

"Charlie Tango," Greg radioed as he began a high-speed descent, "this is umpire on guard. Do you copy?"

The radio remained silent.

"Charlie Tango, come up guard."

*Stay calm*, Scott told himself as he shoved the shoulder straps aside. He attempted to move again, then realized that the sleeve of his jumpsuit was caught on a twisted edge of his seat. His mind, disciplined by years of conditioning and training, began to flash a warning. *Panic in the water is an irreversible behavior.* With his lungs aching in searing pain, he reached for Maritza. She wasn't there.

Scott kicked at his bent door and finally forced it open. He swam free of the cockpit and bashed against one of the twisted main rotor blades, then shoved off into the inky blackness. Near the surface of the lake, the water seemed to glow as Scott saw an array of minuscule organisms drift lazily in front of his eyes. A split second later he surfaced as his oxygen-starved mind screamed for air.

With his lungs heaving, Scott treaded water and frantically looked around the floating debris. The steady surge of electrical shocks continued as he noticed waves of blue electricity shimmering across the water. The pungent smell of jet fuel permeated the air and made breathing difficult.

He was about to call out when someone yanked on his leg. Instantly, Jackie broke the surface of the water and thrashed about as she sucked in the foul-smelling air.

"Where's Maritza?" Scott sputtered.

"I don't know," she gasped, then recoiled from the electric shocks and the sight of the blue light undulating across the water. "We have to find her!" she said on the verge of panic.

"Stay where you are," Scott ordered. Feeling his pulse racing, he took a deep breath and dove eight feet, grazing his head against the crushed nose of the LongRanger. Rapidly feeling his way around the cockpit to the fuselage, he suddenly bumped into something soft. He was immediately clutched around the neck by Maritza. The panic-stricken woman's broken ankle was trapped in the twisted side door.

Fending off Maritza's thrashing arms, Scott discovered what was holding her underwater. With his lungs burning, he braced his back against the mangled fuselage and repeatedly kicked at the jammed door. On the fourth try, the door gave way and she shot for the surface.

Maritza was coughing up water and struggling to stay afloat when Scott surfaced near her and swam to her side. Jackie joined them a moment later.

"What's the"—Maritza choked twice—"blue light?"

"Electricity," Dalton said, then took in a breath of air and dove straight down again. Less than fifteen seconds later he surfaced with the life raft. He quickly pulled the toggles and the raft popped open and inflated.

"We're not far from shore," Scott said as he choked and blinked the fuel-contaminated water from his eyes. He reached for the waterproof survival radio. "Hang on to the side and we'll swim it in."

"Just a second," Jackie uttered as she helped Maritza to the side of the raft. "We're ready," she advised as she kicked with wide, even strokes. The wound on her ankle was only a dull pain.

No one said a word as they paddled toward shore. They were still surrounded by the soft, tremulous glow on the water, but they had adjusted to the tingling sensation flowing through their bodies.

"Umpire, Charlie Tango on guard," Scott radioed in a hoarse whisper.

"Charlie Tango, what's your situation?" O'Donnell said briskly.

"We've crashed." Scott coughed and cleared his throat. "We hit a power line and we're in the lake."

"Oh, shit!"

"We're swimming toward the shore."

"Is everyone okay?"

"Yes," Scott said, then spit out a mouthful of fuel-tainted water.

"What's your position?" Greg asked.

"We're at the southeastern edge of the lake," Dalton said as he studied the barren shoreline adjacent to Site Delta. "It looks like the strip is fairly close to the water, but I don't know how soft the soil is."

"Do you see any obstacles?"

"None, other than the power line," Scott said as his paratrooper boots touched the bottom of the lake. "I'll keep you clear of it."

"Okay," Greg said as he adjusted his night-vision goggles. The emergency airstrip was located at his ten o'clock position, less than two miles. "I'll hold the landing lights until the last second."

"We're almost there."

"Copy."

Nearing the edge of the reservoir, Scott heard the distinct sound of the Cessna Caravan. "Give us a few seconds, and I'll get a pencil flare up."

"Better hurry," Greg warned as he slowed the airplane and lowered the flaps. "I see lights—it looks like three or four vehicles headed your way."

"How far away?"

"I don't know your exact position. They're probably a mile, or more."

"Keep an eye on 'em."

"Will do."

Scott slipped in the mud, then gained his footing and slid the raft out of the water. Wringing wet from their dunking, Scott and Jackie helped Maritza crawl out of the water. Suffering only bruises and superficial cuts, Scott carried Maritza well clear of the shoreline and gently lowered her to the ground near the airstrip.

While Jackie examined Maritza's ankle, Dalton took a quick look around and fired a pencil flare at a forty-five-degree angle to the horizon.

"Hey, Bubba," O'Donnell said as he banked toward the faint streak of light, "I hope that was you."

"Who else?"

"Your visitors are closer than I thought."

Scott darted a look at the faint glow of headlights approaching the reservoir. "Make your approach in the middle of the arc . . . and, ah, it looks like you have at least two—maybe three thousand feet."

"I'm turnin' final. How does two-ten look on the heading?"

"I'd say that's about right."

"How about another flare?"

"You got it," Scott said as he fired another marker across the uneven airstrip. "Keep it in the middle."

"I'll give it my best shot."

Motionless, Dalton watched the first set of headlights crest a small rise and race toward the flats near the shoreline. Scott drew his weapon, dropped to the ground, and took careful aim. He squeezed off several rounds, knocking out a headlamp on the second vehicle, then reached for another clip.

Jackie took Maritza's weapon and quickly added another headlight and windshield to the count.

Scott raised the radio to his mouth. "Land close to the approach end, and I'll guide you by flashlight."

"Hell," Greg said, tossing his NVGs on the cockpit floor, "I'm down in the grass now."

"Hit the landing lights," Scott advised.

"Coming on," O'Donnell said as a brilliant halo of blinding light forced Scott to shield his eyes. "Pull the power! You're almost on us!"

The Caravan hit hard, bounced once, and rapidly came to a halt under max reverse thrust and heavy braking.

Kneeling on each side of Maritza, Jackie and Scott lifted her by the arms and carried her to the open cargo door. As they helped her into the plane, rounds from high-powered rifles began penetrating the fuselage of the utility transport.

"Let's get out of here," Scott yelled as he boosted Jackie up and into the cabin, then jumped aboard at the same moment Greg added full power.

"I'm hit," O'Donnell shouted as another round ripped through the nose wheel tire. "I need some help!"

Dalton raced to the cockpit as the airplane veered to the left and bounced along on the flat nose tire. He leaped into the copilot's seat and simultaneously jammed the right rudder pedal full forward and snatched the yoke back. With the nose wheel off the ground and the powerful turboprop in full song, Scott played the controls like a maestro.

"Hang tight," Scott exclaimed as the driver of a Chevy pickup truck attempted to cut him off and block the airstrip.

Using a combination of short-field and soft-field takeoff techniques, Dalton finessed the heavy Caravan into the air a split second before the right main landing gear smashed through the windshield of the Silverado. Scott deftly countered the violent yaw, then allowed the damaged airplane to accelerate in ground effect. Seconds later, with rounds still penetrating the fuselage and wings, he turned the landing light off and nursed the bullet-ridden airplane into a shallow climb.

Unscathed by the hail of gunfire, Jackie hurried forward and helped Greg out of the left seat. With his assistance, she moved him to the cabin and propped him between Maritza and a nine-man life raft. O'Donnell's left thigh was bleeding profusely and he had another serious wound to his left shoulder. Using one of the Caravan's first-aid packets, Jackie and Maritza dressed Greg's wounds. A few minutes later Jackie used a flashlight to inspect the underside of the wings, then returned to the cockpit.

"How are you doing?" she quietly asked Scott as she slid into the left seat and latched her restraining harness.

"Okay," he answered as they stared at each other's disheveled appearance. "How are Maritza and Greg?"

"She's in fair shape for the time being, but we need to get him to a hospital as soon as possible."

Scott studied the GPS and glanced at the fuel gauges. "Do you think he can hang on until we get to Athens?"

Her strained expression turned into one of regret. "We aren't going to make Athens," she murmured.

Surprised by the tone of her voice, Scott frowned when he turned to her. "What are you talking about?"

"We took some rounds through the bottom of the ferry tank," Jackie answered as she looked at him, her eyes filled with concern. "What isn't spraying the countryside is filling the aft section of the cabin."

Stunned by the disclosure, he looked into the dark cabin, then caught her eye. "Can you plug the leaks?"

"No," she said under her breath. "They're inside the perimeter of the frame that's bolted to the floor."

Scott's expression turned grim. "We're trapped in a flying

bomb," he said with understated calm in his voice. "It doesn't get any better than this."

"Yes, it does," she said lightly, staring at him with close curiosity. "We're also leaking fuel from both wings."

"Great." Scott quickly calculated the approximate time to fuel exhaustion, then turned to her with a sober look in his eye. "Folks, before we land, I'd like to explain our out-of-court settlements."

Jackie reached into a pocket of her wet flight suit and extracted a compact tape recorder. "If this thing is still working, I'm going to debrief Maritza."

"You can get on the sat-phone . . ." Scott trailed off when he saw her slowly shake her head.

"That's the other bad news," Jackie said as she showed Scott the Caravan's shattered satellite-phone that had been blown into three pieces. "I lost mine during the crash."

"Well," Scott said with a shrug, "we'll just have to try to reach the *Permak Express*—stretch the fuel as far as we can."

# 22

## USS *George Washington*

The Persian Gulf lay as flat as a millpond while the carrier and her battle group turned into the gentle breeze. Far to the south of the flotilla, a nearly transparent flame from a huge Iranian oil platform cast an eerie afterglow across the black waters.

Once the warships of the U.S. 5th Fleet were repositioned, *Washington* went to flight quarters. The deck came alive with a choreography of flight crews, airplanes, tow tractors, and deckhands hauling volatile fuel lines, hoisting missiles, loading bombs, prepping the catapults and arresting gear, and chocking and chaining aircraft to their assigned sections of the deck.

An environment particularly susceptible to catastrophic accidents, the mayhem on the flight deck is even more precarious during the black of night. Between the screaming jet engines, and the foul-smelling scent of steam mixed with salt water and jet fuel, duty on the flight deck is not for individuals who are easily distracted.

With the supercarrier steady on course and speed, the pilot of an HS-11 "Dragon Slayers" rescue helicopter lifted his craft into the horizonless, moonless night and flew toward a known Iranian eavesdropping trawler. After flying a wide circle around the surveillance vessel, the SH-60 Seahawk took up station on the starboard side of the carrier. The deadly-serious business of flight operations was commencing, where seconds and inches often spell the difference between life and death.

Flight-deck crewmen in sweat-stained green pullovers hooked the duty E-2C Hawkeye to the port bow catapult, then waited for the launch signal from the air boss in Primary Flight Control. Located high on the port side of the island, Pri Fly served as the ship's control tower during flight operations. The "boss" is the supreme ruler of the flight deck and everything that flies in the vicintity of the boat.

On the slippery flight deck, F-14 Tomcats and F/A-18 Hornets were standing by to protect one of the most formidable fighting machines in the world. Inside the cockpits of the powerful jets, the pilots of the Hornets and the pilots and radar intercept officers in the Tomcats were growing anxious. The growing speculation as to what they were doing in the Gulf had abruptly ended two hours before they manned their planes. Their CO had briefed them; the U.S. was going to send Tehran a wake-up call. If any Iranian fighter planes or surface ships wanted to contest the issue, they were to be dispatched as quickly as possible.

While they waited to taxi to the catapults, many of the pilots and naval flight officers silently went through their checklists a second time. In this unforgiving world, minor details could mean the difference between success and failure—living or dying.

Precisely at the scheduled launch time, Captain Nancy Jensen watched the shooter's night wands signal the Hawkeye pilots to increase power. The aviator's pulse rates rapidly went up as the airframe began to vibrate and shake from the power of the straining turboprops. The copilot keyed his intercom. "It's darker than three foot up a bull's ass."

"Yeah, I love it," the pilot grumbled as he surveyed the engine instruments, checking for any irregularity, anything that might kill them during a night catapult launch. Everything looked in order. "Let's do it."

A second later the E-2C's external lights were switched on. At that second the fate of the flight crew was in the hands of God and a steam-powered catapult. *Kaabooom!* The pilots' eyes literally flattened in their sockets as the aircraft accelerated down the track and disappeared into the gloomy night.

The flight crew of the Grumman surveillance platform, which could detect airborne targets anywhere in a three-million-cubic-mile envelope, checked in with the carrier and the Hawkeye crew they were scheduled to relieve. In addition to the normal flow of commercial air traffic in the Gulf area, the duty "Miniwacs" was monitoring two separate formations of suspected Iranian military aircraft. They were also watching several flights of U.S. warplanes and rescue helicopters that were taking up station over the Gulf.

Below deck in *Washington*'s darkened Combat Direction Center, the ship's brain, tactical action officers monitored computerized wall screens showing the location of every ship, aircraft, and oil smuggler in the area. The air crackled with radio chatter as the men tracked an array of Iranian vessels as they navigated the Gulf's dark waters. Many of the contacts were flagged red on the giant computer screens, including the warships *Peter the Great*, Russia's largest ballistic-missile cruiser, *Pyotr Veliky*, and *Admiral Kuznetsov*. The senior officer in CDC found it curious that the Russian flagship and her escorts had suddenly changed course and were distancing themselves from the U.S. battle group.

Concerned about the unusual concentration of Iranian aircraft, Admiral Coleman and his staff weighed their options. Coleman decided to leave well enough alone unless the airplanes appeared to be a direct threat to the task force. He didn't want to provoke the Iranians into a premature confrontation.

*Washington*'s flight deck became extremely busy while various planes waited to be catapulted into the night sky. In short order, two all-weather electronic surveillance EA-6B Prowlers were airborne and climbing for altitude. The Marine Prowlers could quickly distinguish between friendly and enemy signals, then jam them.

Following the VMAQ-3 "Moondogs," two high-endurance S-3B Vikings from VS-32 were launched and began snooping for submarines. With three of Iran's Kilo subs thought to be at sea, CAG, the commander of the air group, was *very* nervous about their potential threat to the carrier battle group.

Losing a carrier, or other major surface combatants, could rapidly change the balance of power in the Gulf region.

Leading the division of F-14 BARCAP fighters—Barrier Combat Air Patrol—Lieutenant Commander Denby Kaywood and his backseater, Lieutenant Chet Hoffman, were anxious to get airborne. It was show time and the initial four Tomcats and four Marine F/A-18s would be backed by two Alert Five Hornets.

Sandwiched between the BARCAP birds and the Alert Hornets, Lieutenant Ridder Cromwell would be the deck launch interceptor. Cromwell, a former topgun instructor, would be parked on the starboard bow catapult with his Tomcat's engines idling. With his F-14 connected to the fuel pits, Cromwell and his RIO, Lieutenant Fred Singleton, would be ready to launch in a matter of seconds. If the situation became touchy, the Alert Five fighters would immediately go to deck-launch-interceptor status.

## USS *Hampton*

When the executive officer loudly knocked on his cabin door, Commander Bob Gillmore's eyes flew wide open and his heart rate instantly increased. He reluctantly opened the door and recognized the concerned look in Todd Lassiter's eyes.

"It's a go, skipper."

"Okay," Gillmore said as he yawned and rubbed his eyes. "I'll be there in a few minutes."

"Yes, sir."

"Fresh coffee all around."

"It's brewing, sir."

"You do good work."

After closing his door, Gillmore squinted at the multifunction display near his bunk, noting that *Hampton* was loitering in its assigned position in the Gulf of Oman. He quickly brushed his teeth, then dressed and opened his personal safe. He removed the sealed orders and then joined Lassiter in the officers' wardroom.

Over a cup of fresh coffee, the two of them opened the orders and studied the details of the mission. Afterward they called the officers and the chief of the boat for a thorough briefing, then told the crew about the imminent strike on Iran.

Their reactions ranged from stunned silence to open excitement as the young sailors prepared to launch six Tomahawk surface-to-surface missiles. Gillmore and his senior officers went over the mission orders and reviewed the accompanying rules of engagement. When the last questions were answered, the petty officers manning the BSY-1 (busy one) combat system activated the power for the weapons and loaded targeting information and flight profiles into the missile's memory systems. The flight paths of the Tomahawks were programmed to avoid population centers and remain below Iranian radar coverage. Using satellite navigation and sophisticated terrain-tracking electronics, the missiles would strike within a few feet of a target.

Shortly after the combat system was activated, *Hampton* rose to its launch depth twenty-five nautical miles north of the Tropic of Cancer. Moving slowly through the dark water, the attack submarine sprouted a mast to take a final navigational fix from the Global Positioning System satellite constellation. As a precaution, Lassiter used a slide rule, compass, and trigonometry to plan the attacks by hand.

Minutes after the XO had completed his calculations, the hydraulically actuated doors of the vertical launch system opened and an explosive charge propelled the first Tomahawk up through the protective covering over its stainless-steel container. Entering the water, the missile shot upward until the booster rocket fired, thrusting the Tomahawk clear of the Gulf.

The missile immediately tilted over and jettisoned the burned-out solid booster, sprouted wings and a tail, lighted the turbojet engine, made a small directional correction, then headed for its preprogrammed destination near Bandar-e Abbas. Skimming above the surface of the water, the Tomahawk tracked precisely on a course defined by the acutely accurate terrain-following navigation system. When the powerful missile approached land, it would follow the eastern shoreline of the Persian Gulf, then make a tiny heading change to strike its target at the nuclear storage-and-assembly facility adjacent to the port at Bandar-e Abbas.

A half minute later a second Tomahawk rocketed out of the water to follow the first missile to the same target. Like the first Tomahawk, it tilted down and the booster fell off, but the turbojet lighted a second late. The missile almost impacted the water before it gained speed, stabilized in the proper attitude, then flew unerringly toward its destination.

Gillmore tried to ignore his fear of being discovered by an Iranian Kilo-class diesel-powered attack submarine. If one or more of the subs happened to be lurking in the vicinity, they might have detected the extremely loud noises generated by the Tomahawk launches. Feared because of their super-quiet, stealthy traits, the Russian-manufactured 244-foot Kilos were almost impossible to detect passively when they were operating on their batteries.

The task of detecting them was made even more difficult when they were "sleeping" on the bottom of the Gulf in relatively warm, shallow water. Acquired for the purpose of controlling access to the vital Strait of Hormuz choke point, the 3,077-ton (submerged displacement) submarines were intended to be Iran's equalizers when dealing with the overwhelming power of the United States Navy.

The missile launch sequence continued at thirty-second intervals until the last Tomahawk blasted out of the water and turned on course. The final three cruise missiles were targeted at a nuclear research-and-weapons storage warehouse located at Bushehr.

After the sixth vertical launch tube filled with water and the hatches were closed, Commander Gillmore breathed a sigh of relief and ordered a communications mast to be raised. Via satellite, he sent a short confirming message to the Pentagon, then prepared to dive deeper and set course for the middle of the Arabian Sea.

Less than a minute after *Hampton* launched her last Tomahawk, *Cheyenne* began launching her cruise missiles toward the same targets. Stabilized at her launch depth sixty-five nautical miles southwest of the border between Pakistan and Iran, *Cheyenne*'s Tomahawks were programmed to reach Bushehr and Bandar-e Abbas three minutes after *Hampton*'s last missile hit its target.

### Iranian Submarine *Taregh*

Startled by the first explosive noise that reverberated through *Taregh*, Captain Mehdi Rafiqdoust quickly recovered. With his heart racing, the Kilo-class submarine skipper anticipated the next loud report, as did the stunned operator of the acoustic receiver. After the second powerful explosion, Rafiqdoust had no doubt; he'd stumbled across an American submarine. An American sub that was launching missiles. This was obviously the reason Tehran had ordered his crew to go to combat readiness condition one.

His last communication with *Dauntless* confirmed that *Taregh* was loitering in a position where the American battle group had passed many hours before. Aware that U.S. nuclear attack submarines—sometimes more than one—generally accompanied carrier battle groups, Rafiqdoust hesitated a moment. Was the undeclared war between Iran and the United States now a shooting war? The rift had been the lead story on every news program for the past two months.

Rafiqdoust exchanged a glance with Commander Fathi Ashmar, his intensely fierce second in command. The small man's unblinking stare left no question about his feelings. The men nodded in silent agreement. Convinced that his country was being attacked by the Great Satan, Rafiqdoust gave the order to attack the enemy submarine.

"We are at war," he said grimly, then smoothed his thick mustache. "We will sink the American submarine."

Well trained and motivated, the Iranian officers and sailors swung into action on the skipper's command. Two Russian advisers gave Rafiqdoust weak, but polite smiles and made their way to their berthing quarters. The Varshavyanka-class sub experts had strict orders from their superiors in Moscow; they were not to take part in any hostile military engagement.

By the time the American's fifth weapon was away, Rafiqdoust had the range and bearing to the noisy target. Elated by his good fortune, his mind raced in search of anything that might be questionable about his logic. One last analysis before he fired the first torpedo. *Are the Americans launching their weapons at Iraq?*

If so, an unprovoked attack on a U.S. Navy submarine would be a huge political embarrassment. It could end his career and cost him his life. On the other hand, if Rafiqdoust was correct in his assumption, and he managed to sink the enemy sub, he would have enormous leverage to move to the highest circles in the Iranian Navy.

The civilian and military leadership of Iran enthusiastically endorsed the complex and expensive task of operating submarines; now it was time to deliver on the investment. If Rafiqdoust was successful in his efforts to destroy the sub, the U.S. government would think twice about further intervention in the affairs of the Islamic Republic of Iran. He smiled inwardly. *Allahu is guiding me. I have made the right decision.*

With two of *Taregh*'s six 533-millimeter torpedo tubes out of service, Rafiqdoust double checked his firing solution, then ordered four sub-killer torpedoes fired. He wiped the perspiration from his forehead and checked the time-to-target on the first torpedo. Would he be successful in his quest to kill the intruder? He wouldn't have long to wait for an answer.

The control room was deathly quiet when Commander Gillmore gave the order to do a "baffle clear," an S-shaped maneuver to make sure an enemy submarine wasn't lurking in *Hampton*'s baffle zone. "Left ten degrees rudder, come to one-nine-five."

"Left ten degrees rudder, aye," the young helmsman repeated. "New course one-nine-five. Sir, my rudder is left ten degrees."

The only noise came from the hum of the ventilation ducts as the attack sub began a turn to check the deaf area astern of the boat.

"Make your depth two hundred feet," Gillmore said with obvious relief in his voice. His mouth and lips were so dry, he had to swallow before he issued each order.

"Two hundred feet, aye," the diving officer replied.

A low murmur spread through the control room as the tension began to dissipate. The farther away they could get from the launch coordinates, the better chance they would have to evade any hunter/killers in the area.

Gillmore turned to the chief of the boat. "Let's give the men some—" He stopped in mid-sentence, an uncomfortable feeling in the pit of his stomach—a feeling of primal fear. Along with the other men around him, the captain had heard a faint sound. In disbelief, Gillmore heard it again, louder this time. Much louder.

*Ping*-PING!

The sound was unmistakable, striking terror in the hearts of the crew. To a person, their faces contorted in a kind of horror that is something more than mere fright. They were about to die, and there wasn't anything they could do about it.

"Emergency blow!" Gillmore ordered in frenzied desperation. "Let's get on the roof!"

The petty officer at the ballast control panel lurched for the two handles located above his head. Panicked, he activated the controls, sending high-pressure air from the air banks into the ballast tanks. The sub immediately began ascending toward the surface.

The third *ping* came less than two seconds before *Hampton*'s double hull was ripped open by a powerful blast. Like a huge sledgehammer, the concussion-implosion slammed Gillmore backward into a bulkhead, knocking him down. With the wind knocked out of him, he gasped for air and tried to get to his feet. The lights flickered twice and went out as *Hampton* rapidly filled with seawater.

Gillmore groped in the dark as cold water gushed through the control room. He managed to get to his knees at the same time as the second torpedo smashed into the remains of the attack sub. With his eardrums ruptured and his scalp bleeding, Gillmore was swept through an opening in the hull. He frantically tried to orient himself in the dark, but the water was so disturbed he couldn't determine which way was up. Panicked, he clawed at the water in an attempt to reach the surface. Twice, he bumped into other men as they struggled to save their lives.

Gillmore was making progress until the third torpedo detonated, tumbling him through the water. He struck his head against the remains of the forward escape trunk, knocking himself unconscious. He sank slowly, arriving on the floor of the Gulf fifteen minutes after *Hampton*.

The crackling and grinding sounds of a submarine breaking apart were clearly evident to the senior operator of *Taregh*'s acoustic receiver. When he signaled confirmation of the kill, the crew in the control room began to celebrate.

The captain glared at them. "Quiet," Rafiqdoust hissed under his breath. "There may be a second American sub out there."

Commander Fathi Ashmar turned to Rafiqdoust and smiled with unconscious pride. "The Americans are getting their noses bloodied."

# 23

## The White House

Although it was early morning in the Persian Gulf, the evening was still young in Washington, D.C. Freshly shaved and showered, President Macklin entered the wood-paneled bunker known as the White House Situation Room. He'd stopped by the Oval Office to ensure that the TV cameras and lights were positioned where he liked them. If everything went as anticipated, Macklin planned to make a short announcement to his fellow citizens, then enjoy a late dinner with his wife, former foreign news correspondent Maria Eden-Macklin. If things didn't go well, it would be a long night for the commander in chief and his entire staff.

The president took his chair at the head of the wide table and greeted his secretary of defense, the national security adviser, the chairman of the joint chiefs of staff, and Fraiser Wyman, Macklin's chief of staff.

A gaunt man with tightly curled gray hair and deeply set blue eyes, Wyman had been a longtime inhabitant of the political underbrush before Macklin rescued him from obscurity. A late bloomer, Wyman wore small round metal-rimmed glasses and displayed a charming, almost boyish smile. A middle-aged bachelor, he had three passions other than politics; attractive young women, skiing in Switzerland, and expensive foreign sports cars.

"Okay, Pete, tell me some good news," Macklin said cheerfully as he puffed on a fresh Onyx cigar.

Adair hesitated a second, giving himself away. "Well, we have more activity than we anticipated."

"Activity?" Macklin's voice accused Adair.

"Yes, sir."

"Why does that *not* surprise me?" the president challenged.

From previous encounters with Macklin, Adair knew better than to take the bait. "They've launched what appear to be numerous fighter aircraft out of Shiraz and Bushehr. All their forces—air and sea—are in a heightened-alert status."

"Wonderful," Macklin said curtly. The single word managed to indicate his concern and irritation. If the operation backfired, and American lives were lost, he would be in deep political trouble. Heads, of course, would have to roll.

"Les, what do you suggest?" the president asked with venom in his voice. "Should we cancel the strike?"

Chalmers flicked a nervous glance at his watch. "It's too late," he said, somewhat apologetically. "The Tomahawks are in the air. We should have confirmation any second."

Macklin swore to himself, then looked each man in the eye before he spoke. "We underestimated Tehran."

In silence, the men waited for the storm to hit.

"Or," Hartwell Prost finally said in a suggestive voice, "they knew we were coming."

The president frowned and gave him a surprised look. "What are you talking about—what's that supposed to mean?"

Prost tilted his head and half turned to look at his boss. "Someone obviously leaked the plan," he declared with terse calm. "This was a super-secret operation, and the Iranians were waiting for us. That didn't just happen by chance."

No one, including the president, said a word until Fraiser Wyman finally found his voice. "I'm sorry, Hartwell, but I find that difficult to believe."

"Why do you find it difficult to believe?" Prost challenged. "Let's hear your explanation."

"Our relations with Tehran have hit rock bottom," Wyman suggested in a steady, pleasant voice, "and this is simply a reaction to our increased presence in the Gulf. It's that simple."

Hartwell's jaw muscles twitched. "You don't believe that any more than I do. They were *waiting* for us."

"Okay," Wyman taunted in a harsher tone. "Give us some facts."

"You want facts?" Prost snapped back. "How many times have the Iranians launched fighter planes—and gone on alert—when one of our carrier battle groups entered the Persian Gulf?

"None," Prost answered his own question. "They may not have known precisely what our objective was, but they knew something was up."

"They have good surveillance and reconnaissance capabilities," Wyman blurted. "Maybe they picked up something, or the crash of the Tomcat could have spooked them. We don't know what they think."

Macklin raised his hands to Wyman. "We'll discuss this later. Regardless of what the Iranians know or don't know"— he glanced at General Chalmers—"Les says that we have missiles en route to their targets. We're facing a major threat, and we better start making some informed and intelligent decisions for a change."

"Sir," Chalmers said, trying to sound confident, "we have overwhelming firepower in the Gulf. I don't believe the Iranians are going to cross swords with us, even if this operation has been compromised."

The president traded glances with Hartwell Prost and Pete Adair, then turned to Chalmers. "Would you bet your job on it?"

Caught off guard by the taunt, Chalmers managed to keep his composure. "I just did, *sir*."

The secure phone rang, warming the chill in the room. The general lifted the receiver and identified himself. A moment later Chalmers placed the phone in its cradle and looked straight at the president. "It's confirmed. The Tomahawks are airborne, sir."

"Get everything up," Macklin ordered. "If the Iranians counterattack, I want to stop them in their tracks."

"Yessir," Chalmers replied with painful stiffness.

The president reached for the phone with the blinking light. Holding for the chief executive, the speaker of the House of Representatives was on the line.

## The Herdsmen

The last embers of the small fire barely glowed as the lame and partially blind sheep tender struggled to rise from his mangy makeshift bed. He lost his balance and tripped over the man lying on the adjoining sleeping mat. Speaking in Luri, his younger companion grumbled as the older man made his way to a shallow trench to relieve the pain in his bladder.

After he was finished, the native of Baluchistan shuffled to the reddish-orange embers and stirred them with a short stick. He added a few thin pieces of wood to the small fire and warmed his withered, arthritic hands over the warm flames.

A few moments later he heard a strange sound approaching him—one he'd never heard in his seventy-one years. The younger man, with his eyes darting in fear, bolted upright and fought to control the panic that was engulfing him. He listened intently while his mind raced to associate the sound with something he could relate to. The low screech became a high-pitched scream as the Tomahawk missile raced straight at their resting place, then blasted directly over the heads of the frightened men. Shocked by the invisible, screaming monster, they sat in stunned silence for a moment before they began talking excitedly to each other.

They were trying to calm their fears when the same eerie sound approached a second time. Afraid that the monster was returning to kill them, the men huddled in sheer terror and trembled while they frantically tried to extinguish the fire. Unsure if the flames were attracting the flying beasts, the older man yanked off his frayed jacket and quickly smothered the low flames.

With the horrendous sound growing closer and closer, the men sprawled on the ground and began praying to Allahu. Reeling from absolute panic, they covered their heads when the screaming monster roared low over them and flew off in the darkness. Thirty seconds later the sound returned from the original direction, causing the younger man to soil his clothes. At an altitude of seventy feet, the missile flew directly over their campsite and continued on course. Eyes sunken and terrified, the men didn't move a muscle until they could no longer hear the monsters. As the minutes ticked away, their heart rates slowly subsided while they shivered and waited for the first signs of daylight.

## The Situation Room

Shoving the silver coffee service aside, President Macklin gave Les Chalmers an anxious look as they studied the progress of the cruise missiles on a giant, state-of-the-art multicolored screen. According to satellite information, the first Tomahawk from *Hampton* would be striking the nukes at Bandar-e Abbas in less than nine minutes. Lost in his concern, Cord Macklin was only vaguely conscious of the other men gathered in the Situation Room.

An aide stepped into the revamped room and quietly conferred with Fraiser Wyman, then silently left.

Irritation and uneasiness combined to twist Wyman's face. He leaned close to Macklin. "Mr. President," the chief of staff began, then paused for a long moment.

"What is it?" Macklin snapped.

"Sir, CNN, MSNBC, and the Fox News Channel are reporting that we have launched an attack on Iran, and that we are preparing—"

The color drained from the president's face.

"—to engage them in—"

"Damn them!" Macklin bellowed, his teeth clenched in fear and anger. "*Damn* the sorry bastard who leaked this, and *damn* the sonsabitches who aired it!"

## Bushehr, Iran

Unable to sleep, Peter Simchukov rose from his small bunk and walked out of the austere barracks adjacent to the missile storage-and-assembly facility at Bushehr. Formerly associated with Russia's state-run Polyus Research Institute, Simchukov was a highly respected scientist who designed advanced missile guidance systems called ring-laser gyroscopes. A portly man with bloodshot eyes, stringy salt-and-pepper hair, and a mouth full of rotten teeth, he sat down on a wooden bench and glanced at the star-studded sky, then lighted a cigarette and studied the heavily guarded assembly building.

Inside, four North Korean No Dong I missiles and two Chinese DF-25 missiles were being readied to accept the Russian nuclear warheads. The rearmament program was over three months behind schedule, but the stockpile of nuclear-tipped missiles was steadily growing.

Simchukov was one of thousands of Russian scientists, engineers, and nuclear technicians who'd been underemployed and underpaid after the collapse of the Union of Soviet Socialist Republics. The group represented the cream of the former "rocket scientists" at the secrecy-shrouded state-run nuclear laboratories and technical institutes.

Unable to adequately feed, shelter, clothe, or provide medical care and basic needs for their families, the men had cast aside their ethics in order to care for their loved ones. Renegade nations with aspirations of becoming nuclear powers were all too willing to help the downtrodden Russians regain some degree of dignity and pride.

Russian involvement in the development and installation of Iran's nuclear-power-generation industry had made it easy to slip thousands of extra scientists and technicians into the country to accelerate the Iranian nuclear weapons program. The anti-Western regime now had a clear military edge in the Persian Gulf and the Middle East.

Simchukov's thoughts turned to his wife, Katerina, and their two young children, Natalya and Gennady. They were living in a cold, crowded apartment with his parents and grandparents while his wife attempted to make ends meet by working as a clerk at the Center for Conversion and Privatization in Moscow.

Simchukov and three other Soviet scientists were responsible for training a select group of Iranians to become nuclear weapons technicians. The seemingly endless program was expected to be completed in less than two months, freeing the homesick scientists to return to Russia and their families.

Taking a last drag on his cigarette and crushing it on the ground, Simchukov cringed when he heard an eerie sound. He'd never heard a Tomahawk missile, but he instinctively knew it was the sound of death. Simchukov leaped to his feet and ran as fast as he could for the perimeter of the compound. In his mind, he knew it was useless to run, but his every instinct told him to flee. The ensuing explosion blew the scientist through the chain-link fence, killing him instantly.

The conflagration in the assembly yard would be totally out of control by the time the second and third Tomahawks plowed into the warhead storage building. The nuclear storage-and-assembly complex at Bandar-e Abbas had suffered a similar fate only minutes before. While chaos reigned at the demolished nuclear facilities, *Cheyenne*'s cruise missiles began arriving. Fortunately, as General Chalmers had assured President Macklin, none of Iran's nuclear weapons detonated.

# 24

Flying level at 22,000 feet above the Persian Gulf, Lieutenant Colonel Trent McCutchin checked his fuel and noted the time. Between fifty and eighty miles to the west, a U.S. Air Force RC-135 Rivet Joint surveillance aircraft and an E-8 Joint-STARS Boeing worked with an E-3 AWACS Airborne Warning and Control aircraft.

The RC-135 is considered so menacing that senior officers in the Soviet Union's chain of command willingly risked their careers and international scorn by shooting down Korean Airlines Flight 007, a Boeing 747 they mistook for a Rivet Joint aircraft probing Russia's eastern defenses.

The Rivet Joint team focused on coordinating the location of electronic emissions with the AWACS powerful aerial radar and the Joint-STARS ground radar and moving-target indications. With all the elements working in harmony, nothing could hide from U.S. intelligence for over 300 nautical miles beyond an enemy's front lines.

McCutchin's confidence was high even though a glitch had developed in the Joint Tactical Information Distribution System (JTIDS) aboard the AWACS aircraft. Instead of operating in an environment of greatly enhanced situational awareness—a "God's-eye view" of the Persian Gulf—they would be forced to revert to old-fashioned night-fighter tac-

tics. If the Iranians attacked the U.S. fighters, the lack of
JTIDS capability could translate to a lower kill ratio, a lower
percentage of survivability, and the possibility of fratricide
incidents.

Craning his neck, McCutchin glanced toward the coastline
of Iran and immediately saw a bright flash split the night,
followed by a rising fireball near Bushehr. *The Navy folks
are right on the money.* A moment later he heard a hollow
voice speak to him from the bowels of the Boeing E-3 Sentry
AWACS aircraft.

"Ah, Sting Flight, multiple bandits turning into you," the
senior Air Force captain said. "Six hostiles at sixty-two
miles—ah, level your altitude, nine o'clock. Warning Yellow, Weapons Hold."

"Sting One." McCutchin's mouth went dry and his neck
muscles tightened as rivulets of sweat trickled down his tem-
ples. He rechecked his armament panel and listened to the
AWACS controller talk briefly with the combat search-and-
rescue helicopters and their fighter escorts. Seeing another
bright flash at Bushehr, McCutchin tightened his restraining
straps and prepared to defend himself.

The E-3 Sentry operator spoke again, this time with a hint
of trepidation in his soft voice. "Sting Flight, the six hostiles
now at your eight o'clock—your altitude. Come left zero-
seven-zero."

Breathing deeply and forcing himself to relax, McCutchin
keyed his radio. "Sting One, we're coming left to zero-four-
zero."

"Negative, Sting. Zero-*seven*-zero. Come left to zero-
seven-zero."

"Zero-seven-oh."

"Roger, Sting."

Flying in an offset trail position, the other three F-15 Ea-
gles turned in unison with their leader while two flights of
F-16 Fighting Falcons positioned themselves for aerial
combat. In addition to air-to-air missiles, the "Electric Jets"—
Fang Flight and Rock Flight—carried jamming pods and
HARM High Speed Anti-Radiation Missiles to knock out any
SAM sites that locked onto them with radar. The opposing
forces had a closure rate of over 1,000 miles per hour.

## USS *George Washington*

Orbiting northwest of the battle group, the E-2C Hawkeye warned the carrier about the approach of hostile aircraft. "Strike, Screwtop. Seven bogies off the coast of Iran turning inbound to your position. Zero-two-five at seventy-five miles. Angels twelve."

"Roger that," the controller on the ship radioed while Captain Jensen listened to the conversation. Her uneasiness grew as she contemplated the possibility of being attacked. *This can't happen . . . not on my watch.*

"Strike," the Hawkeye controller radioed, "I'm seein' three additional targets. They're really low, eight miles behind the other bogies."

"Copy, Screwtop."

Jensen reached for her direct line to the Combat Direction Center. After speaking to the senior officer in CDC, Jensen took a deep, silent breath and turned to the officer of the deck. "Sound General Quarters," she ordered, and reached for her life jacket and battle helmet.

The heart-pounding sound of general quarters immediately set off a well-orchestrated stampede throughout the ship. In a wild scramble, all hands scampered to their battle stations as a sense of concern turned to raw fear.

Coordinated chaos reigned in Primary Flight Control, the glass enclosed control tower jutting over the flight deck.

"Get the DLI in the air!" Rear Admiral Ed Coleman said impatiently. "Let's move it, Wade!"

"Yessir," Captain Wade Kavanaugh calmly replied as squawk boxes blared and telephones rang.

"And get the Alert Five birds up to the cats!"

"Workin' on it, Admiral."

"The White House"—Coleman popped a stick of gum in his mouth—"wants to kick some ass."

"Yes, sir."

Kavanaugh, *Washington*'s air boss, was used to Coleman's penchant for barging onto the bridge or into PriFly. A laid-back native of Georgia, Kavanaugh tried to ignore the crusty battle-group commander while he talked to the catapult officer. The "shooter" was in the process of launching Lieutenants Ridder Cromwell and Fred Singleton in the duty

Deck Launch Interceptor, call sign Diamond 107.

"Let's get 'em in the air," Coleman barked above the clamor. "This isn't a weekend drill!"

"They're clearing the deck, sir."

Coleman was steeling himself for action. "It's time for Roosevelt to make her entrance—get her planes up here." Without saying another word, the admiral spun on his heel and headed for the bridge.

Kavanaugh and his assistant, known as the "miniboss," glanced at each other and breathed a sigh of relief.

With the fueling hose clear of the F-14, Cromwell exercised his flight controls to the stops and then selected afterburner. With his heart stuck in his throat, he checked his instruments as the screeching, roaring Tomcat shook and vibrated and strained at the holdback fitting. The center of the jet blast deflector glowed reddish orange as twin streaks of white-hot flames shook the steel shield.

Satisfied with the indications on his engine instruments, Ridder Cromwell toggled the external lights, then braced himself for the violent stroke of the catapult. For the next few seconds their fate would be out of his hands. They were just two pieces of adrenaline-charged protoplasm about to go on a rocket ride.

Marauder One and Two, the Alert Five Hornets from VFA-82, were taxiing forward when Cromwell's Tomcat, howling in afterburner, hurtled down the deck in a billowing cloud of steam. Cromwell and Singleton were crushed against their seats until the airplane flew off the bow. The 159-mph shot was normal and a few seconds later the Tomcat was cleaned up and climbing on the assigned intercept heading. Less than two minutes later the F/A-18s were accelerating toward the intruders.

Trent McCutchin turned on his gun camera video recorder, scanned his instruments, and then cast a sweeping look toward the coast. He saw another crackling flash in the distance, followed by a huge explosion, then secondary explosions. Intermittent streaks of light suddenly flashed across the pitch-black horizon as heavy antiaircraft fire erupted along the shoreline. From his vantage point over the Persian Gulf, the AAA looked like thousands of flashbulbs flickering during halftime at the Orange Bowl.

"Sting Flight, bandits at your twelve!" the AWACS officer warned. "Heads up—they're forty-five out and closing fast!"

"Sting One," McCutchin replied, scanning the enemy planes on his radar.

"We're getting too close to shore."

There was a brief, but maddening pause.

"Fangs," the AWACS operator suddenly blurted, "come left to zero-six-zero—we're picking up more activity."

"Fangs coming to zero-six-zero."

Listening to the F-16 flight leader, McCutchin felt a tingling sensation a few seconds before the radar warning receiver began to bleep.

"Weapons hot!" the AWACS coordinator said in a tight voice. "Weapons hot! Bandits on your nose!"

"They're tracking us!" Fang One blurted.

"SAMS!" someone else said excitedly. "Multiple SAMS—at least nine! Right up the pike!"

"Take 'em down, Fangs! *Now!*"

"We're goin' down!"

"They're away," someone shouted.

"Missiles in the air!"

Multiple SAM sites were painting the Falcons and the Eagles. In a matter of seconds seven of the eight F-16s had range and bearing solutions to many of the shore targets, but not all the sites. Moments later the pilots launched their HARM missiles, then activated their jamming pods and countermeasures dispensers.

"More SAMS!" Fang Three advised, hitting the buttons for the chaff launchers. "Over a dozen up—two more comin'!"

"Lock 'em up!"

"Come right, Fangs! Hard right! Keep it coming around."

"I'm hit! Oh, God . . ."

"Who's hit?" Fang One shouted, then cringed when he saw the streaming trail of fire from the remains of an F-16.

"Four. I've—I'm punchin' out."

"We've got one going down!" Fang One transmitted over the Guard frequency. "We need some help! Get CSAR out here."

"Checkmate's floggin' it," a reverberating voice replied

from the Navy helicopter. The combat search-and-rescue team was already en route to the crash site.

"It's Tommy," a muffled voice shouted. "I don't see a chute—too dark to see shit down there!"

"They're still shooting at us," another voice cried out. "They're all over me—gotta get down!"

Prepared for a savage fight, the Iranians were throwing up a wall of SAMs and antiaircraft artillery fire. A series of bright flashes from the shoreline indicated that the HARM missiles were finding their targets. The scene was surreal and reminded McCutchin of his first night over Baghdad, a night of unbelievable surprises and undiluted fear.

"They're—we're gettin' boat-launched SAMs comin' straight up!" Fang One warned, popping off chaff. "Lock 'em up—knock 'em out!"

A millisecond later Fang One's Falcon was blown to shreds in a mushrooming fireball. Bleeding from deep facial wounds, the stunned pilot tried time and again to pull one of the two sets of ejection handles, but he couldn't locate them. *God, get me out of this and I'll never do it again.*

In frustration, he willed his hands to cooperate, but something was terribly wrong. No matter how hard he tried, his arms and hands wouldn't respond. The long fall to the Gulf was filled with pain and agonizing terror.

Worried about the possibility of a midair collision, Trent McCutchin flinched when a brilliant streak of light, too fast to follow, flashed past his canopy. His eyes grew large as the sky suddenly illuminated with more AAA fire. It was like being in the middle of a sizzling lightning storm.

"SAMs!" Tim Cotton radioed. "Sting Two is—" he said before a SAM detonated under his cockpit, killing him instantly.

"Aw, sweet Jesus . . ."

Glancing at the radar, McCutchin saw an array of six bandits closing almost head-on. The hair stood up on the back of his neck.

"Sting One engaging!" He fired an AIM-120 "Slammer" and quickly targeted another enemy aircraft. McCutchin squeezed off another missile and felt a tremendous jolt under the belly of his plane as he maneuvered for another shot. With stark clarity, McCutchin knew he needed to make some quick kills and get the hell out of Dodge before the odds caught up with him.

With his adrenaline flowing at an alarming rate, Major Ali Akbar Muhammud was on overload; there was simply too much to absorb in his first *real* fighter engagement. Frightened and feeling nauseous, he fired a missile, then made a frenzied decision when Major Viktor Kasatkin's plane blew apart in a blinding flash.

"Let's get out of here!" Muhammud radioed to the other pilot, then frantically fired another missile at the U.S. warplanes. Without hesitation, he firewalled the twin Tumanskiis and yanked the MiG into a nose-low, gut-wrenching turn toward the shoreline. "Break off! Return to base!"

"Breaking off," a high-pitched voice replied.

While he quietly prayed, Muhammud selected burner and allowed the MiG to accelerate past Mach 1.2 while his remaining wingman scrambled to catch up. Descending through 8,000 feet at Mach 1.3, Muhammud was hit by a "friendly" SAM.

White-knuckled and shaking, the sweat-soaked pilot gripped the controls and froze while the MiG bucked and yawed to the right. Without warning, the right turbofan exploded and blew a wide hole in the fuselage, causing a raging fire. With the annunciator lights flashing warnings, the aircraft was quickly becoming uncontrollable. When the plane started an uncommanded roll, Muhammud panicked and ejected before he had time to think about the consequences. The supersonic ejection killed him.

The remaining MiG jocks stayed in the hunt and pressed their attack on the Americans. The lead Fulcrum driver shot down an F-16, but not before Rock Three blew one of the Iranian wingmen out of the sky. While the flaming fighter tumbled toward the water, a SAM struck the MiG flight leader and he turned toward the coast, ejecting seconds after a tremendous fireball erupted from the MiG. With afterburners blazing, the last MiG jumped out of the melee and headed for Shiraz as fast as Allahu and two turbojets could take him. Although the Iranian captain thought he was home free, Sting One was closing on the MiG from high and to the left.

Concentrating on the orange-white glow from the MiG's

burners, McCutchin switched to his twenty-millimeter Vulcan cannon. The situation had turned into a confusing, warp-speed furball of fighters, missiles, and cannon shells flying in every direction. The commanders of the Iranian SAM sites were launching everything they had in their inventory. Nothing was being spared. The influx of information and warnings was staggering, beyond the ability of humans to process in such a compressed time frame.

"*Mayday! Mayday!* Sting Four, I've been hit! I can't control it!"

Trying to close on the fleeing MiG, McCutchin keyed his radio. "Get out, Corky! Get out of there!"

"Shoot him!" someone pleaded. "Kill the sonuvabitch!"

"Sting Four—I'm on fire—ejecting!"

"We have people in the water," McCutchin shouted on Guard frequency. "Get out here!"

Working hard to line up a good deflection shot, McCutchin fired a couple of bursts that did little more than alert the MiG driver. Aware that his plane was absorbing cannon fire, the Iranian came out of burner and dove for the deck. Squinting to see his prey in the dark, McCutchin continued to hose the MiG with armor-piercing, explosive fragmentation rounds. The heavy shells tore through the fuselage, ripping the innards to shreds.

The pilot ejected while the airplane was still shedding parts. Slowly, the Fulcrum rolled inverted and plummeted toward the Gulf, streaming burning fuel all the way to impact.

Gasping for oxygen, McCutchin snapped the Eagle into a punishing high-G batturn that caused transonic vapor to erupt above the wings. Rolling level, he pitched the nose up and was clobbered by a SAM. The powerful explosion shattered the canopy and rendered him semiconscious. With his oxygen mask drooping on his chest, McCutchin rode the spinning Eagle to a watery grave.

# 25

## Aboard the Caravan

Flying low over the coastline, Scott glanced at the former Phoenician city-state of Sidon. Graced by Castle of the Sea, the northern harbor of Saida was quiet at this time of the morning. Scott began a shallow climb to improve his chances of contacting the *Permak Express*. Surprisingly, the ship immediately answered the radio call, although the transmission was weak and broken. Seconds later the ship was steaming toward the stricken Caravan.

Out of habit, Jackie and Scott glanced at the fuel gauges as they continuously computed and updated the time and distance to the container ship. At best, the chances of reaching the *Permak Express* were fifty-fifty.

She turned to him and spoke in a low voice. "Well, it wasn't pretty, but we got the job done."

"Yeah." Scott shrugged. "The key word is 'lucky.' "

Jackie remained silent.

"I'm going to check on Greg and Maritza," Scott said as he unbuckled his seat and shoulder harnesses. "You have the airplane."

"I have it," Jackie said as she assumed control of the turboprop. "What are you going to tell them?"

"The truth," he said, then remarked idly, "which I'm sure they've already figured out."

Jackie remained quiet while Scott stepped out of the cockpit. Maritza and Greg were sitting on the bare floor next to the life raft. They were cold, in constant pain, and soaked raw with jet fuel. Neither one had complained.

Scott knelt beside them and spoke in a soft, soothing voice. "Both of you need immediate medical attention, but we're going to have to make some changes in our—"

O'Donnell and Gunzelman interrupted him at the same time.

"Don't worry about us," Greg said steadily. "The mission comes first, so do what you need to do."

Scott reached for Maritza's hand and felt the pressure of her cold fingers. Her eyes reflected a deep sense of fear and emotional pain. "You're going to have to ditch the plane, aren't you?"

"Yes," Scott said without hesitation. He allowed his head to droop. "We don't have many options left, so we're going to get you aboard the container ship as soon as possible."

O'Donnell's gaze inadvertently shifted to Scott's eyes. "Bubba, you can't bluff worth a shit," he said with a ragged smile. "We're going to run out of fuel first, right?"

Scott shrugged his shoulders. "That's a distinct possibility, Captain Optimistic. Aren't you the guy who always has the upbeat, 'top of the morning' attitude about everything?"

An awkward quiet settled over the pungent smell of the cabin.

Maritza finally broke the silence. "Greg tells me that you're the best," she declared in a firm voice. "And I told him that Jackie's the best, so we're not worried."

Scott quietly nodded, then patted her hand and returned to the cockpit. *God, if you have a miracle to spare, we really need one.*

### Over the Persian Gulf

"Diamond One-Oh-Seven," the senior Hawkeye controller radioed to the lead BARCAP pilot, "six—make that seven bogies at your twelve, noses on, at sixty-three miles, Angles fourteen."

"One-Oh-Seven, we've got 'em." Lieutenant Commander Denby Kaywood inched the Tomcat's throttles forward.

"Diamond One is comin' up on the power. Let's go combat spread, Stan."

Stan Greenwich, Kaywood's wingman, clicked his radio button twice and worked his throttles forward while he banked away from his flight leader.

"Three more bogies in trail," the Miniwacs controller said excitedly while another controller notified *Washington*.

"Diamond One-Oh-Seven," the controller said hastily. "Make that five aircraft. They're hugging the deck, seven to eight miles behind the first wave. They're—the wingmen are diverging from the leader. They've jinked out ten—'bout fifteen degrees."

"Roger that," Kaywood answered, scanning his engine instruments. "They gotta be carryin' cruise missiles."

"Yeah, best bet."

"Diamond Three and Four step to the left," Kaywood ordered, trying his best to sound calm. "One and Two goin' for knots, comin' right twenty."

With a *click click* on the radio, the second section leader and his wingman banked and disappeared in the dark sky. They would maneuver in combat spread, ready to splash the oncoming bogies.

In Kaywood's backseat, Chet Hoffman had his head buried in the radar scope, tweaking and interpreting the information displayed on the screen. He was one of the best when it came to anticipating an enemy's moves and visualizing the fight well before the merge. In order to keep the surface of the water from interfering with his radar, Hoffman wanted to get below the adversaries so he would be looking up at the enemy.

"Let's take her down," Hoffman suggested a split second before Kaywood radioed their wingman, then lowered the nose and plunged downward, leveling at 4,000 feet and 470 knots.

"Warning Yellow, Weapons Hold," the Air Warfare Commander ordered. "Repeat, Warning Yellow, Weapons Hold."

"Copy, Diamond One-Oh-Seven."

The U.S. pilots were in an intermediate stage in the process of preparing to fire in self-defense.

Hoffman kept his face glued to the radar scope while Kaywood talked to himself. "Fifty-eight miles, speed 450, Angels twelve."

With his reflexes in survival mode, Kaywood watched the separation shrink at an alarming rate. When the bogies reached twenty-two miles, he keyed his radio. "Master Arm On."

"Master Arm On," Stan Greenwich repeated from Diamond 104.

"Three."

"Four's ready to dance."

Chet Hoffman felt warm perspiration on his forehead. "I can't believe this," he quietly said over the intercom. "And to think I gave up submarines for this kind of crap."

"Centering the T," Kaywood announced as he worked on a steering cue to ensure an optimum missile launch position. "Eighteen miles, centering the dot. Lookin' good, Chet."

When the Iranian leader reached fifteen miles, Kaywood didn't hesitate. "Fifteen miles. Fox One! Fox One!"

"Here we go," Hoffman said, then gulped oxygen as the Sparrow missile rocketed toward its prey. "Stan fired a missile. Two's got a missile off."

"Fox One!" Three declared.

"Fox One," Four said evenly.

"Eleven miles!" Kaywood reported, then stopped breathing a few moments. In the distance, he saw a series of white flashes, followed by a high-pitched warble sound in his earpads. The bogies had launched air-to-air missiles. He felt his heart pound as the adrenaline kicked in.

"Nine miles!" Kaywood announced. "Fox One again!"

"Oh, shit," Hoffman said over the intercom. "This ain't good."

A bright flash, followed by a rapid succession of pulsing explosions lighted the sky as one of the MiGs disintegrated in a shower of white-orange plumes.

"Good hit!" someone radioed. "You nailed him!"

Taking evasive action, the MiGs broke left and right with one of them going straight up. Diamond Three savaged the stray MiG when the pilot pulled through the top of an egg-shaped loop and started down.

"Another hit! Good kill!"

Kaywood snapped the Tomcat into a face-sagging vertical

climb, rolling ninety degrees over the top to position himself for another shot.

"Go Fox Two," Hoffman advised in a ragged voice. "Select Fox Two."

"Okay," Kaywood replied, selecting heat. "Fox Two."

While Kaywood tracked a MiG in an effort to get a missile tone, another flash and explosion lighted the night. Kaywood's instincts told him it was his wingman.

"Stan, you okay? You up, Stan?"

A brief moment of silence answered his questions. With the entire tail missing, Greenwich's F-14 had yawed sideways, departed from controlled flight, then violently cartwheeled across the sky. Stunned by the direct hit, Greenwich and his RIO ejected after the first tumble.

"Diamond One-Oh-Four is in the drink!" Kaywood radioed on Guard. "Get someone out here—do it now!"

"Screwtop copies. CSAR is eight miles and closing. We have a bogie extending away from the area—headed home."

"Roger," Kaywood acknowledged. "We're going to need tankers."

"They've got one up, and one ready to shoot, and we have aircraft from Roosevelt on the way."

"Tell 'em to buster!"

"They're supersonic, fifty-five miles."

"Copy."

Except for the lone defector, the Iranians continued to press the engagement as the remaining Tomcats jockeyed for position. Stationed in a reserve position, the four Hornet pilots were ready to pounce if another F-14 was shot down.

Hoffman worked a merging target while Kaywood maneuvered behind a MiG for another shot.

"Shoot him," Hoffman encouraged. "Fox Two."

"No tone," Kaywood yelled in a strained voice. "Come on!"

Hoffman concentrated on his scope. A different bogie was beginning to gain a slight advantage on Diamond 107.

"Lock him up!" Hoffman said excitedly. "Shoot him!"

Kaywood heard a  rasping sound in his headset, confirming that the Sidewinder had acquired the infrared signature of the bandit's jet exhaust.

"Fox Two," Kaywood said as the "Winder" whooshed

away, then curved upward and went ballistic. "Son of a bitch," Kaywood uttered as he racked the straining F-14 into the vertical to try to counter the bogie stalking him. A loud explosion shook the Tomcat as a missile detonated in the aft section of the starboard engine.

"Shit," Hoffman exclaimed, feeling a twinge of panic. "Let's go! Let's get out of here!"

With warning lights flashing in his face, Kaywood secured the right engine and turned for the carrier.

"Diamond One-Oh-Seven is hit!" he declared as a sizable lump developed in his throat. "I'm disengaging and goin' to home plate."

"Roger, Diamond." The Hawkeye controller paused to inform the carrier, then came back on the frequency. "You have a ready deck. Your bogies appear to be withdrawin'— goin' north."

"One-Oh-Seven," Kaywood replied as a trace of acrid smoke drifted up toward the dome of the canopy. *We gotta get to the boat.*

"Thunderbolt One," the Miniwacs controller radioed to the Marine pilot in the VMFA-251 Hornet. "I'm going to divert you. We're tracking five bogies—low on the deck—eleven o'clock at twenty-eight miles. Looks like they're goin' for the carrier."

"T-Bolt copies," Major Buck Martin replied, and banked toward the approaching planes. "Thunderbolts, arm 'em up."

"Two."

"Three."

"Four."

Martin lowered his nose and shoved the throttles into burner. "I've got 'em tied on radar. Got 'em locked."

"Copy. Diamond One is closing from your seven o'clock, nine miles. Marauder One and Two are off the deck and climbing."

"T-Bolt One."

Martin remained quiet while his flight of F/A-18s accelerated and drifted apart in a line-abreast spread. Armed with AIM-120 missiles with multispectral seekers that can sense both infrared and radar signatures of cruise missiles, the pilots were confident they could handle the bogies.

Approaching the hostiles, Martin keyed his radio. "Guido, shoot the one on the right, Phil and I will take the center three, and John you go for the left one."

In rapid order, the pilots acknowledged the orders.

"Here we go," Martin announced, and fired a missile at the center bogie, then waited a second and fired another. "Fox Two—Fox Two."

In quick succession, four more missiles were streaking toward their targets. The three Mirage F-1s were easy pickings. The Iranian pilots held a steady course while they prepared to fire their Exocet cruise missiles. The left wingman was hit a nanosecond before he fired his missile. The other two pilots launched their Exocets seconds before their Mirages disappeared in huge fireballs.

The U.S.-built Iranian F-4s fired their Chinese cruise missiles, then broke hard to starboard in full afterburner. The flight leader's jet exploded halfway through the turn. The other Phantom, manned by senior officers, escaped unharmed.

"Good hits!" Martin exclaimed. "Good kills!"

"Thunderbolt One, Screwtop, climb and maintain angels ten, heading zero-one-five. Max conserve."

"T-Bolt copies, angles ten, zero-one-five."

"Diamond One, Screwtop is trackin' cruise missiles!" the frantic Hawkeye controller warned. "Two targets at your ten o'clock—both targets boresighted on Mother!"

"I've got 'em!" Ridder Cromwell gasped as he wrapped the big Tomcat into a tight left turn. He worked hard to get a tone, but the missiles were too low to the water. Finally, after a couple of frustrating tracking corrections, Cromwell heard the sweet sound he was waiting for.

"Fox Two," he declared as the missile shot out in front of the F-14. Cromwell immediately banked toward the second target.

The AIM-120 made a series of small corrections, then undulated a couple of times before slamming into the Gulf thirty feet behind the Exocet.

"Come on," Singleton muttered from the rear seat. "We don't have much time . . . lock it up."

Cromwell eased the nose down and heard a feeble tone at

the same time as the Hawkeye controller radioed an urgent order.

"Diamond One, knock it off! Knock it off! Break right—right and reverse course!"

Snapping the fighter into a punishing turn, Cromwell labored under the G-forces. "What the hell's goin' on?"

"You're too close to the ship. They're goin' with 'R2D2'—break—Marauder One and Two, max climb to angels eight, heading three-five-zero. Expedite!"

"Marauders are outta here."

R2D2, the nickname for the Mk-15 Phalanx Close-In Weapons System, is a rapid-fire cannon with six rotating barrels. The self-contained fire control radar is housed in a white dome which jerks into action seemingly without provocation. Mounted on both sides of the carrier, CIWS is the Navy's standard defense against antiship missiles and low-flying, high-speed cruise missiles.

# 26

**B**reathing more rapidly than usual, Denby Kaywood concentrated on listening to the carrier's air traffic controllers as they vectored him to final bearing. His pulse quickened as wisps of smoke began drifting past his crash helmet. Without warning, the horizontal-situation display flickered a few times and then grew dim. He took a deep breath and slowly exhaled, then toggled the intercom switch. "Ah . . . yo, Houston, we have a problem."

"No shit," Chet Hoffman said excitedly as a yellow tongue of flame curled from beneath his instrument panel. "I've got a fire goin' back here! Turn off the port generator!"

Kaywood complied with the request. "Is it out?"

"No! I've got flames comin' out from under the instrument panel!"

"Hang on a second," Kaywood said as he shut off the emergency generator. Using a flashlight to illuminate a standby gyro that was good for less than ten minutes, Kaywood felt his neck and shoulders becoming tense. He turned his head toward Hoffman. "Is the fire out?" Kaywood shouted.

"No!" There was no mistaking the edge of panic in his voice. "We're gonna have to jump out!"

"You gotta be shitin' me."

"Slow this sonuvabitch down!" Hoffman demanded as the snakes of fire started crawling into the cockpit.

Kaywood yanked the left throttle back and started slowing the Tomcat in preparation for a controlled ejection. Cold fear gripped both men, robbing them of their logic and instincts.

"Wait—wait a second!" Hoffman exclaimed as the flames suddenly disappeared from the wire bundle. "I think it's out! Yeah, it's just smoldering—keep truckin'."

"We're almost there." Kaywood swallowed hard as he eased the left throttle forward and brought the emergency generator back on-line. The instrument lighting came on as Kaywood dumped the cabin pressure, then selected RAM air to clear the smoke and fumes. "How we lookin'?"

"Good to go. Let's get back on deck."

"I have the ball," Kaywood said.

He made a minor throttle adjustment as the approach controller in the Carrier Air Traffic Control Center calmly talked to him.

"One-Oh-Seven," the controller said slowly and clearly, "on line slightly right, three-quarter mile, call the ball."

"Diamond One-Oh-Seven on the ball, three-point-nine." Kaywood had the bright orange "meatball" centered, and his fuel state was 3,900 pounds.

CAG Paddles, the landing signal officer, quickly responded. "Roger ball, fourteen knots. You look a little fast."

Kaywood's lineup was good and he was beginning to feel more confident. *Almost home.*

The ball began descending, prompting Kaywood to add a touch of power. "Come on, stay on it."

"Powweeer," the LSO called. "Let's get some power on."

Kaywood shoved the throttle forward and concentrated on the meatball, lineup, and angle of attack. "Easy . . . easy."

"You're fast," Hoffman advised.

"I know."

Something didn't feel right to Kaywood. The ball rose to the proper position and continued to rise. He tweaked the throttle back and made a slight lineup correction.

"One-Oh-Seven, paddles. Check your gear down."

In astonishment, Kaywood noticed the flashing WHEELS light as he slapped the landing-gear handle down. "Shit!" *Terrific.*

"Keep it together," Hoffman coached. "You're doin' fine."

"Yeah, I'm cookin' now." Kaywood fumed. "Sterling performance." Distracted by his embarrassing mistake, he glanced at the gear indicator and allowed the Tomcat to drift left as it slowed and settled below the glidepath.

"Power," the LSO said firmly. "Powwweeer."

Lowering the starboard wing, Kaywood inched the throttle forward as the airplane began to drift back to the right.

"Lineup." Reverting to body English, the senior LSO instinctively attempted to control the movement of the airplane by moving his body in the desired direction. "Watch your lineup."

Approaching the round-down, Kaywood began focusing on lineup and ignored everything else as the F-14 settled toward the water.

"You're low—slow!" Hoffman warned, reaching for the ejection handle between his legs. "Take it around!"

"Powwweeer," the anxious LSO demanded. "Power-power-*power*!"

Shoving the throttle to military power, the left turbofan began to spool up as Kaywood worked to keep the wings level.

In despair, Paddles pushed his pickle switch and the wave-off lights flashed on. "Wave off, wave off, wave off!" he chanted.

It was too late.

"*Holy* Mother of Jesus!" Paddles shouted as he and his assistants dove into the safety net beneath the windswept LSO platform.

For a fleeting moment Kaywood thought they were climbing away from the dark flight deck. He was wrong.

Hoffman gripped the ejection handle and closed his eyes. "We're goin' into the spud locker!"

"Stay with me," Kaywood exclaimed.

Yawing from asymmetrical thrust, the staggering Tomcat slammed into the round-down in a nose-high attitude. The horrifying explosion turned night into day as huge flames engulfed the remains of the demolished airplane. Severed from the rest of the fuselage, the cockpit skidded up the angle deck and plunged over the side of the ship.

Dazed and disoriented by the twenty-G impact, Kaywood

and Hoffman didn't attempt to eject until after they hit the water. When the cockpit rolled on its side and began sinking, Hoffman pulled his ejection handle. The two men were shot sideways through the water, but quickly surfaced and began struggling to keep their heads above water.


## The *Neyzeh*

In a state of high anxiety, the young captain of the Iranian gunboat placed the radio microphone in its bracket and turned to the senior rated sailor in his crew. "Fire the missiles."

Without hesitation, the slender, dark-bearded man shouted orders to the frightened sailors who were responsible for launching the C-802 antiship missiles.

"Fire missiles! Fire missiles!"

In a matter of seconds the Silkworm cruise missiles were rocketing straight toward *Washington*.

Seven miles on the other side of the carrier, another Combattante II gunboat fired two C-802 missiles at the giant flat-top, then raced away at flank speed.

With Admiral Coleman standing in the background, Nancy Jensen watched helplessly while the helmsman executed a maneuver to swing *Washington*'s stern away from Kaywood and Hoffman. The SH-60F Seahawk rescue helicopter was over the flight crew in a matter of seconds. As the pilot stabilized the helo in a hover, a rescue swimmer jumped into the water to help the struggling fliers.

At the same time the air warfare officer aboard the Aegis guided-missile cruiser heard the warning alarms go off. The other warships also sounded warnings and took evasive action.

"Missiles inbound," the carrier's 1MC barked. "This is *not* a drill!"

Jensen gripped the arms of her chair as the battle-force ships began launching Sea Sparrows and firing Close-In Weapons Systems.

More warnings were being sounded from the Combat Direction Center when Captain Jensen saw a flash in her peripheral vision.

"Take cover!" a high-pitched voice said over the 1MC. "Take cover!"

Jensen momentarily froze when two of *Washington*'s powerful CIWS defensive systems opened fire. Spewing twenty-millimeter shells made of depleted uranium, two of the CDC-controlled Phalanx "Gatling gun" cannons put up a curtain of steel between *Washington* and the incoming missiles.

*I don't believe this,* Jensen thought while each of the six barrel cannons howled at 3,000 rounds a minute. Her nerves went tense when another CIWS opened fire from one of the escort ships.

The last-ditch defense systems blew two of three cruise missiles to smithereens. Another missile, flying so low that it made radar acquisition nearly impossible, escaped the blazing fire of the Vulcan Phalanx cannons. Two seconds before impact, the sea-skimming missile arbitrarily pitched up a few degrees and penetrated the hull of the carrier at the main deck level.

In an instant the aft end of the hangar bay and the jet-engine repair shop erupted in explosions and fire. Fed by volatile jet fuel, a series of thunderous explosions destroyed a Marine EA-6B Prowler and blew three sailors off the fantail and into the Gulf. Debris and shrapnel ricocheted off the bulkheads and adjacent planes while frightened crewmen rushed into the inferno to rescue their shipmates and help fight the spreading fire. Flames and dense smoke billowed out of the hangar bay as the blaze spread to nearby berthing compartments.

While the CIWS cannons continued to spew a stream of shells at the incoming C-802 missiles, Admiral Coleman remained uncharacteristically quiet. Fires were raging and lives were in danger when he looked to the commanding officer. In keeping with an honored Navy tradition, only one person was in charge of a ship. It was time to save lives and the carrier. Nancy Jensen responded to the challenge as three of the four Chinese cruise missiles were quickly destroyed in a hail of cannon fire. The surviving missile blew a large hole in an office space adjacent to the intelligence center.

Acting firmly and professionally, she had the repair lockers mobilized, the helicopters airborne, a man-overboard search under way, and reports coming in from damage control.

Satisfied that Jensen was handling the crisis in a satisfactory manner, Coleman returned to the flag bridge as the SH-60F Seahawk landed near the bow of the flight deck. Suffering from minor injuries, Kaywood and Hoffman were quickly placed on stretchers and carried to sick bay.

High above the carrier, Major Buck Martin and his fellow Hornet pilots were being vectored toward the fleeing gunboat *Neyzeh*. Likewise, Ridder Cromwell and Marauder One and Two were setting up for an attack on the other boat. Once the pilots were low and close to the gunboats, it wasn't difficult to spot the frothy wakes of the speeding vessels. When Martin and company rolled in for their first strafing run, the crew of *Neyzeh* abandoned ship while it was running at full speed.

While the stricken carrier's escorts approached to help fight the devastating fire, the Iranian gunboats were sunk by heavy cannon fire from the Tomcat and Hornets. Once the gunboats were destroyed, the fighters tanked from two Air Force KC-10s, then joined the fighters from USS *Roosevelt* to provid protection for the *GW* battle group while other planes diverted to airfields in Bahrain and Kuwait. Two S-3B Vikings remained on station to sniff for subs while the Hawkeye kept a close eye on potential threats from all quadrants.

From the reports she was receiving, Jensen was beginning to feel a sense of relief. The smaller fires were under control and the conflagration in the aft section of the hangar bay was almost extinguished.

When Jim Lomas entered the bridge, Jensen could see the grief written on his face.

"How many?" she quietly asked.

"Nineteen dead, and forty-eight injured—including two of the three men who were blown overboard. They're still searching for the other guy, but I don't hold out much hope for him."

Anger screamed through her nerves, but Jensen gritted her teeth and shifted her gaze to the frantic activity on the flight deck. "*Roosevelt* is launching more aircraft as we speak. They should be overhead before too long."

"The sooner, the better."

Struggling to control her emotions, she turned to her XO. "What a fiasco," she said as her mouth twisted in a rueful grimace.

"Yeah, we sailed straight into a trap."

After receiving a brief message about the condition of the American carrier, Ali Nasrallah, the captain of *Nuh,* raised his periscope and smiled when he saw the faint glow of fire in the distance. On *Washington*'s hangar bay and flight deck, exhausted crewmen continued to fight the last of the fires. Surrounded by her escorts, the big flattop was slowly proceeding toward the United Arab Emirates deep-water port of Jebel Ali, the only Gulf naval support facility where U.S. supercarriers can pull pierside.

Familiar with his operating environment, the brash skipper of the Kilo-class attack sub was confident he could sink the carrier and outwit any U.S. submarine or ASW effort. Operating in his own littoral waters, Nasrallah had the advantage of knowing the layers, the ambient sea noise in the strait, and the shallow areas where he could "sleep" on the bottom.

"The Americans made a big mistake," the captain said derisively. "Now they're going to pay with their lives."

One of the Russian advisers, a former Kilo skipper, gave Nasrallah a few suggestions and stepped out of the way. The captain fired six torpedoes at the crippled warship, then turned seventy degrees to starboard and executed a series of speed, depth, and course changes as he quietly moved away. After reaching a crowded, noisy shipping lane, Captain Nasrallah allowed *Nuh* to settle to the bottom and go into "sleep" mode. Proud of his performance, he nervously waited for the torpedoes to smash into the giant carrier. Nasrallah was supremely confident that he would be hailed as a hero when *Nuh* returned to her base at Bandar-e Abbas.

Nancy Jensen was conferring with her department heads and damage-control experts when the torpedoes were detected. Midway through an evasive maneuver, a torpedo exploded 120 feet forward of the propellers. A second powerful explosion damaged both port-side propshafts and both screws. A third torpedo twisted and jammed *Washington*'s rudder at an awkward angle. The rest of the weapons, with the exception of one that blew a gaping hole in a Mobile Oil supertanker, missed the carrier and a dozen other commercial and military vessels. The double-hulled supertanker, ripped apart by the initial blast, exploded several more times and sank in less than twenty minutes. One crew member survived for twelve days, then succumbed to his injuries.

# 27

## The Situation Room

"**S**on of a bitch," President Macklin said to no one in particular, then thumped his fist on the edge of his chair. "Son of a *bitch!*"

The Situation Room remained deathly quiet until Hartwell Prost cleared his throat. "Mr. President, there's no way around it."

"Around what?" Macklin snapped, and took a quick sip of coffee.

"Tehran *had* to know about our plans."

Outrage bubbled as the president gently shook his head. As the leader of the most powerful nation on the planet, Macklin was dismayed and deeply angered to think that he might have a traitor in his midst.

"We have to find the leak," Prost continued in a quiet, calm voice. "And we need to do it as quickly as possible."

"What do you think?" the president asked Prost. "Has someone, a foreign intelligence service, a computer hacker, or a terrorist group, tapped into the Defense Department Internet?"

"It's possible." He shrugged. "Any breach of security could help level the playing field, but the only Pentagon systems the hackers have been able to compromise are the unclassified ones. They were able to peer into payroll files and personnel records, but no classified information appeared to have been compromised, or so the experts claim."

"Mr. President," Pete Adair interrupted, "we didn't have—"

"Hold your thought a second," Macklin said, struggling to conceal his annoyance and frustration. "What's the worst that could happen?"

"At the very least," Prost said, anxious to talk in private with the president, "there are probably a dozen or more hackers who could potentially compromise the nation's defenses."

"Give me the bottom line."

"If a hacker, or team of hackers, gained access to the DOD computers, they could intercept, delete, and change all the classified messages on the net. They could stop the Pentagon from deploying forces, scramble military telecommunications, and possibly launch a variety of weapons, including nuclear missiles."

"Terrific," the president piped sarcastically. "Do you think a terrorist group would have that kind of capability?"

"Sure. Hackers are highly skilled, arrogant, reckless, and some of them are extremely greedy. We're constantly redefining our vulnerabilities to cyberspace assaults. We now have the ability to camouflage destructive signals within normal transmissions. These infectious signals can ride data streams through fiber-optic cables straight into enemy computer systems. We can disrupt and destroy the global economy and cripple the infrastructure in major metropolitan areas. It's a never-ending journey to Armageddon."

Prost paused when Macklin frowned, then eyed him with icy stiffness.

"The enemy," Hartwell quietly suggested, "may have a system to recognize cyber attacks and launch an aggressive and fatal counterattack to our platforms."

General Chalmers interrupted. "That may be true, Mr. Prost, but I don't think so—at least not at this stage of the game."

Hartwell slowly shook his head. *Game? Computers are going to be our downfall.*

"The first time we use our virus," Prost continued, "the enemy is going to have a tactical meltdown. It'll take them a couple of years to figure out how we did it, then a year or so to turn it on us. By that time, if not sooner, we'll have to have an impenetrable defense for our platforms. The game will continue as long as there are two humans left to play."

Hartwell picked up his glass of water. "The threats are changing rapidly," he said with a troubled expression, "and the terrorists are much more sophisticated than most people believe."

Unconvinced, Macklin furrowed his brow. "Do you *really* believe that terrorists are sophisticated enough to pull off a cyberspace Pearl Harbor?"

"Without a doubt," Prost said boldly. "If they don't have the capability internally, they can hire the expertise. As I pointed out, there are any number of people who can disrupt the air-traffic-control system, wipe out bank records, scramble airline and hotel reservations, shut down major pipelines, send trains on collision courses, disable 911 emergency phone service, or even erase the New York Stock Exchange's trading records. It's an open-ended nightmare, one that includes our defense systems.

"If a single hacker penetrated our defense network," Prost continued, "he or she could craft a virus that would spread literally with the speed of light. It could easily loop and weave from system to system until it strangled our military command-and-control structure."

"Wait a minute," Pete Adair said forcefully, exchanging a glance with General Chalmers. "Before we start trying to solve problems that don't exist, I want to set something straight. Les and I made sure that the orders were *hand-delivered* to Admiral Bowman at La Maddalena and Admiral Holmes at Norfolk. They personally gave the orders to Bob Gillmore, *Hampton*'s skipper, and Forrest Dunwall, CO of *Cheyenne*. And no one at the command center had any idea what the messages were about. Nothing went on the net," he said emphatically. "There was no breach of security at the Pentagon."

The statement was met with silence.

"Well," Macklin said as his mouth tightened, "someone tipped them off, and we're going to find out who is responsible."

"I don't think we'll have to look too far." Prost sighed

grimly. "If the Pentagon is clean, then the leak obviously came from here."

The president cast an angry glance at his national security adviser. "Do you have any factual basis to support your theory?"

"No, sir, but it just seems logical."

"We'll discuss it later," Macklin flared.

"Yes, sir," Prost agreed blandly.

With a look at his watch, the president rose, prompting everyone to rise. "Well," he said in a harsh voice, "it's time for me to tell the citizens of this fine country what a bang-up job I'm doing for them."

Adair glanced at the bank of television sets. "Sir, CNN and CBS are already reporting the story, so you may want to consider making a short statement from the Briefing Room, then turn it over to me."

"I appreciate your consideration, but I think it's best if I stick with my original plan."

"I understand," Adair replied in an undertone.

"Sir," Les Chalmers said glumly, "may I have a private word with you?"

"You bet," the president declared, "as long as we're headed in the direction of the Oval Office."

Accompanied by three Secret Service agents, Macklin and Chalmers walked away from the Situation Room. Acutely aware of the military tragedy in the Gulf, the agents remained a discreet distance from the two men.

"Mr. President, you'll have my resignation on your desk by 0800 tomorrow morning."

"The *hell* I will," Macklin said curtly. "Sacrificing you isn't going to bring a reprieve. Besides, this wasn't entirely your fault. You can shoulder part of the blame, but someone obviously gave the Iranians our game plan."

"Sir, I sincerely appreciate your confid—"

"Not another word," the president declared as he came to an abrupt stop and faced his friend. "You're not going off to lick your wounds. You're going to stay right here and help me find the sonuvabitch who sold us out."

"Mr. President—"

"Cut the crap," Macklin said evenly as the agents quickly

turned away. "The name is Cord, same as it was when we used to get falling down drunk in Saigon."

The president turned on his heel and started walking before Chalmers could respond.

"What's the current status of *Washington* and *Roosevelt*?" Macklin asked as Chalmers hurried to catch up.

"*Roosevelt* is headed into the Gulf. *GW* has dropped anchor, and we expect to take her under tow in the next few hours. She'll be in the shipyard for at least six or seven months."

"If they don't sink her first," the president said curtly. "What are you doing to protect her?"

"We have a solid net of fighters airborne, and every available ASW resource is hunting subs, including helos from *Roosevelt*. She should be in the Gulf by early morning."

"Good," Macklin said evenly, and lifted an eyebrow. "Isn't Nancy Jensen the skipper of *GW*?"

"She sure is, and she's done an outstanding job of saving the ship."

"At least *someone* did something right."

"After they lost steering," Chalmers continued in a flat, decisive voice, "she reacted quickly to keep the ship from drifting into the shipping lanes."

"Yeah, that'd be a hell of a hazard to navigation."

The Oval Office was crowded and humming with activity when President Macklin entered the room. Ignoring the network crews and media representatives, he walked to the bulletproof window framed by the American flag and the presidential flag. He glanced at the family photographs on the credenza, then turned and sat down at his ornate desk.

The embarrassment and anger he felt was evident from the grim set of his jaw muscles. Macklin caught the reassuring smile from the first lady, then faced the lights and waited for his cue.

"Good evening," he greeted the audience in a warm, even voice. "Less than two hours ago elements of our military forces attacked two missile launch sites in Iran. Those installations were equipped with nuclear-tipped missiles and represented an immediate threat to our military personnel and our allies in the Gulf region. Based on our latest intelligence reports, the nuclear facilities received heavy damage."

Macklin's poise was unshakable. "Any nation foolish enough to contemplate using weapons of mass destruction against the United States, our armed forces, or our allies must fully understand the consequences of their actions. Make no mistake about it—*no* mistake. Our response will be swift and devastating.

"I want to reassure every American, our friends around the world, and the citizens of Iran, that we have not declared war on Iran. We *do not* want to declare war on Iran. However, we will continue to respond swiftly to any threat in the Gulf region, be it a military situation, or a terrorist situation."

The president paused, hardening himself for the most difficult part of his job. With the same look of civility and grandfatherly-compassion that helped win him his position, Macklin stared straight into the camera. "Regrettably, American lives were lost during the operation to restore stability in the Gulf region."

## The Florida Keys

After Massoud Ramazani received the initial battle damage assessment from Tehran, he terminated the satcom transmission. Ramazani continued to sip warm orange juice while he watched President Macklin attempt to minimize the severe bashing the American military had taken in the Gulf.

Although the commander in chief mentioned damage to the carrier *George Washington*, he didn't disclose the fact that it was currently dead in the water. The president went on to explain that some "assets" were lost in the strike, but he didn't reveal how many U.S. warplanes were now lying on the bottom of the Persian Gulf.

Ramazani watched the tight-jawed president make every attempt to be upbeat about the results of the surprise attack. When it became painfully obvious that Macklin was spinning himself into a corner, an off-camera media consultant gave the commander in chief a "pull the rip cord" signal. With the precision of a neurosurgeon, the president brought the "live event" to a smooth conclusion and the bright lights clicked off.

Harboring mixed feelings, Ramazani rose from the sofa

and walked out to the island home's spacious dock. He was pleased that the Iranian military had acquitted themselves and humbled the Americans, but the attack on his homeland was stirring a great deal of rage in his gut. He sat down in a lounge chair and allowed his thoughts to run their course while he relaxed under the stars and balmy breezes. *Macklin is a walking dead man.*

## Moscow

President Nikolai Shumenko and Yegor Pavlinsky talked quietly over breakfast on Shumenko's patio. They discussed the warm weather and the protest marches in Red Square while they occasionally glanced at the four heavily armed men guarding the grounds.

The president caught Pavlinsky's eye. "I'm afraid your plan may have grave consequences for us."

Pavlinsky gave him a barely perceptible shrug. "What consequences?"

"You know what I'm talking about."

"We have nothing to lose," Pavlinsky said defiantly, "and the Americans have a carrier out of action for at least six to nine months."

"My friend," Shumenko said under his breath, "I fear we have, as Admiral Yamamoto once said, awakened a sleeping giant."

"We have to survive this crisis," Pavlinsky declared with a solemn expression. "The Americans are becoming overextended and their situation will get worse."

"That's what concerns me."

Pavlinsky glanced at one of the guards and turned to Shumenko. "It won't be long before we'll be filling the void in the Gulf region. It's working in our favor, but we have to be patient. Trust me."

They locked stares before Shumenko broke the silence. "If you trap your enemy in a corner—"

"Yes, yes," Pavlinsky interrupted. "If the enemy has no escape, they will fight to the death. That's not what we're doing."

Shumenko looked down and slowly shook his head. "It would be foolish to underestimate Macklin."

"I know," Pavlinsky said stiffly. "He *was* a fighter pilot, but now he's a president who has to be more reserved."

"This bit of wisdom"—Shumenko sighed heavily—"from a man who never served in the military."

# 28

## Near the *Permak Express*

Using Greg O'Donnell's night-vision goggles, Scott caught sight of the container ship a few miles in front of them.

"I've got 'em," Dalton announced triumphantly.

"Where?" Jackie asked, noting the first signs of daylight in the eastern sky. "I don't see it."

"Eleven-thirty, about three miles," he said as he initiated a shallow climb and keyed the radio. "Easy Rider, Charlie Actual has you in sight. Do you have accommodations and winds?"

"Light and variable with a cork to port."

"We're looking forward to seeing you."

"Easy Rider, aye."

Scott angled toward the ship as he made preparations to ditch the damaged Caravan. The fuselage tank was empty and fuel had stopped dripping from the wings ten minutes after the gauges read empty.

"Jackie," Scott said as he eased the turboprop up to 400 feet, "how about jettisoning the cargo door and handling the life raft?"

"I'm way ahead of you," she said, then glanced at Maritza and Greg. "They're well braced, so I'll toss the door out and stay with them."

"Good," he said as he spotted a motor launch fifty yards

to the left side of the ship. "I'm going to put it down just short of—"

Without any warning, the engine quit and began spooling down.

Scott immediately turned toward the ship and said a silent prayer of thanks. *Thank you, God. I'll take it from here.*

Jackie scrambled to the aft section of the cabin, then heaved the cargo door out and strapped in next to Greg and Maritza.

"At least we made it to the ship," Jackie said as she braced for the impact. "I'm feeling lucky."

"Yeah," Greg said in a pained voice. "We'll be okay."

Scott lowered the flaps and adjusted the bank angle so he wouldn't be headed straight for the motor launch. Two extremely bright spotlights suddenly illuminated the preferred landing area, but Scott couldn't stretch the glide that far.

"Easy Rider," Scott radioed as he ripped off the night vision aid. "I've lost the engine. I'll be dropping in short of your lights."

"Short?"

"I need the lights about three hundred yards out?" Scott exclaimed. "I've lost the engine."

"Will do," a different voice said as the lights panned farther out from the ship. "How's that?"

"Outstanding," Scott said as he smoothly flared the airplane and flipped on the landing light. "You can get the launch under way."

"They're headed your way."

"Great."

Because of the Caravan's fixed landing gear, Dalton had to slow the airplane as much as possible before he plopped the Cessna into the water. If the nose wheel dug in at high speed, it could force the airplane up on its nose and over on its back. Altitude and airspeed control would be critical during the final seconds of flight.

"Here we go," Scott shouted as he held the turboprop a few feet above the water and allowed it to bleed off speed in ground effect. He gingerly worked the trim, nursing the airplane along until it was almost fully stalled. Relying on his seat-of-the-pants instincts, he eased the yoke back when the Caravan stalled with the wheels ten inches above the water.

The big turboprop mushed into the Mediterranean as a huge spray of water engulfed the entire airplane. It rocked up on its nose, then gently settled back as Jackie tossed the life raft out. She pulled the exposed lanyard to eject the raft from its case and fully inflate it.

Scott unstrapped and hurried to the aft cabin to help Jackie get Maritza and Greg into the life raft. The airplane was rapidly filling with water, which made the task more difficult and time consuming. Moments after Scott and Jackie assisted Maritza into the raft, the motor launch arrived. A trained rescue swimmer leaped into the water to help with Greg. Less than three minutes later the motor launch was headed for the ship. Shivering in the bow of the boat, Scott felt Jackie's fingers dig into his arm as the Caravan's tail rose straight up and then disappeared beneath the sea.

He cupped her hand and shrugged. "As soon as we're aboard, we'll contact Hartwell."

Jackie nodded, then took a deep breath and exhaled. "If Maritza is up to it, she can give him the brief."

"Good idea."

"We did it," she said triumphantly, and put her arms around his waist. "I have a bottle of fifty-year-old scotch stashed in my stateroom. Care to join me for a small celebration."

Scott smiled warmly. "That's the best invitation I've ever had."

"My instincts," she whispered in his ear, "tell me that that's not true."

## The Oval Office

Deeply disturbed by the debacle in the Gulf, President Macklin impatiently glanced at his wristwatch while his national security adviser finished his conversation on the "secure" line. Hartwell Prost quickly wrapped up his business and joined the president and two Secret Service agents. With the agents in close proximity, Macklin and Prost began walking toward the executive mansion.

"I just got the word," Prost said, falling in step with Macklin. "Dalton and company managed to extract Ms. Gunzelman."

"Outstanding," the president exclaimed. "At last, thank God, something went as planned this evening."

"Well, *not* exactly."

"What do you mean?" the president asked, mindful of the risks involved in the dangerous rescue attempt.

"They apparently flew into an ambush, like our people in the Gulf."

Macklin bristled, but made no comment.

"Dalton and Sullivan are okay," Prost continued in a business-as-usual voice, "but Scott's pilot was seriously injured, and Ms. Gunzelman broke her ankle."

The president reached inside his jacket and extracted a cigar. "What's the extent of the pilot's injuries?"

"Gunshot wounds to his leg and shoulder," Prost explained, then added, "He flew cover when Dalton was shot down during the Gulf War."

"Get both of them to Bethesda," Macklin said as he lighted his cigar, "and make *damn* sure they have the best of everything, including rehab—whatever it takes."

"Yes, sir."

In silence, the four men continued their journey to the second story residential quarters. Once they reached the presidential living area, Macklin and Prost settled into comfortable lounge chairs on the softly lighted Truman balcony. The president eyed his cigar while the agents fanned out to opposite sides of the railed platform.

Externally calm, Macklin stared across the wide expanse of the South Lawn. "Well, give it to me straight."

Prost paused thoughtfully. "First, I have some other disturbing news."

"The bad news before the bad news."

"I'm afraid so. One of our carrier helos fished the remains of a Russian pilot out of the Gulf. He's been identified as Major Viktor Kasatkin, a Russian fighter pilot who was apparently instructing the Iranians in advanced fighter tactics."

With the smallest of smiles, the president shook his head. "Well, it's time to play hardball with Moscow, and set a date for a summit. I'll take it up with Shannon. Now, tell me about Ms. Gunzelman."

"She has given us a lot of information," he said without expression. "Besides Bassam Shakhar and Khaliq Farkas, a man named Massoud Ramazani has been activated to assist in carrying out the threats issued by Shakhar."

The president narrowed his gaze in sharp question. "What do we know about Ramazani?"

"According to Ms. Gunzelman, he's intelligent," Prost explained matter-of-factly. "He's shrewd, and, until recently, he was a professor at the University of Miami."

"What?" Macklin exclaimed in outrage. "You're telling me that we had a terrorist teaching in one of our universities?"

Prost nodded.

*"Terrific,"* the president said in disgust.

Macklin eyed his friend with a mildly disapproving look. "Are they working in unison, or leading separate groups?"

"We aren't sure, but Ms. Gunzelman thinks it's a team effort. According to the word inside the compound, Ramazani and Farkas have co-responsibility for paralyzing our commercial air transportation system."

The president quietly nodded.

"If her information is reliable," Hartwell went on, "Ramazani and Farkas have established a base of operations somewhere in the Florida Keys, but she doesn't know the exact location."

"Amazing," Macklin said with a throaty laugh. "We have various intelligence agencies, informants, and listening posts around the world. We have the CIA's Global Response Center and Counter Terrorism Center, NSA, and the FBI Joint Terrorism Task Force, and not one of them was aware that Farkas was flying an A-4 attack aircraft over U.S. soil—*and* that we had a terrorist teaching at an American university."

The president suddenly stopped, fixing Prost in his gaze. "I apologize if I'm offending you, but surely you see the irony in this?"

Prost remained unflappable. "Your point is well taken."

"We have all this vast network in place," Macklin said with a theatrical wave of his arms, "and no one in the loop knows shit."

With his anger seething just below the surface, the president continued. "On the other hand, working independent of the government, we have a smart, gutsy young woman who managed to work her way straight to the heart of a major terrorist organization."

Macklin pointed a finger at Prost. "Now that, my friend, is espionage personified. No question about it. We need to get her on the payroll."

"Mr. President," Prost said without any sign of resentment, "I strongly recommend that we tighten air travel security, and do it now."

"I agree," Macklin said, pondering the DFW crash. "What do you recommend?"

"We need to go to Level Four and immediately prohibit curbside check-in," Hartwell stated emphatically. "In addition, we need to use every intel capability we have—military and civilian—to provide aerial recon over and around our major and regional airports."

The president remained quiet for a long moment, then gazed across the South Lawn. "I'll give the order tonight."

"The sooner, the better," Prost said firmly. "These people know our weaknesses, and they aren't like Saddam Hussein's ragtag crew. They're sneakier, nastier, better organized, better financed, and they have a suicidal resolve to complete their missions."

"I share your sense of urgency," the president said, then sighed heavily. "What else did Ms. Gunzelman have to say?"

Clearly uncomfortable, Prost avoided the president's unnerving gaze. "Russian advisers—chemical and biological experts—have been working with Shakhar's terrorist groups."

Macklin's anger showed in his eyes. "Another reason to turn the screws on Moscow and Tehran."

"I couldn't agree more."

"What else from Ms. Gunzelman?"

Prost frowned and took a deep breath, then let it out. "To her knowledge, Farkas and Ramazani have personally been charged with the responsibility of assassinating you, or facing death themselves." He paused, letting the full weight of his words resonate.

"Well, that sure tops off a swell day," Macklin said sarcastically.

Prost spoke in a flat, emotionless voice. "Ramazani and

Farkas have solid reputations for achieving their goals. We can't discount them."

The president's imagination was stimulated. "Give me the whole story, and don't filter anything."

"We have to assume that Farkas and Ramazani *are* indeed spearheading a highly concerted effort to kill you," Prost said in a steady voice. "We've already seen what Farkas is capable of doing, and Ramazani is considered to be even more bold and clever. Working alone, they are very good at what they do. Working as a team, they have the potential to accomplish anything that Shakhar wants them to accomplish."

Macklin calmly blew a smoke ring into the warm night air. "What do you recommend?"

"The same thing I recommended before."

"I'm not leaving the White House," the president announced defiantly.

"That's fine," Prost fired back. "However, if something happens to you, I'm not going to look in the mirror for the rest of my life and know that I was derelict in my duties."

"Consider your duty fully discharged," Macklin said, painfully conscious that Prost was right.

Restless, Hartwell spoke in a subdued voice. "One last thing," he said slowly, and paused. "Shakhar has reportedly sent a Hiroshima-strength nuclear bomb to the U.S."

Macklin's expression took on a stunned look. "Well, you certainly saved the best for last."

Prost remained unperturbed.

A sudden moodiness settled over the president. "He obviously got it from the Russians, so the real question is where did he send it and what does he plan to do with it?"

"According to Ms. Gunzelman, it's onboard a large motoryacht at their base of operations in the Florida Keys. Unfortunately, she doesn't know anything about the yacht, except she believes it's over one hundred feet long."

"What's their plan?"

"She thinks they're going to take the yacht up the Potomac to Washington and blow D.C. flatter than a Kansas wheat field."

"The hell they will," the president said harshly, then softened his tone. "I want this to be your number-one priority. Use whatever resources you need, but get to digging on this."

"Yes, sir."

"Find that yacht!"

"With your permission," Prost went on, "I want to keep this under wraps. I don't want people running in circles and alerting the media."

Macklin's brow furrowed. "You have a point there."

"Before we get anyone else involved," Prost suggested, "I'd like to ask Dalton and Sullivan to see what they can come up with. I want them to comb every inch of the Keys from the tip of the mainland to Key West."

"Do what you need to do," Macklin said dryly. "I want results, and I want them now. They have seventy-two hours—not one hour longer—to produce something of significance, or we'll do it a different way."

"Understood."

"One other thing," the president said stiffly. "Let Sullivan and Dalton know about the nuclear bomb—the possibility that a nuke may be on the yacht."

"Yes, sir," Hartwell said, then cast a look at the Secret Service agents. "Mr. President," he said with a sudden change of heart, "may I have a private word with you on another subject?"

Macklin looked perplexed. "Hartwell, you know you can be candid with me. What is it?"

"Sir," Prost said with a deep sigh, "what I have to say to you *must* be in private. I trust you understand."

Hovering in the background, one of the agents spoke before Macklin could respond. "Mr. President, we'll be inside if you need us."

"I appreciate it," Macklin said, a keenness in his look. He waited until the men were out of hearing distance. "Should I have a stiff drink first?"

"It wouldn't hurt," Prost began with sadness in his voice. "I had planned to sleep on this before I discussed it with you, but I've come to the conclusion that it can't wait."

A sudden tautness claimed the president's expression. "Lay your cards on the table," he said with a wary voice.

Prost hung his head, then looked up. "According to Ms. Gunzelman, we *do* have a leak in the White House."

Taken aback, the president's face hardened into a dark frown. "That's a very serious charge."

A long silence followed, which neither one wanted to fill.

Macklin took a long pull on his cigar and walked to the railing. "You better come clean with me. Who is it?"

"She doesn't know. She's heard Shakhar refer to his 'contact' in the White House, but she doesn't know who it is."

Deeply troubled by the disturbing news, the president turned and faced his close confidant. "What do your instincts tell you?"

Eyeing each other in the soft glow, both men felt the strain of silence.

"Sir, I have to be honest."

"Go on," Macklin demanded.

"I've noticed a subtle change in Fraiser."

The blunt statement shocked the president. "You better explain yourself, and it better be good."

"As you know," Prost began, somewhat tiredly, "Fraiser has a propensity—a desire to live above his means."

"The point?" Macklin demanded in a thickened voice.

"He recently purchased an expensive country estate near Charlottesville." Prost kept his expression bland. "And, last week, he took delivery of a new Lamborghini Diablo roadster."

The president's expression remained impassive. "If he can afford the payments, it's certainly none of our business."

"Sir, his government salary is his primary source of income."

Macklin studied his cigar for a moment. "Hartwell," he said with a look of impatience, "I know Fraiser isn't the most frugal person in the world, but I'm sure he's been investing wisely for a number of years."

"Wisely enough," Prost countered with icy calm, "to pay cash for a two-point-three million country estate, *and* a quarter-million dollar sports car to park next to his '99 Ferrari?"

Macklin stared at him in confusion. "You're positive about this? You checked it yourself?"

"I'm positive."

The president's face reflected a sense of bewilderment. "For the time being, we'll keep this to ourselves."

Prost quietly nodded.

"Before we do anything else," Macklin continued, "I want the FBI to check into this."

"I agree."

The president's eyes bored into Prost. "First thing in the morning," he said with a sharp pitch in his voice, "we'll have the director over for a chat."

In silence, Prost walked to the balcony railing and cast a glance over the grounds. "I hope there'll be a reasonable explanation."

"So do I," Macklin said as he turned to his friend. "It's been one helluva day. How about joining me for a nightcap?"

"Thank you, sir," Prost said in a hushed tone. "I could use one."

# 29

## The Florida Keys

Basking in the warmth of the sweet breezes, Massoud Ramazani watched the sun dip into the turquoise-and-emerald waters. While day slowly faded into twilight, the tranquil bay of the small island was tinted a coral pink.

In the distance, a gleaming white yacht slowed as it approached the expansive private dock. Walking barefoot through the soft, white sand, Ramazani crossed the narrow beach and walked to the end of the wooden pier. He was fascinated by the graceful lines of *Bon Vivant*. The magnificent 126-foot Broward motoryacht was equipped with digital satellite television, twin satellite-communications suites, and an Aerospatiale Gazelle helicopter sitting on the renovated upper sundeck. Sporting a fresh coat of paint, the revamped vessel looked like a new ship.

While the captain edged *Bon Vivant* next to the dock, Hamed Yahyavi, Khaliq Farkas's trusted assistant, acknowledged Ramazani while he and the helicopter pilot studied the tiny island.

Surrounded by a man-made coral breakwater and a cement seawall, the lushly tropical compound consisted of an open and airy four-bedroom home and two spacious guest cottages. Totally self-contained, the residence was equipped with a twin generator system and a backup portable generator, solar heat, and bottled gas for cooking.

Less than a mile from the mainland, the home was close to a small airport that could accommodate most corporate jets. Secluded and quiet, the residence provided security and cover for Ramazani's terrorist cells. The former owners were pleased to learn that the real-estate auction firm they retained had sold the property to a retired banker from Pittsburgh.

Massoud smiled with pleasure when he thought about the role the yacht would play in their assault on the U.S. and their primary target, President Macklin. However, Yahyavi's upcoming trip to Atlanta with Farkas took precedence in the schedule of events. By declaration of Bassam Shakhar, Farkas and Yahyavi would have the first opportunity to become heroes to anti-American groups worldwide.

After *Bon Vivant* was secured to the dock, Ramazani went aboard and greeted Yahyavi and four handpicked three-man special action cells. To a person, the men smiled broadly and exuded a sense of warmth and friendliness to everyone. Dressed in attire ranging from expensive suits to blue denim work clothes, the highly skilled teams would use portable antiaircraft missiles to create chaos in the U.S. airline industry. Farkas would bring the weapons with him in the Citation, then cram Yahyavi and two of the three-man cells into the jet and drop the missileers near their targeted airports. Fifty-eight other cells would be operating from Los Angeles, New York City, Philadelphia, Baltimore, Seattle, Minneapolis–St. Paul, Oakland, Chicago, Newark, Detroit, and Washington, D.C.

Off to the side of the special action cells, three "throwaways" were standing together. The vacant look in the men's dull eyes left no doubt about their fate. Although they were not very intelligent, the men were as dedicated as World War II Kamikaze pilots to their mission of self-sacrifice. They only needed to be aimed in the proper direction.

Ramazani was surprised when *Bon Vivant*'s unsmiling captain grimly eyed him. Tall, with deeply set blue eyes and blond hair, the man was a walking portrait of a crusty Nordic sea dog. Paid a princely sum for shepherding the yacht across the unpredictable Atlantic, the retired cruise-ship captain was anxious to return home. His apprentice first mate, a member of the Iranian Revolutionary Guardsmen, would take over as the captain of *Bon Vivant.*

"Follow me," the skipper said curtly as he motioned to Ramazani.

While Yahyavi gathered his belongings from his small stateroom, the potbellied captain escorted Ramazani through a mahogany-paneled formal dining room to an elegant king-size master stateroom.

" 'Ave a seat," the skipper said coldly, then knocked on a cabin door and walked out of the room.

Smothering his disdain for the captain, Ramazani sat down next to an open wooden crate containing six AK-47 semi-automatic rifles. The Chinese-made weapons were accompanied by twelve thirty-shot magazines. A moment later a stocky, bearded man with tobacco on his breath walked into the stateroom.

Silently, the former director of the MINATOM Defense Complex at Arzamas-16/Sarov, Russia, opened the double doors leading to the teakwood-trimmed sitting room. Without ceremony or emotion, Sergey Plekhanov unlocked and removed the top of a suitcase-size container. Inside, a thermonuclear bomb was securely mounted in steel straps.

Plekhanov, abandoned by his military sponsors, had dismissed his unpaid guards and walked away from the nuclear weapons complex with the powerful weapon. Fearing the worst for his family, he buried the bomb under a dilapidated factory, then gathered his wife and daughter and escaped from Russia during a blizzard. Networking with colleagues who were working on nuclear projects in Iran, Plekhanov and his family made their way to Bushehr, Iran.

Two weeks after leaving Russia, Plekhanov met with two of Bassam Shakhar's agents who struck a deal with him. He gave them a map and detailed instructions to the location of the weapon. A month later Shakhar had a powerful nuclear bomb to use on the Americans and Plekhanov and his family moved into a comfortable apartment in Bushehr.

Transfixed by the sight of the weapon, Ramazani was momentarily at a loss for words. *I can't believe it's here.*

"I show you how to detonate bomb," the Russian scientist announced in an impatient voice. "Then I leave you to your work."

### The *Permak Express*

The tedious, painful process of stabilizing Greg's condition had consumed the better part of thirteen hours. Afterward the ship's male nurse prepared Maritza and Greg for the long flight to the U.S. With the patients resting comfortably in the cabin of the LongRanger, Jackie and Scott waved at the ship's crew, then she lifted the helicopter from the pad and transitioned to forward flight. Navigating by GPS, she set course for Athens and climbed into the hazy Mediterranean sky.

Working with Hartwell Prost and senior White House aides, Scott had arranged for an Air Force C-141 Starlifter staffed with medics to meet their helo in Athens. The long-range Lockheed workhorse would transport Greg and Maritza to the National Naval Medical Center at Bethesda, Maryland.

Scott and Jackie would accompany their friends to the naval hospital, then fly commercially to Miami to start searching the Florida Keys for the terrorist base of operations.

Scott glanced at Jackie, then gave her a mischievous smile. "Are you comfortable with Hartwell's proposal?"

"Sure," she said lightly, "if I don't think about the fact that this yacht is carrying a nuke."

"Put it out of your mind."

"Right, and stop breathing at the same time."

They remained quiet while Jackie scanned for traffic.

"Someone gave Shakhar's people a heads-up," Scott declared in a flat voice. "This time no one will know how we're conducting the operation. It's just you and me and our seaplane."

Catching sight of another low-flying helicopter, Jackie made a slight course correction. "So, when did you get your seaplane rating?"

"Last summer," he said nonchalantly. "I thought it would be an efficient way to complete my biennial flight review."

A knowing smile broke across Jackie's tanned face. "How much float time do you have?"

Dalton gave her a sheepish grin. "About five hours—enough to get my rating. What about you?"

"Zilch-point-zero."

"That's no problem," Scott said with undisguised bravado. "I'll teach you everything you need to know."

"That's what I'm afraid of." She laughed, then rolled her eyes in his direction. "Has it occurred to you that you don't meet the insurance requirements to rent a floatplane?"

"When you're working with the Agency," he said in mock seriousness, "you don't need to *rent* things."

"Oh," she said with a slow smile. "Let me guess. We're going to use one of the toys they've confiscated from the bad guys."

"Actually, it belonged to a seaplane operator who was a little light on his tax returns. The friendly boys at the IRS gave it to the CIA." A look of satisfaction settled over his face. "I'm going to handle this through an old friend from the Agency, so no one but the three of us will know about the arrangement."

"How reliable is your friend?"

"Like the sun coming up in the east."

"That sounds reasonable," she said as they flew over a cruise ship. A few moments passed before Jackie gazed at Scott, her attention focused on his eyes. "At the risk of hurting your pride, I feel compelled to raise an obvious question."

Scott gave her a look of amused indulgence. "You have no confidence in me, right? Is that what you're about to say?"

Jackie arched an eyebrow. "Between the two of us," she said with a straight face, "we have little to zero experience in floatplanes. Wouldn't it be easier and safer if we used a helicopter?"

He hesitated, then smiled broadly and stretched his arms. "And take all the adventure out of it?"

"Seriously."

"We could use a helo," he explained, "but floatplanes and amphibians are a lot more prevalent in the Keys. We need to blend with the surroundings, do the reggae thing—look like free spirits who belong there."

"Parrotheads?" she mused.

"Something like that."

"If you say so, Cap'n." Jackie smiled evenly. "I just want to be on record when we crawl out of the wreckage."

"Duly noted." He chuckled.

"What kind of plane are we going to use?"

"A Maule M-7 on amphibious floats—the same kind I got my rating in—so we're in good shape."

"Yeah, right," she said with typical honesty. "I seem to remember words to that effect in Athens."

Scott's slow smile reflected his usual air of confidence. "He is lifeless who is faultless."

"Too much luck often dulls one's perspective," she suggested gently. "Another old proverb."

"Perhaps," he agreed with a dismissive shrug. "In any event, we're going to use my rule book this time."

She inclined her head to him. "Your book has no rules."

"You got it."

Jackie checked the engine instruments and turned to Scott. "What are your plans for Thanksgiving?"

He gave her a quizzical look and slowly smiled. "That's— what—five months away?"

"I like to plan ahead."

"I haven't made any plans." He grinned. "You have something in mind?"

"How about having dinner with me at my parents' home?"

"Sure," he said with a surprised look. "I'd be honored."

"Not so fast," she said with a chuckle. "You haven't met my parents."

# 30

## Washington, D.C.

The handpicked Marine guards assigned to the White House had exchanged their dress uniforms for battle fatigues and machine guns. With the commander in chief a target of embittered militants, the grounds of the White House were being patrolled by two highly trained platoons of Marines. Led by seasoned first lieutenants, the "tough as nails" veterans specialized in counterterrorism.

Inside the White House, Secret Service agents refined their plans to spirit the president from the Oval Office in the event of an attack by terrorists. At the first indication of an assault, an agent would push a panel on a wall adjacent to the president's rest room, causing a secret door to slide open. A staircase leading down to a brightly lit tunnel provided the president a means of escape to his private elevator, or another exit near an office that had once served as the White House barbershop.

The risk of further conflict with Iran had sent a shudder through the financial capitals of the world. Concern over who would eventually control the Strait of Hormuz had caused oil futures on the Chicago commodities market to triple in value. Reporting the conflict in great detail, the media anchors and pundits were generally lukewarm to President Macklin and his handling of the situation. World reaction to the attack on Iran had been sharply divided, with many nations in the Middle East fearful of a major war erupting in the Gulf region.

The Jockey Club in the Ritz-Carlton Hotel presented a logistical nightmare for the Secret Service, but the president and the first lady insisted on having lunch at least twice a month at the famed power-crowd watering hole. Regardless of the situation in the Persian Gulf, Macklin remained adamant about projecting a calm, relaxed demeanor to the public.

Playing their usual roles in the kitchen and in the dark-paneled dining room, six agents went about their duties dressed as captains, waiters, and busboys. Near the heavy glass door just off the hotel's small lobby, other agents disguised as high-powered Washington insiders and hotel bell captains watched for any signs of trouble.

Earlier, before the club opened, the restaurant had been thoroughly checked for eavesdropping devices and other intelligence-gathering paraphernalia. Satisfied that the club was sanitized, the Secret Service had given the president the standard spiel about lip-readers. In public, Macklin and his wife generally kept their conversations light and pleasant, especially with respect to sensitive matters that could compromise his administration. Today would not be one of those days.

Seated at Table 14, a cozy corner retreat where a couple could dine and not only see, but be seen, the president and his attractive wife were enjoying a glass of wine with their chicken salad. A shapely brunette a decade younger than her husband, Maria Eden-Macklin sat with her long legs discreetly crossed at the ankles. Self-schooled to project the proper image of a first lady, Maria's face seldom reflected anything other than a pleasant expression when she was seen in public. Today, however, the retired foreign correspondent was having a difficult time keeping her emotions beneath the surface.

Maria pushed up the elbow-length sleeves of her tailored designer suit, smiled, then leaned closer to the president and whispered in her ear. "May I speak frankly?"

The president returned her smile and sipped his Chardonnay. "You always do," he said with a chuckle.

She raised her wineglass to conceal her lips: "I don't think you should press your luck." She smiled in a faintly autocratic manner. "You should be forthright about the submarine. If it's missing, have Pete go on television and admit it."

"Maria," the president said lightly, "you know this isn't the time"—he glanced around the room—"or the place to bring up that subject. We'll discuss it later in private."

"You have a full schedule until late this evening," she declared in a quiet, firm voice. "We need to talk about this *now*, before someone leaks it to the press. Pete needs to be honest about the situation."

"It isn't quite that simple." Macklin maintained a hint of a smile and talked in a hushed voice. "Pete and Les don't want to unnecessarily alarm the families of the crew, in case *Hampton* makes contact in the next day or two."

Briefly, Maria studied her husband. "If something *has* happened to it, you're going to come across as deceitful. Remember the Trident that sailed to the wrong station in the Pacific and hid for more than a week?"

"Maria, not now," he said impatiently.

"It was rigged for quiet," she hastily continued, "and so deeply submerged that it wasn't able to send or receive messages?"

"They could receive signals by slow underwater methods."

Again she raised her wineglass to her lips. "Not if the sender is thousands of miles away."

"Let's drop it," the president insisted.

"For nine days," she said in a hushed voice, "the United States Navy was missing a Trident nuclear-missile submarine and no one had any idea where it was."

"Okay, so a mistake was made," he said with a trace of irritation. "No one likes to admit things like that."

"What's more," she went on, "a shrewd reporter got wind of the story and embarrassed the Navy and the White House. Don't be deceitful," she quietly admonished. "You're the commander in chief."

Macklin returned a casual wave from the chairman of the House Ways and Means Committee. "We're going to roll the dice," the president said under his breath. "If it's just a communications failure, then we're okay. No one is going to get upset."

"If it hasn't been a communications problem," she suggested, barely moving her lips, "then what?"

The president felt the hard probe of her gaze. "Then I'll do what I have to do. I respect their advice."

"Even if they're wrong?"

"They're advisers, not prophets." He sensed her faint recoil and reached for her hand. "I appreciate your concern, you know that."

She nodded and raised an eyebrow, then gazed around the room while she asked a question. "If you ask Pete to resign, will he do it gracefully?"

"I'm sure he would," Macklin answered, surprised by the question. "Why do you ask?"

She reached for her napkin and lightly touched the edge of her mouth. "The mood on the Hill is ugly. They're going to want someone's head at the hearings." Maria smiled at two well-heeled socialites as they rose to leave. "They're going to make it tough for Pete, and probably Les, too. You'll be next if you don't shake up the Pentagon and the White House to feed the wolves."

"Maria," the president said in a low, even voice as he acknowledged a senior senator. "Try not to frown."

With a catlike gleam in her eyes, she smiled as if he'd just told her an amusing story, then lowered her voice. "We've been humiliated in Iran twice, and this situation has the potential to be a much bigger debacle than Desert One."

The first lady was referring to the three Marines and five airmen who died in 1980 while attempting to rescue fifty-two American hostages from the Ayatollah Khomeini. The accident happened when a C-130 tanker plane and a helicopter collided in the staging area after a sandstorm and mechanical problems caused the mission to be aborted.

"No one knows that better than I do," Macklin retorted in a hushed voice as he glanced around the room.

"Now," she declared with a troubled look, "one of our newest aircraft carriers is being towed to a shipyard, *and* we can't account for one of our nuclear submarines. It makes you look incompetent."

"Maria, please," the president said a shade defensively.

She calmly ignored him and raised her wineglass. "It's embarrassing to us as a nation, and the committee is going to hold you personally responsible."

"They *should* hold me responsibile," Macklin stated emphatically, and finished the last sip of his wine. Running his fingers back and forth over the red and white tablecloth, the president thought about the members of the Senate Armed Services Committee. To a person, Macklin respected them, but he knew they weren't going to cut him any slack just because of his strong support for the military.

He studied his wife's aqua-blue eyes. "Maria, I don't want you to worry about this situation."

"I'm not worried about the *situation*—I'm worried about *you*," she declared, and then spoke more softly. "The hearing will be extremely contentious. You know that."

"Yes, I do."

"It could cost you a second term in office."

There was a long silence.

"I don't think so," Macklin finally said. "They clearly understand that the security of the Persian Gulf is vital to the United States, and to the economic well-being of the world. They also know that things *can* go wrong during military operations."

"Like bombing the Chinese embassy in Belgrade," she said mechanically.

"War isn't a precise—" Macklin flared, then stopped himself in mid-sentence.

"It's your reputation that's on the line," she said in a hushed voice, "and it's your future at stake."

"Maria, the United States is in the Persian Gulf to stay, no question about it. There is no alternative, and the committee knows that. We're *the* big fish in the pond."

"Apparently," she paused, trying to hide her skepticism, "the top dogs in Baghdad and Tehran didn't get the word."

The president stifled the impulse to respond to her remark.

"The major terrorist groups have announced a call to arms," she said with a vague shrug of her shoulders. "If it were me, I'd try to deflect what happened in the Gulf, and explain what I'd do to keep our country from being held hostage by a bunch of lunatics."

"That's precisely what we're working on," he asserted, and

flashed a quick smile for the sake of the luncheon patrons who occasionally glanced at the first couple. "Now relax and enjoy your lunch."

"Right," she murmured. "We're living in a residence surrounded by concrete barriers and armed men—Marines with real bullets. And, as of yesterday, we have over a dozen men with portable missile launchers on the roof. It's like being confined to a palace in the middle of some third-rate banana republic."

Before Macklin could answer, he noticed the Secret Service agents, in unison, cast a glance at the entrance to the Jockey Club. A moment later Fraiser Wyman walked through the door and headed straight for the president's favorite table.

Macklin felt a sudden flush of adrenaline when he saw the strained look on Wyman's face. *Now what?*

"I apologize for interrupting," Wyman said as all eyes turned toward the president's table. "I have to have a word with you, sir."

"Sure," Macklin said hastily as he signaled the dining-room captain. "We'll make it a threesome."

Arrangements were quickly made and Wyman nervously accepted a glass of wine. He had often discussed sensitive matters in the company of the first lady, but he had reservations about speaking openly in the Jockey Club.

"Mr. President," Wyman said quietly and deliberately, "we need to return to the White House as quickly as possible."

Maria spoke first. "Fraiser, take a couple of minutes to enjoy your wine, then leave as unobtrusively as possible. We'll be along in a few minutes."

"Yes, ma'am," he said with a concerned look.

"And smile," she asserted, then gave a nod to a Secret Service agent dressed as a waiter. He slipped into the kitchen to send the signal that the president would be leaving earlier than planned.

When the first couple sat down in the living room of their private quarters, the president noticed Wyman's new diamond-encrusted Rolex. Macklin gave him a half smile. *Somehow, I have to take him out of the loop until Sandra Hatcher and the FBI finish their investigation.*

"I know you don't have good news," the president grumbled, "so let's have it straight out."

"Sir, they—the Navy—found some debris from the *Hampton*."

The president's face went slack before he promptly regained his composure. "When?"

"About forty-five minutes ago."

"What happened?"

"It was sunk—probably by Iran."

"Where?"

"Very close to where they launched the Tomahawks."

"They're positive the debris is from *Hampton*?" Maria asked with only a trace of her usual smile.

"Positive. Something blew the sub apart."

Macklin shuddered. "Any survivors?"

"No, sir."

Maria gave the president an anxious glance. "Who knows about this?"

"I don't know," Wyman confessed, and faced the president. "Sir, we can't sit on this very long. I strongly recommend you go on television and announce what's happened, before the networks break the story."

"Fraiser's right," Maria said firmly. "It isn't good news, but it comes straight from you, before the media can put you on the defensive. Get the bad news out front, then slowly shift the subject to your Cornerstone Summit in Atlanta. It's a major race-relations initiative, and it's very important to America's future. Use it to dilute the controversy about the Gulf, then get on to a message with familiar themes."

"I agree," Wyman hastily added. "It'll help take the focus off the negatives and move the agenda to the positive side—to Atlanta. And, it may move us up in the polls."

Macklin stared at the floor, not really seeing it. *I have to guide this with a steady hand.* "Get the Oval Office ready," he ordered coldly, then glanced at Fraiser's shiny Rolex President.

Wyman caught Macklin's eye. "It's ready sir."

## High Above Georgia

Wearing a uniform adorned with wings and four gold stripes, Khaliq Farkas carefully reviewed the approach procedures

for the William B. Hartsfield Atlanta International Airport.
This was the last leg of his long day, having dropped portable
antiaircraft missiles and terrorist units in other cities.

Drowsy from the afternoon sun warming the cockpit, Farkas yawned, then finished the water in his plastic bottle. The
flight from the Florida Keys had been smooth and uneventful,
and he wanted to keep things that way. He could ill afford
mistakes that might draw critical attention from the en route
air traffic controllers.

After receiving clearance from Atlanta Center, Farkas
eased the Citation I/SP into a gradual descent toward the
bustling airport south of Atlanta. Once established in a stabilized descent, he listened to the automatic terminal information service for Hartsfield International. Afterward he
buttoned his collar and adjusted his tie, then glanced into the
richly upholstered cabin. "Hamed, wake up. We're almost
there."

"I am awake." Dressed in a pricey Giorgio Armani suit,
Hamed Yahyavi casually opened one eye. "How could I possibly sleep?"

Concerned about flying into a major airport, Farkas looked
back a second time. "I want you to help me watch for traffic."

"I'm on my way." He shrugged, then unfastened his seat
belt.

Yahyavi's facial features and body were almost perfect,
including his manicured fingernails and well-groomed dark
hair. Educated in Europe and at the California Institute of
Technology, the electrical engineer appeared to be a normal,
well-adjusted person. However, behind the sensitive, soft
brown eyes and disarming smile was a true psychopath.

Yahyavi made his way to the cockpit, then settled into the
right seat. Looking at the sprawling city, Yahyavi smiled
when he thought about their plan. He and Farkas had per-
fected the procedures in Tel Aviv during May of '96. The
Ben Gurion International Airport was shut down for three
hours while they panicked pilots and flight controllers. If they
had conducted their experiment at night, or in bad weather,
the results could have been even more spectacular.

The weather conditions for the Atlanta operation looked
extremely favorable—low ceilings and rain—but no one
could predict with absolute certainty whether the atmospheric

elements would cooperate on any particular morning. If the aviation forecast came to pass, tomorrow morning would be a memorable one for a number of people.

Initially, Yahyavi had argued against the bold plan, pointing out the high risks involved, and the lack of total control over the outcome of the venture. However, Farkas had convinced him that the scheme could be executed without fear of detection.

Arriving at Hartsfield International, Farkas cleared the active runway and taxied to the Mercury Air Center fixed-base operator. An energetic customer-service representative met the airplane and quickly made arrangements for a rental car to be brought to the corporate jet. When the car arrived, Farkas and Yahyavi carefully loaded their equipment into the Crown Victoria.

Afterward Farkas placed the engine covers on the Pratt & Whitneys, locked the airplane, and then chauffeured his "boss" to the registration parking area at the Atlanta Airport Marriott.

After they checked into separate rooms using the names on their counterfeit credit cards, Farkas closely observed a bellhop while he pushed a baggage cart to the rental car. The talkative teenager loaded the two plywood-and-steel containers on the cart, tossed the other luggage on top of the trunks, then followed Farkas to his room overlooking the airport.

# 31

The early morning was aglow in shades of soft pink and pastel gray when Scott taxied the Maule M-7 floatplane away from the seaplane base. With a high power-to-weight ratio, the Short Takeoff and Landing (STOL) aircraft is virtually unmatched in any other high-wing-strut-braced airplane.

In the right seat, Jackie was organizing the charts, binoculars, cell phone, and camera for quick access. With the seventy-two-hour deadline running out, they were anxious to start searching for the terrorist's yacht and their base of operations. Uncomfortable with the possibility of encountering a nuclear bomb on the yacht, they had avoided discussing the subject.

Dalton was attired in oversized khaki shorts, deck shoes, and a loud, extra-large, multicolored aloha shirt. Multiple magnetic "pierced" earrings, and a Cubs baseball cap, worn backward—completed his eclectic ensemble. His nine-millimeter Sig Sauer was concealed at the back of his baggy shorts.

Jackie's fashion statement included faded denim short-shorts, a revealing sequined tank top, red-and-white sandals, an assortment of inexpensive rings and flashy earrings. Topping off the eye-popping garb, Jackie sported classic Douglas

MacArthur aviator sunglasses, a glitzy straw hat with a dozen yellow flowers on one side, and a large canvas tote bag that contained her nine-millimeter Glock.

After energizing the landing light, anticollision beacon, and navigation lights, Scott advanced the power to do a brief run-up, then allowed the floatplane to weathervane into the light breeze. He set the flaps, made sure Jackie's seat belt was secure, checked the trim and rudders, then surveyed the area for boats and other floatplanes. Satisfied that the area was clear of obstacles, Scott brought the yoke fully aft and added full power to raise the propeller out of the spray.

"Here we go," he announced in a confident voice.

As the speed rapidly increased, he shoved the yoke forward to force the amphibious floats up and "on the step" much like a speedboat skims across the surface of water.

"This is great," Jackie exclaimed as the floats slapped the water. "Mind if I follow through on the controls?"

"You might as well fly it," Scott said firmly as he removed his hands from the throttle and yoke. "Can you reach the rudder pedals?"

"Yes—no problem," she answered as she smoothly took control of the airplane. "I've got it."

"Just a touch of back pressure," he coached as the Maule skipped twice and gently lifted into the smooth morning air. "Carry on. I'll handle the sectional chart"—referring to their Miami aeronautical chart.

"Okay by me," Jackie said as she took in the aerial view of cruise ships in the port of Miami. "How high do you want to cruise?"

"Let's try three hundred feet."

"Sounds good." Jackie glanced at the Miami skyline and turned to take in the Atlantic. "I have a question?"

"Shoot."

"Should we concentrate on yachts in the one-hundred-foot-or-larger range, or should we check everything over fifty to sixty feet?"

"I'd say eighty feet and over," he suggested. "It's just a hunch, but I don't think anything smaller would have the cruising range to make it across the South Atlantic."

Jackie scanned the horizon. "Unless they installed extra fuel tanks."

"That's a possibility, but I think we should concentrate on the larger yachts on the way down. If we don't have any luck, we'll check the smaller boats on the way back."

"Sounds like a plan."

The sun began inching above the horizon as they flew low over Biscayne Bay, then followed the intracoastal waterway past Soldier Key and Islandia.

"You might want to step up to five hundred feet," Scott said as he studied a private airstrip east of Card Sound. "We'll drop down again after we cross Highway One."

She added power, then glanced back in both directions. "We're venting fuel over the right wing."

"I know. This thing has been sitting neglected for a long time and the fuel cap is slightly warped."

"Well, that's comforting news. I wonder what else is wrong with it?"

"Hey, if it craters, we'll plop it on the water and find another ride."

"Yeah," Jackie said under her breath. "We haven't crashed anything for almost a week."

Ignoring her ribbing, Scott used the binoculars to study the Florida Keys as the coral-and-limestone islands and reefs curved southwesterly into the Gulf of Mexico. At this hour of the morning, traffic was light on the Overseas Highway that runs from the mainland to Key West, the southernmost settlement in the United States.

Flying over the emerald hues of Key Largo's pristine waters, Scott searched for anything that looked suspicious, including large yachts, and homes on private islands.

"Okay, we can step down to three hundred feet."

Jackie eased the nose down.

Scott focused his attention on Rock Harbor. "Let's drift over by the ocean side and take a look."

"Okay."

Banking toward the Atlantic, Jackie surveyed the greenish blue seas. As the warm sun rose above the ocean, the sky turned azure and highlighted the clear waters and white sweeps of beach. The day promised unlimited visibility and typical balmy breezes.

Approaching Plantation Key, Scott focused his binoculars on a magnificent Hatteras motoryacht named *Princess Fa-*

*tiya*. The passengers relaxing over breakfast on the aft deck were unquestionably of Middle Eastern lineage.

"How about a wide three-sixty to the left?" he asked as he reached for his Pentax. "I'm gonna snap a few pictures."

"Coming around," Jackie said as she checked for other aircraft. "See anything interesting?"

"I thought I did, but they have small children on board."

She stretched to see over Scott's shoulder. "It might be a ruse."

"That's possible, but I have my doubts." He took a few more pictures as they completed the circle. "Terrorists don't operate that way."

Rolling out straight and level, Jackie glanced across a wide expanse of hazy green water. "Florida Bay looks pretty shallow."

"It's very shallow. Three to four feet in some places, and it's full of coral that'll tear the bottom out of a boat."

Jackie looked west as far as she could see. "That explains why there aren't any boats out there."

"At least not any on the surface," he declared with a grin.

Concentrating on the dock and ships at Plantation Key, Scott took numerous pictures of the million-dollar yachts. "I don't think we're going to find anything here. Terrorists aren't into world-class sportfishing, or socializing over cocktails."

Continuing southwest over a private seaplane base, they passed Islamorada, on Upper Matecumbe Key, then flew low over Craig and Long Key State Park. Scott photographed yachts and homes along the way and reloaded his camera as they neared Marathon, the largest town in the middle of the Keys.

"They have a nice airport here," Scott said as he keyed the radio and gave an advisory call to other aircraft to report the Maule's position and Jackie's intentions.

"That looks interesting," he said, pointing to a small island with a sprawling home on it.

"It sure does."

"I'll take it," Scott advised as he assumed control of the airplane.

"You have it."

"Complete with a seagoing megayacht," Scott uttered as

he banked the Maule to investigate the remote home. "They even have their own helicopter on the yacht."

"That's the only way to travel," Jackie observed dryly.

Scott was intrigued by the impressive home. "Not a bad shack."

Protected by a coral breakwater and a moat, the estate was situated in the middle of an acre of plush tropical landscaping. Surrounded by emerald-and-turquoise waters, the isolated home and both guest cottages appeared to be in excellent condition.

Caught off guard by the distant sound of an airplane, Massoud Ramazani barked commands to the men loading supplies on *Bon Vivant*. One of the team leaders quickly grabbed a tarp and covered two portable antiaircraft missiles lying in the bottom of a utility boat.

"Hurry," Ramazani exclaimed as he rushed across the crowded dock. "Get out of sight!"

Within seconds, everyone disappeared inside the yacht or ran for cover inside the home. Wearing white slacks and a double-breasted blue blazer, Ramazani casually strolled onto the main deck of the yacht and walked toward the bow. He glanced up and smiled as the yellow-and-white floatplane banked overhead. *Where's the blue-eyed, blond-haired captain when I really need him?*

With a show of lazy indifference, Ramazani cast a slow glance at the Maule and waved in a cordial manner.

"Jackie," Scott said as he studied the man on the yacht. "Do you see anything unusual?"

Her eyes narrowed when she noticed the rows of unweathered wood at one end of the pier. "It looks as if they've recently extended the dock to accommodate the yacht."

"Yeah, like in the last month or so." He gently rocked the wings in recognition of the friendly wave. "Take a look at the boxes stacked on the ship and the dock."

Jackie leaned around Scott for a better view. "It looks like they're preparing to get under way, but—"

"Where's the crew?" he inserted. "Would you mind taking some shots while I circle the place?"

"I'm already on it," Jackie said as she snapped photos of

the yacht and the helicopter. "Try to keep the wingtip slightly above the horizon."

"Okay," Scott said as he eased into a shallow turn. "That's an odd color for a helicopter."

She focused her attention on the helo and took more pictures. "It looks like desert camouflage that's been painted over."

"Yeah, with brown stripes that don't match where they join at the tail."

"That's odd."

Scott concentrated on the small flag displayed on the side of the helicopter. *That looks familiar.*

Jackie scanned the water and sky, but her peripheral vision caught a reflection and movement off to her side.

"We have traffic," Jackie exclaimed as she instinctively reached for the controls. "Level at one-o'clock—*watch it!*"

Glancing at the oncoming floatplane, Scott racked the Maule into a tight, knife-edge turn as the red Cessna 206 ripped past only feet away.

"Holy shit," Dalton gasped as he rolled wings level. "Did you see a landing light?"

"No, nothing," Jackie said breathlessly as she keyed the radio. "Cessna Two-Oh-Six near Marathon," she said with cold rage, "do you copy Maule Seven-Three Bravo?"

A long silence answered her question.

Scott took a deep breath and slowly exhaled. "I'd like to have a chat with that guy, if he lives long enough."

"Maybe we'll run into him later," Jackie said with clenched teeth. "No pun intended."

Scott nodded grimly as he turned the plane back toward the secluded home. "We'll look for him along the way."

Wide-eyed with anger, Jackie slowly shook her head. "We're lit up like a Christmas tree, and he didn't even see us."

"Asleep at the wheel," Scott said as he began another circle around the island home.

"I wouldn't doubt it."

Dalton set up for a low pass along the starboard side of the yacht. "*Bon Vivant.* I want to check the name and see where the ship is registered."

"I'll work on it," Jackie said as she reached for her new

satellite-phone. "I don't know what it is, but something seems amiss."

"I have the same feeling," Scott said as he pulled up to make one more circle around the plush estate. "We'll press on to Key West, see what we find, then head back this way."

After a second's hesitation, she glanced at him. "We'll have to wait until the photo shops open."

"Not this morning," he said with a fleeting smile. "I have a friend who'll process our film and deliver eight-by-tens in less than an hour."

"You know," Jackie said as she studied the yacht and the helicopter. "You amaze me at times."

"Well"—he laughed aloud—"that's a start."

After investigating the area around Bahia Honda State Park, Scott pointed his finger toward the northern shores of the lower Keys. "That entire area is a refuge for the great white heron."

"It's beautiful," Jackie remarked as she folded the sectional chart into a smaller rectangle. "There's an unmarked balloon cable off to the right."

"I see it."

"The cable goes up to fourteen thousand feet," she warned.

"Castrovision," Scott said as he flew toward Pine Island. "We'll check out these smaller Keys, then cross the highway and fly around the south side of Key West." He banked to the right to pass north of the treacherous aerostat location.

Skirting the balloon cable, they looked for anything that might resemble a remote base for terrorist operations.

Jackie reached for the sat-phone when it rang, then signed off after a brief conversation.

"The yacht is registered in Liberia, of all places," she announced, and watched him give her a questioning look.

His reaction was tempered with doubt. "I have a strange feeling, but I don't want to set off any alarms yet."

"Let's head for Key West," she said decisively, and glanced at the fine mist of aviation gasoline venting over the right wing. "We need to get some fuel and head back to that island."

Scott glanced at the gauges. "Yeah, there aren't too many places to get fuel out here. If you'll take it for a minute, I'll call Cindy. She'll take our film to her shop while we get some fuel and grab a quick bite of breakfast."

Jackie gave him a sly smile as she took the controls. "That's what I'd call *concierge* service."

"Hey, she's a special friend."

"I can only imagine."

Passing close to the private airport on Sugarloaf Key, Scott took control of the Maule and contacted Naval Air Station Key West for VFR traffic advisories. With no reported traffic, he made contact with the tower at Key West International while he circumnavigated the southwestern end of the Key and returned to land at the international airport.

"You want to make the landing?" Scott asked as he lowered the landing gear out of the floats.

"Sure, talk me through it."

"Slow to eighty, and ease the power back to 1,700 rpm."

Jackie made a smooth transition as Dalton calmly coached her.

"Flaps to twenty-four," Scott said as he looked in vain for the red floatplane they had encountered near Marathon. "I guess the Cessna driver must have gone on to the Dry Tortugas."

"Just as well," Jackie said as she concentrated on flying the approach. "We have enough on our plate."

"Flaps to forty," Scott said as he scanned the area for other air traffic. "Slow to seventy-five."

"I'm a little high and fast."

"You're doing just fine," Scott advised as they reached a point approximately ten feet above the runway. "Start an easy flare."

"I'm not sure about this," Jackie protested.

"Ease the power back, ease the power, bring it to idle, and hold the attitude you have. Lookin' good, stay with it."

"I'm trying."

The wheels touched down with a surprising softness.

"I have it," Scott said with a wide smile. "Great job."

"Thanks."

Dalton changed the subject when he saw a petite, blond-haired young woman waving at them.

"That's Cindy Simmons," Scott said as he returned the greeting. "She's a real *conch*."

"A what?"

"She's a local—a native," he explained. "Born and raised here."

Looking at the attractive, softly feminine woman, Jackie suddenly felt embarrassed about her own appearance. "I hope we're not going anywhere fancy for breakfast."

"Fancy?" Scott asked, managing to keep a straight face. "I was thinking about Marriott's Casa Marina Resort, if you think we're not too overdressed."

"You wouldn't dare."

# 32

## Hartsfield International Airport

After Khaliq Farkas ordered breakfast from the room service menu, he glanced out his twelfth-floor window at the dense fog and then dialed a telephone number in Washington, D.C. Identifying himself as a current member of the Warehouse Discount Club, Farkas scribbled a few notes while his contact with the carefully modulated voice gave him an update on the flight schedule for *Air Force One*.

The sequence of confidential information, including the estimated time of arrival in Atlanta, was delivered to Farkas in the form of a brief sales pitch for outdoor furniture and garden tools. The lavishly appointed blue, white, and silver jumbo jet was due to land precisely on schedule.

When his room-service order arrived, Farkas quickly polished off the poached eggs and orange juice, then called Hamed Yahyavi. Over coffee and dry toast, they studied the latest weather forecast for the Atlanta area. Although the atmospheric conditions were creating dense fog, which was perfect for their plan, they fervently hoped it wouldn't cause a problem for the arrival of *Air Force One*.

Next, they opened the two custom-crafted plywood-and-steel containers. The trunks housed twelve Bendix/King VHF aircraft radios, six military UHF radios, and three fully charged aircraft batteries. The radios were capable of receiving or transmitting on any military or civilian/general aviation frequencies.

Farkas would be able to listen to transmissions from any aircraft approaching or departing the Atlanta area. He could simply change the frequencies to listen to the Atlanta control tower, clearance delivery, ground control, approach control, departure control, and the Atlanta air-route traffic controllers, including the en route, feeder, and final controllers.

The radio package allowed them to transmit to the pilots on any of the frequencies, or block transmissions on any frequency by pressing and holding the transmit button. Yahyavi had built the special containers to enable them to close the prongs on the side of the boxes to press and hold the transmit buttons, thus freeing them to operate unused radios while the other transceivers disrupted important radio calls between pilots and controllers.

With eighteen radios tuned to a variety of extremely critical frequencies, they could transmit bogus orders to many flights while they blocked all communications on the other sensitive channels. The situation would not be disastrous in clear weather during the daytime because the pilots could visually confirm other conflicting traffic and take corrective measures to avoid midair collisions.

However, in inclement weather, when the flight crews are flying in instrument conditions, they can't see each other. Vectoring a number of converging aircraft toward one another, and assigning them to the same altitude in a reasonably confined area, would be chaotic and most probably catastrophic. The chances of a midair collision would be extremely high.

Placing a particular airplane—*Air Force One*—in a precarious position would be the easy part. Like a crapshoot, the outcome would be impossible to predict because the circumstances are beyond one's total control. But the chances of *Air Force One* swapping paint with another airplane were frighteningly high.

In addition to the radios, Yahyavi had purchased folding antennas that would increase the range of the radios. From their vantage point overlooking the airport boundary, they would be able to disrupt the majority of normal aviation communications and create havoc with the flow of air traffic into Atlanta/Hartsfield International.

They also had two portable radio scanners that allowed them to listen to the various aviation frequencies while they monitored police- and fire-department communications on the public service band.

"Here's an update," Yahyavi said when a revised local weather forecast came on the television.

The conditions were so bad that Delta Air Lines was reporting one-hour delays and twenty-nine of their arriving flights had been diverted to other destinations.

"Almost perfect conditions," Yahyavi said excitedly. "Who could ask for more?"

"No one," Farkas replied as a tiny grin creased his face.

Yahyavi stared into the dark eyes of his accomplice. "Death to the enemies of the revolution! Death to Macklin!"

"With Allahu's blessing," Farkas said bitterly, "the president of the United States will not see another sunrise."

## Andrews Air Force Base, Maryland

Among many other important missions, the Air Mobility Command's elite 89th Airlift Wing is responsible for the operations of the special aircraft used by the president, vice-president, cabinet members, members of Congress, high-ranking dignitaries, and senior members of the U.S. military. The dedicated men and women of the 89th pride themselves on providing the safest and very highest-quality service.

Before leaving his office at Andrews Air Force Base, the 89th Operations Group commander finished his morning coffee, then stepped in front of his full-length mirror. Colonel Curtis Wayne Bolton checked his shiny black shoes, adjusted his tie, and straightened his immaculate blue tunic. Along with the silver command-pilot wings, the colorful rows of decorations were perfectly aligned and centered on his left breast.

The tall, silver-haired officer donned his hat with the scrambled-egg insignia sprawled across the visor, then closed his chart case. It was time for the presidential pilot to board *Air Force One*.

The flight to Atlanta's Hartsfield International Airport had been coordinated with the applicable air-traffic-control agencies, including the Andrews control tower, Washington departure control, en route air-traffic-control centers, and the appropriate Air Force command posts. Every detail of the flight had been double- and sometimes triple-checked.

Approaching the Boeing 747-200B, designated a military VC-25, Bolton returned the crisp salute of Chief Master Sergeant Willard T. Brewer. The good-natured sergeant, whose ancestors included slaves and sharecroppers from the Mississippi Delta, always greeted his pilot with a wide smile. Being associated with transporting the president to the Cornerstone Summit made Brewer's smile seem even wider than usual.

Like the rest of the crew of *Air Force One*, Sergeant Brewer had been individually screened and selected by Colonel Bolton. The well-organized, highly professional team represented the best of the best in the United States Air Force.

Entering the spotless state-of-the-art cockpit, Bolton was greeted by his copilot, Lieutenant Colonel Kirk Upshaw. The young, clean-cut Air Force Academy graduate was a highly motivated officer with a bright future. Upshaw's career aspirations were greatly enhanced by the fact that his father had been an Air Force combat fighter pilot who rose to be chief of staff at Supreme Headquarters, Allied Powers Europe.

"Everything ready to go?" Bolton asked Upshaw while he glanced at the navigation charts and instrument approach plates.

"All set. We have our clearance and we're ready to start engines."

"Good." Bolton gave the flight deck a cursory inspection. "I'm going to take a walk-through—see how we're doing."

Upshaw nodded as he adjusted his seat.

Leaving the quiet surroundings of the cockpit, Bolton chatted with various security personnel, Secret Service agents, and members of the news media while he made his way through the giant airplane. Along the way, he took time out to visit with a group of influential black leaders and a key senator from Georgia.

The amicable politician never tired of having the opportunity to arrive in his home state aboard the royal chariot known as *Air Force One*. He knew the value of an appearance in the company of the president of the United States, especially to his constituents and the media. The wily and charming senator thoroughly enjoyed regaling his public with stories about the times he had coached presidents while he'd been onboard the flying White House.

Continuing his tour of the airplane, Bolton inspected the 4,000 square feet of living/working space, including the two galleys, the medical suite, the six passenger lavatories, and the mission communications center. Packed with an array of cryptographic equipment, radios, and computers, the sophisticated comm center provided worldwide secure data and voice communications. The presidential 747 also had triple redundancy in cockpit communications, including UHF and VHF radios.

Paying special attention to detail and cleanliness, the command pilot checked on the plush executive suite that provided the president and his family with a private office, dressing room, bathroom, stateroom, and conference/dining area. The personal attention to detail aboard *Air Force One* would rival the most prestigious hotels.

Separate accommodations were provided for aides, guests, Secret Service agents, security specialists, and representatives of the news media. The flight crew had their own lounge and minigalley.

Designed to carry seventy passengers and twenty-three crew members, the long-range 747 was equipped with nineteen television monitors, eleven VCRs, a thermonuclear shield, and eighty-five telephones. Every inch of the 238 miles of onboard wiring has been specially shielded to protect it from electromagnetic pulses that would emanate from a thermonuclear blast. The shielding also protects the wiring from more common electromagnetic interference.

Cruising at 560 mph at an altitude of 35,000 feet, the big jet could fly over 9,000 statute miles without refueling. Using the in-flight refueling capability, the presidential platform could safely remain airborne for two weeks or longer if necessary.

Bolton was pleased to see that every task and request had

been taken care of, including the specially prepared breakfast for the president. Fresh newspapers and magazines, excluding the publications banned by the first lady, were onboard the jumbo jet. In addition, a navigation chart with the plane's course was on the president's desk.

Even though the exterior of the airplane had been carefully preflighted, Bolton walked back down the boarding stairs to make a final inspection. After exchanging greetings with the Air Force guards and the Secret Service agents, he strolled around the outside of the flying White House.

He never failed to look at the words "United States of America" emblazoned along the fuselage of the spotless 747. With sunlight sparkling from the highly polished silver, white, and blue surface, the graphic symbol of freedom and democracy filled him with pride.

His practiced eye continued to survey the huge airplane from nose to tail and wingtip to wingtip, including the self-contained baggage loader. Bolton didn't detect any damage or blemishes, and, most important, all the essential components were securely attached to the airframe. *Air Force One* was ready to take to the skies.

### Key West

Closer to Havana than to Miami, the oddly picturesque town was coming alive when Scott and Jackie entered the gaily decorated bar and grill. They ordered the "Bone Islet" breakfast and tall Virgin Marys, then unfolded the sectional aeronautical chart and plotted the coordinates of the island home near Marathon.

"What do you think?" she asked innocently. "What if we're wrong and there *isn't* something sinister going on at the island?"

"That's why we're going to check it out before we contact anyone." He gave her a dismissive shrug, then looked into her eyes and smiled. "I don't want to charge in like John Wayne, then look like a fool if the place turns out to be a retreat for corporate executives."

She lowered her gaze. "You have a point." A smile spread slowly across her lips. "Bad form after our show in Lebanon."

He looked away, seeking a diversion. "That's why I'm using *my* rule book this time," he declared in a quiet, flat voice. "No one knows where we are, or what we're doing."

Jackie chuckled. "Sometimes, I wonder what we're doing."

"That makes two of us."

The place was becoming crowded by the time Jackie and Scott finished their Virgin Marys. Less than a minute later a mousy, gum-chewing waitress delivered their fresh conch chowder and fritters to their beer-soaked wooden table.

"Thanks," Scott said as he glanced at the object above his right shoulder. The saloon's soft neon glow highlighted a Ray-O-Vac leakproof battery advertisement over their booth.

"Nice place," Jackie said as she surveyed a strange assortment of local Key Westers, two of whom had live lizards perched on their shoulders. "Lots of ambience—sort of a drenched-in-decadence atmosphere."

A slow grin spread across Scott's face. "Hey, look at the upside." He gestured to their collective attire. "We fit in with the crowd."

"Yeah, that's the scary part." Jackie cast a look at a rail-thin woman who was braiding another skinny woman's hair. Both of the locals were smoking cigarillos and wearing huge clear plastic earrings that flashed like strobe lights. "You'd have to be naked, wearing snowshoes and a life jacket, and have your head stuffed inside a glowing pumpkin not to fit in here."

"At least I didn't take you to the Marriott," Scott said as a mischievous smile spread across his face.

"For that, I can be thankful."

Jackie tasted her chowder and looked around. The walls were covered with endorsements for Philco appliances, Indian Motorcycles, Bell & Howell eight-millimeter movie cameras, Remington Rand typewriters, Cushman Eagle motor scooters, and a large replica of a "Harry Truman for President" campaign button. From millionaires, to the last of the hippies, to sex-starved sailors on Cinderella liberty, the bar was a gathering place for many of the characters who gravitated to the cozy little island.

"Only in Key West." Jackie laughed out loud. "Thousands of free spirits living in their own quaint little world."

"And," Scott added, "they're genuinely happy."

Jackie nodded. "Party time round-the-clock."

"That's the beauty of it," Scott remarked, then tossed a look at a drunken musician with a graying ponytail and a Taylor guitar. The man had a face that looked like it had worn out three bodies. Barely able to balance on his bar stool, the hollow-eyed crooner was doing an unconscionable injustice to a Johnny Mathis ballad while two couples stumbled and lurched around the dance floor.

"That should be a felony," Jackie said, barely able to keep a straight face. "It sounds like someone is sticking him with a cattle prod."

Scott studied the lanky singer with the fluorescent tan for a few moments. "Probably too much shock therapy."

A tall, full-bosomed waitress with a mouthful of pearl-white teeth approached their table. "Are you Scott?"

"Yes."

"This just came for you," she said as she handed him a large photo mailer. "Cindy is tied up at her shop."

"Thanks."

"Anytime, handsome," she said suggestively as she deliberately brushed against him.

"Very subtle," Jackie said derisively.

Scott opened the mailer and began sorting through the photos. He quickly surveyed the pictures of the island home and yacht, then stared at a photo of the helicopter for a few seconds. "Dammit," he exclaimed.

"What is it?"

"You called traffic—the Cessna we almost creamed—about the same time I noticed the flag on the helo."

"And?"

He pulled back and looked at her. "Take a gander at this," Scott said as he shoved the picture across the table. "That was what was bothering me after we flew away. I couldn't remember if the flag's green, white, and red stripes were vertical or horizontal."

"Mexico's stripes are vertical—same with Italy," Jackie said as she studied the photo, then stopped and stared at Scott. "That's an Iranian flag!"

"Let's go," Scott said as he gathered the pictures together.

"We'll head back and check the island before we call in the troops."

Jackie rose from the table. "I'll take care of our bill—you grab a cab."

# 33

## The White House

With cheerful smiles on their faces, President and Mrs. Cord Macklin walked out of the mansion and waved to a cluster of reporters near the South Portico. A few correspondents waved back, but most of the media ignored their friendly gestures.

The first lady nervously glanced at the snipers on the roof, then turned her attention to the plethora of Marines and Secret Service agents deployed around the grounds.

Under the chief executive's left arm, he carried a leather folder containing a copy of the Cornerstone Summit speech he planned to deliver in Atlanta. Unsatisfied with a couple of items in his speech, he intended to polish the rough edges during the short flight to Georgia. Political pundits had branded his last discourse on race relations as "a meandering journey in search of a destination." His address to the diverse audience in Atlanta had to come from the heart.

After crossing the freshly manicured south lawn, the president kissed his wife good-bye, then turned and walked up the steps to the gleaming Marine Corps VH-3D *Sea King* helicopter. Seconds later the main rotor blades began turning while the commander in chief settled into his seat. A few moments later, in the early cool of morning, *Marine One* smoothly lifted from its landing pad and turned toward Camp

Springs, Maryland, home to Andrews Air Force Base.

The president vacantly stared out the window as he thought about the trip to the heart of the south. Citing security reasons, Hartwell Prost wanted to cancel the trip, but Macklin had persisted on showing up for the important summit. The money people were committed, operatives were committed, and national and local politicians were committed.

In addition, three former presidents would be there, along with scores of governors, mayors, business leaders, clergymen, and well-known celebrities. Regardless of Hartwell's concerns about safety, there wasn't any graceful way for Macklin to renege on his promise to lead the racial initiative in Atlanta. Besides, people expected presidents and fighter pilots to be the type of individuals who routinely fulfill their obligations.

As the Anacostia River passed beneath the helicopter, the chief executive's thoughts shifted to the responsibilities of his office and the fact that he couldn't escape them, regardless of where his travels took him. He also reflected on the threat of more terrorism engulfing the nation. Finally, he focused on the unanswered questions about Fraiser Wyman. *I'm going to have to be patient and let the FBI complete their investigation.*

Aboard *Air Force One*, Colonel Bolton immediately received a message from the mansion. The commander in chief's helicopter had lifted off the White House lawn. The president was en route to Andrews and would be arriving at the shiny 747 in approximately eight minutes, depending on the route *Marine One* was using this particular morning.

Bolton strapped into the left seat and glanced out the window. Now that the president was airborne, the level of activity at the Air Force base was rapidly increasing. The gates to Andrews were closed and all vehicle traffic on the terminal ramp was stopped. In the tower, the ground controller had halted the various planes taxiing on the airfield. An Air Force vehicle traveled the length of the duty runway, looking for debris that might get sucked into the 747's behemoth engines.

During the ground search of the runway, security personnel with dogs patrolled the areas adjacent to the taxiways. At other locations, Air Police were on alert for anything that appeared suspicious. Rescue equipment and rescue personnel, fire trucks, ambulances, and medical specialists were in position to render help in the event of an emergency. In addition, a rescue helicopter was standing by to lend assistance if *Air Force One* crashed during takeoff.

Counting the minutes since the commander in chief departed from the White House lawn, Kirk Upshaw spotted *Marine One* as it approached from the northwest. He was surprised to see the helo flying lower than usual.

"I see them."

Bolton nodded. "Got 'em."

Everyone was in place when the presidential helicopter made its approach to the landing area. The aircraft commander eased the wheels on the ramp and stopped in the assigned parking spot close to the big Boeing.

As the main rotor blades began winding down, a handful of Air Force brass walked toward the entrance to the helo. Seconds later the door swung down to form a stairway to the ramp. A Marine sergeant hurried out and popped to attention, then rendered a snappy salute.

The president concluded a conversation with an aide before he walked down the stairs and greeted the welcoming committee. Two Secret Service agents followed the chief executive out of the helicopter and remained close to his side as they made their way to *Air Force One*.

Once the commander in chief and his aides started up the stairway, Curt Bolton gave the order to start engines. When the first two engines were idling, Chief Master Sergeant Brewer closed the cabin door as the mobile stairway was taken away. With the last two engines on-line, the ground crew chief smartly saluted the presidential pilot. Returning the gesture of respect, Bolton released the brakes and allowed the plane to begin rolling as Upshaw contacted ground control.

"*Air Force One* is taxiing."

"Ah roger, *Air Force One*."

As the 747 rumbled along the taxiway, the flight crew completed their checklists. The powerful General Electric turbofans—each rated at 56,750 pounds of thrust—were purring like kittens. Weighing well below the maximum take-off weight of 836,000 pounds, the huge airplane would become airborne after a relatively short roll. Approaching the runway, Bolton noted the various security personnel and safety equipment standing by for their departure.

Upshaw called the tower.

"*Air Force One*, ready for takeoff."

The tower controller gave clearance for takeoff as Bolton simultaneously guided the Boeing onto the runway and smoothly advanced the four throttles. With the thundering engines spewing red-hot exhaust, *Air Force One* quickly gathered speed while the flight crew carefully monitored the engine instruments. Everything looked good.

When the big jet reached rotation speed, Bolton gently eased back on the yoke and raised the nose to the prescribed attitude. As if in slow motion, the giant airplane lifted off the runway and began its ascent to 35,000 feet.

Two minutes after the 747 was airborne, a flight of four Air Force F-15 Eagles rendezvoused high and behind *Air Force One*. Working with a Boeing E-3 AWACS, the air superiority fighters would provide protection for the presidential airplane until it was within eyesight of the Atlanta airport. At that time, if there was not an obvious threat to the president, the fighters and the AWACS would break away and land at Dobbins Air Reserve Base.

Winging southwestward toward Atlanta, the president chatted with the senator and the delegation of national black leaders for a few minutes, then excused himself and headed for his special place of refuge. Carrying a steaming cup of fresh coffee, the chief executive glanced at the gold-and-blue presidential seal as he entered his private office aboard *Air Force One*.

He sat down and began eating his breakfast while he studied the aeronautical chart on his desk. He followed the straight green line as it paralleled the Appalachian Mountains, passed over Lynchburg, Virginia, Hickory, North Carolina, the western tip of South Carolina, and into the Atlanta area, terminating at Hartsfield International.

Considering all the amenities *Air Force One* afforded him, the president paused to look around his office. The gleaming airplane was truly the ultimate symbol of the power and majesty of the presidency. The fabulously appointed Boeing was the envy of other chiefs of state and royalty, regardless of their fortunes and holdings.

Nothing on earth could eclipse the special magic and the raw power and authority that *Air Force One* represented. Providing escape and adventure for the president, this symbol of the United States of America easily surpassed all the other benefits of his office.

### Near Marathon

"Damn, it's gone," Scott exclaimed as the island residence came into view. "They sure as hell got under way in a hurry," he said as he began a shallow descent toward the lushly tropical compound. "They can't be too far away, not even at top speed."

"True," Jackie admitted as she reached for the binoculars. "The question is, which way did they go?"

He raised the right wing and searched the horizon, then repeated the same maneuver with the left wing.

"Were they planning to leave anyway," Scott asked rhetorically, "or did we spook them?"

Jackie scanned the water in every direction. "I don't see anything except small boats. Nothing the size of the yacht."

She turned her attention to the coral breakwater, then studied the home. "I don't see any signs of life."

Setting up a wide orbit, Scott continued descending while he observed the island estate. "Let's land and take a look around."

"Are you sure?"

"Absolutely."

Jackie carefully investigated the grounds of the estate. "If we run into any bad guys, they're probably going to have a lot more firepower than we do."

He began slowing the Maule and lowering the flaps. "I don't think we have much choice. We're looking for a nuclear bomb and we're running out of time." His claim was impossible to deny. "Our deadline is almost up."

"Like you said in Alaska, it's your show," Jackie conceded as she checked her nine-millimeter Glock. "Let's do it."

Scott made a long final approach parallel to the dock. The

Maule splashed down near the pier and Dalton came off the step thirty feet from the dock. Swinging the airplane around near a seventeen-foot Boston Whaler, he opened the door and leaped on the float, then shut down the engine just before he grabbed the pier.

"Nice job," Jackie said as she climbed out and cautiously surveyed the area. "The hair is standing up on the back of my neck."

"Same here," Scott said as he secured the airplane to the dock. "Keep your eyes open."

While Dalton climbed onto the pier, Jackie slid across the cockpit and crawled out the left door.

"Be careful," she said under her breath.

Without warning, a man of Middle Eastern descent appeared from behind a planting of thick tropical foliage.

Although he felt a stab of adrenaline, Scott smiled in a relaxed manner. "Hey, man, wha's happenin', dude?"

"This is private property," the muscular man said as he walked onto the dock. "I must ask you to leave."

"Well," Scott began slowly, "you see, man, we'd like to accommodate you, but we've got a major-big-time problem with our flyin' machine."

"That is none of my concern," the unsmiling man said curtly. "You will leave at once, or I will be forced to call the authorities."

Scott looked at Jackie, then broke into a wide smile and turned back to the grim-faced man. "That's who we're trying to contact." He laughed overzealously. "We'd appreciate some help."

Out of the corner of her eye, Jackie saw a rugged-looking man with a weapon approaching from the side of one of the guest cottages.

"Ah . . . Scott," she said in a quiet, clear voice. "We have an armed visitor at our eight o'clock."

"Take him!" Dalton exclaimed at the same instant he drew his Sig Sauer and pointed it at the first man. "Hit the ground! *Now!*"

Stunned, the well-built man hesitated until Scott fired a round that grazed his right sandal. He hit the pier like a bag of cement.

"Freeze," Jackie shouted at the other man. "FBI! Drop your weapon! Drop it *now!*"

The man raised his semiautomatic as Jackie fired three rounds, striking him in the leg and chest. He stumbled backward, then fell to the ground and groaned in agony.

"Who else is here?" Scott barked as he placed the barrel of the nine-millimeter to the first man's temple. "You have three seconds."

"There's only two of us," the frightened man uttered. "You're not FBI."

"That's right—they're a lot nicer."

"Take what you want and leave," the man pleaded.

Scott caught a glimpse of Jackie while she hurried to retrieve the Intratec semiautomatic from the wounded gunman.

"What I want," Dalton said impatiently, "is some answers."

"About what?" the man said with a trace of sarcasm.

"Tell you what," Scott said as he pressed the barrel to the bridge of the man's nose. "You better change your attitude, or you're going to be seeing your Maker a lot sooner than you thought."

"What can I tell you?" the man asked while perspiration rolled down his cheeks. "I am a simple caretaker."

"Right," Scott said contemptuously. "Where's Khaliq Farkas?"

Suddenly full of fear, the militant hesitated. "I don't—I have never heard of the man, honestly."

"Never heard of him, huh?"

"Never."

Scott glanced around the compound. "Well, ol' buddy, you must've been on the moon for the last twenty years."

"I don't know what you're talking about."

"How about Massoud Ramazani?" Scott asked while Jackie carefully watched for other gunmen. "Does that ring a bell?"

The question had a profound impact. "I . . . don't know anyone by that name. What do you want?"

"Let's try this," Scott said firmly. "Where did the yacht go?"

"Who *are* you?" the confused man asked.

"I don't think I'm getting through," Scott said as he slowly shook his head and smiled. "Now pay attention."

"Please, I don't *know* anything."

Without taking her eyes off the other man, Jackie moved closer to Scott. "The yacht is getting further away."

He nodded and tapped the man's head with the Sig Sauer. "I'm only going to ask you one more time," Scott said with raw conviction. "If you don't answer, you're not going to like the alternative."

"I am prepared to die," the militant said curtly, then broke down. "Go ahead and kill me," he blurted in an anguished voice. "I am prepared to die for Allahu and the revolution."

"If you want to die, we might as well make it memorable," Scott said, eyeing the empty utility boat. Equipped with a 112-horsepower Evinrude outboard, the Boston Whaler looked almost new.

"You know something?" Dalton said as he grabbed him by the collar. "I'd be willing to bet that you're not a water-skier."

The man's face turned to stone and his eyes reflected abject fear.

Scott got down next to him. "Am I right?"

"I don't swim."

"No problem," Dalton said innocently. "Swimming is optional—same with the water skis. I'm going to teach you how to body-ski."

The man's eyes grew wide.

"Since we don't have a lot of time," Scott went on in a calm voice, "I'm going to start you out with the advanced lessons."

"I'm not going anywhere," the militant said with a trace of panic in his voice. "You will have to kill me."

"Jackie," Scott said evenly, "if you'll cover Ski Cat and his friend, I'm going to rig the boat for body skiing."

"He's gonna love that," she said in a husky undertone, then pointed her gun at the man. "I just hope he isn't bleeding by the time you get him into the water."

"Me, too." Scott smiled. "There's a lot of hungry sharks out there."

# 34

## Hartsfield International Airport

Khaliq Farkas attached a small suction plunger to the lower left side of the window and skillfully used a glass cutter to extract an eight-inch square of glass. He repeated the same steps on the right side of the glass, then stepped back to admire his work and the view. Looking over the top of a hotel and Interstate 85—even with the restriction of low clouds and fog—he had a bird's-eye view of the sprawling international airport. He estimated that he was approximately one mile from the west end of the south runways.

Feeling more confident by the minute, he unpacked a spiral notebook, two ballpoint pens, and the portable radio scanners. He cautiously surveyed the hotel grounds, searching for anyone who might be looking up at the building. Most everyone entering or leaving the high-rise hotel was looking at the pavement in an attempt to dodge the multitude of water puddles.

Across the room, Hamed Yahyavi unfolded the long radio antennas and attached the mass of tangled cables to the aircraft radios, then carefully divided the antennas between the two openings in the window.

The weather was still rotten, but the light rain had abated for the moment. The fog and low visibility were continuing to cause flight delays, but air traffic was flowing reasonably well now that the early-morning rush hour was over. Not quite ideal conditions for what he wanted to achieve, but good enough to take a chance on inflicting mass casualties and creating fear about where and when an attack might occur next.

Checking the current United States Government Enroute Low Altitude navigation charts, Farkas tuned in the frequency for the airport arrival ATIS—the automatic terminal information service. He immediately learned that Hartsfield/Atlanta International was using both Runways 8 Left and 9 Right for landing aircraft. The reported weather during the past hour was slightly above the minimum ceiling and visibility needed to execute the standard Instrument Landing System precision approaches to the two runways.

Switching the radio to the ATIS frequency for departing aircraft, he was informed that outbound flights were using Runways 8 Right and 9 Left.

Farkas switched one of the radios to eavesdrop on the Atlanta Control Tower frequency for the runways on the north side of the airport—8L-26R and 8R-26L. He then tuned a second radio to monitor the tower operator controlling the runways on the south side of the field—9L-27R and 9R-27L.

Checking his wristwatch, he calculated where *Air Force One* would be at the present time. The gleaming wide-body jet would most probably still be cruising at 35,000 feet, communicating with a high-altitude en route air traffic controller. According to his estimate, the specially configured Boeing 747 would commence its descent in approximately twenty minutes.

He tuned the remaining radios to keep track of clearance delivery, both ground-control frequencies, departure control, and various approach-control frequencies, including the feeder and final radar controllers. The last VHF transceiver was set to 121.5—the general aviation emergency frequency guarded by most civilian control towers, radar facilities, and flight service stations, while a UHF radio was tuned to 243.0—the military emergency "guard" frequency. The other UHF radios were tuned to Hartsfield approach, tower, ground, and departure control.

Farkas monitored the tower frequency and watched the

string of aircraft taking off while he listened to the approach controllers handling the inbound flights. This allowed him to get a feel for the flow of air traffic so he could time his actions to cause the most significant consequences.

He drew a square in the center of a fresh page in the notebook and began writing the flight numbers down adjacent to where they were located in relation to the airport.

Mentally placing himself in the control tower at the center of the bustling airport, he visualized what was transpiring in the dark clouds high above the sprawling city. When an airliner approached Atlanta, an en route controller in the Atlanta Air Route Traffic Control Center "handed off" the flight to a feeder controller in the terminal radar-control facility.

The feeder controller had the responsibility of sequencing air traffic into a smooth flow before he turned the airplanes over to the final controller. The final controller's job entailed spacing aircraft for the final approach to the airport before he "handed" the flights to the local controller or to the control tower.

From studying the flow of air traffic at Hartsfield, Farkas knew the Atlanta north feeder was controlling two narrow corridors of inbound traffic. One route was devoted to traffic arriving from the northeast, while the other busy corridor handled inbounds from the northwest. Both routes converged north of Atlanta International, where the final controller took control of the flights.

"What a great setup," Farkas said as he checked his watch. "We just have to be patient, and think clearly."

"You're the pilot," Yahyavi observed with an amused smile. "I'll take care of the scanners."

## The Island

"FBI?" Scott whispered as Jackie helped him tie the boat's severed anchor line to the stern of the Boston Whaler. "Was that a moment of panic, or are you really with the Bureau?"

"It just came out," Jackie admitted, her voice barely audible. "I'm not keeping anything from you."

Scott smiled widely, then winked. "That's good, because I was beginning to have my doubts."

"Well, rest easy."

"Are you about ready, Ski Cat?" Dalton asked as he turned to the militant sitting on the dock.

The man's hands were tied behind his back and his ankles were tied together. The end of the anchor line was securely fastened around and through his bound ankles. Scott cinched the man's life jacket as tight as he could.

"I'm telling you," the militant pleaded, "I don't know anything."

"You don't sound very convincing," Scott said lightly. "You could sure save us a lot of time and energy, and save yourself some—how should I phrase this?—*real* discomfort."

"I can't tell you what I don't know," the man cried out as his eyes burned from the salty perspiration.

"Then make something up, and it *better* be good."

A seasoned water-skier, Dalton jumped into the boat and started the powerful Evinrude outboard.

"Keep an eye on things," he said to Jackie, then turned his attention to the pleading man. "I'm gonna take out some slack, then I'll pop you off the dock and have you flying high in no time."

"No! Please don't do this!"

"Relax and enjoy the ride."

Without warning, Scott firewalled the throttle and braced himself. The Boston Whaler lunged out of the water and snatched the terrified man off the dock. He plunged into the emerald waters and disappeared for a few seconds, then popped to the surface as the boat rapidly accelerated.

Reaching top speed, Scott made a sweeping left turn as the man violently bounced along the surface of the water, twisting and spinning wildly over the edge of the wake on the outside of the turn. Nearing the dock, Dalton tightened the turn and flung the man out into smooth water.

"Hang in there, guy!"

Skipping across the surface like a flat stone, the man accelerated to a speed that was faster than the speed of the boat. When the militant's head was skirting the edge of the pier, Scott eased the power back and spun the Whaler toward the desperate terrorist.

Jackie grabbed a boat hook and snared the sputtering

man's life jacket, holding his head above water until Scott roared up in the boat.

"Hey, you're doin' great!"

Panic-stricken, the terrorist gasped for air, then spewed vomit and seawater down his life jacket. "I—please," he pleaded as his head slid to one side. "I can't tell you something that—"

"Okay," Scott interrupted. "You have real potential, guy, no question about it. I'm betting that this time around, you can manage some five-and-six-foot bounces off the water."

"No!" he begged as he gasped for air. "Please don't do—"

Dalton interrupted him. "We're just gonna have to get the speed up a little higher, that's all."

"Okay," the man said, then choked and coughed. "Okay," he sputtered. "I'll tell you what I can."

"Oh, no," Scott said as he leaned near the militant's twisted face. "You'll tell me everything. One lie and you'll be going for the double whammy—the big one. Got it?"

The man nodded and coughed.

"Where's the yacht?"

"Headed for the Potomac River."

Jackie's eyes widened. "What are they planning to do?"

"Set off a bomb as close to the White House as—"

"What kind of bomb?" Scott interjected.

The man hesitated, then began coughing again.

Scott grabbed him by the life jacket and hauled him halfway out of the water. "Answer me, dammit!"

"A nuclear bomb."

Jackie and Scott made eye contact.

"Where's Ramazani?" Dalton asked.

"On the boat."

"Where's Farkas?"

"In Atlanta."

Jackie and Scott shared a startled look before Dalton stared into the man's frightened eyes.

"Is he planning to harm the president?"

"Yes."

"How?"

Another hesitation.

"Okay," Scott said evenly as he turned toward the controls. "I'll make this ride *extra* special."

"They are going to do something to his plane."

"What *exactly* are they going to do?" Jackie asked.

"I don't know," he said with a pleading look on his face. "Farkas was here to pick up a person to go with him to Atlanta. I don't know what they are planning to do—honest."

Scott smiled broadly. "Relax, Ski Cat."

After they hauled the man out of the water and securely tied him to a tree, Jackie motioned Scott aside.

"The other guy died while you were in the boat."

Dalton glanced at the inert form lying on the ground, then looked around the property. "From the array of antennas here, I'd say these boys have some pretty sophisticated communications gear."

"We better take it out of service," Jackie suggested. "Just in case any more of these characters are around."

They quickly destroyed the communications center and knocked the antennas to the ground.

"Let's get out of here," Scott said as he ripped the electric cords out of the generators. "We have to get in touch with Hartwell. The president is expected to be in Atlanta today."

Jackie nervously glanced at her wristwatch. "Actually, he should be en route right now."

"Let's get airborne," Scott said as he turned and sprinted for the floatplane. "We'll use the sat-phone."

Scott started the engine and quickly configured the airplane for takeoff while Jackie frantically tried to contact Hartwell Prost in Washington. After two unsuccessful attempts to get through to his office, she finally heard a ring as the Maule lifted off the water and began climbing. After a delay to interrupt a staff meeting, the conversation with Prost was short and ended abruptly.

"He's going to contact *Air Force One*," she announced as they searched for any sign of the yacht. "I told him about Farkas being in Atlanta, and confirmed that a nuke was on the yacht."

"What's his thinking?"

She reached for the binoculars. "He wants us to find the yacht and keep it in sight until the Coast Guard or Navy can intercept it."

"What about the two guys we left on the island?" Scott

asked as he glanced at the mist of fuel spraying over the right wing.

Jackie turned an air vent directly toward her face. "Hartwell's contacting the FBI. He's keeping us out of the picture."

"Good."

Jackie slowly swept the horizon with the binoculars. "We have to find that yacht."

"Yeah, mucho pronto," Scott said as he leveled the plane at 500 feet. "It shouldn't be too difficult now that we know where they're headed."

Morteza Bazargan, the leader of the special action cell on the island, crawled out of the moat and pulled himself up the coral breakwater as the Maule disappeared in the distance. Wet and frightened, he reentered the water and waded across the chest-deep moat, then hurried to check on his two comrades.

"What did you tell them?" he yelled when he found his second in command tied to the tree.

The man mumbled incoherently.

"Speak up!" Bazargan said as he backhanded the man across the face. "You told them about the boat, didn't you?"

"Yes," the man said feebly. "They were going to drown me."

Without saying another word, Bazargan untied the traitor from the tree, but left his hands tied behind his back. He yanked him to his feet and shoved him toward the dock.

"No!" the frantic man pleaded as he desperately tried to maintain his balance. "I didn't tell them anything that—"

Bazargan shoved him off the pier and turned toward the home. He had seen the antennas crash to the ground and he had heard the communications equipment being destroyed. Somehow, Bazargan had to make contact with the ship and warn Massoud Ramazani before the people in the floatplane located *Bon Vivant*.

Unfortunately for Bazargan, a private pilot flying over the island spotted a bloody body lying on the grounds and another body floating beside the dock. The pilot contacted Miami Air Traffic Control Center and they alerted the Coast

Guard. Minutes later a Coast Guard HH-65 Dolphin arrived while Bazargan was changing into dry clothes. The helicopter crew entertained the suspected murderer and drug dealer until the FBI arrived.

# 35

## Air Force One

Cruising in relatively smooth air at 35,000 feet, the 747 was rapidly approaching Atlanta. Noting that they were 105 nautical miles from the international airport, Colonel Bolton nodded to Kirk Upshaw. The copilot spoke into his microphone.

"Atlanta Center, *Air Force One* is ready to start down."

"*Air Force One,*" the controller said clearly, "pilot's discretion to flight level two-six-zero. Advise leaving three-five-zero."

"*Air Force One* discretion down to two-six-zero, report out of three-five-zero."

Curtis Bolton gingerly eased the outboard throttles back, descending with an imperceptible change in aircraft attitude and engine sound. He worked hard to make the speed and attitude transition from level flight to the approach configuration almost unnoticeable to the passengers.

"Atlanta, *Air Force One* is out of three-five-oh."

"Ah, roger, *Air Force One,*" the controller acknowledged, and gave them a new radio frequency.

Delicately working the inboard throttles to match the number-one and number-four throttles, Bolton called for the descent checklist. The pilots went through their normal briefing for a descent and reaffirmed their approach and landing speeds.

Above and behind the 747, four F-15s began descending with *Air Force One.* The flight leader could see that he and his charges would have to abandon the flying White House before they had planned to. In the next minute or two, the president's plane would be entering a wide band of dark clouds. The pilot checked in with the AWACS, then contacted the 747.

*"Air Force One,"* the Eagle flight leader radioed, *"Shotgun One* and flight are breaking off and heading for Dobbins. Have a good day."

"Roger, *Shotgun*," Upshaw replied. "Appreciate the escort."

The F-15 pilot clicked his radio twice as the fighters turned toward Dobbins Air Reserve Base. Seventeen miles east of the fighters, the Boeing E-3 AWACS began descending toward Dobbins.

Nearing the murky cloud layer, Bolton and Upshaw listened to the Hartsfield Automatic Terminal Information Service. The latest ATIS recording provided them with information on ceilings, visibility, obstructions to visibility, temperature, dew point, wind direction, wind speed, altimeter setting, remarks about the airport, and instrument approaches and runways in use.

Bolton gazed at the thick, dense clouds as they began to descend into the dark maze. The sensation of speed mixed with nature's handiwork made him feel euphoric.

Ken Kawachi sat in the quiet, darkened room in the Atlanta Terminal Radar Control Facility and concentrated on his cluttered radarscope. With the burden of responsibility for hundreds of lives in his hands, Kawachi, like other air traffic controllers, paid very close attention to the constantly moving blips on his radar screen.

To the uninitiated observer, the ghostly radar returns with their associated tiny letters and numerals appear to be minuscule particles slowly drifting in a sea of molasses. But to the trained air traffic controller, each radar image represents a single airplane, the flight identification, and the speed and altitude of the aircraft.

The hushed atmosphere in the gloomy control room reflected the intense, serious environment the controllers work in while they steadily and efficiently handle multiple inbound flights. Working with a multitude of computers, radar, aircraft transponders, and radios, controllers and pilots work in unison twenty-four hours a day 365 days a year to make air traffic flow smoothly and safely.

Inclement weather conditions, like snowstorms, thick fog, and violent thunderstorms, have the potential to create tension so palpable that nerves are stretched to the breaking point and mouths suddenly go dry. It isn't the kind of work environment for those who have a low threshold for pressure. In fact, many aviation experts consider the profession one of the most stressful in the world.

Kawachi was working four airliners and a corporate Learjet when he accepted two more flights, United Flight 1147—a Boeing 727 arriving from Chicago, and *Air Force One* en route from Andrews Air Force Base.

Customarily, the flying White House received kid-glove treatment from air traffic controllers when the commander in chief was onboard. However, the custom had been relaxed when President Macklin took office. Having been a seasoned military pilot, he had requested that the Federal Aviation Administration treat the world's most famous airplane like any other aircraft; no special considerations, no excessive separation from other aircraft, and no holding other flights on the ground until the big Boeing departed. In other words, no protective bubble. The word went out, but controllers still provided preferential treatment whenever possible. No one wanted to be remembered as the individual who caused a problem for the president of the United States.

Kawachi handed two other air-carrier flights to the final controller earlier than usual and quickly switched his attention to his new charges. Although the feeder and final controllers share the same working space, they don't have direct voice communication and they communicate with the flight crews on separate radio frequencies.

The final controller, Louis Traweek, was becoming overloaded by the multitude of inbound traffic. He was handling six aircraft when Kawachi dumped two more flights on him.

Traweek had to reduce the number of aircraft he was controlling before he could accept any more flights. He was becoming saturated and begining to lose his situational awareness.

Recognizing that he had a fast-moving Sabreliner corporate jet overtaking a twin-engine Cessna 310 he had turned eastbound onto the final approach for runway 8 Left, Traweek quickly ordered the jet crew to slow to their final approach speed and turn left to a heading of 350 degrees.

Preoccupied by the latest two air carriers that had entered his airspace, Traweek momentarily forgot about the Sabreliner and gave his attention to the airliners.

Although Ken Kawachi had passed control of the two flights to Traweek, the final controller hadn't acknowledged the handoff. In essence, no one was providing positive separation for the two airliners. The jets were descending and rapidly closing on the preceding aircraft when Traweek remembered the Sabreliner.

"Sabreliner 324 Zulu Romeo," Traweek tersely radioed, "turn left to two-three-zero and maintain normal approach speed."

"Sabre Twenty-Four Zulu Romeo, two hundred on the heading and, ah, normal approach speed."

"Negative! Heading two-three-zero for Sabreliner Two-Four Zulu Romeo. Repeat—two-three-zero!"

"Copy, two-thirty on the heading—Twenty-Four-ZR."

Listening to the various approach frequencies and the tower frequencies, Khaliq Farkas and Hamed Yahyavi were ecstatic when they heard the copilot of *Air Force One* check in with the approach controller. The 747 was precisely on time, as the Iranians expected the crew of *Air Force One* would be. Determined to undermine public confidence in U.S. civil aviation, Farkas seized the moment to test his radio equipment and further exacerbate the already congested air traffic system.

A Delta Air Lines MD-88 arriving from Dallas–Fort Worth was descending out of the low clouds on an Instrument Landing System approach to Runway 9 Right. Farkas quickly scanned his notes and selected the radio tuned to the tower frequency for the south runways and pressed the transmit switch.

"Delta One-Seventy-Six," he said in an urgent voice, "go around! I repeat—Delta One-Seventy-Six, go around! Fly heading three-six-zero, maintain five thousand."

"Delta One-Seventy-Six on the go," the surprised voice replied as the MD-88 captain abandoned the ILS approach. He rotated the airplane to a normal climb attitude and reentered the darkened clouds. While he initiated a smooth turn to a northerly heading, the first officer raised the landing gear and the flaps.

"Delta One-Seventy-Six, disregard the previous trans—" The frantic controller was cut off as Yahyavi quickly secured the transmit switch to the transmit position. The frequency was now unusable since no one could receive or transmit on it.

"This is going to be better than we anticipated," Farkas said excitedly as he looked at his scribbles and broadcast another pirate radio transmission on one of the approach frequencies.

"United 1147," he said in a bold, authoritative voice, "turn left heading zero-eight-zero and maintain five thousand."

"Ah, 1147 heading zero-eight—"

The radio transmission was interrupted when Yahyavi repeated the same steps as before. Another blocked radio frequency meant fewer options for the pilots and air traffic controllers. At the most critical moments Farkas was taking away their ability to secure the safety of scores of airplanes and thousands of passengers.

Feeling the effects of a sudden surge of adrenaline, Farkas glanced at his sheet of paper and transmitted another order.

"*Air Force One*," he barked in a taut voice, "descend and maintain five thousand, turn right to two-eight-zero. Now!"

"*Air Force One*, five thou—"

Yahyavi interrupted the transmission and set all but one of the radios to transmit. No one would be able to use the majority of the normal frequencies used by the tower and air traffic controllers. Using the last available approach frequency, Farkas radioed an American flight inbound from Dallas–Fort Worth.

"American Eight-Sixty-Four," he said impatiently, "expedite your descent to five thousand and fly heading zero-one-zero."

"Five thousand and zero-one—"

The first officer of Flight 864 tried to acknowledge their instructions as Yahyavi stowed the last radio in the transmit position and reached for the two police scanners. With a few pirate directives and twelve blocked radio frequencies, he and Farkas had created pandemonium in a dynamic and lethal environment.

Listening to the scanners, Yahyavi monitored the police- and fire-department communications while Farkas counted backward from sixty seconds. The longer *Air Force One* and the multitude of other aircraft groped around in the clouds without any directives, the more frantic everyone would become.

The pilots and flight engineers who had maintained their situational awareness to other aircraft would be even more concerned; there were a number of planes, including *Air Force One*, on a collision course at the same altitude.

A feeling of great satisfaction suddenly swept over Farkas. "The friendly skies aren't going to be so friendly this morning."

"Allahu is with us," Yahyavi declared in a soothing voice. "The infidels are going to get a taste of real terror."

# 36

## Atlanta

C aptain Fred Oliver, commanding United Flight 1147, gave his first officer a curious glance and then saw the concern written on the face of the flight engineer. Buffeted by light turbulence, they were flying in solid instrument conditions and suddenly couldn't communicate with anyone on their assigned frequency. Worse, they were headed straight for the northeast corridor of inbound traffic to Hartsfield/Atlanta International, one of the busiest airports in the country.

"Pete," Oliver said as evenly as he could, "try our previous frequency. Get *someone* on the horn."

"Okay."

Recently promoted to copilot, First Officer Pete Taylor frantically switched the radios and made three calls to the air traffic controller who had been working them. The only thing he heard was a high-pitched screeching sound. He turned to meet Oliver's questioning eyes.

"There's something weird going on," Taylor declared in a hollow voice, "and we're right in the middle of it."

They exchanged anxious looks.

"Try twenty-one-five," Oliver said firmly.

"Okay."

Taylor switched to 121.5 and tried the emergency frequency. Finding it blocked, he gave Oliver a blank look.

"Nothing, boss. We better get the hell out of here while we have a chance."

"Yeah," Second Officer Zeke Ingraham added, "before we end up scratching some sheet metal."

Fred Oliver, a former Navy F-4 Phantom pilot and distinguished military test pilot, nodded his agreement with his crew. "I don't know what to tell you, except we've got big problems."

"No shit!" Ingraham grumbled.

"Pete," Oliver began in as calm a voice as he could muster. "Keep transmitting on guard, and squawk emergency, then lost comm."

"I'll try Flight Service, too," Taylor responded while he set the transponder to squawk 7700.

"Good idea," Oliver said briskly.

The special 7700 transponder code would notify the air traffic controllers that United 1147 had an emergency situation in progress. Taylor then tried the nearest Flight Service Station. The FSS frequency was clobbered with frantic requests for information and directions. Everyone was attempting to talk at the same time, which was completely obstructing the frequency. The frightened flight crew of United 1147 weren't the only people in trouble.

"No luck," Taylor reported.

Oliver glanced at him. "Great—just what we need."

Zeke Ingraham groaned and absently studied his flight engineer panel. Along with his fellow pilots, Ingraham knew that for every second they remained in this predicament, the chances of having a midair collision went up exponentially.

*We've got to do something, skipper!* Ingraham's mind was screaming. *We can't screw around out here.*

Without waiting a full minute, Pete Taylor switched the transponder to squawk 7600—the code for lost radio communications—and gave Oliver a pained look. "We better get outta the area, or we're gonna get our asses smashed."

"Yeah," the shaken captain answered. "You're right."

Ingraham leaned forward. "You got my vote!"

Fred Oliver hesitated a moment to analyze the situation. He knew *his* radios were working because they could hear the frantic calls to the Flight Service Station. However, he didn't have any idea what was going on with the approach, departure, and tower frequencies. If there was a massive blockage of communications and everyone attempted to follow the FAA regulations pertaining to radio failures while operating in instrument flight conditions, Captain Oliver knew there was going to be a lot of aluminum fluttering to the ground.

Unable to see beyond the nose of the airplane, Oliver decided to do something unorthodox. He turned north-northwest toward Dobbins Air Reserve Base and descended to 4,500 feet—a Visual Flight Rules cardinal altitude that was 500 feet below and 500 feet above standard Instrument Flight Rules altitudes of 5,000 feet and 4,000 feet. He could only pray that no one else was trying the same evasive tactic—and that no one was climbing or descending through their altitude. He silently cursed both his bad luck and the miserable weather. *This isn't really happening, is it?*

"Pete, try Dobbins Approach while we test the 'big sky theory.' "

"You got it."

Zeke Ingraham looked ill. "We're in the goddamn Twilight Zone."

"Traffic! Traffic!" warned the computer-generated voice of TCAS, the Traffic Alert and Collision Avoidance System. "Traffic! Traffic!"

An airborne-collision-avoidance system, TCAS is based on radar beacon signals which are beamed outward from the host aircraft. The collision warning system operates independent of ground-based equipment and provides conflict resolutions to pilots.

In a frenzy, Pete Taylor searched his charts for the proper approach frequency for the military base. *What a clusterfuck.*

"Traffic! Traffic!" TCAS blared.

Ingraham momentarily closed his eyes and prayed that he'd be able to see his son's softball game the following day. A few moments later he opened his eyes and stared at his wedding band. *If I survive this, I'm going to find a ground-based job and stick to it.*

"Uh-oh," Kirk Upshaw said nervously. "Someone is deliberately interfering with our communications."

"Sabotage," Curt Bolton declared.

"What?"

Bolton spoke slowly. "We're being sabotaged."

Upshaw's eyes reflected his fear. "Should we declare an emergency and climb to VFR on top, then sort this mess out?"

"Let's hold on declaring an emergency. Get out the Dobbins charts and get ahold of a controller—try UHF and VHF."

"Okay." Upshaw reached for his approach plates and paused. "Do you want to contact Washington?"

"Absolutely. Fire off a message."

"Yessir."

Upshaw quickly thumbed through his flight information publications. "You wanna squawk lost comm?"

"Yeah—go ahead."

Upshaw punched in 7600 on the transponder.

"I want to get the president on the ground," Bolton loudly declared. "Then we'll find out what the hell is going on."

A moment later the senior Secret Service agent onboard rushed into the cockpit. "Colonel, we've just received a warning from Washington that we may be flying into a terrorist trap."

With a small turn of his head, Bolton cast a lazy glance in his direction. "You're a little bit late, Sam."

"Oh, shit," the agent said with an anguished look. "What's going on?"

Bolton concentrated on his flight instruments. "Someone is giving bogus instructions over the radio, then jamming the frequency."

Gripped with acute fear, both the feeder and final air traffic controllers sat helplessly and watched scores of moving radar blips beginning to merge while they frantically tried to establish radio contact on different VHF and UHF frequencies. Warning devices for the special transponder codes and the airborne conflict alert systems were sounding their alarms, adding more distractions to the utter confusion in the control room.

Through trial and error, the frustrated controllers found unblocked local frequencies, but the desperate flight crews had no way of knowing what radio frequency they should be monitoring.

In the enormous Atlanta Air Route Traffic Control Center, frenetic en route radar controllers were quickly attempting to stem the flow of air traffic descending into the Atlanta area. Some flights in the high-altitude structure were being placed in holding patterns, while other flights were being diverted to other major airports or held on the ground.

The sudden breakdown in communications near Hartsfield/ Atlanta International had reverberated all the way to the Air Traffic Control System Command Center located at Herndon, Virginia, near Dulles International Airport. Approximately 130 ATC personnel at the 29,000-square-foot building monitor and manage more than 150,000 flight operations daily in the contiguous United States. With a click of a computer key, FAA specialists can scrutinize eight large screens with pictorial displays of air traffic and weather conditions nationwide.

If a major midwestern airport was expecting a blizzard, ATC Command Center would be able to regulate the time flights could depart for the area. The idea is not to allow more aircraft in the air than can be safely controlled without having to resort to "stacking" the airplanes in holding patterns. The system was designed to hold planes on the ground until the FAA feels it is reasonable to expect that the flight can proceed directly to the destination airport and land. Holding flights near an airport is an added complication for controllers and pilots and consumes a tremendous amount of fuel.

At the moment the planners and controllers at Command Center were scrambling to slow the arrival sequence of 287 aircraft headed for the Atlanta area. Safety was the paramount consideration on their minds. Restoring order was the only way to achieve that goal. Everyone was cooperative, but no one had anticipated this type of communications breakdown and the system couldn't cope with the blocked frequencies. Simply stated, there wasn't a contingency plan to deal with this magnitude of sabotage.

Louis Traweek sat in stunned silence and stared at a radar symbol that represented American Airlines Flight 864—a

Boeing 727 carrying 124 people that was passing over the airport and flying almost straight at the corridor for traffic inbound from the northwest. A reformed chain-smoker, Traweek reflexively reached for his empty breast pocket as he visualized the midair collisions he believed were imminent.

While chaos was spreading through the darkened control room, Traweek snapped out of his daze and repeatedly tried to call Delta Flight 176—the MD-88 that had been given a counterfeit order to go around as the captain was preparing to flare for a landing. With the hapless crew unable to see out of the airliner, or communicate with an air traffic controller, the airplane was now flying straight north toward the combined inbound traffic congestion from the northeast and northwest.

What concerned the shaken controller most was United Flight 1147. For whatever reason, the crew had changed course and, according to their current altitude readout, had descended to 4,500 feet without receiving an ATC clearance to deviate from their assigned heading or altitude. Under the circumstances, the captain had elected to play a deadly game of airborne Russian roulette.

The cluttered radarscope indicated another frightening catastrophe in the making. After losing communications when they were told to turn to a heading of 280 degrees, the pilot of *Air Force One* had obviously decided to use his command prerogative to declare a lost communications situation and proceed toward Dobbins Air Reserve Base. They were squawking 7600 on their transponder while the Boeing 747 was rapidly merging with United Flight 1147.

With his insides twisted from stress and sheer frustration, Traweek helplessly watched the United flight and *Air Force One* close on each other. He knew the only salvation would be if each maintained their current altitude. More midair conflict alerts went off as nine airplanes converged near the airport and occupied a one-square-mile section of airspace.

Louis Traweek and his fellow controllers wanted to close their eyes and block out any thoughts of the high probability that they were about to witness multiple collisions in the skies over Atlanta.

For most air traffic controllers, their worst recurring nightmares were about personal miscalculations that resulted in two jumbo jets colliding over a highly populated area. The present situation was even worse than their most frightening dreams. They were actually living the nightmare, and *Air Force One* was in the center of the flail.

Involuntarily, Traweek flinched when two blips indicating the same altitude merged for a long moment before separating on the scope. *They couldn't have missed each other by more than 100 to 200 feet vertically or horizontally.*

# 37

"Traffic! Traffic!" TCAS warned as Bolton and Upshaw stared at the screen, then made a minor correction in both course and altitude. Eleven seconds later Bolton cringed when his airplane was buffeted by American 864 as it passed overhead in the dark clouds. Flying in these conditions was like being in a submarine and unexpectedly having another sub scrape across the top of the hull of your boat. For Bolton and Upshaw, the near midair experience was too frightening even to contemplate.

Bolton was a cool customer by nature, but his present predicament was unnerving and unprecedented in his accident-free aviation career. Even the most shocking emergencies he'd faced weren't as stressful as flying blind in a dark sky full of metal objects traveling hundreds of miles per hour in many different directions. With no positive control, Bolton and his crew and passengers were in the hands of fate.

Bolton glanced at Upshaw. "This could only happen when the president is onboard."

"No shit," Upshaw said while he yanked open his approach plates and selected the military ATIS frequency for Dobbins. "We're *all* passengers for the time being."

The cockpit became eerily quiet while they listened to the

Dobbins information. The weather wasn't any better than what had been reported at Hartsfield/Atlanta.

"Traffic! Traffic!" TCAS warned.

"Curt." Upshaw hesitated while he tuned in the busy approach-control frequency at Dobbins, then carefully framed his question. "Do you think we ought to step down a couple of hundred feet, get below our cardinal altitude?"

"Maybe miss a fender bender?" Bolton calmly asked.

"It might give us a better-than-even chance."

Bolton stared at the altimeter for a few seconds and initiated a slight descent from their assigned altitude of 5,000 feet. "What the hell—it's a roll of the dice any way you look at it."

"Yeah, a roll with our eyes closed," Upshaw said cryptically as he selected the UHF frequency for approach control. "Dobbins approach, *Air Force One*."

"Stand by, *Air Force One*—all aircraft on this frequency, stand by!" the controller blurted in an exasperated voice and then addressed two flights he was trying to work into the traffic flow for Dobbins. "Northwest Seven-Twenty-Four, descend and maintain four thousand. Delta Six-Ninety-Nine, turn right to two-eight-zero and continue your descent to six thousand."

Unlike the normal pattern of communications between controllers and pilots—where instructions issued by a controller are read back to him by the flight crews—this controller was issuing a constant stream of instructions and expecting the pilots to respond instantly to the orders. There wasn't time for the usual clarification procedure.

Summoning his courage, Bolton leveled *Air Force One* at 4,700 feet and listened to the harried controller trying to sort out the flights in the most immediate danger. The controller's problem reminded Bolton of a triage surgeon in the process of sorting victims to determine priorities for action in an emergency. He fervently hoped the tormented controller would find time for the president's plane. *I'd give up my retirement pay if I could just see what the hell was happening.*

Kirk Upshaw involuntarily ducked his head to the side. His sudden action caused Bolton to twitch.

"What'd you see?" Bolton asked while his pulse raced.

Upshaw was trying to find his voice. "I thought I saw something converging from the left—it passed right in front of us."

"Steady at the helm," Bolton said quietly in an effort to calm the jumpy copilot. "We'll be on the ground soon."

"If we survive this," Upshaw said through clenched teeth, "I'm going to church every Sunday, so help me God."

"I'll go with you," Bolton said in a tight voice.

Stirred by his intense anxiety, Chief Master Sergeant Brewer made small talk. "I remember a tanker crew who had a religious awakening," he said in a nervous voice. "They were descendin' at night to ten thousand feet over the ocean. The moon wasn't out and the night was pitch-black. When the pilot leveled off at what he thought was their assigned altitude, the crew felt a series of continuous bumps—sort of like they were in light turbulence. They turned on the ice lights and discovered they were flyin' in ground effect only a few feet above the water."

"Wonderful," Upshaw observed, unamused.

Ignoring the interruption, Brewer continued. "The engines were blowin' spray off the ocean when the major began climbin' away from the water. Ground effect was the only thing that kept them from becomin' shark food."

Kirk Upshaw gave Bolton a fleeting glance, but found he'd suddenly lost his voice. *I wonder what the president is going to say when we taxi in at Dobbins instead of Hartsfield?*

Bolton shook his head in frustration. "Kirk, try Dobbins again. We're *Air Force One.* We can't waste any more time."

"Yes, sir."

"We have the president onboard," Bolton said dryly. "We *have* to have positive control—don't take no for an answer."

Upshaw nodded. "You want to go ahead and declare an emergency?"

"Damn right! The president is onboard and we're flyin' blind."

Relaxing in the elaborate presidential office, the chief executive sat his coffee cup down and wrote the final words to his speech on racial harmony. Pleased with his efforts at spearheading a major race initiative, he unfolded his morning paper and studied the New York Stock Exchange composite transactions. Turning to look out the window, the president was shocked to see an airplane flash beneath the wing.

Captain Fred Oliver could occasionally see a few hundred feet in front of United 1147, but he couldn't see the ground because of the haze and thick clouds. The continuous choppy turbulence prompted him to recheck the seat-belt sign. Pleased to see that it was in the on position, Oliver didn't consciously remember toggling the switch. He also checked to make sure he had all the 727s external lights on.

Pete Taylor momentarily swallowed his fear and looked at Oliver. "I've never seen anything like—"

"Traffic! Traffic!" TCAS suddenly warned as Oliver, Taylor, and Ingraham shot a look at the TCAS scope. "Traffic! Traffic!"

Oliver glanced through his side window. "We've got one at ten o'clock."

"I'm looking," Taylor replied in a voice laced with fear. He scanned the dark clouds out the left side of the cockpit, hoping to get a glimpse of the conflicting traffic. "I can't see a damn thing."

"Keep looking," the captain said as he deactivated the autopilot and took manual control of the airplane. "He's probably level at five thousand."

"He's closing on us," Zeke Ingraham warned while he joined in the search efforts. "He's headed straight for us!"

"Descend! Descend! Descend!" ordered TCAS.

Both pilots shared a quick glance as Fred Oliver began a smooth descent from 4,500 feet. He felt remiss in not telling the flight attendants about the situation. There wasn't anything they could do to alleviate the problem, and he didn't want to worry them needlessly.

"Increase descent!" shouted TCAS at a level that shocked the flight crew into instantaneous action.

"Oh, shit!" Taylor yelled.

The relatively smooth ride was over for the time being. Oliver reduced power and forced the yoke forward while he cross-controlled the tri-engined jet. The Boeing sliced downward as the TCAS continued its urgent warning.

"Increase descent!"

"There he goes!" Pete Taylor said with genuine relief in his voice.

"Increase descent!"

"Okay, goddammit!" Oliver swore in frustration.

A half second later, while passing through 4,200 feet, Oliver saw the lights of a large aircraft as it roared over the top of their airplane. The encounter with the Delta jet was extremely close. The captain of the other airliner was also cheating on the altitude rules in order to increase his chances of avoiding a midair collision.

It's getting exciting up here," Pete Taylor uttered, and looked at the TCAS scope. "I'll try Dobbins again."

"Okay," Oliver replied while he added a small amount of power and began a smooth climb back to 4,500 feet. "We gotta get somethin' going or we're going to be in deep shit."

"Dobbins approach," Taylor radioed when the controller paused for a breath of air. "United Eleven-Forty-Seven."

The controller again ignored him and rapidly issued commands to a number of flights that were in close proximity to each other. "American Two-Sixty-Two, turn west and slow to your final approach speed. Citation Six-One-Charlie Mike, turn to zero-three-zero and give me your safest slow speed. American Four-Sixteen, turn east and give me your slowest speed. Delta Eight-Twenty-Eight, turn west *now*! Descend and maintain six thousand—give me your best rate!"

"Traffic! Traffic!" advised TCAS as Oliver and Taylor stared bug-eyed at the scope.

Zeke Ingraham forced himself not to look at the screen, thinking instead about his wife and son.

"Traffic! Traffic!"

"Here we go again," Taylor commented as he studied the collision avoidance system.

"Do you see him?" Oliver asked.

"No!"

"Keep looking."

"I am."

"Traffic! Traffic!"

With his attention riveted to the TCAS scope, Oliver took his eyes off the altimeter for a few seconds. "Where is he?"

"I'm not sure. Looks like, ah, four to five o'clock at—"

"Descend! Descend! Descend!"

"United Eleven-Forty-Seven," the air traffic controller screamed, "turn left two-three-zero *now!*"

"Increase descent!" shouted TCAS. "Increase descent!"

Oliver pulled the throttles back. "Gotta do it."

"This is getting crazy!" Taylor exclaimed.

Ingraham stiffened and glanced at his flight engineer panel. "Yeah—too damned crazy."

"Increase descent!"

"Eleven-Forty-Seven turn left!" the controller shouted as he saw two blips on his radar screen merging at the same altitude. "Turn left *now!*"

"Increase descent!" screamed TCAS.

Pete Taylor attempted to answer the controller while Oliver immediately initiated a steep, descending turn to the left.

"Aw, shit!" Oliver swore to himself when he saw that he'd drifted up to 4,700 feet. "Pay attention—fly the airplane."

"Dobbins approach," Taylor tried again. "United Eleven-Forty-Seven is coming left to two-three—"

The urgent radio transmission was abruptly interrupted when the two left engines and the bottom of the fuselage of *Air Force One* smashed through the first-class section of United 1147, ripping the entire flight deck of the 727 away from the rest of the airplane.

The frightened passengers in the first-class section of the United jet died instantly as the airliner exploded in a huge fireball. The violent collision produced a reverberating sound similar to a thunderclap. Fiery scraps of metal plummeted from the skies as the aircraft tumbled tail over nose toward the ground.

The stunned pilots died when the remains of their cockpit slammed into the roof of a home a quarter of a mile from where the main wreckage of Flight 1147 landed.

# 38

*Air Force One*

Shocked by the violent collision, Colonel Bolton froze on the controls when the Boeing rolled slightly left wing down and yawed to the left. He instantly recognized what had happened, but his mind was reeling from the seriousness of the situation. *Air Force One* had had a midair collision and he was the pilot in command. It was hard to comprehend the magnitude of the accident.

The cockpit was aglow with warning lights as he and Kirk Upshaw mechanically went through the emergency procedures to secure the two left engines. Upshaw maintained his professionalism while handling the checklist, but he was suffering from a combination of disbelief and horror.

"Get us priority at Dobbins!" Bolton exclaimed as he struggled to fly the 747 on the two starboard engines. "We're goin' straight in! I can't hold this—I can't maintain altitude!"

"Mayday! Mayday!" Upshaw urgently radioed. "*Air Force One* has had a midair! I repeat—*Air Force One* has had a midair collision! We've been hit. We're turning . . . we're heading straight in to Dobbins. The president is onboard and we need priority handling and the equipment standing by!"

"All aircraft stand by," the astounded controller replied. "*Air Force One,* you're almost abeam the runway. I'll have to take you out for a right turn to Runway Eleven, Runway

One-One. Maintain two-eight-zero on the heading and descend to three thousand."

Upshaw repeated the instructions. "Two-eight-oh and down to three thousand, *Air Force One*. Roll the trucks—roll everything you have!"

"Roger."

Racked with guilt that he suggested they change altitudes, Kirk Upshaw listened while the controller told him the latest weather conditions. If they were lucky, they'd break out of the clouds during their turn to final approach.

"*Air Force One,* the equipment is rolling."

"Thanks," Upshaw said briskly, then ordered Chief Master Sergeant Brewer personally to inform the senior Secret Service agent of their emergency situation.

"Yes, sir," Brewer said stiffly as he rushed out of the cockpit.

With his mind reeling, Curt Bolton glanced over his left shoulder and saw the scores of jagged holes in the leading edge of the wing. The number-one engine had literally been ripped from its mount, and the second engine was crushed and canted downward at a precarious angle. A greasy trail of blackish-gray smoke poured from the heavily damaged General Electric turbofan.

Bolton pushed harder on the right rudder pedal, banked slightly into the operating engines, and added power to the number-three engine to slow the increasing sink rate. He managed to level the airplane at 2,900 feet.

"Curt," Upshaw solemnly reported, "we've got hydraulic problems . . . and we're losing fuel at a hell of a rate."

Bolton responded in the most calm voice he could muster. "Just take care of the priorities, okay?"

"I'm working on it."

"We gotta concentrate on getting down in one piece," Bolton said with an expression of frustration. "Get another message off to Washington. Tell 'em we have heavy damage—that we're going into Dobbins."

Upshaw nodded and answered a question from the controller. "We've got two engines out and marginal control authority. We're losing hydraulics and we've got fuel pouring out."

"Copy, *Air Force One*. The equipment is in place."

Bolton was beginning to catch glimpses of the ground, but the visibility was still patchy. "What's the field elevation?"

"It's—let's see," Upshaw muttered as he grabbed the Instrument Landing System Runway 11 approach plate. "A thousand and sixty-eight."

When the controller advised them to turn and descend to 2,500 feet, Bolton prayed that they would break out of the clouds. He desperately wanted to get the airplane on the ground as quickly as possible. In its present condition, the wounded Boeing was extremely difficult to handle.

He recalled the United Flight 232 crash landing at Sioux City. After an engine component in a DC-10 disintegrated, the tail-mounted engine exploded and severed the hydraulic systems that powered the primary flight controls. Constantly adjusting the thrust of the wing-mounted engines, the pilots skillfully maneuvered the airplane to the Sioux City Airport, but lost control in the final seconds of the approach. The horrifying crash landing killed 111 people, while 187 survived. Bolton desperately wanted to avoid a similar fate.

"Air Force One," the controller said in an even voice, "I'm going to set you up with the ILS Runway One-One approach—keepin' ya in close."

"Appreciate it."

The president knew they'd had a midair collision. It was obvious that the airplane was staggering through the air. Along with the other passengers, the president was suddenly startled when another airplane thundered close over the top of *Air Force One*. The sound of the passing engines was extremely loud, and a sharp jolt from the severe turbulence of the wing tip vortices shook the huge Boeing. For an instant Macklin allowed a tinge of panic to grip him. He wanted to talk to the pilots, but he knew they had their hands full trying to get the airplane on the ground. Macklin had a gut feeling. *Something is very wrong.*

The president started to get up, then sat down when two Secret Service agents pounded on the door.

"Come in," he uttered.

The agents rushed in and almost fell over Macklin.

"Sir, are you okay?"

"I think so."

"Mr. President," the senior agent exclaimed in a commanding voice, "we've had an accident, and we're going to be landing at Dobbins."

"Is everyone okay?"

The agent ignored the question. "We need to seat you in a different section of the airplane. Please follow us."

Staring into the hazy, opaque clouds, Curt Bolton wrestled the controls of the unsteady 747 as he worked hard to level the aircraft at 2,500 feet. He and Upshaw had performed a flight control check and decided to increase their approach speed by fifteen knots. The flaps were set for the airplane's current configuration, and the pilots were delaying the lowering of the landing gear until they were sure they could make it to the runway.

While Upshaw used the PA system to brief the president and the other passengers about the impending emergency landing, Bolton made judicious throttle corrections to follow the heading changes issued from the new approach controller.

*"Air Force One,* keep it comin'."

The sudden utterance of a drawling, experienced voice was a comforting surprise for the VIP pilots. The senior controller at Dobbins had been placed in charge of *Air Force One.*

On base leg to Runway 11, Bolton finally made visual contact with the surrounding terrain. Seconds later he saw the 10,000-foot runway in the distance. A sigh of relief swept over him as he nursed the battered Boeing toward the air base. For Upshaw's benefit, Bolton jabbed a finger in the direction of the airfield.

"I see it," the copilot exclaimed, staring through the light, intermittent rain. "Thank God and General Electric!"

Lieutenant Colonel Skip Tornquist, the flight leader of the F-15s that had escorted *Air Force One* to Atlanta, taxied to a halt on the ramp at Dobbins ARB. He watched the E-3 AWACS land, then raised his canopy and glanced at the fire trucks racing toward the runway. Seconds later, as he egressed from the cockpit, Tornquist stopped and stared at a lumbering 747 as it emerged from the rain-swollen clouds.

"Oh, my God," he said to himself as he recognized the

famous Flying White House. *Jesus, they're missing an engine.*

In obvious trouble, the airplane was flying in a strange, wing-down, nose-up attitude. *What happened?*

When Tornquist reached the pavement, he and his fellow pilots stared in total shock as *Air Force One* staggered toward the runway. Tornquist clenched his fists. *They aren't going to make it.*

Curt Bolton spotted the sprawling Lockheed Aircraft complex, then saw the array of fire trucks and emergency equipment awaiting them. "They've rolled out the welcome mat."

"Let's hope we won't need it."

"*Air Force One*," the relaxed controller said in a monotone, "continue your turn to . . . right to one-one-zero. The runway'll be at your twelve o'clock, four and a half miles."

"We have it in sight," Upshaw reported with a rush of excitement as he rechecked and identified the localizer frequency. The inbound course was set on 109 degrees and the glideslope and localizer were coming to life. They were intercepting the final course low and in close.

"I'm keepin' you in tight," the controller stated in a confident voice. "You're cleared ILS Runway One-One."

"*Air Force One*—cleared for the approach!"

"Good luck."

"Thanks!"

The approach controller "handed" them off to the tower operator. In turn, the tower controller cleared the flight to land before he gave them the wind direction and speed, followed by the current altimeter setting.

"We're getting slow," Upshaw prompted.

"Okay," Bolton replied while he gently added power on the starboard inboard engine. "We're lookin' good."

Like a sparrow hawk stalking its prey, Upshaw closely monitored the airspeed indicator and other instruments. Bolton now had the approach speed and ILS needles almost pegged.

"Just a second," the colonel said, tight-lipped. "Stand by for the gear."

"Okay."

"Gear down," Bolton finally ordered while he fought to

stay on the glidescope and localizer. "Keep it nailed."

Nine long seconds passed and the nose gear still indicated unsafe.

Wide-eyed with concern, Upshaw hesitantly glanced at Bolton. "We've got an unsafe nose gear."

"That's the least of our problems."

Upshaw shot a look at the airspeed. "We're bleeding off! Power—get some power on! Power!"

Curt Bolton didn't reply as he inched the number-three throttle to the stop. The lumbering 747 yawed ever so slightly as the engine came up to speed and then howled at maximum power.

"We're still slow," Upshaw announced, breathing faster than normal. "Gotta have more power—power!"

Bolton eased the number-four throttle forward and felt the airplane yaw farther to the left. At this slow speed, he couldn't add enough right rudder and right bank to overcome the yaw to the left. He was behind the power curve and he was committed to land on this pass. He couldn't go around for another try. This was it; no second chance.

"Gotta hold my lineup," Bolton admonished himself as the 747 began to sink slowly toward the ground. "Dammit! I should've held the gear until we had the runway made!"

"Do you want to raise the gear—belly it in?"

"No—it's too late," Bolton said through clenched teeth. "We'll hold what we've got—stay with it."

"We're gonna be a little short!"

"Just a tad," Bolton responded stiffly. As much as he tried, he couldn't block out the flashing warning lights on the annunciator panel.

"Airspeed—airspeed!" Upshaw blurted. "We're losing it!"

"Hang on!"

"Raise the nose!"

Low and slow with the wing flaps partially extended, Bolton was struggling to maintain runway alignment and salvage the landing. With more power thundering from the screaming right outboard engine, the 747 was beginning to respond to the excessive sink rate, but the nose was slowly yawing to the left.

Passing between the Navy ramp and the Lockheed Aircraft facility, Bolton increased the angle of bank to the right in a final, desperate attempt to align the sluggish airplane with the runway before *Air Force One* smashed into the ground.

The president sat in stunned silence. Although his mind was having trouble accepting what was happening, he sensed that things were going from bad to worse.

Suddenly the disabled airplane slammed into the overrun just short of the runway threshold. The tremendous impact collapsed the main landing gear and ripped the right outboard engine from under the wing. Jet fuel spilled along the wreckage path, then ignited in a blinding flash. Leaving a long trail of reddish-orange flames and thick black smoke, the stricken Boeing skidded onto the runway and began a long slide on its crushed belly.

Shocked by the incredible force of the crash landing, Macklin and the two Secret Service agents turned to identify the source of the dull orange glow in the cabin.

An eerie ball of bright fire traveled the length of the aisle and mushroomed into a thick cloud of oily smoke near the tail of the 747. The president could hear crackling sounds, then noticed sparks from wires and cables. Macklin recoiled in horror when he realized that his clothing was saturated with jet fuel. *Oh shit! We have to get out of here!*

"Fire!" someone shouted. "We're on fire!"

"We've gotta get out!" an unidentified voice shouted in panic. "We're soaked with fuel!"

"We're gonna die!"

"Don't panic, goddammit!" the senior agent yelled.

"We've got fire in the cabin!"

"Where's the president?"

Panic broke out as more passengers began screaming and yelling, some unfastening their seat belts to scramble toward the nearest door or emergency exit. A well-known reporter from *Newsweek* tripped and fell on his side, causing a group of journalists to go down like bowling pins.

"Get out of the way!" the senior agent ordered passengers as he grabbed the president by the arm. "Move aside!"

"We're on fire, for God's sake!" a woman cried out.

"Move aside!"

"Get us out of here!"

•    •    •

Gripping their control columns, Bolton and Upshaw watched in horror and total exasperation as the careening airplane swerved off the left side of the 300-foot-wide runway. Engulfed in a blazing inferno of jet fuel, the out-of-control plane continued its sickening slide across the ground toward Base Operations and the control tower. Off to the side, fire trucks, ambulances and rescue equipment were accelerating to chase the heavily damaged jumbo jet.

Macklin and the two agents were savagely thrown sideways across a row of seats when the flaming Boeing dug a wingtip into the ground and lurched to a jolting, crunching stop northeast of the helicopter pad at taxiway Juliet.

All the passengers who were out of their seats or had been trying to open escape hatches were forcefully launched down the aisle and over the seats as chaos and panic spread. A mass of tumbling bodies smashed into other passengers, breaking bones and causing other painful injuries and bruises.

Dense black smoke began pouring into the passenger cabin where the aircraft had been torn apart near the middle of the fuselage.

The agents helped the disheveled president to his feet.

"We're on fire!" one of the agents gasped as he shoved people out of the way. "Comin' through! Get out of the way!"

"Get the doors open!" someone yelled.

Trapped by the surge of people trying to get out of the burning plane, the agents forced their way through the frantic passengers. With the president securely in tow, they clawed their way toward the nearest exit. It was clear that no one except the two agents had any interest in being second to the chief executive when it came time to abandon ship.

"Get out of the way!" the first agent said as he shoved a senior White House aide to the side. "You're blocking the aisle!"

Reaching the exit, the agents tossed the president out of the plane. He landed heavily on his back and slowly sat up when the agents hit the ground beside him. Scraped and bruised to the bone, the commander in chief stumbled to his feet and tried to wipe the smudge off his face. He could hear the cacophony of sirens as fire trucks and rescue vehicles quickly responded to the unfolding disaster.

Shaken by the crash landing, an ashen-faced Macklin followed his handlers to the nearest ambulance. While the medical personnel treated his cuts and abrasions, the president watched the firefighters struggle to extinguish the flames pouring out of *Air Force One*.

When he saw the flight crew scramble from the cockpit, Macklin turned to the senior agent. "I want to talk to Colonel Bolton."

# 39

## The Marriott

With his nerves on edge, Khaliq Farkas had switched off all his aircraft radios a few minutes before he heard a remote rumbling sound north-northwest of him. On the one hand, it sounded like rolling thunder coming from many miles away. On the other hand, it sounded like a deep, somewhat muffled explosion, but he wasn't sure what the source was.

He considered the odds that it might have been *Air Force One* impacting the ground, then dismissed the thought as wishful thinking. At least he'd managed to disrupt the arrival of the presidential jet. That was reward enough, knowing that he had sent the foolish president into harm's way. Perhaps next time the leader of the infidels wouldn't be so lucky.

Farkas and Yahyavi moved to the window and cautiously looked around the immediate area surrounding the Airport Marriott. As far as they could see, nothing appeared out of the ordinary. No one was looking up at the building. Everything appeared to be quiet and normal.

Yahyavi unhooked the folding antennas and closed the window shades, then quickly packed the equipment and turned the volume up on the radio scanners.

Seconds later he and Farkas heard a frenzied police report over the public-service band; at least one airplane—possibly two—had crashed near Smyrna. Leaning closer to the scanner, the terrorists listened closely as the first accounts of the accident began pouring in.

They promptly switched the television on and began flipping through the channels. A few scattered reports concerning the crash of an airplane were interrupted by fresh news flashes that indicated that more than one plane had been involved. There were interspersed reports that prior to the crash, Hartsfield/Atlanta International had experienced a major communications failure and that many flights had been diverted to other airports, including Dobbins Air Reserve Base.

Farkas selected another channel and heard the familiar musical interlude that accompanied the bright red "Breaking News" logo.

"This just in to CNN," the vivacious blonde reported. "We're receiving information that *Air Force One* has been involved in a collision and has crash-landed at Dobbins Air Force Base."

Bug-eyed, Farkas and Yahyavi stared at each other, then turned back to the television screen.

"Repeat, *Air Force One* has crash landed. We have unconfirmed reports that the president was aboard at the time the plane went down. CNN will bring you more details when we receive them."

Farkas switched to another station in the metropolitan area.

After a brief explanation of the breaking story by the anchorwoman, a grim-faced local reporter confirmed that an airplane had crashed on the outskirts of Smyrna, Georgia. A moment later the first live television pictures began coming in from the crash site.

Farkas and Yahyavi concentrated on listening to the reporter.

Holding an open umbrella in one hand and a microphone in the other, she was clearly astounded by the devastation surrounding her. Not prepared for the extent of the disaster, the commentator was relaying information as quickly as she was receiving it. Distracted by a low-flying media helicopter, the woman continually glanced at the helo while she answered questions from the news anchor at the Atlanta studio.

•  •  •  •

A smile of immense satisfaction spread across Farkas's face. "We brought down *Air Force One*. We did it!"

"Praise Allahu," Yahyavi said in a trembling voice as he repeatedly poked his thumb into the air. "Death to enemies of the revolution!"

Before Farkas could respond, the police scanner suddenly broadcast a terrorist-threat alert. Transfixed, Farkas and Yahyavi listened to the warning of "potential terrorist activity" in and around the international airport. The woman repeated everything twice, then paused to receive an update.

Every available law enforcement officer was descending on the Atlanta airport and the immediate area surrounding Hartsfield International. According to the dispatcher, the FAA flight controllers believed that the bogus radio instructions had come from somewhere near the airport. Farkas and Yahyavi stared at each other for a moment, then scrambled to gather their belongings and make a run for the rental car.

"What about the equipment?" Yahyavi asked in a frightened voice.

"Leave everything here," Farkas said curtly as he donned his captain's uniform. "Let's get moving."

Abandoning the radio equipment at the Marriott, they drove their rental car straight to the Mercury Air Center building and made a mad dash for the Citation. Both men noted the lack of activity on the aircraft parking ramp. There was no sign of people and no airplane engines running.

Surprised that the crowded parking ramp was deserted, Yahyavi quickly yanked the engine covers off the Citation while Farkas brought the jet to life. With the second engine coming up to speed, Yahyavi jumped through the door and locked it while Farkas called ground control for permission to taxi to the runway.

"Negative, Citation Two-Two Tango Whiskey," the controller said bluntly. "The airport is closed at this time. Do not taxi or reposition your aircraft. I repeat, remain where you are."

Farkas was about to respond to the controller when he and Yahyavi saw two police cars slide to a halt near the fixed-base operation. Farkas's survival instincts were honed to a razor-thin edge.

With their weapons drawn, three officers jumped out of the patrol cars and cautiously approached the idling Citation. One of the men was carrying a high-powered rifle with a scope mounted on top.

"What do we do?" Yahyavi insisted with an anxious expression. "You can't let this happen to us."

"Shut up," Farkas snarled as he shoved the throttles forward and released the brakes. With animal keenness, he wheeled the jet around and raced for the taxiway parallel to runway 8L-26R. Three rounds penetrated the Citation's fuselage as Farkas lurched onto the taxiway and added full power to takeoff downwind.

Once airborne, he sucked the landing gear up and raced northward under the dark clouds. With his transponder turned off, Farkas flew low to avoid radar detection. Fifteen minutes after the frantic escape, Farkas banked sharply to miss a tall tower. Startled by the close call, he zoom-climbed to 1,500 feet and kept a close watch for other traffic. He turned to glance at his accomplice.

Ashen-faced, Yahyavi sat in the cabin and stared at the rays of light coming through the bullet holes.

Farkas grinned as he scanned the hazy sky. If the dice continued to roll in his favor, the jet would soon be hidden in its camouflaged hangar in West Virginia.

# 40

"There's a good-sized one," Jackie announced as she pointed to a large yacht straight ahead of the Maule. "It looks like the same kind of yacht."

Scott lowered the nose and descended toward the gleaming ship. From the wake the yacht was leaving, it was making good speed.

"Only one problem," Dalton said as they rapidly closed on the ship. "They don't have a helicopter onboard, and there isn't a name on the stern."

Jackie raised the binoculars and closely studied the yacht. "It looks exactly the same, except for the blue canopy over the afterdeck."

Scott leveled off at 200 feet. "And the inflatable boat where the helicopter had been on the other ship."

"Let's do a three-sixty," Jackie suggested as she reached for the camera. "That's an exact replica of the other yacht."

"Coincidence?"

"Who knows?"

Abeam the yacht, Scott initiated a climbing turn to circle the craft. *Why are they steaming so fast?*

"No name on the stern," Jackie said mechanically as they banked over the ship. "And no name on either side of the upper deck. What does that tell you?"

"Well, it might be on a delivery cruise to its owner."

"Headed northward?" she asked as she snapped photos of the yacht.

"It could be a West Coast boat," he advised as he allowed the Maule's nose to drop toward the water. "That's why they have that ditch that runs through Panama."

Checking the number of exposures left in the camera, Jackie turned and glanced at the yacht. "Humor me and make a low, slow pass parallel to the stern."

Scott nodded and rolled into a tight, descending turn. "If Ski Cat wasn't telling the truth, we could be chasing a phantom."

Jackie gave him a questioning look. "Even if he *was* telling the truth, the captain could have taken it out in the Gulf."

"Or," Scott suggested as the floatplane skimmed low over the water, "they could've headed toward Cuba or straight out to the Bahamas. Who knows?"

After three quick photos, Jackie leaned back in her seat. "Scott, this just doesn't feel right. Too many coincidences."

"Yeah, I know what you mean." Dalton pointed the Maule toward Key Largo. "If we don't see anything between here and the Ocean Reef Club, we'll contact Hartwell."

A restlessness settled over Jackie as she scanned the horizon. "They have to be out here somewhere."

"On second thought," Scott began slowly, "what we have here is a yacht full of terrorists who, oh-by-the-way, just happen to have a nuclear bomb onboard."

"I believe you have the picture."

He turned to her and raised an eyebrow. "Yeah, it's time to get the Coast Guard and Navy involved in the search."

For a few seconds she gazed at him, then reached for the satellite phone. "The sooner, the better," Jackie declared as she punched in Hartwell's number.

After the Maule made the low pass and turned toward Key Largo, Massoud Ramazani slowly let out his breath and said a prayer to Allahu. Besides the wet paint running down the stern, the helicopter had barely been out of sight when the floatplane suddenly appeared. Still shaking from the close call, Ramazani turned to the inexperienced captain. "Put in at Plantation Key."

The Revolutionary Guardsman made a small course correction. "Do you want me to contact the helicopter pilot?"

"No!" Ramazani blurted with pent-up anger. *You fool!* "He's not coming back to the ship!"

The neophyte skipper hunkered down and paid strict attention to his boat handling. He and his apprentice first mate were still smarting from scraping the hull when they hurriedly cast off from the dock.

After gathering the crew on the bridge, Ramazani laid out his plan. "As soon as we get into port, we'll paint another name on the stern, and we'll paint the deck blue. We'll make all the cosmetic changes we can to the ship this afternoon, and get under way as soon as the sun goes down."

One by one the Maule flew over dozens of yachts and fishing boats, none of which compared with the motoryacht Scott and Jackie were searching for. As they approached the Ocean Reef Club, it was obvious that the terrorists had won the first round.

Hartwell had made arrangements to have a Bell Long-Ranger delivered to them at the Fort Lauderdale–Hollywood International Airport. In addition to Jackie and Scott's efforts, the search for the yacht now included the combined assets of the military and Coast Guard.

Uncomfortable with the fine spray of aviation fuel venting over the wing, Jackie leaned back in her seat. "Let's get this thing on the ground and have a professional photographer look at our negatives."

"No argument from me," he stated emphatically. "I'm just wondering if they went out far enough to be over the horizon."

"That's a possibility."

### Near Huntington, West Virginia

Khaliq Farkas brought the Citation I/SP to a smooth halt on the grass runway and taxied to the hangar. As the engines quietly spooled down, two men hooked the small utility tractor to the jet and quickly pushed it backward into the hangar.

When Farkas and Hamed Yahyavi stepped out of the Citation, Yahyavi went straight to the rest room while Farkas issued the order to paint the corporate jet a different color and change the side number. Afterward he paused to inspect the A-4 Skyhawk. Sporting two Sidewinder air-to-air heat-seeking missiles, the attack jet was also loaded with a full complement of twenty-millimeter cannon shells. Farkas was checking the missiles when one of the cell members rushed into the hangar to report that Bassam Shakhar was on the satellite-phone.

When Farkas lifted the receiver, Shakhar grandly congratulated the terrorist on the downing of *Air Force One*, then sharply chastised Farkas for not killing the president. Shakhar reported that Macklin survived the crash landing, then went on to loudly reiterate the specific goals he had set forth.

"The entire operation," Shakhar said impatiently, "is centered around killing Macklin. Creating chaos and panic throughout the U.S. ranks a close second on my list of priorities, but killing Macklin is your *primary* responsibility. The president is your *primary target*," he said angrily. "Do you understand?"

Not one to take a dressing-down from anyone, Farkas did a slow burn. "My record speaks for itself," he said curtly.

"Your record has a blemish," Shakhar loudly retorted. "You are supposed to be the best, but I have my doubts."

Farkas gripped the phone so tightly that his hand trembled.

"Our goal," Shakhar angrily blurted, "is to kill Macklin and cripple the Americans until the last U.S. soldier is out of the Middle East."

"Islam will prevail," Farkas said loudly and firmly. "The next event is about to start."

# 41

## Washington, D.C.

For security reasons stemming from the Atlanta tragedy, the Secret Service had enlisted the Navy to fly President Macklin back to Washington in a nondescript C-2 Greyhound transport plane. In an effort to keep the security profile as low as possible, the afternoon flight was listed as a routine cross-country training mission.

Accepting the president's invitation, Colonel Curtis Bolton flew home with the commander in chief while the rest of Bolton's crew flew on an Air Force transport. Fortunately, all the passengers onboard Air Force One survived the accident. Macklin assured Bolton that he would continue to be the pilot of *Air Force One.* The two men discussed every aspect of the tragic accident, then talked about Bolton's impending meeting with members of the National Transportation Safety Board.

The president also talked to Bolton about rescheduling the Cornerstone Summit in Atlanta. With the focus of the nation riveted on the Dallas crash and the deadly midair collision involving *Air Force One,* the race initiative had been overshadowed by more pressing concerns.

Later, over a standard flight-crew box lunch, Macklin and Bolton talked about their upcoming trip to California. The president, who was scheduled to give a speech at a mega-bucks fund-raiser in San Francisco, was determined to fulfill his obligation. To that end, Macklin had contacted General Chalmers and set the plan in motion.

Working as a close team, the Marines and the Air Force would supply fighter coverage for the flying White House on the way to the West Coast. On the way back from San Francisco, Air Force and Navy fighters would escort the 747. Every detail of the flight would be kept confidential, including the departure time.

After the twin-engine turboprop landed at Andrews Air Force Base, the chief executive had been transferred to an undistinguished military helicopter for a trip to the National Naval Medical Center in Bethesda, Maryland. When the thorough checkup had been completed, the president had been driven in a nondescript utility van to the White House to recuperate from the harrowing experience.

Wearing a pair of dark sunglasses to cover his bruised right eye, the president strolled into the basement Situation Room and wearily sat down. He was determined to deal a stunning blow to the terrorists and their sponsors.

Waiting for Macklin were Pete Adair, Hartwell Prost, and General Les Chalmers. The president paused, casting a glance at each individual at the table. "I'm declaring a state of national emergency."

Silently, the men exchanged concerned looks.

Macklin looked straight at Adair and Prost. "Use your own judgment in deploying the Reserves and the National Guard, but secure all military installations. I want all of our bases at 'Threatcon Alpha' and I want a massive security clampdown at sensitive federal installations, including nuclear weapons labs. Also, use whatever means you need to surround every airport that has scheduled air service."

In the heat of the moment Adair kept his skepticism to himself. "We better include seaports," he said in a tight, nervous voice.

"Do whatever you think is appropriate," the president said, then changed the subject. "From the ATC tapes and the descriptions from eyewitnesses at the hotel and the airport, the FBI has confirmed that our information from Dalton was right. Khaliq Farkas was one of the two men who were involved in sabotaging the communications in Atlanta. And, in their panic, they left their radios and other equipment at the Marriott."

Macklin's facial muscles grew rigid. "The first thing I intend to do is declare war on terrorism, *and* the states that support them. I'm going to carry the war straight back to the people who have sponsored Farkas and Ramazani and the rest of the lunatics."

Prost looked uneasy, but remained silent.

The president glanced at Prost, then continued. "I intend to demonstrate to the leaders who use, sponsor, or protect terrorists that they will pay a deadly price for their misdeeds. I may not be able to prevent all the terrorist attacks, but I can sure as hell put the fear of God in their sponsors."

The president took a deep breath and slowly exhaled. "This evening, I'm going to make my case to the American people. Congress—for the most part—will follow the polls. I will emphasize that my actions to combat terrorism will be carried out in a manner consistent with our nation's laws, values, and interests. I intend to underscore our basic premise; those who would attack the United States, or her citizens, can expect swift and devastating retribution."

Lighting his cigar, Macklin studied Prost and Adair. "I'm going to instruct the secretary of state to notify the Iranians, the Lebanese, the Afghans, and the Syrians—through the Swiss and other allies—that Tehran, Beirut, Kabul, and Damascus are to close every single terrorist training camp in their countries in the next seventy-two hours. If they aren't closed by the appointed time, I will destroy the camps and any form of opposition we encounter."

Prost had a question. "What about the Palestinian Authority, Libya, and the other rogue states that support terrorism?"

"The secretary of state will send a diplomatic message to Libya informing them that within seventy-two hours they must close all terrorist training camps, expel all terrorists from Libya, and cease construction on their chemical and biological weapons plants. If they don't comply, we'll eradicate their camps and weapons facilities."

The president puffed on his cigar. "The same for the Palestinian Authority. Either dismantle the terrorist wings of Hamas and Islamic Jihad, or the United States will do it for you—and it isn't open for discussion."

Prost glanced at Macklin, then surveyed the other men. "Another matter we need to address is the Sudanese. What the Barbary Coast was for pirates, Sudan has become for terrorists. I recommend the same time frame for them to close every terrorist camp under their control, or they'll feel the brunt of American military power."

"I'm in complete agreement," Macklin said evenly. "Is there anyone who doesn't support this course of action?"

Silence engulfed the room.

Macklin turned to his SecDef. "Pete, I'd like your assessment."

"For the most part, I concur. If the sponsor states fail to comply with our demands, I strongly recommend that we use conventional cruise missiles on the first round of attacks. However, I have to add a caveat."

The president's eyes narrowed. "Let's hear it."

"If the terrorism continues, we better be ready to use our 'bunker busters' to destroy their high-value underground complexes, like Libya's chemical weapons plant at Tarhuna and the deep caves in the mountains of Afghanistan."

"Whatever it takes," Macklin said firmly.

"After the Gulf War," Adair continued, "most everyone in the region buried their most important assets, made their weapons more mobile, and fabricated triple-redundant communications systems. It's going to take more than conventional weapons to destroy them."

"As I said, whatever it takes." Macklin turned his attention to General Chalmers. "Do you have any reservations about using the B61s?"

Chalmers hesitated a moment, thinking about the wisdom of deploying the new, needle-shaped, earth-penetrating hydrogen bombs. Packaged in depleted uranium 30 percent heavier than lead, the 340-kiloton warheads would detonate three to six meters below the surface, creating a massive shock wave capable of obliterating targets hundreds of meters wide and hundreds of meters deep.

Weapons experts believed that most of the radiation would be contained underground, *if* the slender bomb impacted at the proper angle and velocity. If the angle of entry was too shallow, the bomb could slice under the ground, then skip back out and cause extensive collateral damage from a surface blast.

Chalmers quietly cleared his throat. "Using nuclear weapons is a high-risk option, but I'm confident that we can achieve the desired results without contaminating too much surface damage."

Macklin gazed steadily into Chalmers's eyes. "What kind of surface damage are we talking about?"

"Depending on the wind conditions, it's possible that lethal radiation could be spread over eight to ten square miles."

"Mr. President," Prost said with a pained expression. "The International Court of Justice has ruled that any threat or use of nuclear weapons, other than where the very survival of a nation is threatened, is against international law."

"When our country is being invaded by terrorists," Macklin said drolly, "I supersede the court."

"You might want to reconsider," Prost advised.

"Understand this very clearly," the president retorted in a strained voice. "I *am* going to put a major damper on those thugs."

Unfazed by the harsh treatment, Hartwell's expression remained the same. "It's your choice, sir."

"You're damn right it is," Macklin exclaimed, and turned to face General Chalmers. "Put the Fifth Fleet on alert and have the Roosevelt battle group ready for action."

"Yessir."

"I'd also like for you and the joint chiefs to give Secretary Adair and me an up-to-date target list in twenty-four hours."

"You'll have it in twelve hours," Chalmers said with great enthusiasm. "I'll be here at 0730."

"I'll be expecting you," the president said evenly. "Meeting adjourned."

When Macklin rose from his chair, Prost caught his eye. "Can you spare a few minutes?"

"Sure," Macklin said as he puffed on his cigar. "Let's get out of this hole. I need some fresh air."

## The South Portico

Ignoring the sage advice of the section chief of the Presidential Detail, the commander in chief and Hartwell Prost sat down in rocking chairs near the South Portico. Macklin was a stationary target for any madman with a high-powered rifle. Add a scope to a weapon having a muzzle velocity high enough for hunting elephants, and the assassin could be miles away before anyone could figure out where the round came from.

Troubled by the accident in Atlanta, the special agent in charge of the Secret Service contingent was extremely unhappy about being overruled by the president. Agent Tim Oberlander, like many other special agents who served in the White House, had warm feelings for the man they were responsible for protecting twenty-four hours a day. The agents were bound by an oath to ensure the safety of the president, and it made their job more difficult when the chief executive did not cooperate with them.

Although the sun had set a few minutes earlier, a reddish orange hue hugged the horizon and provided ample light for some nutcase to train his sights on the president. Uncomfortable about the situation, Agent Oberlander took up his position and carefully viewed the area overlooking the portico.

Along with his fellow agents, he couldn't wait to get his charge inside the mansion and tucked in for the night. Once POTUS—the president of the United States—was put away in the family quarters, the men and women of the detail could take off their shoes and relax, even share a few laughs over a beer and a pizza.

Prost glanced at the Marines guarding the White House, then noticed that Macklin's jaw muscles were grinding back and forth. The president forced a smile as he took in the lights beginning to twinkle in the nation's Capitol.

"What's on your mind?"

"Fraiser Wyman," Prost said mechanically. "His sudden wealth came from a trust fund his grandfather set up years ago. Apparently the old man knew his grandson fairly well. Fraiser couldn't collect the money until his forty-fifth birthday, which was two months ago yesterday."

"I'll be damned," the president said with obvious relief. "What's the flip side—who's in bed with the Iranians?"

"I don't know," Prost groused. "We'll just have to keep digging. Sandra Hatcher and I will stay on it."

Macklin quietly nodded.

"New subject?" Prost asked.

"Sure."

"Sir, after this incident in Atlanta, it's time to take some extraordinary measures to ensure the safety of you and the first lady."

"Hartwell," the president declared impatiently, "I have the Marine Corps guarding me, I ride around in an armored car, and we've closed part of Pennsylvania Avenue to public traffic. My home is a fortress with reinforced walls, electronic sensors along the fence, metal detectors that screen all visitors, bomb-sniffing dogs running around, over a million and a half dollars' worth of armored glass, and round-the-clock security. Oh, I almost forgot—I have a bombproof subbasement, too."

"Sir, I know you don't like the idea of limiting the public's access to the White House, and to yourself, but you know it's absolutely necessary."

Prost's impassioned words evoked a strong response from Macklin.

"Christ," the president snorted in protest. "We have snipers and antiaircraft batteries mounted on the roof. What's next—gunships circling the White House?"

"That's exactly what I recommend."

Macklin gave Prost a questioning look. "You can't be serious."

"Until we have Farkas and the other nuts in custody," Prost said slowly and clearly, "I strongly suggest that armed aircraft—or helicopter gunships—accompany you wherever you go."

"Why not put me in Leavenworth?"

"That's an option," Prost said firmly, then cracked a smile. "Raven Rock would be my choice."

The president was stubbornly persistent. "The people feel more and more estranged from their government. I'm trying to make government smaller—make myself more approachable. At a time like this—a national emergency—I can't afford to distance myself from the public. It sends the wrong message."

Prost lowered his voice so the agents could not hear him.

"Mr. President, I'm asking you to do this as a personal favor to me."

Macklin cringed at the thought of hiding from cowards. "Hartwell, I'm the leader of the country. I can't lead from the back lines."

"Allow the military," Prost said with a steely-calm voice, "to provide air cover until we have the terrorists behind bars, or in the morgue."

The president leaned his head back and pointed skyward. "There are fighter planes orbiting overhead as we speak, twenty-four hours a day."

The sensitive discussion came to an abrupt halt while the two men stared each other down.

"Okay, dammit," the president said with open irritation. "But I don't want fighter planes to be seen anywhere near *Air Force One* when we're taking off or landing."

"That won't be a problem."

"Let's keep it low-key and quiet."

"Fair enough, sir."

# 42

## Fort Lauderdale

Recovering from the shock of the tragic events in Atlanta, Scott and Jackie were having dinner at the Pier 66 Resort and Marina. Having exchanged their Key West "costumes" for more traditional garb, they were deeply enmeshed in the details of the crash landing when an attractive young lady approached their table.

"Are you the Dalton party?" the sultry brunette asked Scott.

"That's us," Jackie cheerfully chimed in. "What can we do for you?"

"You have a couple of urgent messages," the woman said coldly as she handed Jackie two slips of paper.

"Thank you."

"You're welcome," the flirtatious woman said as she smiled at Scott and sashayed out of the restaurant.

"This one's from the photographer," Jackie said as she flipped her cell phone open and punched in the number.

"I hope he has something," Scott commented as he looked at the other message. The Bell LongRanger had been delayed by unexpected maintenance, but it was due to arrive in Fort Lauderdale by seven P.M. Dalton slid the note to Jackie, then polished off the last bite of his dessert.

She quickly finished her conversation with the certified

aerial photographer and snapped the phone closed.

"We were duped," she admitted with a pained look. "We flew right over *Bon Vivant*, but the name had been painted out."

"You have to be kidding," Scott said in a quiet, hollow voice. "How could he tell it was the *Bon Vivant*?"

"He placed the negatives under a microscope and there was a telltale pattern of letters underneath what he figures was a light coat of paint. He said that another layer of paint would have completely concealed the name."

Scott slowly shook his head. "Does he suspect anything?"

"I doubt it." Jackie smiled serenely. "I told him it was a divorce issue, my husband was trying to hide assets from me."

"What a gal." Scott chuckled softly, then turned serious. "We have to get copies of the photos to Hartwell. They need to be distributed to the military and Coast Guard as quickly as possible."

"Relax," Jackie said soothingly. "In about an hour he's going to bring me three prints of each picture of *Bon Vivant*."

"Good," Scott said with obvious pleasure. "Hartwell can make arrangements for a military plane to fly them to Washington tonight."

Jackie sipped her iced tea. "After we get the photos headed in the direction of Washington, let's go check out the helo."

Scott leaned back in his chair and raised his napkin. "That sounds good to me."

"We also need to reserve our survival gear," she commented. "Then we'll be ready to go at first light."

"Yeah, we want at least a four-man life raft and two life vests." Scott struggled to conceal the frustration he was feeling. "This deal about Farkas having an A-4 really bothers me."

"It's a nightmare."

"What do you think he plans to do with it?"

Jackie paused a moment. "I don't know, but you can hang a lot of ordnance on it—enough to flatten the White House."

### Houston Intercontinental Airport

Dressed in an expensive suit and new shoes, Ruhollah Ferdowsi calmly presented a phony driver's license, a Sam's

Club picture ID card, and a fake UN diplomatic pass to the ticket agent. The smiling woman behind the counter accepted his traveler's checks and issued Ferdowsi a ticket in the coach section of Continental Flight 460 to New York City.

A controversial computerized profiling system identified Ferdowsi as a possible security risk. His large leather bag was thoroughly searched and matched to him. After he boarded the MD-80 and took window seat F in Row 26, his bag was stowed aboard the airplane.

Forty-nine minutes after the 6:55 P.M. departure, Ferdowsi excused himself and clambered over the two businessmen sitting in the aisle and center seats. The shy-looking man ambled back to the rest rooms, entered the one on the left side of the airplane, and locked the door.

Ferdowsi closed his eyes and spent two minutes in quiet meditation, then opened his eyes and sat down on the toilet lid. He removed his shoes and socks, loosened his tie, and opened the small plastic container of anthrax taped to his ankle. It was time to complete his mission for the revolution.

One minute later the plastic explosive the "throwaway" had taped to the bottom of his right foot blew the entire tail off the jetliner, including the aft galley and the passengers in Rows 29 through 33. A flight attendant was also sucked out of the airplane by the explosive decompression.

Amazingly, the pilot managed to keep the aircraft under control for almost twenty seconds. When the captain pulled the throttles back, the loss of equilibrium finally overwhelmed him and he lost control of the stricken airplane. The ensuing crash on a small farm northwest of Jackson, Mississippi, killed all 117 souls onboard. Another ninety-four firefighters, rescue workers, paramedics, law enforcement officers, and media personnel died from exposure to the anthrax germs.

### Minneapolis–St. Paul International Airport

Thirty minutes after the Continental jet went down, three members of a special action cell monitored their aircraft radio as the controller gave the pilot of a Northwest Airlines Airbus permission to take off. The Iranians had patiently waited for this particular flight to depart.

Less than a minute after rising from the runway and climbing into the evening sky, the A320 was hit by a Swedish Bofors RBS-70 antiaircraft missile. The fiery explosion blew the starboard engine into thousands of glowing pieces and started a raging fire in the wing.

While the flight crew frantically struggled to return to the airport, another portable missile struck the same engine, blowing the power plant completely off the airplane. Seconds later the right wing exploded in a fireball, sending the Airbus into a slow-motion spin.

The horrific crash took the lives of everyone onboard, including a former Iranian clandestine agent in the CIA's Directorate of Operations. The terrorists had done their homework in finding the turncoat who had caused the deaths of four of their leaders.

The members of the terrorist cell were almost caught as they made their getaway from the perimeter of the airport. Two police officers happened to see a streak rise into the sky from the vicinity of a Budget cargo van. Seconds later another streak flashed skyward as the vehicle quickly accelerated away from the scene. While the patrolmen were pursuing the van, the Airbus crashed with a thunderous explosion.

Suffering from shock, the officers chased the speeding vehicle through heavy traffic. As they closed in on the van, they called for backup, then swerved when the rear doors of the cargo van flew open. The officer driving the patrol car locked the brakes, but both policemen died at the scene from a fusillade of rounds from an automatic weapon.

## 1600 Pennsylvania Avenue

Like a caged lion, the restless president prowled the White House Treaty Room while he waited for Hartwell Prost to arrive. Located on the second floor near the presidential living quarters, the former Cabinet Room was Macklin's favorite place to discuss sensitive issues with his closest advisers.

Seconds after he arrived at the White House, Prost was quickly ushered to the Treaty Room. The ashen color of his face gave away the fact that he had heard about the crash in Mississippi.

"Have a seat," the president said after the special assistant closed the door behind him.

Although he was disconcerted, Prost maintained a reserved, dignified aura about him as he took a seat.

"I assume you've heard about the Continental crash," the president said impatiently.

"Yes," Prost said clearly. "I just heard about it."

"Do you have any doubt?" Macklin asked with a hint of rage in his voice. "Any *fraction* of a doubt that it wasn't terrorism?"

"No." The veins in Hartwell's neck were protruding. "We can't afford to wait seventy-two hours for the Iranians—or anyone else—to make a decision to call off the attacks. If we don't send an immediate message to the sponsor states— every one of them—we run the risk of having our nation and our citizens held hostage to regimes bent on destroying us."

The president paced the floor, then sat down. "*Dammit,* I have to think this through."

Prost nodded, but kept quiet. *We're at their mercy . . . you have to do something.* From previous difficult experiences with the president, Hartwell knew it was better to let the storm blow itself out before he attempted to explain anything, or to defend a course of action he had recommended.

"They've gone too far," Macklin said bitterly. "I'm going to shut down their military, their infrastructure—electricity, water, fuel—knock them on their asses without a huge loss of life."

"I concur, Mr. President."

Macklin stared at Prost for a moment, then looked down at the floor. "We need to convene the NSC and have the joint chiefs lay out—"

A sudden knock on the door interrupted the president as the first lady stepped through the door. "There's been another crash," she exclaimed breathlessly. "They said something about the Minneapolis–St. Paul area."

In disbelief, Macklin and Prost stared at Maria.

"An airliner?" the president asked.

"Yes. It was a Northwest Airbus," she said, then sat down on the edge of a chair next to her husband. "Witnesses have reported that it was hit by a missile—right after takeoff."

"Hartwell," the president said with icy stiffness. "I want all the players in the Situation Room on the double."

"Yes, sir," Prost said as he hurried toward the door.

Maria reached for her husband's hand and held it tightly. "You're going to have to tell the American people something."

"I know," he conceded reluctantly. "When it's the proper time."

"Cord," she said boldly, "there's a sense of panic out there, and it's spreading faster by the minute."

Macklin's nerves went tense. "I have to set some military responses in motion before I go on television," he quietly said with a determined expression.


## Pier 66 Resort and Marina

Having made arrangements for their survival gear, Jackie and Scott were taken aback when they entered the lobby of the resort. Everyone was talking loudly and many of the guests seemed to be agitated and frightened. Scott politely interrupted a conversation between a bell captain and an elderly couple who were checking out of the hotel.

"Excuse me," Scott said to the young man. "Can you tell me what's going on?"

"The terrorists have downed another airliner," he said in a rush as he quickly loaded bags.

"Possibly two planes," the older gentleman exclaimed. "That's what the newspeople are saying."

Scott exchanged a concerned look with Jackie, then excused himself and took her by the arm. They made their way through the crowd and went to his room. After he closed the door, Jackie turned on CNN while he called the Jet Center fixed-base operator at the airport. He asked the customer services manager to top off the LongRanger with jet fuel and place the life raft and life vests in the lobby.

Turning to the television, Scott watched while the stunned anchor recapped the tragic events that were capturing the attention of the world. Another accident had just occurred near St. Louis when a TWA MD-80 crash-landed after reporting an explosion in the forward section of the passenger cabin.

"Many of the airlines are grounding their planes," Jackie announced. "There's a nationwide run on rental cars, and it's pure pandemonium at most of the major airports."

"Jackie," Scott began slowly as he kept his eyes on the television. "We need to head for Key West tonight. We don't have time to locate a UHF radio and have it installed."

"You're right," she said while she watched the breaking news stories. "If we have to, we can have the controllers relay information from us to the military."

"Yeah, we'll work around it." Scott began packing his bag. "At first light, I want to be looking for Ramazani's yacht. If they have a nuke onboard, the entire East Coast is at risk. We'll keep going north until we find it, or run out of daylight."

"Between the Coast Guard and the Navy," Jackie said as she reached for her room key, "we're going to have a lot of competition."

"I thrive on it."

Jackie rose from her chair and headed for the door. "I'll meet you in the lobby in ten minutes."

"I'll be there."

## The Yacht

Renamed *Sweet Life*, the 126-foot Broward was forty miles northeast of Ft. Pierce, Florida, when the first signs of daylight appeared on the eastern horizon. With the main fuel tanks and auxiliary tanks filled to capacity at Plantation Key, the splendid motoryacht had more than enough range to steam nonstop to Washington, D.C.

Manning the bridge, the tired and inexperienced first mate was sitting in a wide, elevated chair monitoring the autopilot and radar. His eyelids would slowly droop shut, then snap open when his head suddenly fell forward.

After undergoing a complete face-lift at Plantation Key, *Sweet Life* appeared to be a completely different ship. Along with the name change and extensive repainting, Ramazani had invited two comely passengers to join him on the cruise. Twins, Robyn and Kara Proctor had been overwhelmed by the offer of a free round-trip vacation to Washington, D.C., on a magnificent yacht.

Former students of Professor Massoud Ramazani, the shapely, blue-eyed blondes were on vacation from the University of Miami. They had quickly thrown their things together and raced from North Miami Beach to Plantation Key. When they arrived, Ramazani had explained that a wealthy uncle—a Saudi Arabian prince—had given him permission to take the ship on an extended cruise. He also encouraged the sisters to spend as much time as possible on the large, open-sky lounge.

The skeleton crew was belowdecks having breakfast when Ramazani walked onto the bridge.

Having succumbed to the insidious effects of fatigue, the first mate had fallen asleep at the wheel.

Ramazani forcefully slapped the back of the man's head, knocking him out of the captain's chair. "Get out of my sight," he exclaimed in a rage. "Send that other moron up here!"

Less than two minutes later the disheveled skipper appeared on the bridge. He was still tucking his shirttail into his trousers as he climbed into the captain's chair.

A deep frown crossed Ramazani's face. "If either one of you ever fall asleep on duty again, you will be shark shit an hour later."

Red in the face, the captain clenched his jaws shut and stared out to sea. *One more threat and he will be the one who has an accident.*

Ramazani spun around and left the bridge, then began a leisurely tour of the yacht, stopping to chat with Kara and Robyn for a few minutes. Afterward he went below to check the security of the nuclear bomb, then returned to the bridge.

An hour later, while the twins were lounging on the open sundeck, a Coast Guard HH-60J Jayhawk flew over the ship and circled back for a closer look. When the helo slowed to a crawl, Ramazani's pulse raced as he stepped away from the passageway leading to the bridge.

"Wave at them," he said loudly to Robyn and Kara. "They love for people to wave at them."

The sisters smiled and waved at the crew. Both pilots and a crewman waved back as the twin-engine Sikorsky gained speed and continued northwest toward Jacksonville.

Ramazani let out a sigh of relief and eyed two fully loaded AK-47 semiautomatic assault rifles propped against the starboard bulkhead. Next to the AK-47s were two portable antiaircraft missiles. He gazed at the attractive young women. *At least they'll have a good time before they die.*

# 43

## The Persian Gulf

Along with surface ships of the U.S. 5th Fleet, the attack submarines USS *Jefferson City* and USS *Annapolis* launched Tomahawk cruise missiles at selected targets in Iran, then stood by for further orders from the White House. Within the time span of an average lunch break, the primary terrorist training centers used by al-Islamiyah, the Revolutionary Guard Corps, Hamas, Hezbollah of Hejaz, and al-Gamaat were reduced to smoking ruins and twisted metal.

One compound in particular, the Imam Ali Camp in east Tehran, was leveled by seven Tomahawks from the USS *Gonzales*, an Arleigh Burke–class destroyer. A fourth missile went astray and hit the Azadi Hotel, formerly the Hyatt Hotel, knocking a huge hole in the decaying building.

In addition, eight more cruise missiles from the destroyer USS *Stout* pulverized a safe house used by a cell of Bassam Shakhar's lieutenants. Another U.S. warship destroyed buildings used by senior members of the Iranian intelligence service. A minute later the top-secret Iranian Defense Technology and Science Research Center near Karaj was destroyed by three Tomahawks.

Thirty miles to the north, other ships of the 5th Fleet were launching wave after wave of Tomahawk missiles at terrorist compounds and runways and taxiways at military airfields in

Iran. The mission was simple; make it impossible for Tehran to launch any fighter aircraft.

Minutes later a second round of cruise missiles destroyed or damaged a large number of Iran's military aircraft, including many of the 121 jets Tehran inherited from Iraq during the Persian Gulf War. While the jets were burning to the ground, other Tomahawks were destroying missile plants in Semnan and Esfahan and design centers at Kuh-e Bagh-e-Melli, Sultanabad, and Lavizan.

## The Red Sea

Three U.S. ships fired missiles directly into Sudanese airspace. Nine Tomahawks slammed into suspected terrorist base camps and support camps and a chemical weapons plant in Khartoum. Another missile malfunctioned and hit an apartment building, killing sixteen innocent victims and setting fire to an adjacent bakery.

## The Arabian Sea

The submarine USS *Boise* joined surface ships to cause heavy damage to terrorist training camps and support facilities in three remote areas of Afghanistan. Twelve Tomahawks shattered a command-and-control building at a large base ninety miles south of Kabul. Other missiles flattened terrorist housing, indoctrination, administrative, and logistics centers, including storage buildings containing weapons and ammunition.

## The Mediterranean Sea

Sixth Fleet attack submarines and surface combatants rained Tomahawk missiles on selected terrorist compounds in the Bekaa Valley. Despite two missiles that malfunctioned and crashed harmlessly into the sea, every target was obliterated, including the Shaykh Abdallah Barracks, a military training facility used by the Iranian Revolutionary Guards and Hezbollah fighters. Key areas of infrastructure supported by Bassam Shakhar and his followers were hit especially hard, including the compound where Maritza Gunzelman had gleaned so much valuable information.

A volley of missiles hit terrorist training camps, support camps, and safe havens in the Palestinian Authority-ruled West Bank and Gaza. Thirty-seven terrorists who were training in tactics and weaponry were killed by Tomahawks that carried cluster munitions designed to explode shrapnel bomblets over a large area.

Operating separately from other U.S. ships in the Mediterranean Sea, the Ticonderoga-class cruiser USS *Vella Gulf*, the attack submarine *Montpelier*, and the destroyers *Ramage* and *Hayler* joined the assault on terrorist facilities and selected military targets in the Bekaa Valley. One of the submarine's Tomahawks malfunctioned and went off course, barely missing a Greek cruise ship forty-five miles from the *Montpelier*. Many of the startled passengers, including a large group of Americans, watched in horror as the errant missile plunged into the sea 200 yards off the ship's port bow.

## Los Angeles International Airport

Although the freeways were clogged, the normally bustling airport was unusually quiet this morning. Except for a string of corporate planes and jumbo jets from foreign airlines, few domestic airliners were taking off or landing. Even the smaller commuter airlines were operating less than twenty percent of their flights.

Tempers were running short as frightened and disgruntled passengers scrambled to get refunds from airlines and travel agents. Hordes of people who were trying to make alternative travel arrangements found that it was an exercise in futility. The demand had quickly exceeded the available seats on buses and trains. Rental cars were almost nonexistent and commanded exorbitant rates.

Wearing the uniform of a baggage handler who had been murdered a few minutes earlier, Ahmad Quraishi walked to the US Airways Boeing 737. He cautiously surveyed the immediate area while he helped load bags, then scrambled into the cargo hold when the other loader was not looking. He crawled into a corner and covered himself with luggage. Knowing that he was playing an important role in the Islamic revolution, Quraishi was confident that he would be remembered as a warrior.

Twenty minutes after US Airways Flight 36 departed from Los Angeles for Philadelphia, the deceased baggage handler was found by his supervisor. Every airplane on the ramps at Los Angeles International was grounded, while the few flights that had departed during the previous hour were quickly notified of a potential threat to safety. Two of the planes diverted to the nearest suitable airport while the other flights continued to their destinations.

After the first officer of US Airways Flight 36 took a stroll through the cabin and didn't see anyone who looked suspicious, the captain elected to continue to Philadelphia. Although there were only twenty-seven passengers onboard, the captain was determined to give them the best service he could provide.

In the baggage compartment of the 737, Ahmad Quraishi flicked on his tiny flashlight and checked his wristwatch, then made himself comfortable. The "throwaway" had his orders and he intended to do exactly what he had been instructed to do in the name of Allahu.

As the flight progressed toward Philadelphia, both pilots began to relax. They were evading thunderstorms and discussing the captain's tennis game when the airplane suddenly exploded, raining bodies, anthrax, and flaming debris across the Indianapolis Motor Speedway.

### Melbourne, Florida

After flying and searching all day, Jackie and Scott were exhausted and frustrated. From Key West to Melbourne, they had seen only two yachts that vaguely resembled the former *Bon Vivant*.

With the sun dipping below the horizon, Jackie checked the fuel and reluctantly turned toward the coastline. "That's it—we're too low on gas."

"We've been too low for twenty minutes," Scott said flatly, then lowered his binoculars and glanced at Jackie. "I can't believe we haven't seen anything that even remotely looks like the yacht."

"They may have ducked into the Intracoastal Waterway,"

she suggested, "or found a way to camouflage the ship in one of the yacht basins."

"I don't think so."

"Why not?" she asked as she gazed at the setting sun. "They may want to lie low for a while—wait for things to cool off."

Scott glanced at a large sailboat as it flashed under the helo. "I think this whole operation is organized around a sequence of scheduled events. If that's true, we should overtake them tomorrow."

"Unless"—Jackie pointed at their sectional chart— "they're steaming a hundred miles or so from the coast."

"We can't cover everything."

"That's why we have the Navy and Coast Guard," Jackie said, then changed course to check out a large yacht. "The Guard's HH-60Js can fly three hundred nautical miles out to sea, refuel from a ship, then search for extended periods of time."

"I still think they aren't going to stray too far from the coast."

"You may be right." Jackie turned the volume up on the VHF radio and started to say something, then stopped and listened in shock to the terse message from a controller to a pilot.

Stunned by the news of the US Airways crash, Scott turned to Jackie. "How are they getting the explosives through security?"

"I don't know, but this is totally out of control."

Scott glanced at the last rays of sunlight. "We're in deep trouble."

"No kidding," Jackie declared. "What's more, we have Farkas on the loose."

"Oh, yeah. He'll surface again."

"I don't even want to think about it," Jackie said, then looked at Scott. "Even with all the safeguards they have around the White House, it wouldn't take much creativity to flatten it."

"That's right, and Farkas knows how to pull it off."

She pointed out a low-flying airplane, then contacted Patrick Air Force Base Approach Control.

Unbeknownst to Scott and Jackie, *Sweet Life* was cruising at eleven knots thirty-two miles northeast of Melbourne.

# 44

## The Oval Office

Maria Eden-Macklin slipped into the Oval Office a few seconds before the president was scheduled to speak. Concerned about the toll the terrorist crisis was taking on her husband, she gave him a smile and a discreet thumbs up.

Dressed in a dark blue suit and gray silk tie, Cord Macklin returned the gesture with a slight nod before he looked straight at the television camera. *Okay, stay relaxed and calm. Image is everything.*

"Fifteen seconds," the director advised.

The president took a long, deep breath and forced himself to relax his facial muscles. It was difficult to do since he couldn't stop thinking about the latest tragedies. The American 757 that crashed near Little Rock, Arkansas, after being struck by a portable missile had been devastating, but the Southwest jetliner that was shot down during its approach to Dallas Love Field had left absolute carnage on Hines Boulevard. Both terrorist cells escaped unharmed. A few other potential disasters had been averted by excellent CIA and FBI intelligence, combined with incompetence in the ranks of the militants, but the terrorists were still scoring heavy blows.

Macklin let out his breath. *Speak clearly and slowly.*

The red light came on.

"Good evening," Macklin said with a solemn look. He paused to school his voice. *Don't frown.*

"My fellow Americans, and our friends around the world, I come to you this evening with a heavy heart. Our nation and our citizens are being attacked by governments that substitute terrorism for statesmanship and anti-Americanism for religious belief."

Viewers were spellbound. On every continent, in homes, businesses, hotels, resorts, and bars, most conversations came to an abrupt end.

"The despicable acts of terrorism that have killed and injured so many of our citizens will not be overlooked or forgotten. As we mourn our dead and injured, I want to explain some important facts to those who choose to be our enemies."

Macklin's eyes were riveted on the camera lens.

"Terrorism will not be tolerated," he said with deep passion in his voice. "Not while I'm president of the United States of America. As I speak, the sponsors of these cowardly attacks *are* paying a stiff penalty for their transgressions. If the terrorist attacks continue, their sponsors *will* pay even greater penalties. If we apprehend these barbarians, we will prosecute them to the extent the law allows. Make no mistake about my commitment. No one, and no amount of condemnation, is going to dissuade me from the course I have charted."

An eerie quiet pervaded the Oval Office.

"We *do not* have a dispute with the citizens of the countries that support terrorism. However, if your leaders allow these deliberate and murderous acts of terrorism to continue, lives will be lost on your side, innocent lives."

The president paused to swallow.

"My fellow citizens, the United States of America is under siege. As long as I reside in the White House, your country will remain safe and secure. Our military, the finest and best-equipped military in the world, stands by to protect each and every one of you. These contemptible acts of violence have shattered our peaceful lives for the moment, but we're Americans, and, we *will* rise to the challenge of vanquishing the terrorists and their backers."

Macklin's jaw hardened.

"Before I close my remarks, I must make one thing crystal clear to the terrorists and to their sponsors. We know who you are, and we have you in our crosshairs. If this cowardly assault on our country continues, I promise you that I will punish you round-the-clock. I will punish you until you have no military assets or infrastructure left. You will rue the day you attacked the citizens of the United States of America."

The president clenched his jaw muscles. *Easy, nothing dramatic.*

"My fellow citizens, I pledge to you that I will stop this reign of terror. Good night, and godspeed."

### Whiteman Air Force Base, Missouri

Nine minutes after the president made his promise, the B-2 Advanced Technology Bomber *Spirit of South Carolina* lifted off the runway and climbed into the moonlit sky. In the space of six minutes, five more stealth bombers from the 509th Bombardment Wing were on their way to the "rogue" nations that supported international terrorism.

The $2.3-billion warplanes were carrying assorted bomb loads, including the Joint Direct Attack Munition, 4,500-pound deep-penetrating bombs, and the B61 "bunker buster" hydrogen bombs. Two of the front-line aircraft, call signs Darth 66 and Darth 63, were configured to carry eighty 500-pound bombs in the two weapons bays.

The most survivable U.S. aircraft in the fleet, the sinister-looking "batplane" is virtually undetectable to acoustic signatures, infrared and radar. With the assistance of KC-10 advanced tanker/cargo aircraft from the 60th Air Mobility Wing at Travis Air Force Base and the 305th AMW at McGuire AFB, the B-2 bombers can take part in a battle mission anywhere in the world within twenty-four hours, then return safely to their base at Whiteman.

### Holloman Air Force Base, New Mexico

Eight F-117A Nighthawks from the 9th Fighter Squadron of the 49th Fighter Wing were in the process of taking off for the long flight to the Middle East. Another eight warplanes from the "Black Sheep" of the 8th Fighter Squadron were preparing to take off. With a radar cross section of one one-hundredth of a square yard—the size of a small bird—the "Wobblin' Goblin" is an invisible bomber that can hit a target the size of a coffee table.

The unique design of the single-seat stealth airplane provides incredible combat capabilities. Loaded with laser-guided weapons, the sleek strike fighter can destroy hardened targets with devastating accuracy. The pilots had been given extremely high-resolution KH-11 spacecraft images of their target areas and specific objectives. Like the B-2s, the Nighthawk aviators would use KC-10 and KC-135 tanker aircraft to complete their mission.

### Dyess Air Force Base, Texas

*Oh Hard Luck* and seven other supersonic B-1B bombers from the 28th Bomb Squadron roared into the star-studded sky and set course for targets that included terrorist training camps, logistics centers, chemical and biological weapons plants, underground command and control centers, and safe houses for international terrorists.

While the strategic warplanes climbed to altitude, six additional B-1B Lancers from the "Bones" of the 77th Bomb Squadron at Ellsworth Air Force Base lifted into the night and began their long flight to the Middle East. All of the intercontinental planes contained conventional 500-pound and 1,000-pound bombs.

Four additional B-1B bombers based in Thumrait, Oman, would fly multiple missions to destroy terrorist training centers and weapons-storage facilities.

### Barksdale Air Force Base, Louisiana

After one of the B-52 pilots aborted his takeoff because of a faltering engine, five other long-range strategic bombers from the 2nd Bombardment Wing departed for a thirty-six-hour, nonstop combat mission to the Gulf region. With an unrefueled range in excess of 8,800 statute miles, aerial refueling gives the eight-engined "Stratofortress" a range limited only by crew endurance.

Although the airplane can carry a significant array of

weapons, the heavy bombers from the 20th Bomb Squadron were configured with revolver-type launcher systems to carry eight subsonic Conventional Air Launched Cruise Missiles. This arrangement, coupled with worldwide precision navigation equipment, gives the B-52H an incredibly accurate "drive-by shooting" capability.

## Melbourne International Airport, Florida

The sun was barely above the horizon when Jackie and Scott donned their life vests and boarded the LongRanger. She quickly brought the ship to life and contacted the control tower while he arranged the charts and energized the hand-held VHF marine radio.

Seconds later Jackie lifted the helo into the air and headed straight toward the beach. Scott checked his Sig Sauer before he picked up the binoculars and began scanning the vast ocean. Since few pleasure boats were out at this time of the morning, he was looking forward to covering a lot of water in the next hour or two.

Jackie gave him a fleeting glance. "Let's try about ten miles out at a thousand feet. That way we'll have a wider reference."

"That sounds fine."

"What does your intuition tell you?" she asked with a faint smile. "Will we locate them today?"

"According to my calculations," Scott said while he searched for large yachts, "we should catch up to them later this afternoon."

"I hope you're right."

"Trust me," he said confidently, then smiled broadly.

Jackie rolled her eyes as she leveled the helo at 1,000 feet.

## Boeing 99HP

The first officer of the corporate-owned Boeing 737 listened to the ATIS information for the Chicago-O'Hare International Airport, then contacted the Air Route Traffic Control Center. The controller cleared the flight to descend and maintain 11,000 feet. He cautioned the crew about reported turbulence below 10,000 feet.

Nearing their assigned altitude, the captain advised the two flight attendants to secure the cabin due to turbulent conditions. One of the young ladies entered the cockpit to collect the pilots' lunch trays, then quickly returned to the plush passenger cabin.

After the en route controller handed the flight to approach control, the first officer contacted the controller and requested a visual approach to Runway 14 Right.

"Boeing Nine-Nine Hotel Papa," the controller replied, "expect visual Runway One-Four Right, continue your descent to four thousand feet. Winds one six zero at two two, gusts two nine."

"Visual one-four right, down to four thousand, Ninety-Nine Hotel Pop."

The first officer turned to the captain. "It's kind of spooky, you know, coming in here with no traffic to worry about."

"Yeah, it's gotta be killing the 'cattle car' shareholders."

The faded blue-and-gray Chevrolet Suburban parked adjacent to Landmeier Road looked innocent enough. Up front, the driver and passenger nervously watched for any sign of trouble. Along with the local and state police vehicles and the military Humvees patrolling O'Hare, groups of local citizens were banding together to keep an eye out for suspicious people.

In the back of the big Suburban, the leader of the terrorist cell used an aviation receiver/scanner to eavesdrop on the O'Hare Control Tower. After hearing the tower controller give Boeing 99HP clearance to land, the the wiry man uncovered a portable antiaircraft missile and opened his side door.

"Make it good," the driver encouraged as he adjusted an air-conditioning vent. "It's the last one we have."

The Islamic militant lifted the Swedish Bofors RBS-70 from the floor and stepped outside. Because the airlines had grounded themselves, the civilian 737 became a juicy target. The man took a breath and held it while he watched the airplane approach. As it passed over the Suburban, he patiently waited until the missile was tracking, then gently squeezed the trigger. With a smile on his smooth-shaven face, he watched the missile accelerate toward its innocent prey.

"Go," he said to the driver, then tossed the missile launcher on the floor. "Let's get on the freeway."

With the 737 configured for landing, the first officer was about to ask the tower controller for a wind check when both pilots felt a tremendous impact accompanied by a loud report.

"Shit," the captain swore as the nose of the airplane began dropping. "I can't control this thing," he said as he hauled back on the control yoke.

"We've lost the right engine," the first officer exclaimed as a "sink rate" warning sounded.

"Get the nose up!" the copilot pleaded. "Get it up!"

The ground-proximity warning system activated. *"Whoop Whoop, pull up! Pull up!"*

"Get the nose up," the first officer yelled.

"I can't," the captain exclaimed. "What the hell is goin' on?"

The copilot was frantic. *"Power!"*

The captain firewalled the throttles and pulled the control yoke back as far as it would go. "We're goin' around! Clean it up!"

As the first officer reached for the landing-gear handle, the nose began to rise, but not enough. They were staring death in the face.

"Oh, shit," the captain exclaimed, fighting the onset of panic. "We're goin' down, tell 'em we're going in!"

"Ninety-nine Hotel Papa is goin' in short of the runway!"

"Say again," the tower controller said.

"Oh, God, no-no-no!" The captain agonized a second before the Boeing slammed into the ground and exploded, killing everybody onboard.


## Darth 68

After the long flight from Whiteman Air Force Base, the B-2 mission commander and the pilot were tired as they approached their primary target in Libya. Using specific combinations of food, drink, and sleep, the stealth-bomber crews could fly forty-eight-hour missions. It was not an ideal situation, but the pilots were trained and conditioned to operate in that type of environment.

"You ready to go, Frank?" Lieutenant Colonel John Otterman asked from the right seat of the *Spirit of California*.

The pilot, Major Frank Korecky, took one last look at his four color multifunction displays. The B61 "bunker busters" were ready to go to work. "All set."

"Here we go," Otterman said as they initiated the attack on the camouflaged chemical weapons plant located in a hollowed-out mountain forty miles southwest of Tripoli.

With the bomber's master mode switch in the "Go to War" setting, the radio emitters were turned off, the quadruple-redundant flight controls now operated in a "stealth" mode, and the weapons systems were readied.

Six minutes later the huge nerve-gas plant near Tarhuna ceased to exist. A short time later a major underground command post was completely flattened. Only a trace of radiation reached the surface.

At the same time, Darth 66 destroyed two of Libya's re-activated terrorist training facilities and a weapons-storage facility. Their secondary targets included a radar site and two military installations used by nuclear scientists and technicians from the Ukraine.

Darth 63 bombed two terrorist camps in Sudan while Darth 65 dropped earth-penetrating B61 hydrogen bombs on Iranian "hardened" underground targets, including the Hemat Missile Industries production facility.

Ten minutes later, Darth 70 flattened a severely damaged terrorist support camp and logistics center southeast of Tani, Afghanistan, then bombed a terrorist base camp and weapons storage facility near the border of Pakistan.

Suffering from an electrical anomaly, Darth 60 successfully bombed terrorist facilities in Lebanon and Syria.

When the B-2s completed their missions, they headed for three KC-10 tankers loitering over the Bay of Bengal and the Nicobar Islands. After a top-off, both the *Spirit of Texas* and the *Spirit of Missouri* would fly directly to Guam while the other B-2s returned to Whiteman AFB.

Only minutes after the stealthy F-117 Nighthawks dropped the last of their precision-guided bombs on their targets, including the Shahid Hemat rocket research facility on the outskirts of Tehran, the B-1B Lancers hit other targets with devastating accuracy. Following the newer strategic bombers, the venerable Vietnam-era B-52 Stratofortresses put the finishing touches on the hourlong, wide-ranging air raid.

Staggered at different intervals, more U.S. bombers were en route to the Middle East. At Minot Air Force Base, Ellsworth AFB, and other Air Combat Command bases, numerous aircraft were taking off to continue the saturation bombing.

### Moscow

President Nikolai Shumenko was staring morosely out his window when Yegor Pavlinsky was ushered into the dacha.

"Have a seat," Shumenko said in a tired voice.

Without saying a word Pavlinsky sat down in a large leather recliner.

Silence strained the atmosphere.

"You're remarkably quiet this morning," Shumenko observed, then turned to look his friend in the eye.

Suffering the effects of a skull-pounding hangover, Pavlinsky cleared his hoarse throat. "Things don't always go as planned."

Suppressing his intense anger, Shumenko ignored the remark. "Many of our arms-and-service buyers are now being pulverized by the U.S. military, the same military that you, in your immeasurable wisdom, said would be driven out of the Middle East."

Feeling defensive Pavlinsky raised his chin in his usual arrogant manner. "We stand to gain millions by selling more planes and weapons in the Gulf region."

Another period of silence engulfed the room.

"The White House," Shumenko began slowly, "has demanded a summit in Paris in ten days."

Pavlinsky started to speak.

"No," Shumenko said stiffly, and raised his hand. "Let me finish. The White House has requested that we send someone to escort the body of Major Viktor Kasatkin—one of our flight instructors assigned to Iran—back to Moscow."

Curious and confused, Pavlinsky frowned. "I don't understand."

"Major Kasatkin was flying a MiG-29 in combat and was shot down by one of the American pilots."

Pavlinsky had a blank look on his face. "But our pilots have strict orders not to engage in combat on behalf of Iran."

"The major elected to disobey the order," Shumenko said in a tired voice. "You will accompany his body home."

Stunned, Pavlinsky searched for words. "This—it is not my responsibility."

Frowning, Shumenko glared at Pavlinsky. "You *will* accompany the body home," he growled in disgust.

# 45

### The South Lawn

Accompanied by Hartwell Prost, Pete Adair, and three un-smiling Secret Service agents, the president rushed out of the mansion and opened his oversized golf umbrella. The steady drizzle was threatening to turn into rain as the afternoon wore on.

Dressed in a long, tan raincoat buttoned snugly around his neck, Macklin gave the drenched reporters a casual wave as the six men approached *Marine One*. As soon as the president and his party were onboard, the gleaming helicopter climbed away from the landing pad and turned toward Andrews Air Force Base.

With only a few minutes available to catch up on events, Prost and Adair wanted to cover as many topics as possible. Thus far the bombing missions had been a resounding success, with mixed reactions from allies and foes. Washington-based representatives of the countries being bombed were alternately howling in protest and threatening swift retaliation.

"The first lady is safely inside Raven Rock," Prost advised as he opened his attaché case. Site-R is a major military bunker located inside Raven Rock Mountain in Pennsylvania. A presidential apartment, affectionately known as the Lucy and Desi Suite, is provided for the president and his spouse.

"Good," Macklin said flatly as he vacantly stared at the steady stream of water flowing across the side window. *This is, without a doubt, the worst day I've had in my life.*

"Are you okay, sir?" Prost queried.

"Yes," the president said absently as he thought about the gut-wrenching visit he had had with Sandy Hatcher an hour before he left the White House. After experiencing a shocking revelation, Macklin had summoned the director of the FBI to the Oval Office. Without taking his eyes off the rivulet of rain, the president sighed. "I'll be fine this evening, you can count on it."

Adair and Prost exchanged concerned looks. Macklin's face was chalky white and he seemed listless.

With sadness in his eyes, the president turned to Adair. "What happened to the B-2 we lost?"

SecDef was fatigued and it showed in his eyes. "General Chalmers said it collided with a tanker while they were trying to refuel in severe turbulence. From what I understand, the primary tanker developed a fuel leak, so the B-2 continued on to rendezvous with another tanker northeast of the Spratly Islands.

"The bomber was on the verge of flaming out when the pilot attempted to refuel while they were flying through heavy thunderstorms. The B-2 rammed the back of the KC-10, then dropped straight out of sight."

"What happened to the tanker?" the president asked.

"It was severely damaged," Adair conceded, trying to hide the yawn he couldn't suppress. "The pilot managed to land it in one piece in Manila. The boom operator sustained major injuries during the collision, but they expect him to make a full recovery."

A frown creased Macklin's forehead. "What about the B-2 crew?"

"We don't know," Adair admitted with a pained expression. "The plane went down in the South China Sea, and we haven't heard anything about the pilots. We have every available resource looking for them."

Lost in his thoughts, Macklin did not respond.

"We also had a B-52 shot down over Iran."

Solemn-faced, the president stared out the window. "Any survivors?"

"There was one, sir."

"Was?"

"They shot him to death while he was descending in his parachute."

"Sonuvabitch," Macklin said bitterly, then fell silent.

Prost took advantage of the pause. "Two of the terrorists who shot down the civilian 737 are dead, and the third one is in critical condition."

The president made eye contact.

"Two undercover FBI agents," Prost went on, "happened to see the missile as it started up. They were in a limo a block away and spotted a Chevy Suburban lurch onto the road and accelerate at full throttle. The agents gave chase and the terrorists fired at them. While our guys were calling for backup, the Iranians ran a red light and got creamed by a dump truck full of scrap iron."

"How's the truck driver?" Macklin asked with a dull expression.

"He's fine, just a few scratches."

"Good," the president said, and turned to Adair. "I want to continue to pound the hell out of the primary terrorist targets and military targets you and the joint chiefs have selected."

"Yes, sir."

The president's spirit was bouncing back. "Regardless of the cries and threats coming out of the UN and the Middle East, I'm going to stay focused on Iran, Libya, Sudan, Afghanistan, Syria, and the terrorist facilities in the Bekaa Valley until Bassam Shakhar and the rest of his loony pals call off their thugs."

The veins in Macklin's neck were protruding. "I want the bombing to go on every day from sundown to sunup, but at random intervals, keep 'em off balance and in shock."

"I understand, sir," Adair said as they approached Andrews. "As we speak, B-1s from Dyess are hitting terrorist strongholds, while B-52s from Barksdale and Minot are carpet-bombing the Bekaa Valley."

"That'll get their attention," the president said as the helicopter began a smooth descent toward the air base.

Prost allowed himself a moment of pleasure. "They're crying foul at the top of their lungs."

"That's what I want to hear," Macklin said with a trace of sarcasm. "As long as we're being terrorized, the sponsors are going to get pounded into the dirt. I *will* break them."

Prost glanced at Adair, then caught the president's eye. "That's what you have to do with this kind of mentality. You have to treat them in the only way they understand."

"That's what I'm doing," Macklin said resolutely, then changed the subject. "What can you tell me about the yacht and the nuclear bomb?"

"Nothing," Prost said lightly. "They're still searching."

Macklin glanced at his wristwatch, then stared out the window and addressed Adair. "What's happening in the Gulf?"

"The *Roosevelt* is conducting cyclic-ops and we haven't had any serious threats to the battle group."

"Good." The president spoke slowly and clearly. "When you return to the White House, I'd like the two of you to have dinner there and wait for me to contact you."

Taken by total surprise, both men looked at each other, then cautiously turned to the president.

"May I ask what's on your mind?" Prost asked while Adair hesitated.

"Not yet," the president said coldly, and continued to stare out the window. "I need time to look into a few things first, okay?"

"Yes, sir," they said as one.

## Andrews Air Force Base

When Colonel Bolton received the message that *Marine One* had departed from the White House, he took his place in the left seat of the backup *Air Force One*. The gates to the sprawling base were closed and all traffic on the terminal ramp was stopped, including airplanes. Fire trucks, rescue personnel, and ambulances were in position.

Three companies of Marines patrolled the perimeter of the air base, and another thirty Marines with portable surface-to-air missiles watched the overcast, rainy skies. Inside the base, double the normal amount of Air Police were on alert. Nothing had been left to chance.

A few minutes later *Marine One* made a gentle landing and came to an imperceptible stop in the assigned spot close to *Air Force One.* While the main rotor blades wound down to a halt, Macklin hurriedly finished his business with Adair and Prost, then grabbed his umbrella and walked down the stairway to the parking apron.

A poster-perfect Marine sergeant gave his commander in chief a snappy salute as a Secret Service agent tried to shelter the president from the rain. Macklin, who preferred to carry his own umbrella, waved him away as a half-dozen Air Force brass paid their respects to the president.

After the friendly greetings were exchanged, Macklin and his Secret Service retinue hurried toward *Air Force One.* The *Marine One* pilots would wait until the 747 departed before they flew Prost and Adair back to the White House.

Once the president started up the stairway, Colonel Bolton gave the command to start engines.

Thirty seconds after Macklin walked aboard the airplane, a chief master sergeant popped an umbrella open and stepped out of the 747, then hurried down the mobile stairway. The cabin door was closed and the ground crew chief smartly saluted Colonel Bolton a second before *Air Force One* began rolling toward the runway.

High overhead, four immaculate F/A-18Cs from Marine Fighter Attack Squadron 232, the Corps' oldest and most decorated fighter squadron, waited for the flying White House. The commanding officer of the Red Devils and three of his most experienced pilots would escort *Air Force One* on the first segment of its flight to San Francisco.

# 46

## Near Ponte Vedra Beach, Florida

After refueling the helo late in the afternoon at Daytona Beach, Jackie and Scott continued searching for the elusive yacht. They passed a number of Coast Guard and Navy helicopters that were zigzagging in search of the 126-foot *Broward*. Scott and Jackie also encountered the Coast Guard cutter *Legare,* the CG patrol boats *Metomkin* and *Key Largo*, and the Navy frigates *Taylor* and *Samuel B. Roberts* combing the waters along Florida's stunning upper east coast.

Abeam the Ponte Vedra Inn & Club, Scott trained the binoculars on a distant yacht. "Come port about ten degrees."

"What is it?" Jackie asked as she made a small heading change.

"Here," he said, handing her the binoculars. "I'll take it for a minute."

She relinquished the controls and focused on the ship. "It looks like the same one, with a different paint scheme and name."

"Let's check it over," Scott said as he gave her the controls. "Figuring their normal speed against ours, this may be the jackpot."

"I hope you're right." Making a gentle descent, Jackie rapidly closed on the yacht and looked at the name boldly painted across the transom. "*Sweet Life* sure doesn't look like the one we photographed."

"That's probably why no one has been suspicious of it."

Jackie made a small course correction to fly by the right side of the yacht. "You'd think someone would have at least investigated it."

"Not if it doesn't fit the description," he suggested. "Yachts can spell trouble for a skipper, especially if you stop one and find a bevy of congressmen on a 'monkey business' cruise."

"Yeah, that could destroy a career, depending on who happened to be onboard the yacht."

As they approached the ship, Scott caught sight of a pair of shapely blondes lounging on the large sundeck. "That's interesting," he said lightly as the young women waved at the helicopter.

"Well, don't fall out," Jackie teased as Scott returned the friendly waves. "This is obviously not the same one."

"I don't know," Scott said as he placed his Sig Sauer next to his right leg. "There isn't anyone else on the deck."

"So?"

"Have you ever seen two attractive young women on a boat—any kind of boat—who weren't surrounded by guys?"

A long silence followed before Jackie banked the LongRanger to the left and headed back to the yacht. "I never thought about it that way."

"That's because you're used to it." Scott chuckled. "You've always been surrounded by guys who were drooling over you."

Her glance sliced to him. "I haven't seen you drool."

"I only do that late at night," he said with a brief smile. "Let's slow down and circle this baby a couple of times. Maybe someone will come out on deck to see what we're about."

"I don't want to get too slow," Jackie cautioned as she banked into a gentle turn. "It's too hard to regain energy quickly enough."

"You sound like a fighter pilot." He grinned good-naturedly.

She turned her head and gave him a slow smile. "That's because I *am* a fighter pilot."

• • •

After a slight hesitation, Massoud Ramazani reached for an AK-47 and stepped to the side of the short passageway leading to the bridge. He glanced at the captain and saw the fear in the man's eyes.

"Stay on course," he ordered as his heart pounded a little harder. "There's something familiar about the people in that—" He stopped in sudden shock when he recognized the woman. "It's them, the man and woman who were flying the floatplane!"

Temporarily paralyzed, the skipper found his voice a few seconds later. "The people who flew over us after our helicopter left?"

"Yes," Ramazani said curtly.

"What are we going to do?"

Ignoring the question, Ramazani checked the ocean in every direction. The closest boat, a smaller yacht, was at least two miles from *Sweet Life*.

"Come left five degrees and slowly increase our speed." *If I walk out on deck, they'll recognize me.*

"I'll take the wheel," Ramazani said as he stepped toward the captain's chair. "Take our guests some water or something, and wave and smile at the helicopter."

"Are you sure?"

"Yes," Ramazani snapped in a sharp voice. "Act like you're having the time of your life."

The nervous skipper looked confused.

"Do it!" Ramazani ordered as he selected VHF on the aircraft scanner and increased the volume of the VHF marine radio. He noted the side number of the helo and gradually advanced the throttles. *Just go away and don't cause any problems.*

Jackie and Scott were about to start the second circle when a man with four gold stripes on each shoulder walked out of the bridge, waved a couple of times, then headed toward the built-in wet bar on the sundeck.

"If he isn't from the Middle East," Scott said with concern in his voice, "I'll buy you dinner every night for the next month."

"That's the same kind of boat, no question about it," Jackie said as she kept the turn fairly tight. "What do you make of the blondes onboard?"

"Who knows? Most men—regardless of their persuasion or age—enjoy attractive young women."

She studied the yacht for a few seconds. *Other than the color of the paint, how many yachts look like the one we saw in the Florida Keys? Not many of this size.* "Maybe we should notify the Coast Guard and keep this guy in sight until they can check him out."

"That's probably the best thing to do," Scott agreed as he reached for the handheld marine radio, then keyed the transmit button to talk to the closest vessel they had seen. "Coast Guard cutter *Legare*, this is Bell Three-Niner-Five-Tango. Coast Guard cutter *Legare*, LongRanger Three-Niner-Five-Tango."

Ramazani's eyes flashed cold fear when he heard the call go out to the Coast Guard. Reacting from a combination of instinct and desperation, he grabbed one of the two portable antiaircraft missiles and raced for the passageway leading to the door. Without slowing down, he ran out on the wide sundeck and launched the missile at the LongRanger.

The missile tried to make a tight course correction, but it had been launched too close to the helicopter. When it flashed by the cockpit, Jackie and Scott flinched.

"Whoa," Jackie exclaimed as she instinctively lowered the nose to gain speed and put some distance between the helo and the yacht. She was nursing maximum power out of the LongRanger when another missile slashed over the top of the helo.

"Stay low and accelerate!" Scott insisted as he turned to look at the yacht. "Let's get tail-on to him!"

"Who's flying this thing?" Jackie exclaimed.

"I believe we just found Ramazani," Scott said loudly as he reached for his Sig Sauer.

"You *really* think so?" she asked with a hint of sarcasm.

He twisted around to catch a glimpse of the yacht. "Start a level turn to the left and we'll approach from the bow."

"Are you nuts?"

"Not completely."

Pulling all the power she could muster from the Allison

turbine, Jackie banked the helo into a tight left turn.

The marine VHF radio suddenly came alive. "Bell helicopter calling Coast Guard cutter *Legare*, say again."

Scott grabbed the radio. "Bell Three-Niner-Five-Tango has come under fire from the motoryacht *Sweet Life* three miles northeast of Ponte Vedra Beach! There are terrorists onboard the *Sweet Life*, and we request immediate assistance! Do you copy?"

"Stand by," the startled radio operator said.

"We don't have time to stand by!" Scott shot back. "I need to speak to your commanding officer! This is an emergency!"

The urgent request was met with silence.

"Damn," Scott said as he tossed the radio aside and looked at the two women. "They don't have a clue," he said to Jackie as the two college students scrambled down a ladder leading to the yacht's wide transom. "We have to try to persuade them to jump before Ramazani kills them."

"Or takes them hostage," she added, glancing at the frightened women. "He's on his way to the transom!"

Scott raised the binoculars to his eyes. "He's carrying a rifle, so they may be out of missiles."

"Start a climbing left turn to take us over the yacht," Scott said as he unlatched the door. "At the apex of our climb, let it drift over the top while I fire straight down on him."

Jackie nodded as she called Jacksonville Approach Control and flew the helo into a position where Scott could get a clear shot.

With the AK-47 in his hand, Ramazani was crossing the open aft deck when Scott opened fire, startling the Islamic militant. He fled into the main salon as the two women cowered in a corner of the transom.

"Make a low pass across the stern," Scott said as he gave Jackie the marine radio, then clambered into the back of the helicopter.

"Here we go," Jackie warned Scott as she explained the situation to the surprised air traffic controller.

Scott opened the aft door and waited until they were almost directly behind the yacht, then shoved the door open and put his hands together in a diving motion.

Confused and panicked by the sudden arrival of the helicopter and the unexpected chaos, the women froze in place.

"Oh, shit," Scott said as he saw Ramazani emerge from the salon and wave the rifle at the women. Scott opened fire, striking Ramazani in the right forearm.

"They jumped," Jackie exclaimed as the two women leaped off the stern. "They're in the water."

"I'll toss them our raft!" Scott said as he reached for the bright yellow carrying case. "Put me slightly upwind from them."

"You got it," she said, ignoring the Coast Guard calls and the Jacksonville approach controller. "I have to get on the sat-phone and see if I can reach Hartwell."

Before Scott could answer, a round shattered the right passenger door window while small geysers of water began erupting around the women.

# 47

## The A-4 Skyhawk

Angered by the short notice about *Air Force One*, Khaliq
Farkas was over ten minutes behind schedule, but the late
takeoff was not a showstopper. If he didn't run into any
problems with the weather, or being recognized as an A-4
Skyhawk instead of a Falcon jet, he would have a reasonable
chance of completing the most important assignment he had
ever undertaken.

The operative who had had the responsibility for notifying
Farkas when *Air Force One* departed Andrews Air Force
Base would never have another assignment with the terrorist
group. No excuse was acceptable, not even the traffic vio-
lation he had been stopped for just before the 747 lifted off
the runway. Farkas had killed people for lesser infractions.

Cruising toward Des Moines, Iowa, at 35,000 feet, the
single-seat attack jet was carrying two drop tanks, two
twenty-millimeter Mk-12 cannons, each with 200 rounds of
ordnance, and two Sidewinder, AIM-9 close/medium-range
air-to-air missiles.

Mounted on underwing pylons, the heat-seeking weapons
were ideal for close stern engagements at high altitude in
good visibility. They were less effective at low altitudes, or
in cloudy or rainy conditions. Sidewinders also showed a

propensity to lock on to the sun if the opponent was pointed at the self-luminous sphere.

The Sidewinder would give a growl when it acquired a target. If it was squarely positioned behind a hot jet exhaust, the growl would become a fierce screech until the aviator fired the missile. Accelerating to two and a half times the speed of sound in 2.2 seconds, the Sidewinder's range is between two and eleven miles.

The payload of the missile is an annular blast/fragmentation warhead with a passive IR proximity fuse. Known for its accuracy once it locks on, the missile generally tracks straight into the tailpipe of its prey and reduces the jet engine to scrap metal.

Checking his high-altitude navigation chart and the GPS, Farkas decided to wait until *Air Force One* checked in on the Chicago Center frequency before he requested a return to his "home field" at Columbus, Ohio.

As the seconds ticked off, he became increasingly concerned. Finally, after three minutes, Farkas heard the flying White House check in with Chicago Center. He sucked in a deep breath of cool oxygen. If *Air Force One* was on a direct course to San Francisco, Farkas knew exactly where it should be in eight minutes. He listened to the radio exchanges as he armed his weapons system, then keyed his radio. "Chicago, Falcon One Hundred Lima Bravo with a request."

"One Hundred Lima Bravo, Chicago. Say your request."

"Lima Bravo has developed a radio problem and we would like to change our destination to Port Columbus."

A short pause followed. "One Hundred Lima Bravo, can you accept a higher altitude?"

"That's affirm, Lima Bravo."

Another pause while the en route controller coordinated the change in destination for the troubled corporate jet.

"Falcon One Hundred Lima Bravo is cleared direct to the Port Columbus airport, turn right on course, climb and maintain Flight Level 370."

"Coming right and climbing to 370, Lima Bravo."

Thirty miles north-northwest of the A-4 Skyhawk, Air Force Lieutenant Colonel Clem Haskell and his fellow F-15 Eagle pilots were orbiting at 35,000 feet. Each aircraft was armed with AIM-9 Sidewinder missiles, AIM-120 AMRAAM missiles, and over 900 rounds for the M61A1 Vulcan twenty-millimeter cannons. Having recently topped off their fuel tanks from a KC-135 Stratotanker, the pilots quietly waited to accept the responsibility for escorting *Air Force One* the rest of the way to San Francisco. They would tank again en route.

Based at Mountain Home Air Force Base, Idaho, the pilots from the 366th Wing's 390th Fighter Squadron were considered to be some of the best fighter jocks in the business.

Colonel "Eddie" Haskell glanced to his right, then keyed his UHF radio for a chat with his wingman, Major Bodie Maxwell Wilson. "Beemer, did you hear the Falcon driver's request?"

"I *shore* did," the former Crimson Tide quarterback said.

"Did it seem a little strange to you?"

"Does a cat have climbin' gears?"

"I think we better go have a look-see," Haskell replied hastily, then selected the UHF frequency for the air traffic controller. "Chicago Center, Bulldog One and pups would like to have a look at the Falcon you just cleared direct to Port Columbus."

"Ah . . . Bulldog flight," the controller said as he prepared to change the altitudes and flight paths of other aircraft, "you're blocked from Flight Level 350 to 430—go for it."

"Bulldog One, 350 to 430," Haskell repeated, then glanced at his wingman. "Bulldogs, let's put the pedal to the metal."

Farkas heard the radio call from Bulldog One. His mind raced as he calculated how long it would take for the supersonic fighters to catch him. *This is going to be close.* He inched the throttle forward and started scanning the sky for *Air Force One.* As always, the adrenaline rush was exhilarating when he approached his prey. He lowered the clear visor from his helmet and locked it in place.

Accelerating through Mach 1.12, Lieutenant Colonel Haskell closely watched his radar screen while he and his three charges rapidly gained on the "questionable" target.

"Chicago Center," Haskell radioed, "Bulldog One will have a visual on the Falcon in approximately two minutes."

"Ah, roger, Bulldog."

Haskell waited a few moments, then keyed his radio. "Center, Bulldog. You might want to steer any traffic in our area away from us."

"Will do, Bulldog." The controller studied his radar screen. "Falcon One Hundred Lima Bravo, Chicago Center."

No answer.

The controller made three more attempts to reach the Falcon, then waited a few seconds before trying again.

"Falcon One Hundred Lima Bravo, if you read center, ident."

Nothing happened.

Ignoring the radio calls, Khaliq Farkas absently shoved on the throttle in an attempt to coax more speed out of the subsonic A-4. His palms were sweaty and his mouth was dry. *Two minutes . . . where is* Air Force One?

As the seconds ticked off, Farkas became more desperate. With little hope left that he would be able to find and attack the 747 before he was identified and blown out of the sky, Farkas pickled his two drop tanks. He waited a few seconds, then keyed his radio.

"Chicago Center, Falcon One Hundred Lima Bravo is having a major electrical problem."

"Do you wish to declare an emergency?"

"Negative," Farkas said as he switched off his transponder. "We'll be off the freq for a minute."

"For traffic separation," the controller said hastily, "turn right twenty degrees and report back on."

"Lima Bravo."

The A-4 suddenly disappeared from the controller's radar screen, but Farkas would not be able to hide from the F-15s. They had him locked on radar and they were rapidly merging.

Marine Lieutenant Colonel Gary Darnell, the skipper of the VMFA-232 Red Devils, was monitoring the center frequency and visually searching for the Bulldogs and the corporate jet. *What's the deal with the Falcon?*

Darnell had the civilian jet and the four Air Force F-15s on his radar and expected to see them in a matter of seconds.

He glanced ahead at *Air Force One* and then checked the other F/A-18s in his flight. Although it was difficult to see the gray-colored Hornets against the gray undercast, the other pilots were in their assigned positions.

Concerned about the sudden lack of radio chatter, Darnell decided to get a comm check with his pilots. "Devil check," he said briskly.

"Two."

"Three."

"Four."

Sitting in the left seat of the shiny 747, Colonel Curtis Bolton turned to his copilot, Kirk Upshaw. "Do you have a sense that something strange is going on? That it's too quiet?"

"Yeah," he said flatly as both of them searched the sky. "I don't like the feeling of being in—damn!"

"What?" Bolton said stiffly.

"That's the same voice—the Falcon pilot's voice—that was on the tapes in Atlanta! It's the same guy!"

Bolton's face turned pale. He was about to contact the Marine flight leader when the radio crackled to life.

"Chicago," an agitated voice exclaimed, "United Four-Oh-Eight *damn* near hit a couple of drop tanks—what gives?"

"Did you say drop tanks?"

"That's affirm."

A short pause followed before another voice came over the radio. "Ah . . . we'll check with the military flights in your area."

"United Four-Oh-Eight."

"Bulldogs and Red Devils," the controller said on UHF, "did anyone kick off their fuel tanks?"

"Negative on the dogs."

"Ditto the devils."

"United Four-Oh-Eight," the controller radioed on VHF, "none of the military planes dropped anything. I don't know what to tell you, sir."

"Well, we aren't hallucinating."

"I understand, sir. You might want to file a report."

"I suspect someone on the ground will be doing that fairly soon—if they live through the impact."

• • •

Farkas saw *Air Force One* at the same instant the radio went wild with everyone trying to talk at once. The 747 and her Marine escorts were going in the opposite direction at 35,000 feet. The Hornets appeared to be spread out from two to three miles behind the big Boeing. Farkas had to make a slight course correction and wait for the flying White House and the F/A-18s to pass beneath the Skyhawk.

Zooming upward 1,200 feet, Farkas rolled the A-4 inverted and began a split-S maneuver to place himself two miles in trail behind *Air Force One*.

"Ah, shit," Bulldog One suddenly blurted as he spotted the bogus corporate jet diving straight down.

"The Falcon is an A-4 doing a split-S!" he said curtly over the Chicago Center frequency. "Bulldogs and Red Devils go tactical!"

The eight fighter pilots switched to a preplanned radio frequency.

"Devil One," Haskell exclaimed, "the Skyhawk is coming right down on top of you—going to go right through your troops!"

"I got him!" Darnell radioed.

"You'll have to bag him!" Haskell said, breathing hard. "I can't get a clean shot from here!"

Caught off guard, Gary Darnell was livid when he looked up and saw the Skyhawk pulling heavy Gs to bottom out of the split-S 400 yards in front of his Hornet. *We got suckered.*

If Darnell attempted to blast the A-4 with a missile or his Vulcan cannon, he could easily miss and blow *Air Force One* out of the air.

"Check switches safe—noses cold!" Darnell ordered his pilots as he shoved both throttles into full afterburner. "I'm gonna get that crazy sonuvabitch!"

Pulling out slightly below the Marine F/A-18s, Farkas heard the Sidewinder give a low growl as the 747 filled his windshield. The growl turned into a high-pitched screech a second before Farkas fired the missile. As the heat-seeking weapon accelerated to two and a half times the speed of sound, Farkas fired the second Sidewinder. He saw a flash under the right wing of *Air Force One* as he snapped the A-4 inverted and dove straight toward the undercast.

"Cover the president!" Devil One ordered as he rolled the Hornet over and chased the Skyhawk toward the dark gray clouds. Darnell started to fire a missile at the terrorist, but checked himself when he thought about the civilians beneath the clouds. *I have to take a chance! I can't let him get away!*

Just before the A-4 reached the clouds, Darnell fired a missile and watched it track straight into the tailpipe of its prey. The engine exploded in a giant reddish-yellow fireball that blew the airplane in half. Tumbling wildly and leaving a trail of flames and dense black smoke, the Skyhawk disappeared into the clouds.

Bolton and Upshaw were frantically trying to extinguish the fire in the number-three engine when Chief Master Sergeant Willard Brewer rushed into the cockpit.

"Colonel!" he said in his booming voice. "We have flames all the way from the right wing to the tail!"

Bolton was about to answer when the men felt a second, then third explosion. In slow motion the left wing started to rise as Bolton tried to correct for the uncommanded roll. He knew it was hopeless, but his survival instincts took command.

Upshaw and Brewer watched helplessly as Bolton fed in full left aileron and full left rudder. *Air Force One* slowly rolled over on her back and continued to roll until it was almost upright. Bolton tried to catch it, but the 747 rolled to the right even faster this time. The flight-deck crew had become passengers.

# 48

Frantic to salvage his mission, Massoud Ramazani fired another volley at the helicopter and ran for the ladder leading to the pilothouse. He wiped the blood from the flesh wound on his forearm as his frightened crew of four gathered on the sundeck.

Topping the ladder, Ramazani almost ran into the captain. "Head straight for the Mayport Naval Station," he said breathlessly. "I want full power from the engines!"

"The engines are showing signs of strain."

"Full power," Ramazani bellowed.

Following the skipper to the bridge, Ramazani grabbed the other AK-47 and impatiently waited for the yacht to reach full speed. He picked up a pair of binoculars and scanned the coast, then stopped when he saw the top of the mast of the aircraft carrier *John F. Kennedy*.

He studied the chart-plotting GPS receiver and the radar, then turned to the captain. "Set a course straight for the channel leading to the naval station," Ramazani ordered. "From there, program the autopilot to head straight for the carrier."

While the frightened man was entering the way points into the autopilot, Ramazani briefly considered the possibility of navigating the yacht through the St. Johns River to the heart of downtown Jacksonville, then quickly discarded the notion.

Time was his enemy. Besides, *Kennedy* was a much more tempting target.

If the yacht could ram "Big John" just prior to the detonation of the nuclear bomb, it would sink the giant warship and destroy the naval station and most of Jacksonville. *It might not be Washington, D.C., but it will be a tremendous blow to the infidels.*

When the yacht was vibrating from maximum power, Ramazani rechecked the chart-plotting GPS. At their current speed, *Sweet Life* would plow into the supercarrier in fourteen minutes.

He went below and walked through the mahogany-paneled formal dining room to the master stateroom, stepped over the open crate of AK-47s, then opened the double doors leading to the sitting room. Working rapidly but carefully, Ramazani unlocked and removed the top of the heavy metal container. He set the timer on the nuclear bomb to thirteen minutes, then activated the master arming switch and relocked the large metal container. *Now it's just a matter of time.*

## The Longranger

While Jackie smoothly hovered the helo inches above the water, Scott waited for the right moment, then pulled the exposed lanyard on the life raft and shoved it out the door. The raft automatically ejected from its carrying case and fully inflated within three yards of the panicked women.

"Let's go," Scott exclaimed as Jackie banked and climbed away from the raft. "We'll give the Coast Guard their position."

The rotor wash from the LongRanger shoved the raft toward the women and they quickly scrambled into it.

"They've changed course," Jackie said as she chased the yacht. "It looks like they're headed for Mayport, and there's a carrier in port."

"That figures." Scott kicked out the rest of the shattered passenger window. "Toss me the sat-phone." *If they have a nuke onboard, we can write Jacksonville off the map.* "I hope Hartwell is in his office."

"I'm sure he can be reached," Jackie said as she handed him the phone, then gave the Coast Guard the position of the

raft. After she explained the situation, she contacted Jacksonville approach control and asked them to notify the FBI
and the Navy. They immediately relayed the information to
the proper authorities, then had a short conversation with the
tower controllers at Jacksonville International Airport. All
airplanes and helicopters on the ground would be held in
their places while incoming flights would be diverted to other
airports.

Scott was off the phone in less than a minute. "Hartwell
is pushing all the buttons at his end. He wants us to keep the
terrorists in sight and slow them down if we can."

"We aren't flying a gunship," Jackie said as she glanced
over her shoulder. "How are we supposed to slow them
down?"

Scott took a seat by the open window. "Let's get out in
front of the yacht, then make a low, head-on pass and I'll
see if I can take out the people in the wheelhouse."

Jackie slowly shook her head, then belatedly turned to
Scott. "I think you need to double up on your Xanax," she
said as she positioned the helo for a high-speed strafing run.

Ramazani watched the helicopter pass *Sweet Life* high to the
port side. He studied the horizon for 360 degrees around the
ship, then went inside the bridge to check the chart-plotting
GPS. When the captain suddenly pointed up to the left, Ramazani turned to take a look. The LongRanger was diving
to gain speed and headed straight down the center line of the
yacht.

In one quick motion, Ramazani grabbed the AK-47 and
hurried out to the sundeck. He raised the weapon and began
firing short bursts at the rapidly approaching helicopter.

"There's someone with a—" Jackie flinched as a round came
through the windshield and shattered the left earcup on her
headset.

"Jesus," she exclaimed as another round tore a hole in the
instrument panel. "He's ripping us apart!"

Leaning out the passenger window, Scott held his Sig
Sauer with both hands and squeezed off five rounds. He was
astonished when two sections of the bridge's windshield im-

ploded. As Jackie pulled up, Scott fired his last rounds at Ramazani and ducked back into the cabin.

She took off her mangled headset and reached for Scott's headset in the left seat. "He's going to blow us out of the air if we aren't careful."

Scott looked down at the speeding yacht. "Jackie, if you can make a steady descent directly over the bridge, I can keep them pinned down until I can jump on the roof."

"Are you crazy?"

"Can you do it?"

"Yes, but this is insane."

Scott stuffed his Sig Sauer into the crevice of a passenger seat. "I'm going to need your weapon."

She handed him her Glock and banked toward the motor-yacht.

"Do you have another clip?" he asked.

"No," Jackie said as she slowed to match the speed of *Sweet Life*. "I hadn't planned to start a war today."

Traveling at the same speed as the motoryacht, Jackie flew the LongRanger directly over the bridge and then began a rapid descent. As she slowed the rate of descent, Ramazani stepped out and looked up, fired a quick burst from the AK-47, then ducked back into the pilothouse.

The yacht suddenly heeled over in a tight port turn, forcing Jackie to make large corrections to stay in place. Thirty degrees into the turn, the ship rolled out on its original course.

"I'm going for it," Scott shouted as he stepped out on the helicopter's right landing skid and braced himself. When Ramazani appeared again, Scott fired two rounds through the roof of the wheelhouse. The terrorist darted inside and retaliated by firing a long burst straight up through the roof. Scott heard rounds puncturing the belly of the helicopter.

"Take it up," he yelled. "Get outta here!"

"What do you think I'm doing?" Jackie shouted as she pulled every ounce of power she could from the straining engine.

As they climbed away, Scott stepped forward to the cockpit. "If you'll make an approach straight at the stern, I think I can keep him pinned down until I can jump on the transom."

"Scott," she said in an even, calm voice. "That's over-the-top. What are you going to do *if* you get aboard?"

"I'll figure that out after I get there," he said with a slow smile.

She frowned, then checked the engine instruments. "This is not a good idea, believe me."

"If you have a better idea, I'm willing to listen."

Without uttering another word, Jackie flew a wide arc to approach the yacht from the rear.

While the captain of *Sweet Life* wiped blood from his face and neck, Ramazani looked around the shattered pilothouse. There were holes in the overhead and glass and debris scattered everywhere. He turned to the first mate. "Get below and secure the hatch to the engine room!"

Without saying a word, the hollow-eyed man ran to the companionway leading to the main deck.

Ramazani checked the time and distance to the impact point with the supercarrier. Eight minutes and twenty seconds. *If I could just knock that helicopter out of the air.*

Jackie flew low and fast as she approached the yacht. Scott kept the Glock trained on the aft opening to the wheelhouse. When Ramazani suddenly appeared, Scott fired four rounds as the terrorist fired a short burst at the helicopter and ducked inside.

"Keep it coming," Scott said as he stepped out on the landing skid. "We're almost there."

Nearing the transom, Jackie rapidly slowed the Long-Ranger while Scott kept firing rounds through the opening to the bridge. At the last second he leaped off the skid and landed on the sundeck, then slid off the aft end of the deck and fell on the transom.

Seeing Ramazani reappear, Jackie quickly banked the helicopter to make a 180-degree turn as a round ricocheted off the copilot's door. A second later two more rounds penetrated the engine compartment. Completing the turn, she cringed when another round ripped through the cabin.

Scott entered the main salon and came face-to-face with a man brandishing a rifle. Both men fired at the same instant and the Iranian slumped backward and fell over an L-shaped lounge. He was dead before he hit the carpet.

With a rivulet of blood running down the outside of his thigh, Scott raced forward through the mahogany-paneled dining room. He was about to climb the ladder leading to the pilothouse when a fusillade of rounds ripped into the bulkhead next to him. Scott dashed into an elegant king-size master stateroom and froze when he saw an open crate of AK-47s.

He grabbed one of the rifles and stuck the Glock down the small of his back, then opened the double doors leading to a teakwood trimmed sitting room. Scott stopped and stared when he recognized the Russian nuclear symbol on the large steel container. *They* do *have a nuke.*

"Give it up," Ramazani ordered from the master stateroom. "Your friend crashed the helicopter and you're trapped."

*He's lying,* Dalton told himself as his heart stuck in his throat. He could feel his pulse pounding. *I hope he's lying.*

"There *is* no way out," Ramazani declared with confidence in his voice. "It's time for you to make peace with your God."

Scott spied a carpet-covered hatch.

"You and this boat," Ramazani said contemptuously, "are going to be vaporized in six minutes."

With no other way out of the sitting room, Scott fired a few rounds into the stateroom and opened the hatch. He dropped into a narrow, softly lighted passageway leading to the engine room. *If I can disable the engines, the detonation isn't going to obliterate Jacksonville.*

When he reached the T in the passageway under the main deck, he stopped and silently cursed. The hatch leading to the engine room was chained shut with two interlocking chains and three heavy-duty padlocks. *This son of a bitch is clever.*

A second later Ramazani sprayed the access space with rifle fire. "Drop your rifle and come out."

"I don't think so," Scott said as he held the AK-47 out in the main passageway and fired a burst in return.

"Don't be a fool," Ramazani cautioned. "If you toss down your weapon, you can swim for your life."

"I don't trust cowards," Scott said sarcastically as he frantically looked around. He saw two things that gave him hope—a hatch directly above his head and a bronze under-water through-hull fitting. Moving swiftly, he checked to see if the small overhead hatch would open. He shoved it up a couple of inches and discovered an aft stateroom.

"You are trying my patience," Ramazani said in a threat-ening voice. "You cannot escape from here, unless I allow you to leave. Surely you would like to leave before the ship explodes, wouldn't you?"

"Massoud, that's a stupid question," Scott said as he squeezed off another few rounds down the passageway, then opened the full-flow seacock. Seawater gushed into the yacht as he used the butt of the assault rifle to break the handle off the seacock. *I hope we're taking on water faster than the bilge pumps can pump it overboard.*

Scott turned and shoved the rifle up through the hatch, then scrambled into the stateroom. He cautiously opened the door and spotted a deckhand carrying an AK-47.

"Take a hike," Scott growled as the startled man dropped his weapon and ran toward the aft deck. Dalton fired a few parting shots as the terrorist jumped over the transom and disappeared in the churning wake.

Without warning, Ramazani stepped out of the master stateroom. Scott pulled the trigger and nothing happened.

# 49

## The Longranger

Jackie watched a man jump into the yacht's wake, then bob up and flail the surface of the water as he disappeared under the belly of the helicopter. Unsure if it was Scott, she made a tight, spiraling descent and buzzed the man. Stricken with panic, the deckhand was churning the water in a desperate attempt to keep from drowning.

Jackie pulled up and glanced at the aircraft carrier in Mayport Basin. *Hurry, Scott. Take control of the yacht.* She gazed at the channel leading to *Kennedy.* If the yacht maintained her present course and speed, she would enter the channel near the shoreline in approximately five minutes.

"Jax approach," she radioed. "LongRanger Three-Niner-Five Tango has been hit by gunfire, but I'm going to stay close to the yacht."

"Niner-Five Tango," an excited voice said, "we have help on the way!"

Jackie scanned the water in every direction. "I don't see anything that's going to be able to stop the yacht."

A calmer voice broke in. "There are two armed F/A-18s that have been recalled from a training mission. They've been ordered to sink the yacht."

"Oh, my God," Jackie said to herself, then took a breath and keyed the radio. "On whose orders?"

"The Pentagon, ma'am," the controller answered in a pleasant voice. "From what we understand, it came straight from the secretary of defense."

Taking time to compose herself, Jackie spoke slowly and clearly. "We have a friendly on the yacht. Repeat, we have a friendly operative on the yacht. Do *not* fire on the yacht until he's clear. Do *not* fire on the yacht. Copy?"

"Stand by."

"Let me speak to management."

"Stand by."

Jackie darted another look at the carrier and commenced a shallow descent toward the yacht. She estimated four minutes until the yacht entered the channel. *Come on, Scott. You don't have much time.*

A hail of gunfire rang out as Dalton leaped sideways into the stateroom and slammed the door. He drew the Glock from the small of his back and made an educated guess as to where Ramazani was standing in the passageway.

"Well," Scott said loudly, "I guess you win."

"I always do."

The terrorist leader sounded as if he was in front of the entrance to the stateroom. Scott fired three rounds through the thin wooden door and heard a clatter as Ramazani's rifle hit the deck.

Scott kicked the splintered door open and caught a glancing blow as Ramazani swung the rifle upward. Dalton grabbed both ends of the weapon and slammed the terrorist against a bulkhead. Although Ramazani was bleeding from a stomach wound, he fought back with brutal ferocity.

Calling on all the strength he had, Scott threw the terrorist into the opposite bulkhead, then caught him with a vicious uppercut. The blow fractured Ramazani's jaw and rendered him semiconscious.

Nose to nose, Scott held him against the bulkhead. "I think this cruise is about over, don't you?"

Ramazani mumbled a few incoherent words as Dalton released his grip on him. When the terrorist leader slid to the deck, Scott grabbed the AK-47 and rushed into the master stateroom to get a fresh magazine. After checking the passageway for other crew members, Scott stepped over Ramazani and headed for the aft ladder leading to the sundeck.

"Jax approach," Jackie said, then fell silent when she saw Scott climbing the ladder leading to the sundeck and bridge. *Thank God.*

"Who's calling approach?"

With a sense of relief, she aimed the helo toward the yacht. *I have to get him off the yacht.*

"Jax approach," she said mechanically. "Niner-Five Tango has the agent in sight. I'm going in to pick him up."

"Negative! Negative!"

Jackie ignored the controller and started her approach to the sundeck. The yacht appeared to be riding lower in the water. *It looks like we're down to about three minutes.*

"We have two fighters closing from eighteen miles," the controller exclaimed. "They're supersonic and cleared to fire on the target."

"Dammit!" Jackie radioed in a flash of anger. "Listen up! There's an American agent onboard! He works directly for the national security adviser! Do *not* open fire on the yacht until the agent is clear!"

"Ma'am, we don't *give* the orders. We just pass 'em along."

Jackie concentrated on leveling off thirty yards behind the yacht. "Well, pass this along to the fighter pilots. The operative is a former naval aviator—a Marine Harrier pilot."

Reaching the sundeck, Scott crouched behind an inflatable dinghy as the first mate fired a burst at him, then ducked into the pilothouse. Dalton waved Jackie away and fired a few rounds through the door to the bridge. A moment later the first mate stumbled out on the sundeck and fell to his hands and knees. Bleeding from wounds in his chest and neck, he crawled forward a few feet and collapsed facedown on the deck.

Scott was about to rush the pilothouse when something clamped around his ankle.

## The Hornets

Lieutenant Commander Carl Zukowski keyed his radio. "Easing the power, easing the power," he said to his wingman, Lieutenant Alan Swindell.

"Stand by the boards . . . boards," Zukowski said as the pilots "popped" the speedbrake to rapidly decelerate as they approached the yacht.

"We'll get a visual ID," Zukowski radioed in a laid-back voice, "then set up for a firing pass."

"Ah, roger."

"Wildcat Four-Fourteen," the Jax approach controller said to Zukowski, "be advised that a government agent is onboard the yacht. A civilian helo is in the process of picking him up."

"Copy," Zukowski said as he searched for the yacht and the helicopter. "Tell 'em to hurry 'cause we're runnin' outta gas."

"I'll pass that along." The controller paused a moment. "By the way, the agent on the yacht is a former Marine pilot."

Swindell glanced at his flight leader's plane, then keyed his radio. "That won't be any loss."


Startled by the unexpected attack, Scott lashed out at Ramazani as the terrorist stabbed him in the lower leg with a six-inch Kalashnikov bayonet. Swinging the rifle with both hands, Scott mashed Ramazani's face flat, breaking his nose. The stunned man fell off the ladder and landed headfirst on the wide transom, snapping his neck. Although Ramazani was still alive, he could not do any more damage.

Grimacing from the searing pain in his leg, Scott yanked the blade out of his calf, then heard a familiar sound above the beat of the LongRanger's rotor blades. He looked up to see two Hornets screeching low over the water in tight formation. *Uh-oh, it's time to check out.*

Scott turned and looked toward the Mayport Naval Station. The *Kennedy* was a tempting target and the speeding yacht was turning into the channel. *We're going to hit the boat in about two minutes.*

Struggling to his feet, Scott again waved Jackie away and

limped toward the pilothouse. Firing short bursts through the open door and the aft bulkhead, he was halfway to the entrance when the captain suddenly opened fire.

Jackie watched in horror as Scott dropped to the deck and returned fire. A man in a blood-soaked shirt stumbled onto the sundeck, then staggered backward in a series of spasmodic jerks. His legs crumbled under him as he dropped his AK-47, then fell against the wheelhouse and tumbled head over heels into the water.

She looked up to see the two Hornets rolling in for a firing pass. "Jax approach," she frantically radioed, "tell them not to fire! The agent has gained access to the bridge! He's in command of the yacht!"

"Wildcat One is rolling in hot," Carl Zukowski radioed, then talked to his wingman. "Alan, hold your fire on this run. I'm going to shave the bow off and hope our Marine friend is bright enough to jump ship."

"Copy," Swindell replied. "I'm in cold."

"Jax approach," Zukowski said. "Wildcat One and Two are running on fumes—we gotta have answers."

A long pause followed.

"Wildcat Four-Fourteen," a deep voice said with the sound of authority, "your orders are to sink the yacht . . . at all costs. Do you copy?"

"Oh yeah, we copy," Zukowski said as he and his wingman mentally prepared to eject from their Hornets.

Scott was approaching the pilothouse when— *buuuuuuurrrrrrpp*—the bow of the yacht exploded in a hail of twenty-millimeter Vulcan cannon fire. Able to fire 6,000 rounds per minute, the Hornet's six-barreled rotary cannon literally sawed off four feet of the bow. With the front of the yacht open to the sea and the powerful diesel engines churning at full throttle, *Sweet Life* was rapidly filling with water.

*Time to punch out.* Cringing from pain, Scott limped out to the edge of the sundeck and dove over the side. He quickly surfaced and frantically swam away from the thrashing screws.

Jackie saw Scott surface and immediately began slowing

and descending toward him. "He's jumped overboard—he's safe!" she radioed. "The agent is clear of the yacht!"

"He's off the boat and well clear," Zukowski reported to Jax approach, then added, "the helo is closing on him."

"Great," the deep-voiced controller said with obvious relief. "The word is sink the ship—ASAP."

"We're workin' on it," Zukowski radioed, then talked to Swindell. "Alan, I'm going to work on the bow. You take the stern."

"You got it, boss."

Maneuvering the helicopter closer to Scott, Jackie skillfully brought the LongRanger to a hover near him. She would have to be extremely careful about lifting Scott out of the water.

The powerful rotor-blade downwash whipped the surface of the water into a frothy gale, sending sheets of spray in every direction as she moved closer to Scott. With absolute concentration, she lowered the landing skids into the water, then gasped.

Two large sharks were approaching Scott from his right side. Unable to remove her hands from the controls to point at the danger, she pulled up a couple of feet and hovered toward the sharks. Once she was in position, Jackie eased the LongRanger down until the belly was almost in the water.

Treading water and turning to keep Jackie in sight, Scott was stunned when he saw the dorsal fins. He faced the sharks and saw the fins disappear. *I'm bleeding like a butchered hog.*

Quelling his rising panic, he pulled his knees up to his chest and waited for Jackie to move toward him. With surprising power, something slammed into Scott's lower back, then veered away. *Oh, shit—this isn't good.*

Reaching for the landing skid, he saw a shark coming straight at him. Using both legs, Scott viciously kicked the predator in the snout, then threw his good leg over the skid and grabbed the brace aft of the pilot's door. He pulled himself up and straddled the skid.

As Jackie was lifting the helo out of the water, Scott saw

the two Hornets pulverize the yacht with deadly streams of cannon fire. When the pilots pulled up from their firing run, the 126-foot Broward was twelve feet shorter and rapidly turning into a submarine.

While Jackie flew toward Atlantic Beach at low altitude, Scott maintained a death grip on the brace protruding from the fuselage. He watched the yacht as it neared the slight dogleg channel leading to Mayport Basin and the *Kennedy*. One of the yacht's engines was still thrashing the water into foam, but only the sundeck and the bridge were visible.

The Hornets came in for a third pass, then split when Alan Swindell's F/A-18 flamed out. While the flight leader headed straight for Runway 31 at Jacksonville International, his wingman pointed his lifeless Hornet out to sea and waited until the last second to eject.

*Sweet Life* slowly came to rest at the entrance to the basin and sank in approximately forty feet of water.

Waiting until the helo slowed to a hover over a crowded stretch of beach, Scott dropped five feet to the sand. Jackie moved off to the side and gently lowered the landing skids onto the beach, then motioned Scott to get in. He hobbled around the front of the LongRanger and climbed into the left seat.

Scott's eyes reflected his pain and fatigue. "Take off and fly straight south as fast as you can," he gasped as he buckled his straps.

She gave him a quizzical look. "What's wrong?"

*"Go!* The bomb is on the yacht, and I think it's set to go off at any moment. Let's get outta here!"

For a shocked instant Jackie stared toward the naval station, then applied power to lift off. At the same moment they saw a huge geyser of water shoot hundreds of feet into the air above the entrance to the naval basin. A visible shock wave preceded a blossoming mushroom cloud as the helicopter lifted off the beach.

With the LongRanger barely four feet in the air, the passage of the shock wave slammed the helicopter into the sand with such force that it ripped one of the main rotor blades off and collapsed the slender boom leading to the tail-rotor pylon. The remaining rotor blade thrashed the beach, flipping the battered helo onto its side and sending the crowd running for cover.

When they crawled from the wreckage, Scott and Jackie sat up and stared in disbelief. A low, rolling cloud of debris obscured everything in the direction of the naval base except for one thing; the mast of the carrier *Kennedy*. The nuclear explosion, for the most part, had been diminished by the depth of the water in the channel. The sinking of the yacht had saved thousands of lives.

"Are you okay?" Scott asked as he spit sand and blood out of his mouth.

"I think so," she replied, dazed by the crash. She glanced at a handful of shocked beachgoers running toward them. Actually, the people were running at an odd angle, staring at the mushroom cloud with wide-open eyes.

"Well," Scott began sadly, his spirits nearly flattened, "I sure as hell mucked that up."

"The end result is what counts," Jackie insisted, then looked at his bleeding leg. "I need to get you to a hospital."

"What *we* need," Scott suggested with a rueful grin, "is a nice, quiet vacation in St. Thomas."

Jackie looked sideways at him and nodded. "As a matter of fact, you *do* owe me a ride on a sailboat."

### Naval Medical Center, Bethesda, Maryland

Maritza Gunzelman and Greg O'Donnell were visiting in his room when the familiar bright red logo appeared on the television. They fell silent when the surprised anchorwoman turned to the camera.

"This just in to CNN," she said briskly. "We are receiving initial reports that *Air Force One* has crashed. Again, our sources are reporting that *Air Force One* has crashed north of Springfield, Illinois."

She paused a long moment and looked away, then turned back to the camera. "It is believed—we're getting unconfirmed reports—that President Macklin was onboard at the time the plane went down. These are unconfirmed reports. It is not known what caused the crash . . . wait, I'm getting an update."

A stunned look crossed her face. "We have another breaking story just into our newsroom—this from the Associated Press. A nuclear explosion has taken place at the Mayport Naval Station near Jacksonville, Florida. Initial reports indicate that a nuclear bomb may have exploded aboard the aircraft carrier *John F. Kennedy*. We are receiving conflicting reports about the accident. Our sources are saying that casualties may be very high."

Greg lowered the volume on the television and turned to Maritza. Both were shocked and horrified.

"I hope Jackie and Scott aren't involved in any of this," Maritza said with a distant look in her eyes.

"So do I," Greg replied in a tight voice. "The sponsors of terrorism have grossly miscalculated this time."

"God, if the president is dead . . ." Maritza trailed off and closed her eyes. "It's time to destroy the cowards, eradicate them like a swarm of locusts."

A stir was created in the hallway as word of the horrifying news spread throughout the hospital.

# 50

## The White House

Still dressed in the uniform of an Air Force chief master sergeant, President Cord Macklin approached the office of his chief of staff. The attorney general had called Fraiser Wyman and asked him to remain at the White House until she arrived.

Accompanying the president were Hartwell Prost, Pete Adair, Sandra Hatcher, two Secret Service agents, and two FBI agents. The entourage, like the rest of the nation, was outraged by the terrorist acts that had destroyed the reserve *Air Force One* and devastated the *John F. Kennedy* and Mayport Naval Station. Although their guns were holstered, the four agents were unusually apprehensive.

Enraged by the growing death toll, including everyone aboard the flying White House, Macklin viciously threw open the door and caught Fraiser on the telephone.

Hearing the whisper of the guillotine, Wyman's mouth dropped open as he fumbled to place the phone receiver in the cradle. "Mr. President, I thought you were—"

"Don't say anything," Macklin threatened in a trembling voice. "A few hours ago, before I left for Andrews, I began thinking about the Dallas crash."

"Sir, I know—"

"Shut up," the president said with acid in his voice. "I

found it strange that you happened to know that Senator Morgan was aboard the plane long before the passenger list was released."

Seeking an avenue of escape, Wyman's deeply set blue eyes darted from person to person. There was no way out.

The veins in Macklin's neck looked like they were going to explode. "Then I thought about the odds against Tehran knowing exactly when and where one of our recon planes would show up. A very strange coincidence, wouldn't you say?"

Wyman's face turned chalky white. "Sir, let me expla—"

"Then," the president loudly interrupted, "the surprise in the Persian Gulf was just *too* much of a coincidence."

Wyman's eyes looked huge behind his round metal-rimmed glasses.

With pure malice in his voice, Macklin stared into Wyman's frightened eyes. The president grabbed Wyman by his tie, then savagely yanked him face-to-face. "You're a despicable piece of trash."

Shaking and perspiring profusely, Wyman's mouth opened and shut, but no words came out.

"You already had a fortune," Macklin said bitterly. "But that wasn't enough, was it?"

Wyman's eyes were downcast.

*"Was it?"* the president yelled at the top of his lungs.

"No," he whispered.

"Who paid you?"

"Bassam Shakhar," Wyman said weakly.

"How much did you charge to sell out your country?"

Wyman hesitated, then looked away. "Fourteen million," he uttered in a hollow, frightened voice.

"Where's the money?"

"In Argentina—Buenos Aires."

With all his strength, Macklin shoved Wyman back into his chair. Shaking from rage, the president turned to face the FBI agents. "Get him out of my sight."

"Yessir," they said.

Macklin started for the door, then stopped and looked at Wyman. "You treasonous bastard," the president said in disgust. "May God have mercy on your worthless soul."

•  •  •

Focusing on the primary sponsors of international terrorism, President Macklin orchestrated a campaign of round-the-clock bombings of military targets and civilian infrastructure. For three weeks, seven days a week, bombs and cruise missiles rained down on airfields, naval installations, radar sites, ammunition dumps, missile sites, command-and-control complexes, military storage facilities, and selected civilian targets that would not cause mass casualties. Nothing was spared, not even military headquarters buildings.

Bassam Shakhar and his closest lieutenants rode out the pounding attacks in an underground home in northern Afghanistan.

After the blistering bombing raids, President Macklin delivered a brief but poignant speech to the perpetrators of terrorism and the sponsors of terrorism. Broadcast on MSNBC, Fox, and CNN, the message was short and straightforward. The United States was at war with terrorists. In the event of another terrorist attack on U.S. citizens, at home or abroad, American bombs and missiles would pulverize *all* the sponsor state's major airports, highways, roads, railways, bridges, dams, and power plants. Signing off, President Macklin vowed to make acts of terrorism against the United States too expensive for sponsor states to condone or conduct.

# 51

## New Orleans

Tanned and refreshed after their leisurely vacation in St. Thomas, Jackie and Scott invited Greg and Maritza to join them for a relaxing weekend in New Orleans. Even though Scott, Maritza and Greg were still recuperating from their injuries, the foursome enjoyed their tour of the Vieux Carré. What they hadn't seen Friday night, they saw the following morning, including Jackson Square, the French Market, Royal Street, Dixieland Hall, and the expansive Riverwalk.

They wrapped up the pleasurable tour with a river cruise on the magnificent *Natchez*. With a calliope playing a jaunty melody and its huge paddle wheel thrashing the muddy Mississippi, the colorful steamboat had glided downriver past charming moss-draped oak trees and Chalmette Battlefield. By the time *Natchez* returned to the Riverwalk, the quartet had worked up a voracious appetite.

Repairing to a small, quiet restaurant, they dined on dirty rice and plump links of freshly grilled Louisiana-style sausage, tender and tangy in a rich roux-based sauce. Framed black-and-white photographs hanging on the brick walls depicted a variety of scenes of Bourbon Street during Mardi Gras circa the 1950s and 1960s.

Greg's curiosity finally got the best of him. "Okay," he

said, looking at Scott and Jackie. "What's the story on Farkas?"

Scott glanced at Jackie and shrugged. "You know as much as we do."

"Come on," Greg insisted. "Did they kill him or not?"

Dalton swallowed a sip of cold beer. "Hartwell says they found the ejection seat fairly close to the plane, but there wasn't a body or a parachute anywhere for miles around the crash site. That's all I know, honestly."

"I'll tell you what I think," Maritza said as she caught a whiff of the tantalizing aroma of blackened catfish. "Farkas got away, and he isn't finished with his mission."

Jackie nodded in agreement. "Apparently, the president agrees with you. That's why he's running the country from Raven Rock."

"*If* Farkas is still alive," Scott drawled as he listened to the four-four rhythm of Dixieland jazz drifting through the open door, "he's probably apoplectic over what has happened to Iran and the other sponsors of terrorism. That could make him even more dangerous."

Greg listened to the enchanting music and thought about Farkas. "I think the little bastard's ego is crushed—his reputation is tarnished. He didn't assassinate the president."

"That's right," Scott said with obvious pleasure. "But one thing is for sure. He won't stop trying until someone takes him out."

A faint smile edged Jackie's mouth. "Hey, guys, lighten up. The airlines are flying again, the stock market bounced back, and we haven't had another terrorist attack since the president demonstrated his position on the issue."

"Yeah, we're on vacation." Scott smiled, then let his attention drift toward the languid hoot of a tugboat plying the Mississippi. "Let's have another round," he said as he caught the attention of their waitress.

"I'll second that," Greg exclaimed with an easy smile.

Relaxed and mellow, Scott listened to a sidewalk band belt out Count Basie's "One O'Clock Jump" while another melancholy hoot from a tugboat drifted up from the river.

Scott glanced at his fishing buddy. "My favorite—Count Basie."

Greg gave him a perplexed look. "You mean the vampire guy?"

"Exactly," Dalton said with a grin. "How's the rehab going?"

"Better than I figured," Greg said enthusiastically. "Two more weeks and I'm going to be wetting a line in the Gulf of Mexico."

A small, thin man sitting alone at the bar swallowed an oyster and darted a glance at the wall mirror. He was looking straight into the faces of Maritza Gunzelman and Scott Dalton. Downing another raw oyster, the man with the long white hair and thick white beard carefully wiped his hands on an oversized cloth napkin. He adjusted his sunglasses, then tossed some money on the cluttered bar and donned his French beret. Khaliq Farkas smiled inwardly and walked out of the restaurant.

Visit Joe Weber's web site at:
http://www.JoeWeberNovels.com
E-mail: joeweber@aol.com